THE END OF ALL ROADS

The Sixth Book of Outremer

CHAZ BRENCHLEY

ACE BOOKS, NEW YORK

THE END OF ALL ROADS

A Berkley Book / published by arrangement with
the author

PRINTING HISTORY
Ace mass-market edition / November 2003

Copyright © 2003 by Chaz Brenchley.
Cover art by John Howe.
Cover design by Rita Frangie.
Interior text design by Julie Rogers.

ISBN: 0-441-01114-4

ACE®
Ace Books are published by The Berkley Publishing Group,
a division of Penguin Group (USA) Inc.,
375 Hudson Street, New York, New York 10014.
The name ACE and the "A" design
are trademarks belonging to Penguin Group (USA) Inc.

PRINTED IN THE UNITED STATES OF AMERICA

10 9 8 7 6 5 4 3 2 1

This one's for Jean and Roger,
who liked the books so much
they built the website.

For now I see through a glass, darkly;
but then face to face:
now I know in part; but then shall I know
even as also I am known.

— The First Epistle of Paul the Apostle
to the Corinthians, 13, 12

ONE

The Healing Heart

ELISANDE STOOD ON the terrace of her grandfather's palace, which had once been her home also and was still the one place that she would always come back to, whether she belonged here or not.

Two steps on Surayon ground had always been enough to make her feel sunk soul-deep in the land. That had never been a feeling of unadulterated good—in some senses, in some moods, it was like being hugged by her father—but today the air had a stranger taste, there was a sourness to the moist earth's scent, even the sunlight seemed a little dark.

She stood on her grandfather's terrace and gazed out across his country, her best hope; and she saw fire and death, the imprint of war all over.

More even than that, there was a hollowness at the heart of her, an empty place where something had been ripped from her body. Her blood's beat echoed there, hammer-hard and hurting, *he is dead*. Never mind blame, never mind consequences: only the fact of it pounded through her brain, *he is dead . . .*

He was dead and it really shouldn't matter, but it did.

FROM HERE SHE could see all the heart of the principality, from Surayon-town below her to the river's rush and the climbing slopes beyond. When she'd been very little, she had thought that it was all the world; even after she'd grown bigger, she still insisted that it was all the world that mattered.

It was always possible to go higher and see further. The palace was built into the slope of a hill so massive that she used to call it a mountain; they took her to the top of it and showed her the real mountains, but they were distant shadows and she couldn't understand how they were bigger than this, or how what was far away could matter more than what she stood upon. More importantly, she still felt that she could see the country better from her grandfer's terrace below.

She'd felt so then, and she felt so yet. The air couldn't actually be clearer down here, but it seemed so; and when she stared at any particular distant thing, it seemed to come nearer and more sharply into sight. A faint smudge of movement on a track so far away that it looked hair-thin and half imagined: a moment's concentration and she could see the bullock-cart and the woman who rode it, the boy who led the bullocks, she could almost say what was in the sacks that piled the cart so high. Her grandfather always would say, and she never doubted him.

He'd spent long hours here all her life, gazing out across his penned princedom, watching literally over his people. He must have woven some touch of his power into the stones of the terrace or into the balustrade, perhaps into the air itself, so that what lay far off could be brought closer to the eye. It had worked for her then, before she knew it; it worked for her now, and she truly wished that it would not.

She stood and saw her land in flames, her people slaughtered. That should matter more than anything, more even than Marron still sick, still unhealed, still dying in the room at her back. So why, *why* was it her father who so possessed her thoughts, when he was only one man and dead already, a cold waste of passion?

WHEN SHE MOVED at last, she had to rip herself out of stillness like a tree tearing itself from its deep-buried roots. She felt very like a tree indeed, silent and suffering; she thought she might carry that eloquent silence a long time, years, a lifetime. *He is dead*: the thought led nowhere, had nowhere else to go, so she had to take it with her.

She turned and walked slowly towards the high arch of the open door, pausing to touch the rough-worked stone of the wall for luck before she passed within. She'd done that all her life, picking at lichen-flakes and loving the contrast with the smooth plaster of the inner walls. No ice-slick marble here, no age-worn sandstone or brute blunt defensive rampart. The palace was built of a creamy-pale stone, shot through with veins of blue that glittered where they were cut. That fiery light reminded her of all the secret resources, and of all the secret resources of Surayon. Besides which, these walls were an open invitation for a light and nimble-fingered, nimble-toed girl to climb, all the way up to her mother's garden on the roof. How could she not have loved that, a private access to a private place that was entirely barred to her father?

There were several rooms that opened onto the long terrace. At the further end was the Princip's library, where even she never dared to venture without invitation. Next came the wide audience-chamber, a space of pillars and light with many windows; then there was this, the solarium they'd always called it, a quiet bright room where Elisande's mother had loved to sit with her ladies over her needlework and talk until the sun failed.

Now, today it was a hospital. All the furniture had been cleared to one side; soft pallets had been laid on the floor, and there lay Marron and Hasan, their drawn faces cruelly exposed by the fall of light through the casements. The one was fighting still, she thought, or being fought over, while the other simply faded. The battle raging within Marron was clear to be seen on his skin, fire and shadow surging against each other; Hasan was grey, chill, quite unwarmed by anything that man or sun could offer. The gouges on his face showed like black bars, like a fresh brand.

Julianne sat on the floor by his head, as still as her husband and fading just as fast. Elisande should be similarly sitting beside Marron, grieving as deeply and as silently, except that Jemel had claimed that place. It had been his aching distress as much as her own pain that drove her out onto the terrace.

In the Princip's absence, other men had come to tend the patients: old men, wise men, helpless men. They had touched and probed, had laid hands on Marron and Hasan individually and then by twos together, all at once. And had shaken their heads, spoken in soft voices, advised patience until their lord's return.

Patience was a slow, grinding torment to them all. A table in the far corner had been laid with refreshments, quite untouched; Elisande went over there to pour a beaker of well-watered wine, and carry that to Julianne.

"Here, sweet. You won't eat, I know, but you could drink, at least. You still remember how to swallow."

"You're not eating either."

"No. But I'll share your drink."

Julianne sipped without interest, then looked a little surprised at what she tasted. "I thought it would be *jereth.*"

"No. Not for this. We'll drink *jereth* later, when they're well. And I won't share a drop of mine with you."

The badinage was unthinking, meaningless except to say *we have a friendship that goes deep, deeper than pain, and we will recover it. Later. When they're well.*

Julianne shook her head. "When they're well," she said slowly, borrowing Elisande's determination only to show how weak it was, "we still won't want to celebrate. Only to weep together, for how much we've lost." But her eyes moved to the view of the far horizon, the far side of the valley, and suddenly she sounded weak herself, weak as a child's arguments, as though she had completely misunderstood herself. "He will come, won't he?"

"Of course he'll come, sweet. He lives here, this is his home." She wrapped her arms around her friend, chin on shoulder for a tight hug and said, "He will come, Julianne, I promise. He promised. As soon as he can. But he doesn't have the King's Eye," *though he has the next best thing out on the terrace there, whatever spells he's woven on the wind to bring far-sightedness,* "and all his country is under attack, he had to go out to see . . ."

"Of course he did," on a sigh, reaching a faltering hand out to stroke the bitter cold of Hasan's brow and then snatching it back, as though to touch him hurt as much as not to touch him. "And perhaps he also had to go out to be alone an hour, after the other news you brought him. Rudel was his son, as well as being your father. You can't mourn him properly, you're so tied up inside. I can't, because—because of Hasan, I can't feel anything clearly. Someone has to."

Men should not outlive their children, she was saying, though old men did it as a matter of course in time of war or famine or disease, which meant in Outremer and in the Sands. Not in Surayon. Julianne was right, of course, or partly right, and Grandfer might indeed prefer to shed his tears ahorseback, hidden behind a riding-veil or a visor. But Elisande could be mulish, even now.

"He was a soldier before he was—well, what he is now. Princip, sorcerer, philosopher, what you like. As your own father was, Julianne. Coren kept his tears back and would use Rudel's body if he could; my grandfer would have done the same. Of course they will mourn, but not yet. Not when there's fighting today and a battle tomorrow, and all this country lies beneath the sword."

If Julianne thought her cold or hard, so be it; at least it would give the girl something fresh to think about. Elisande might crave such a heart-whole pain as Julianne was feeling, but she knew too the exhausting weight of it.

She supposed she ought to welcome her own distractedness, her fear for Marron offset by her fear for Surayon, and both of them outmatched by the unexpected ache of grieving for Rudel. She couldn't do it, though, she could find no sense of balance. She yearned to be like Julianne, like Jemel, utterly absorbed in their distress; and was not, and couldn't fake it even to herself.

Restless anxiety dragged her to her feet again, away from her friend. She barely glanced towards Marron and his attendant Sharai, she couldn't take a step in that direction. Instead she went back to the doorway and on to the terrace again, desperate and driven. *He will come,* but she needed him, they all needed him to come soon; and yet he had the defence of all this land to organise. Their troubles were small and individual, his were vast and overmastering. They shouldn't be so selfish as to look for him; and yet they were, she most of all. He might be Princip of a state that stood on the very edge of destruction, but he was still her grandfather, her beloved Grandfer who had been her secret treasure all these years.

She gripped the parapet with both hands, glad of roughness against her skin, something to rub against, something to feel. She stared out across the valley, scanning, searching. There were fires on the flanks of the northern hills, and when she squinted she thought she could see terror beneath the smoke, running men being ridden down. When she stretched all her senses, she thought she could smell burned flesh and hear screaming that was not the screams of men.

She drew back suddenly. It must have been imagination, surely; she was fantasising, turning nightmare tales into truth in her foolish, stupefied head. Or else that had been the screaming of horses, perhaps, trapped in a burning barn. Not women, no, surely not children . . .

The preceptor had burned children at the Roq, she remembered bleakly, chillingly. But these were her own people here, and their own people too, they were all Patrics. Even the most devout Ransomers would not burn their own. Would they . . .?

She remembered Marshal Fulke's preaching against Surayon, and couldn't doubt it longer. And turned, shuddering, to look eastward for her grandfather; and saw instead—or thought she saw—the tribes of the Sharai spread out from wall to mountain wall, doing wicked work with scimitars for the greater glory of their god.

And didn't want to look any more, westward or anywhere; didn't want to go back inside either, to face the other tragedy of the day and try to persuade herself again that it was lesser, when it hurt as fiercely and as deeply. So she stayed, she stood where she was and closed her eyes against the terrors before her and found no rest and no hope of evasion there either, only her father's dreadful death played out freshly behind her lids, a tragedy too many.

WHEN AN ARM laid itself across her shoulders, when iron fingers gripped her tightly through the sleeve of her robe, she choked painfully on a sob that was hard as a pebble and filled her throat as thoroughly; she twisted vainly against the strength that pulled her close. Soft fabric, cloaking a man's body. A small, lean body that had her blinking upward to find his face, when she'd been just about to topple into the security of his hug, except that suddenly he was not the man she'd thought him.

"*Coren?*" Well, Coren was good enough, a splendid second-best; she'd let him hug her as much as he chose and dry her tears willingly against his shoulder, so long as he promised to mention them to no one else.

"Aye, lass. I've brought your father home."

Which made her choke again, because it could never be home again without him and without her loathing of him, a necessary counterbalance to her love.

But choking made her turn her face away from his, and turning made her see. Another man had come out onto the terrace from the cluttered chaos of the library, and was standing gazing at her. Built like a woodcutter, short and broad, with a barrel chest and legs like firkins; crowned with thick white curls beneath his hood and bearded like a hedge in snow; scratching at that beard now with thick, spatulate fingers that looked so much better suited to gripping an axe than a pen or even the sword that he wore half-hidden under his cloak . . .

"Grandfer!"

Elisande wrenched free of Coren, who laughed softly as he let her go. She flew into her grandfather's arms, and no matter that he was wearing chain mail too beneath his surcoat. Even if he couldn't mend what was irrevocably broken, he was still a solidity that she could cling to, where all else had proved so frail. She did cling, and might have cried again now that she'd found access to such a well of tears, except that through her mindless mutterings and his gentle soothing she heard something else, Julianne's voice say, "Elisande . . .?"

She turned against her grandfather's rough hand, where it was stroking her hair in animal comfort. Her friend was standing in the solarium doorway, leaning against the stonework as though that were all that was keeping her upright. Coren moved swiftly to his daughter's side, to take that duty on himself; for a moment, gazing at their matched elegance, Elisande was sharply aware of the contrast. She had always secretly enjoyed her grandfather's peasant appearance, been glad of his rude strength. She'd inherited his lack of height, but her mother's elfin bones; that had been one more thing to welcome, to thrust like a banner in her father's face.

All the bitter triumph of those memories was ashen now. As ashen as her friend, who hung on to her own father's arm much as Elisande herself was hanging on to her grandfather: two girls who had come too far under too great a burden, and needed now to have it lifted from them. Despite everything that was happening in Surayon, the Princip had made time to return to them; Elisande tried to find some hope in that as she lifted her eyes to her grandfather and said, "Please, you can help them, can't you, Marron and Hasan? Say that you can . . ."

"I can try," he said, which was far short of the promise that she was looking for. She'd tried herself, others had tried and failed; Rudel had declined even to try. But the Princip was stronger, wiser, more practised than any. She'd believed in him all her life, when faith was such a hard thing for her to achieve; surely he couldn't let her down now.

"Take me to them," he said, for all the world as though he were the guest here rather than the host. Elisande unwound herself from him, except for keeping tight grip on one arm; she led him past Julianne and Coren and into the bright solarium, thinking that desolation ought never to be so well lit.

For a minute, her grandfather only stood and looked down on the two sick men, where they lay on their pallets in the fall of sunshine.

When he spoke, his voice was quiet and conversational. "A wise man would do nothing," he said, "for either of these, except perhaps to help them into their deaths. The boy is a danger to himself and all around him; the man is the leader of that army, one of those armies that are laying my own land waste. If he is restored, he will seek to destroy Outremer itself, and he is likely the only man who could do that. Without him the tribes will splinter, loot and scatter. Why should I save his life, even assuming that I can?"

"Because he saved mine, and all ours," Elisande said quickly, desperately. "We were attacked by ghûls at the Dead Waters, but Marron fetched Hasan"—she couldn't resist slipping in a small word for her own boy, in hopes of its having weight later—"and he slew them, he and his men . . ."

"Well. That is a reason, certainly, if not a good one. It may not be enough. Honour is a tentative idea in times of war."

"He is my husband," Julianne said, her voice as faint as her colour. "Perhaps, if I speak to him, he will lead the Sharai out of your land for my sake."

"Perhaps, though I doubt it. That is a better reason. His sense of honour may be greater than mine. Now if you had said, 'He is my husband and I love him,' that would have been sufficient without the other."

Julianne's eyes widened. "Do you want me to say that?"

"No need, little one," though she overtopped him by a hand's breadth or more. "It is written all through you. I hope you will find a way to be glad of it, though I think that journey will be a hard one. Keep back, now. There is danger in this. Hope, too, you may certainly hope if you wish to; without that, you wouldn't have brought him to me, and the 'ifrit's work would have been wasted. But that creature has left something of itself inside him, and it may be fit for mischief yet."

Elisande gripped Julianne's arm and hauled her bodily backwards, but not too far. She wanted still to be able to see, and she wanted Julianne to see also. Success or failure, life or death, it seemed important that they both stand witness. If Hasan did not survive, it would be too easy for trouble-minded tongues to spread lies about the manner of his death under Patric hands.

Easier than she'd imagined, even: she blinked, when she saw what her grandfather did. Kneeling down beside Hasan's pallet, he touched the Sharai's grey face and sighed. Elisande knew how cold and lifeless that skin felt; she shivered a little in sympathy for him, for his having to send even his strong spirit into that chilly body.

Except that he didn't, or not immediately. First, he drew a dagger from his belt and a gasp from his grand-daughter as he laid it against Hasan's unresponsive wrist and cut deeply.

Blood followed the blade, sluggish and dark, as though it were thickening inside Hasan's body, almost starting to clot.

Julianne made one soft, unstructured sound. Elisande scowled ferociously, reached up to snatch the hand that she was biting on, held it tightly in both her own and hissed, "Show some faith, girl—that's my grandfather over there! I've been telling you for months how he's not a man at all, he's a demigod . . ."

"You have. Wiser than the djinn, was it, and tougher than the mountains at their roots? He still wants to let Hasan die."

"No, he doesn't—that's the one thing he wants not to do. He was desperate for you to feed him an excuse. If you hadn't, he'd have saved him anyway, just out of curiosity to meet the great Hasan; I know my grandfer. Though he might have locked him somewhere very safe afterwards, for all the rest of his life. He might do that yet, unless you plead for him." *Whether you plead for him or not* was what she actually meant—she knew her grandfer—but this wasn't the time for Julianne to learn that particular lesson.

"Well, whatever he wants or doesn't want, Hasan's going to die in any case. See how he bleeds? That's not human harm, that's sorcery . . ."

"Of course it is, it came from an 'ifrit. That's why we brought him to the greatest sorcerer in the Kingdom for his healing. Grandfer may look like an old braggart soldier your cooks wouldn't welcome in your kitchen; that's because he is an old braggart soldier your cooks wouldn't welcome in your kitchen, but he could still chew up an 'ifrit and spit the shells out. He'd pick his teeth after, mind, he's really uncouth that way. Hush now, hush and watch."

Now the Princip spread his hands across Hasan's chest, every fingertip on a separate rib; he took a slow, careful breath and closed his eyes and sent his thoughts, his will, his spirit questing for the source of so much damage.

Elisande knew that journey well. She knew how hard it could be to seek out the subtleties of damage, how easy it was to become lost. She felt her muscles tense and her thoughts try to follow her grandfather. Hopeless at this distance, not even touching, but still she was dizzy at the spiralling down and down, still she was sick at the cloying, engulfing surge of corrupted blood.

You are not there, you are not him . . .

Julianne had taken a bear's grip on her, crushing, dragging her back into the world. Nothing to do but stand, then, support her friend and trust her grandfather. So she did, she did both and felt herself rewarded, or at least relieved beyond measure, to see at last a hint of smoke rise from the coagulating blood on Hasan's wrist.

The Princip grunted, clamped his hands tight around the Sharai's chest, twisted his face into a dreadful grimace; the wisp of smoke thickened and tightened, drawing itself together even as it was forced out of its stolen body.

Except that it was black, it looked almost like a djinni, hanging in the air above Hasan. Some fragment of an 'ifrit, with at least some vestige of life left in it; and yes, she believed her grandfather entirely when he said that this was still dangerous. It was still dangerously close to him, and he looked exhausted suddenly, slumping where he sat.

She was encumbered, but Coren was not. Before she could shake off Julianne, he had stepped forward; she saw him make the smallest of gestures, heard him murmur the quietest of words.

Sharper than any dagger, his slender and courtly fingers; more deadly than any imam's blessing, his gentle voice. She saw that corporeal shadow dissipate into shreds and nothing, she heard her own slow sigh of tension released, she felt that she could have copied her grandfather in his collapse if Julianne hadn't been so wrapped around her, still taut as a strung wire. It took all her will to force her head to turn, and her voice was little more than a whisper as she said, "I didn't know you could do that."

Coren smiled faintly. "Against such as that, yes. It was only a fragment; malign, but struggling simply to hold itself together in a world not its own. It had no true life, no spirit. It might have sought to infect another body; Marron is always vulnerable, with that open wound on his arm. Even the Daughter could have lost its fight then, and who can say how much we might have regretted that?"

Marron, yes. There was still Marron, and the Princip was exhausted. She stole a glance towards Jemel and saw him sitting beside the young Patric, his eyes fixed on her grandfather, his gaze burning. *Give him time, let him recover, he's an old man*—but she couldn't say it aloud, to make a hypocrite of herself. The same urgency was scorching her.

First, though, there was Julianne. She looked into her friend's eyes and smiled.

"Is it, is it over now, is it done?"

"It's done, sweet. Come . . ."

She led her forward on stumbling feet, to the pallet where Hasan lay. Julianne gave another of those wordless little cries and dropped to her knees beside him. The dreadful grey cast was gone from his skin, and the blood ran bright and fresh now from the gaping cut on his wrist. That at least Elisande could attend to. She crouched beside him, reached to touch and felt the warm tingle in her fingertips as her own healing ability was awoken.

She knitted flesh to flesh and skin to skin. It was easy, it always had been easy here at the heart of her life. She could see the tremble in Julianne's fingers as they touched Hasan's face, as they confirmed the new-risen warmth in him; she heard the gasp of disgust and wonder as the black scabs on his cheek crumbled and fell away to show healthy tissue beneath, if dark seamed scars were ever healthy.

"Those he'll keep," Coren said behind her. "I'm afraid he's spoiled for looks, though he won't think so and neither will his women. His other women. If you'd wanted pretty, you should have stayed with Imber."

She all but ignored that, as was only right that she should; she had one fear left, and addressed it to Elisande. "Why doesn't he wake?"

"He will, sweetheart. That was a deep working; they ought both to sleep a while now, your Hasan and my grandfer. He is only sleeping, though. We could wake him if you want."

"No. No, leave him be. But—Elisande, could you send your djinni to fetch someone for me?"

"Yes, of course. Anyone, from anywhere. Who do you want?" Actually she knew already, she'd only been waiting for Julianne to realise who she wanted. Let the girl think it was her own idea, she'd benefit the more.

"Bring Sherett here from wherever she has gone, if it can find her. He, he would like to see her, when he wakes."

"Esren will find her, and she will come. She won't even argue." Much. Probably . . .

*   *   *

IN THE BRIEF time that it took her to summon the djinni, send it on its errand and elect to ignore Coren's quiet amusement, the Princip had roused himself, at least a little. He called a page into the room and sent the boy running for a towel and a ewer of water, then pushed himself slowly to his feet, ran both hands through his mane of hair and stood looking sombrely down at Marron.

Also, inevitably, at Jemel: who stared back, silent and demanding.

"Patience, lad. I will attend to your friend, but that will be a delicate matter, and I need to think a little first. There are other matters than his health to be considered."

Not for Jemel, plainly; and not for Elisande either, though she did understand her grandfather's hesitation. He was like Rudel in that, seeing the boy only as a vessel for what he carried, and a weak vessel too. A dozen times or more, she'd heard her father as good as say that Surayon and the whole Kingdom would be better off with Marron dead.

He never had tried to kill him, though, and no more would the Princip. She thought that she knew what her grandfather would do instead; it was the most dangerous choice, but she thought he would do it anyway. Grandfathers were like that, like their sons, so little inclined to listen that there was seldom any point in talking . . .

THE PRINCIP SPLASHED cold water liberally over his head, till his hair and beard were dripping. He gave them a brisk rub, then tossed the towel over his page's shoulder and dismissed him.

Elisande fetched her grandfather his preferred drink of fruit juice laced with wine, doing a page's service herself to hurry him just a little, to give him a gentle nudge. As ever she wanted to be doing, or at least to see things done; delay was an animal that gnawed at her bones. She could pretend to the Sharai's desert patience, but only in the desert, where it was more necessity than virtue. Here, even Jemel's showed signs of cracking; her own was in shards already.

The Princip took the beaker she brought him, with a glance that spoke. He would do what he must to Marron when he was refreshed and ready, and not a moment sooner; would she have him botch the work, because he was still weak and ill-prepared?

She scowled up at him, and his lips twitched in a transient, knowing smile. He did drain the beaker in a single draught, though, before handing it back; and then he did make a gesture with his arms that was sure to draw everyone's attention, as if he didn't have it all already.

"I said that last exercise was risky, and it was, despite Coren's talent at waving away trouble. This is worse, this could be lethal. I have to free the Daughter, before I can treat Marron's sickness; we dare not hope that he can control it, which means that I must. I should ask you all to leave, except that I know you would not go. However, I will do nothing until I am satisfied that you are at least as safe as you can be. Hasan is no longer bleeding; if any others among you have a cut, a scratch on your skin, say so now. Be sure."

None of them spoke. The Princip nodded heavily.

"Very well, then. Even so, I want you all at a distance. You must forsake your place at his side, Jemel; not for long, but I cannot have you close. Help to carry Hasan out onto the terrace, then watch from there. Coren, be ready to come in if I call you, but not otherwise. Even you are not immune to this thing. I don't wish to find myself explaining to the King how it came about that his Shadow is now the Ghost Walker, or else spread messily all across the walls of my solarium."

THE PRINCIP STARTED with Marron much as he had started with Hasan: the little touch to the face, a first ten-

tative contact, and then the knife. Just a nick to the endur-
ing wound on Marron's arm, much as Elisande had done
herself in the cell at Revanchard.

Now as then, the Daughter came seething out with the
first drop of blood. Her grandfather stood up to face the
shifting cloud of red as it shaped itself into the blurred
echo of a creature, hinting at a body as monstrous as any
'ifrit. Elisande held her breath. She'd taken a terrible risk
when she'd loosed it in the cell, gambling on her ability to
draw Marron back. Her grandfather was gambling only on
himself and his knowledge of its ancient and mysterious
nature, and she wasn't sure how deep that knowledge ran.

Deep enough, it seemed, at least for now. He raised
both his hands palms-out, as if they defined a wall; he
spoke a few soft words and pushed his hands slowly forward. The smoke-drawn creature seemed to eddy for a
moment, then drifted away from him. Elisande thought it
was losing its definition; she found herself straining to
make out the sketchy lines of its implicit body.

"Grandfer . . .?" The appeal slipped out before she
could bite it back. This was no 'ifrit-shadow, the half-
aware remnant of a dead spirit, to be dispersed to nothingness by a touch of Coren's power. It was something far
stronger, and far stranger; and it was intimately linked to
Marron. He hurt, she knew, when he sent it too far from
his body. She couldn't imagine what would happen to him
if it were scattered or destroyed.

"Don't be alarmed. I have simply confused it—much
as you would confuse the mind of a man you wanted to
slip by unseen. This was more chancy, as it has no true
mind to be played with; but I have left it only the slightest knowledge of itself, and none at all of us. That frees
me to work unfettered with your friend. There is still danger here, though. I must do something that I think has
never been done before, and the less you hinder me with
questions, Elisande, the better my hopes of success."

She nodded silently, uselessly; he wasn't looking at

her. He had crouched down beside Marron once more, and laid his hands on the boy's pale ribs.

It was Jemel who spoke, if thinly. "What does he mean to do to Marron?"

"Heal him," she murmured. "Heal him completely, I mean. He's trying to break the link between Marron and the Daughter. Hush now, and watch. Pray if you can. I can't, I've been trying, but I've forgotten how."

Whether Jemel did pray, she couldn't tell. But he did fall quiet again, withdrawing a little way from her and standing alone, standing straight as he watched and waited.

Elisande was sorry for him, glad for herself, tired of being leaned on.

THE PRINCIP DIDN'T labour so hard over Marron's body as he had over Hasan's. A worm of doubt turned in her gut, for all that she tried to dismiss it as unworthy. She loved him, she understood him, she distrusted him mightily; she thought that he wasn't seriously trying to drive the darkness from Marron's blood and bone. Even when she saw the faintest possible mist of grey rise from the pin-prick in his arm, she didn't believe it would be enough. Hasan had carried a half-living thing inside himself, which had taken strong magic to disperse; this was less than a warm breath on a cold morning, the waft of a moth's wings would scatter it . . .

Certainly Coren made no move to trouble it; neither did it appear to trouble him. It wavered in the room's tugs and shifts of air, which she thought would be too light to disturb a falling feather. When her grandfather shifted, she took her eyes from it for a moment; when she looked again, she couldn't find it.

"Grandfer, that can't be all." *At least tell me straight if you're going to let him die, I don't want your kindness.* And Jemel was Sharai, desert-made, as soft as camel-hide and just as tough. He'd seen one lover go down into death, and had sworn an oath of vengeance that she thought still lingered behind his silences; she feared that he might swear another, if he ever felt he'd been deceived.

"Truly, child, there's nothing in him now that is not his. He was infected by a breath, not a blow as Hasan was. The Daughter had kept it weak and denied it any nesting in his body; now it is driven out and gone. The question is whether I can deny the Daughter its desire to return—and how it will react, if I do so. Keep you back, girl, the danger is not over yet."

No, that she knew. She tried to look in two directions at once, at her grandfather where he held Marron's arm across his lap and at the Daughter where it was little more than a hot and heavy cast to the air, as though a forge were venting into that corner of the chamber.

There would be little even her grandfather could do about the scarring on Marron's forearm. More likely he was trying to feel out what bonds there were connecting him with the Daughter, seeing if he could sense some affinity between the wound and it. Elisande thought that the affinity was with Marron's blood; she was sure that her grandfather would feel nothing, because there was nothing there that human fingers were capable of feeling. Certainly the Daughter was sensing something, though. There was a sudden turbulence throughout the thin cloud of its apparent body. It seemed to seethe against a wall of wind, like an insect that batters senselessly at door and shutter. Elisande had never been truly frightened of the thing before, surely not frightened enough, but she was frightened now. Since it had been—what, hatched?—it had always been Marron's, almost a part of Marron, his will woven in blood and smoke; and she had always somehow trusted Marron, even where he was stupid, even where he was blind.

Her grandfather's fingers were moving inward now,

into the rawness of the open wound, the flesh that never would skin or scar.

Grandfer, be careful . . .

She knew just what he was doing now: how his mind was reaching into the beat of Marron's blood, how it followed that tide through his body till it found the damage in his arm, how it interfered. She had done the same herself or tried to, but only when the Daughter was in him, and so she had failed again and again. She'd never dared to risk this. She was frightened for all of them, terrified for Marron; she could almost hate her grandfather for taking such a chance, if she hadn't understood him so well.

His fingers moved inside Marron's gaping wound, to mirror how his awareness moved, so much deeper within. Slowly, carefully, thoroughly he would be mending what was ripped, sealing what lay open to the world; slowly, carefully, thoroughly he would be closing off the Daughter's gateway to its human host.

Elisande felt the sun's heat against the back of her neck, and hugged herself hard against a terrible chill.

Sometimes she remembered to breathe, or her body did: great wracking gasps that shook her like sobs, as though she were weeping after all when she was so determined not to do that.

Occasionally she remembered her friends and where they were, around her. She thought she might look about to find them, but she never did. There was a separation between thought and action, between mind and muscle. She was as harshly cut off as the Daughter, lacked the power to move at all.

IT WAS THE Princip who released her at last, by moving himself: by sighing, stretching, rising from his place at Marron's side. Even now, though, she'd barely taken the smallest pace forward before he was glancing at her, glaring at her, gesturing her back beyond the doorway.

"Grandfer . . ."

"No, Elisande. There is nothing that you can do but harm. The boy is well enough, for now. Whether he stays so is not in your hands to determine. Neither yours, Jemel," sharing his glare around. "Coren, again I may need you, but wait my call."

When the King's Shadow bowed in acceptance of the command, she could do nothing more than fidget and fret, chew on a fingernail, watch as she had been watching. Her eyes followed the Princip across the chamber, towards where the Daughter billowed against its constraints. Had she thought that there was danger before? She had deceived herself, too scared to see ahead. Now it was truly unfettered, it had no home, no master, and her grandfather was setting himself against it. He couldn't tame it, no man could. It was a wild thing, a spirit, beyond mortal managing. She had no idea what it would do when he released it from its current cage. Perhaps it would flee to Marron's body, find that shelter closed against it and so destroy him in its fury. Or perhaps destroy her grandfather; perhaps it would destroy them all.

Her breath came in whispers, and she resented even so much noise. It was louder than the soft grating of the Princip's boots on the grit on the flagstone floor, and that was too loud already. For his sake she wanted utter silence in the world, she wanted the birds on the hillside to stop singing, the wind not to blow.

IT HAD BEEN an anxious time recently; she could find no nails left to chew. Instead she reached her hand out and snatched at Julianne's just as the Princip reached his own hands out towards the Daughter.

In the same moment, his mind must have unpicked the bonds that held it so diffuse. It drew together suddenly into that familiar insect-shape, sharp and deadly.

She thought it would attack him, mindless and desperate; instead it only hung in the air, potent but undriven, apparently adrift.

Her grandfather held his hands high, on either side of the thing, perilously close to touching where the wisps of its blurred edges frayed into the air. At the same time, he startled her by starting to sing.

Even before her ears had caught the words, the cadence and rhythm of his voice had sent her mind hurtling back to childhood, to those nights when she was too hot or too excited to sleep. Sometimes her mother had come to her, and that was always good; sometimes her father, and in those days that was better. Sometimes, though, occasionally it had been her grandfather who came, and that was best of all. He'd talk to her a little, cuddle and kiss her out of tearfulness, then he'd lie her down on her tummy and his strong peasant hands would caress her head and back, rough skin but a gentle and tender touch, while his voice sang this same song in a whisper that seemed to gather up her soul and carry it swiftly away into restful dreaming.

At the time, she didn't even understand the words. It wasn't until she'd made the trip to Rhabat and learned much from the women there that she'd finally recognised it as a form of the Sharai *sodar*. Her mother sang her lullabies to help her into sleeping; her child's mind had thought this just another kind of lullaby.

Which it was, she supposed, in a way. That it was also tribal magic had been a revelation; that she could find no tribe familiar with that particular song had been a curiosity, a question she'd have liked to put to her grandfather if she'd had any hope of winning an answer from him.

To hear it used now, and to such a purpose, was bewildering. The *sodar* was a way to quiet fretful minds and bodies, to sway them into sleep; surely he didn't think that he could lull the Daughter as he'd lulled a restless girl?

He could, though, and he did. While she watched, aghast, while she listened and still felt the seductive tug of it, her grandfather sang his song.

The Daughter felt it too, or appeared to. It contracted slowly, its colour deepening and the lines of its body becoming clearer, more solid-seeming. The Princip's hands closed in around it as it curled into itself, much like an insect withdrawing into its shell; it looked almost as though he were guiding it, even pressing against it as its red skin turned hard and textured . . .

Touch was always an important, even the crucial element in the *sodar*. Even so, she couldn't hold back a gasp when she saw that he was touching the Daughter for true, holding it firmly in both hands as his song died in his throat. The lightest touch was lethal, when it was bloodbound and alive. Never mind that she'd seen it handled before in this passive state, never mind that Julianne had carried it all through the Roq, never mind the logic that said her grandfather must be safe or else he would be dead already; she gasped regardless, and then she did the other thing that she'd been aching to do against all wisdom and instruction. If he wouldn't be wise, then neither need she.

She plunged forward through the doorway; she hurtled across the chamber to her grandfather's side and tried to wrest the thing—the globe, the sphere, the red ochre ball, the Daughter—from his hands.

He held on to it, as though he'd been expecting just such an assault.

"Elisande, stop it. You're being foolish."

It was the unexpected mildness of the rebuke that stalled her, that quelled the ferocity of her tongue, that left her with nothing to do but stutter feebly, "If, if you'd been bleeding, anywhere at all; or if you'd touched it at all before it was ready, before you'd made it safe—"

"—Then I'd have died, or else it would have conjoined with me instead of Marron. Yes, I know. But neither of those things happened, and therefore I have made it safe, and therefore I can hold it perfectly well without your help."

She let go then, realising only as she did so that her fingers had been quietly exploring the ridges and runnels, the glossy segments and the abrasive hollows of the Daughter's enclosing shell. She'd only seen before, she'd never touched. She remembered how it had been before, how Marron had woken it all unknowing; from that memory she found the resilience to scowl at her grandfather and say, "You still shouldn't hold it like that, you don't know what might happen. You could tread on a nail, bite your tongue, stumble and fall and graze your knee . . . It isn't safe, it's never safe when a man is near it; and you especially, you shouldn't take such risks, your people need you . . ."

Especially now, she meant; and *I need you, especially now,* she meant that too.

"It's precisely because I'm fit to take such risks that my people need me as much as they do."

"Did you, did you know that the *sodar* would make it sleep?"

"No, I didn't know. I knew that it had slept within the Roq, therefore I knew the thing could be done; I guessed a while ago that the *sodar*—that particular *sodar*—might be an influence on it. The words are very old and hard to understand, but they are clearly more than a convenient way to hush a noisy child. I thought it worth the experiment."

"Not worth your life! Marron has carried it a long way—"

"—And should carry it no further. This kept him alive, to be sure, but he must have been a living ghost. Look at him, Elisande."

She shook her head. Jemel would do that, was probably doing it already. She'd seen Marron before in fatigue, in weakness and in pain; she didn't need to see him now, she'd rather look at her grandfather. Who looked suddenly weak, exhausted, deeply hurt.

This man lost a son today, his only child, and very possibly his country too . . . Slowly, respectfully, she reached out and took the Daughter from his grasp, so that he could at least afford to fall if he must.

This time, he let her take it; she'd been sure that he would. She saw herself reflected in his eyes, and thought that she'd grown since last they'd stood together.

It was surprisingly light in her hands, but he seemed to be stronger for being relieved of it, if only marginally.

"You should sleep," she told him, "recover your strength." That was how she needed him, how they all needed him: bull-strong, the spirit of his land.

"I should; but when will I get the chance?" The glimmer of a smile accompanied the words. That was reassuring, but not enough.

"Right now, while I find somewhere secure to stow this."

He shook his head. Even so little movement had him rocking on his feet, but Coren was abruptly there to steady him.

"No, child. I have one duty more, before I can think of resting. And so do you. The King's Shadow has kindly brought my son, your father home to me; it is for us to see to his resting now."

AND SO SHE found herself going down, down many stairs to the crypt below the palace, with the Daughter still clutched like a talisman in her arms. Although she didn't like to use the slightest magic so close to something so old, so powerful, so little understood, she made a witch-light shine to show their way where no lamps burned. Her grandfather was past raising a glow, and Coren didn't have a hand free to hold a torch, too busy using both to help the Princip on the stairs.

Down and down, into the chill, still air that the hills hoarded in hidden caves. The crypt had been just such a cave once, which had been found by digging; quite how the Princip had known just where to dig, Elisande had never bothered to ask.

Now it was a place prepared, though never yet occupied. The walls were smoothly plastered white and set with sconces, with niches for lamps, with shelves for coffins or shrouded bodies. There were biers of white stone on the floor; on one of those lay Rudel, still in his travelling clothes, still in his blood.

On another were set bowls of steaming, scented water, cloths and oils, cerements of linen. Elisande thought this was a test, at Coren's instigation; she glowered at him, and he gazed neutrally back. Then she was certain.

Well, she could do this. With her grandfather at her side, she had to do this.

She set the Daughter to one side, lit the lamps in their niches and let the witchfire die. If she had to do it, she'd do it properly and with no distractions, nowhere to hide. Let these men see how grown she was, how ready.

She and her grandfather stripped Rudel's body, slowly and ceremonially. They washed blood and dirt from his skin, bound up the dreadful gaping hole that should have been his throat, anointed him and dressed him for his long sleep. At some point, one or the other of them had started to hum the *sodar*; now they were both doing it, though it was no part of any ritual that Elisande knew, Sharai or otherwise.

When they were done, the Princip said, "It should have been his task, to lay me here. I never thought to do the work for him. I built this place for me and mine, but they should follow me . . ."

"Grandfer?"

"Yes, child."

"Don't leave him here. It's cold. Too quiet for him, too far from, from Cireille." Largely at Elisande's own sobbing insistence, her mother had been carried home to her family's estate on the other side of the valley, where she lay in warm earth in a grove of olives. "Let him lie with her. Please? He'd have liked that so much more."

"I built this place for me and mine," again. "Am I to be lonely here, when I come?"

"No, Grandfer. I'll follow you," *if I don't come ahead.* "Keep a place for me."

"Would you not choose to be buried with your husband, little one, wherever he may lie? It is the custom. I miss my own wife's company, more even than I'll miss my son."

Her grandmother was long dead, long buried in another land than this; she had never seen Surayon.

"I'll not marry," she said softly, almost thankful for it as she gazed at the empty niches, that might otherwise have waited for her own children. "I'll live and die as I am, and when I'm dead I'll come to you, Grandfer, and our ghosts can guard Surayon above till the stars fall."

"If it's there yet, if we can guard it now," was the dry response. "Coren, I'm too weary for all those stairs again . . ."

Coren smiled, and they all stepped into light; and she thought, remembered, realised that they could have done this coming down, he could have brought them here in a moment. Which meant he'd had a reason not to do it, which her grandfather had understood. Old men, they were hateful sometimes; it sometimes seemed to her that they had planned her every word and action. After the long toil of the descent and the hard reality of her father's body waiting at the bottom, of course she would rebel against leaving him here in the cold alone. They must have known that, they had known it. And so he would lie where he had wanted, where they wanted, where she had spent half her life insisting that he should not be, at his dead wife's side. They'd made her ask it; she felt used, manipulated, nothing new.

It was a small gesture towards a petty independence, but she needed something and she needed it now; so without asking consent, without even saying what she'd done, she left the Daughter where it was, in a vacant niche in the wall of her family crypt. It was, she thought, as safe as anywhere, now that Surayon was no longer safe at all. They would realise or remember soon enough, if they didn't know already; but just for this little while she could pretend, she could convince herself that she had made her own choice and acted on it. She could even make believe that her father was not entirely lost from her story, that she left him on watch over the Daughter, though she'd never let him watch over her.

TWO

A Blade For a Boy

SERVANTS CAME, WITH an offer to carry Hasan and his pallet back inside the chamber. Julianne said no, persuaded them rather to help Jemel bring Marron out to join him. They would wake sooner, she thought, man and boy, with the sun on their faces and the whisper of a breeze across their skins. The breeze whispered 'war', even she could smell the taint of smoke though it came from miles off; she would have spared them that if she could, but thought grimly, bitterly that they were warriors both. They should rouse to that, if nothing else.

She had more trouble with the servants when they brought her food, and she refused to eat it.

"I'll eat when my husband eats," she said softly, stubbornly, wiping the vivid scars on his cheek with a cool cloth and willing him to wake soon, now, before Sherett arrived. Soon or late, though, he should not wake to find her face-full and chewing. "What would he think, that I was here by duty and heedless of him, just taking my pleasure in the sun?"

"No, he'd think he had married a girl with sense enough to eat when she was hungry." This from a blunt, solid woman in her middle years, simply dressed and simply spoken. "No better way for him to wake, child, it'll have him thinking about his own belly and its emptiness. I like a hungry patient."

"I can't . . ."

"Oh, don't be so foolish. If you're too delicate to eat alone and that Sharai boy won't join you, then I will. There's plenty here for all." She set her tray on the parapet and plumped herself down beside it, picked something from a platter and passed it to Julianne.

Golden-brown pastry, sticky and flaking between her fingers; the sweet savour of ground meat and spices flooding her senses, flooding her mouth. She had bitten before she knew it, had swallowed without chewing and bitten again; the meat-cake was gone in moments and she was licking her fingers and looking for more.

"That's better, isn't it? *I* knew," the woman said smugly, as her fat, nimble fingers filled a plate. "You've a starved look about you, girl. Take this and set about it while I put some water in the wine, it'll go to your head else and make you foolish."

The last good food she'd seen had been at her wedding-feast, and she hadn't eaten that. The last of any food she'd seen had been in her cell, and yesterday: far away, a different world—bleaker, more frightening but less doomed, she thought, sitting in the sunshine and smelling smoke—and suddenly very, very long ago.

She ate like a starveling indeed, ravenously, with both hands and no manners. Shadow's daughter, Hasan's wife—*and Imber's wife too, just as much, just as little*—she shrugged off a lifetime of courtly graces and barely contrived to keep one eye on her sleeping man. Let him wake now—please?—and she'd greet him with delight, with her mouth full and her hands greasy, her lips coated in crumbs . . .

WHEN SHE HAD breath enough to talk again, she asked, "What's your name? I'm Julianne . . ."

"I know you are, pet. The Lady Julianne, and all your titles too, but I can't be troubled with that. They call me Gerla. Who's the Sharai?" *And how can I make him eat?*

"Leave Jemel to me," she said. "You don't need to wait on us, Gerla. I may be the Lady Julianne with enough titles to trip over, but I've grown used to looking after myself. And others." *Stubborn boys a speciality . . .*

"Oh, yes. Grown used to going hungry because you lack the sense to eat, I suppose. But it's a girlish trick, and feeding boys is another. Aye, I'll leave him to you, if I have your promise for it. There's plenty else for me to be doing."

"Gerla, tell me something, before you go?"

"Aye, lass. Anything."

"Why are you still here? In the palace, I mean. Fetching trays of food to awkward children, when . . ."

When a wave of her arm was all that she needed, to say that Surayon was burning.

"What, should I run away?"

"Not run, no—not unless you chose to." Though running from the Sharai was no bad idea, and running from the Ransomers was a better. "But there must be something you'd rather be doing than this, somewhere else you'd rather be . . ."

"By all the saints and martyrs, girl—do you think we're saints or martyrs ourselves, to stay to serve our lord when we're crying to be gone?" She seemed genuinely incredulous; Julianne found herself blushing. "Listen, then, and mark it: you were raised to another understanding, maybe, but you're in Surayon now. All the men fit to bear arms—yes, and some of the women, too—are long gone, to fight or find their families. The rest of us, from Pym the page-boy to old Shalira in the laundry, we're here because we want to be. You couldn't chase Pym from the Princip's side, not if you carried a battle-axe and had a hundred 'ifrit howling at your back. And me, well, I've no family that I care a button for, and I can be useful here. Not just to feed foolish children, either. The hurt will be brought here, as swiftly as may be. I'm not the Princip, but I have some skills in healing, and there'll be too many for him to tend them all. This is my place, Julianne; I wouldn't be anywhere else, a time like this."

Julianne felt better than reassured, somehow, she felt as though a promise had been fulfilled. She'd never expected to find Surayon a haven for all that was good in the world. What she had wanted, what she had needed to find was a country that was simply different from what she'd known thus far: the cruel subtleties of Marasson, the chill dedication of the Ransomers, the hot but fickle fires of the Sharai. There was loyalty everywhere, of course, from the Roq to Rhabat, even in the Emperor's court; but everywhere it was shaded by desire or duty or tribal allegiance. Here it seemed to be freely given, won by love. To Julianne, today, that was a plashing fountain in a dry, dry garden.

She stood up and stooped over Gerla to give her a gentle kiss on the cheek. "Actually," she murmured, "I think, neither would I."

Then she picked up the tray and carried it over to where Jemel sat next to the unconscious Marron.

"He won't be stirring for a while yet, love. Hasan was healed first, and he shows no sign of waking. So take your eyes off Marron for a moment and look at this instead. You're desert-bred, you don't believe in waste; the Sharai feast in time of plenty, and there's plenty here. Besides, if you eat your fill now, you'll be ready for when he does wake, you'll be able to tend to him without feeling faint from hunger . . ."

That won her a sort of startled glare at the suggestion that a Sharai should ever feel faint, for whatever feeble reason. She grinned, and kissed his cheek too.

"Jemel, you'd feed a camel before you took it into the Sands, wouldn't you? Well, feed yourself, then. I don't know what kind of mood that boy's going to wake into, but it's going to be something different from anything you've seen before. He's going to be a different person, all himself instead of half the Daughter, only that I don't know if he'll remember what self that is. It could be a long journey to find out, and you've got to stay with him. So eat, you'll need your strength."

That was the argument that swung him. He fell to among the meats and pastries; purely for companionship, she squatted down beside him, picked up a soft almond biscuit and nibbled on it. She was just wondering if perhaps she might try to make him talk, when he glanced up and then a little further up, above her head. His eyes widened; she could hear the effort that he had to make, to speak normally. "Elisande's djinni is returning, with your husband's wife."

It sounded so odd, when he said it like that. It wouldn't seem odd to him, though, that Hasan was much-married. Harder for Jemel to understand was her own uncertain status, with two husbands living. To be sure, it was quite hard for her also. By Sharai custom her marriage to Imber was annulled, because it had not been consummated—but then, neither had her marriage to Hasan. *Not yet . . .*

She was confident that no church court in Outremer would recognise that annulment, if only because they had been Sharai who decreed it. So in the Kingdom she was married yet to Imber, in the Sands she was married to Hasan; that seemed to be the easiest way to think of it. Privately, personally, it was more complicated. In her body, she was married to neither; in her heart, she thought, to both. Here in Surayon, where Sands and Kingdom met, she would have spun like a dizzy dancer between the two, except that Imber was not here and Hasan was in need. That made things easy, for today and perhaps for tomorrow. She didn't dare look any further forward.

SHE GOT TO her feet again to greet her sister-wife with a proper dignity, a proper respect. Turning to see her, though, and finding how her mind tried to see a bird instead, except that it was impossibly large and unlikely, she felt all propriety slip away. She stared, rather, in wonder doused with a cold shudder of sympathetic terror.

She watched Sherett glide down towards the terrace, seeming utterly unsupported in the air; she wondered how the woman could look so calm, how she could bear to keep her eyes open as she hung so high with nothing for her hands to grip to.

Julianne walked a few steps away from Jemel, away from the sleeping on their pallets. Squinting, she could just see the djinni as a spinning thread of distortion. She could see also that Sherett's veil was demurely in place below her hood. That brought a soft, unexpected snort of laughter. An insistence on the decencies was part of what she loved about the woman, along with her fierce independence of thought and her open delight in her husband, their shared husband. Those should all have been contradictions, Julianne thought, but somehow were not in Sherett.

Bare feet touched to ground, as lightly as a falling feather; curse her, she didn't even stumble as she turned graceful, impossible flight into graceful, stalking walk along the terrace.

It was Julianne who stumbled a little, suddenly running: hurling her arms around Sherett's neck when she'd meant to be so cool and dignified, brutally disarranging that modest veil as she kissed a greeting, almost sobbing as she mumbled, "Oh, Sherett, thank you for coming . . ."

Dark eyes flashed in the sunlight, hard hands hugged

her too briefly, a caustic voice said, "I wasn't offered a choice. Snatched from our tent, under the eyes of all our family—they'll be talking about it still, and blaming me. Or you, perhaps."

Julianne's family, too, although she didn't know them; there were still two senior wives she hadn't met, and children also. To her shame, she realised suddenly, she'd never even asked their names.

Well, there would be time enough. A lifetime, possibly. For now, "They can blame me, if they choose. I asked for you. Do you, did the djinni tell you why?"

"It said Hasan was sick, no more than that. I didn't ask further."

No, of course she hadn't asked. For swift mercy's sake, Julianne forced a smile. "He should be well now, only he hasn't woken yet. He was very ill, though, an 'ifrit wounded him and he might have died; I thought you'd want to be here, I thought he'd want to see you . . ."

"You were twice right, then—but what you mean is, you wanted me." A hand gripped hers, and, "Take me to our husband, then; and while I watch him, shameless, you can find yourself a veil."

"Oh, Sherett, you don't need to wear it here—!"

"In a stranger's house, for my husband to see me exposed before princes and slaves? Indeed I do, and so do you."

Julianne groaned inwardly, but found a sudden determined stubbornness. "I will not leave him," she muttered forcefully, "to go bothering servants in a house at war to fetch me a useless length of cloth. Sherett, I will not!"

"You are married now, we are married together—and you will dress and behave as a wife ought, and you will do as I say. I will teach you that, if I teach you nothing else. However," relenting abruptly, surprisingly, "there is perhaps no point in chasing a veil until someone brings you a decent robe to replace that rag you're wearing. This is too fine a house for such neglect—but as you say, they are at war. I have seen that, though I barely know where I am. Here . . ."

Hands tugged at her clothing, and she remembered with a sinking heart just how filthy it was, and how filthy she was herself beneath it. Just at the word she could feel all the grime and the greasiness on skin and fabric both, the lank mats of her hair; no doubt she smelled quite rancid to one newly come from the dry clean air of the Sands.

Sherett pulled the hood up over her head, found a way to twist the robe so that there was an extra fold that could be pulled across nose and mouth and held there, so long as she remembered to hold it.

"For now, that's sufficient. Till he wakes, till he's seen you and spoken to you. He's been hunting you so long, he won't want to wait. He has no more patience than a puppy, that one."

That was so untrue that she might have protested it, if she hadn't been so grateful not to be sent away.

She guided Sherett over towards where their man lay quiet on his pallet. First there was Jemel, with his own quiet man; the two Sharai greeted each other, exchanged compliments and hopes, for all the world as though they had met by chance on neutral ground in the heart of the *mul'abarta*.

Then on, and much the same treatment for Hasan. Sherett squatted beside his pallet, laid one hand on his brow and spoke in a normal, everyday voice, as though halfway through a conversation with him.

"Well, you my man, you've been sleeping long enough. The tribes are riding, and it's time to wake. What, will you let them ride without you? Their head is yours if you will take it, man . . ."

For a moment, he seemed to shift beneath her touch. Sherett merely tutted and went on talking. "Very well then, laze. If you will sleep deeper than my *sodar* could have sent you, I'll rouse you ruder than your mother ever did . . ."

And she set her two hands on his head and began to sing, soft and slow and gentle. Simply overhearing—in sunshine after a long night and a heavy meal, when she could and should have been drifting, drowsing, even solidly asleep despite every duty and summons of the day—Julianne's blood was stirring and her skin alive, crawling beneath the strata of her dirt.

Hasan frowned, and his whole body shifted on the pallet; he opened his eyes and blinked up at his wife, while her hands shielded him from the sunlight and incidentally from any glimpse of Julianne. Well, perhaps it was incidental. "What, still no rest?" he murmured, sounding more amused than querulous, more awake and aware than he had any right to be.

"Too much, already. Besides, God and the tribe and all the tribes together have claimed all the common hours that you have; and yet you are a husband too, though you are inclined to forget that. Is it any blame to us poor abandoned wives, if we seize what stray minutes we may?"

He must have heard that deliberate plural as clearly as Julianne did. He lifted his hand slowly to touch Sherett's brow in a gesture that was simple, private, modest and somehow heartshakingly erotic all at once; then he said, "Where is she?"

"Here, Hasan."

He tried to turn his head, against the strict constraint of his elder wife's fingers; and failed, and said, "May I not look on what is my own, Sherett? Has she become ugly, since I saw her beauty last? Or is she marked," seriously now, a tug of anger in his voice, "has that demon Morakh done her damage . . .?"

"Oh, you may look all you like, so long as you lie still to do it. You are the one who has been marked, Hasan," and a thumb stroked lightly over the triple scar on his cheek. "You have been walking with death, and are barely back from the journey. What you may not do is move about, until the Princip has seen and spoken with you."

"The Princip, is it? Am I in Surayon?"

"You are."

And so is your army, Julianne thought, though she said nothing. Hasan gave a short, soft sigh that might have meant anything. All he said was, "That family seems to be dogging me. The son, the granddaughter, now the old man himself . . ."

Now she had to speak, and did. "We brought you here to save your life, Hasan. Rudel lost his, in fetching you through the Folding."

"Is Rudel dead? I am sorry, though my people may not be. These are stories that need to be told; later will do, if it be not too late. For now, immediately, show me my recovered jewel, Sherett. I promise, I will lie as still as—well, I had meant to say death, but not that. As still as an ailing man in the presence of his newest lady, not wishing to make a flailing, whimpering idiot of himself . . ."

Sherett took her hands away and Julianne slid forward, to where he could see her easily without turning his head or squinting into the sun's glare. She remembered to hold the cloth across her face as a substitute veil; he reached up and touched his fingers to her brow, much as he had saluted her sister-wife.

"Julianne. Wife. I looked for you . . ."

"I know you did. And found me," *in a manner of speaking, and too late.*

"Did I? I remember finding a madman . . ." He frowned, and she could almost see the memory slip from his tenuous grasp. "Well. Later. Show me, I said . . ."

His hand had no stronger grip than his mind, but it served to nip the veil from her unresisting fingers and ease it aside.

"Don't worry," he said, "I won't be scolded. There's only Sherett to see, and it'll be you that she blames."

Now he smiled, and it had been worth long waiting for. Now he stroked her cheek, and pushed back her hood to draw her long hair free. She knelt patient while he played, not daring to risk a glance at Sherett. It was all she could do not to kiss at the inside of his wrist, where the skin might smell sourly of his recent illness but was still his, was a part of him and so near, so tempting, so easily reached for kissing after so long. There had been only the two men come this close to her, and thus far they'd both escaped her kisses.

Thus far, and just a little further: she did resist the yearning, not to shock Sherett beyond bearing. Then she did take her husband's hand and lay it firmly back on the blanket that covered him; and she did tuck her hair back inside her robe, and draw the hood up over, and pull her makeshift veil across her face again.

"You're too thin," he said, reaching out again in defiance of her discipline, folding his hand loosely around her wrist. "A girl should be slender, but not hollow. Were you much mistreated?"

She shook her head, but not in denial of anything he'd said. They were all of them too thin, she and all her friends; each of them had their reasons. "Later," she said, throwing his own word, his own decision back at him. "Time enough for all our stories then. I'm being fattened up again, in any case. And you still need rest—"

"—And food," he interrupted.

"Yes, and food. Fit food," with a little gentle malice. "No meat, no sweets, no feasting. Not till you're recovered."

He groaned superbly. "How shall I ever recover, if you starve me on slops?"

"Slowly," Sherett said, reinforcing Julianne. "In your sleep, largely. We're going to leave you for an hour now; will you lie still and rest, or shall I call up my *sodar* to enforce you to it? I'll fetch the Princip after, and then if he allows it you can sit up, take a drink and a little to eat."

"Where is the Princip?"

"With his granddaughter," Julianne said. "With Rudel."

"Then go, by all means, wherever it is that you are going. I have Jemel for company."

"And you're not to plague him with questions. Jemel, if he tries, you have your own *sodar*—"

"—And will use it. I promise." She believed him. He ached visibly for silence, for solitude, so long as he could share them both with Marron. This all-but-empty palace was too populous for him, as Rhabat had been before. He wanted his friend fit and the open Sands, a spare camel and his wits and skills to live on, nothing more.

Perhaps he could have that now, she thought, with an unexpected flare of hope. Marron was harmless without the Daughter, meaningless in the machinations of the wise. They had no reason to keep him, and he surely had no reason to stay. So he would go, and Jemel would go beside him; and they would find no welcome anywhere in Outremer, so they would be bound for the desert in the end. For the desert and perhaps for happiness, in some scale.

As was she, perhaps, in some scale. Hasan could make her happy, she thought, if only he didn't seek to instal her in Ascariel, junior wife to its tyrant overlord of her conquered people. If he did that she would be useful, yes, but not she thought happy.

Sherett could make her happy also, in other ways. Sometimes quite unexpectedly, as now, plucking her up by the elbow and wrenching her away. As she was towed through the solarium, she asked, "Where are we going?"

"In search of a bath, and fresh clothing. I have been caught in a sandstorm and felt cleaner afterwards than that djinni has left me, with all the wind's dust in my hair; you stink worse than a midden. Patrics may not care about such matters, but you will learn that we Sharai are a fastidious people."

It might not, surely it could not last; but for the moment at least, Julianne felt blindingly, blisteringly happy.

*   *   *

IT WAS QUICKLY apparent that the palace was all but abandoned. They hustled through halls and corridors and found no one; Julianne was just beginning to think they'd have to stand still and shout for attention, when at last a boy appeared, carrying a tray heaped with dirty pots.

He blinked at them, shifted his burden in a vain attempt to hide his damp and grimy shirt, and said, "Ladies? Can I help at all? My name is Roald, I serve the Princip here."

"If you would lead us to the bathing-chamber," Sherett said, "and then perhaps find us a change of dress, or ask a woman to do so. We don't need hot water, cold will do."

Julianne shivered at the thought of a hard scrubbing in icy well-water. That surely wasn't the flicker of a wink that the boy gave her in response; there was certainly the flash of a smile, though, before he suppressed it. "No need for that, my lady. Of course the baths are ready, and the fires hot. If you will come with me . . ."

No surprise, that he was entirely eager to abandon his pots there and then; Julianne suspected that Gerla was wrong, that there was one scullery-boy at least who had been kept in the house against his will. To judge by the way he crouched, the cautious way he straightened, it was an edict that had been reinforced with bruises.

They couldn't be that bad, though; they hadn't marked his curiosity, nor his confidence. He shifted his shoulders beneath his shirt, found a slouching way to walk that didn't hurt too badly and demanded boldly, "Ladies, is it true that you flew in here this morning on a magic carpet?"

Julianne choked on a sudden, startled giggle. When she'd recovered, she said, "I don't know. Is it? I suppose it could be. Didn't you see?"

"I was in the stables," he said disgustedly, "and everyone else ran off, but I had my hands full with the Princip's brute of a stallion, and I couldn't just leave him loose, could I? By the time I had him stabled, I was the last left, and the master wouldn't let me go."

"No, I don't suppose he would."

"And then the Princip wouldn't let me ride out with the other men, even as a messenger. He *needs* messengers . . ."

"I'm sure he does, but he also needs to feel that those in his charge are as safe as they can be. The time will come when he'll have to answer to your family, Roald, for his care of you."

"I haven't got a family, that's why I'm here. The Princip takes us into the palace, until he can find us another home; some of us he keeps. I've been here five years," which was obviously a source of pride rather than humiliation, except that his voice turned suddenly as he went on. "I'm not a *child*, though! He sent the little ones away this morning, up into the hills, and he tried to send me with them, only I wouldn't go."

"So what did you do?" Julianne asked, knowing the answer already, feeling guilty already for dragging it out of him.

"I hid," and surely he couldn't get any redder. "Until they'd given up on me and gone. Then I came out, I was sure they'd let me ride messenger now—but Baris caught me before I got to the Princip, and he took me to the kitchens."

And beat him into the bargain, but Roald was clearly not going to mention that.

"And then we came."

"And then you came, and the baths are just here, and I'll build up the fires for you, lady, because the other lady's Sharai and you both came from the desert and I expect you like it really hot—but tell me about the magic carpet? Please?"

Julianne laughed. "It's not really magic. A djinni brought us here, and there were so many of us, it was just easier"—*easier for me, and Elisande thought of that, even while everything else was happening*—"if it carried us in on a carpet, like half a dozen glasses on a tray. It fetched

Sherett for me later, and she flew in with nothing to stand on at all."

"Oh." That was obviously something of a disappointment. A djinni was one thing, a magic carpet something else entirely. A boy might dream, she supposed, of finding or buying or stealing a magic carpet, but not a djinni. Emphatically, not a djinni. "Why would the djinni do that? They're not usually so . . ."

Helpful? Cooperative? Exciting? Involved? A gesture filled the space of the missing word.

"Never mind why," Sherett said sharply, as they came into the first cool chamber of a simple hammam. There was a shelf of oils and unguents there; she inspected it while the boy ran off to tend to his fires.

He came back sweating under the weight and hammer-heat of an iron basket full of scorching rocks, which he carried through to the inner chamber. When he came out, following billows of scented steam, Sherett ambushed him with a grip on his elbow, a push towards a long bench and a brisk command: "Take off your shirt, and lie down."

"What? Lady, no . . ."

"You might as well," Julianne said, amused. "She'll do it for you, else. And give you more bruises on the way."

Sherett snorted. "I wouldn't beat a boy useless, on a day like this."

"I'm not useless!" A furious protest from Roald, even as he clung desperately to his dignity and his shirt, wrapping his arms tight around his body in an effort to keep them both together.

"You will be when you start to stiffen up, unless you let me at you now. I found a salve here that'll help to soothe the burning. And don't tell me it isn't burning. I know all the stages of a beating, me."

Of course she did, and from both sides, most likely. The boy was mulish, though, eyeing the door in hopes of a getaway, determined to keep his clothes on and his privacy secure. It was Julianne who found the weapon to break down his resistance.

"If you won't be medicined, you must be healed; there's no room here for a boy who can't work. Can Gerla do it, do you think, or must I ask the Princip . . . ?"

The horror of such an idea struck Roald mute, as it seemed; he made no answer. Slowly, though, very slowly he unlaced the neck of his shirt and pulled it off over his head.

Julianne deliberately turned her head aside, not to increase his mortification, and didn't look back until Sherett was done with him, until he was easing his shirt on again and flinching as the worn linen fell against his skin. She thought the salve might be doing some good, by the wary surprise on his face; she thought she had a salve for his soul, which might do even better.

"Roald, come here."

He came, bristling with suspicion, wary of some further degradation. She smiled and said, "I have a task for you. A secret task, can I trust you not to shout it?"

"Of course, lady!"

"Good. Who guards the Princip, with all the men gone to the war?"

"The Princip never has a guard, lady. He is . . ." Again a gesture, in lieu of the word he didn't have; the gesture seemed to mean all-powerful, invulnerable, perhaps simply "Princip".

"Well, he may need one now. There is more than one army in Surayon, and creatures more subtle and more evil than men; even the Princip may have his mind distracted, and his eyes not watching his back. I want you to do that for him, as much as you may. The older boys have gone, his little page is too young for this, and who else is there? Here, take this."

Roald eyed the blade that she offered him, with something close to yearning on his face. All he said, though, was a stout, "Lady, I have my own knife."

"I'm sure you do." She was sure she knew its type, too: a nocked blade handed down through generations of lads, hollow from too many years' rough sharpening on any convenient stone, its handle split and bound with fraying string. No doubt he cut his meat with it, and his nails, too, when he thought to cut them; she doubted strongly whether it was good for much besides. "This knife is special, though, for more reasons than you can see," and he should be able to see plenty in the chased steel blade, the wicked double edge, the haft inlaid with mother-of-pearl. "It has been blessed by priests, to be proof against 'ifrit and other spirit-creatures. This blade will protect the Princip, where perhaps nothing else can do it. Will you take it? For him, and because I ask you to?"

She pressed it into his hands before he could answer, to let him feel the cold smoothness of the hilt, the vicious edge. Even so, he hesitated.

"Lady, this is too good for a kitchen-boy . . ."

"Yes, it is. But it's not too good for the Princip's ward; and it's essential for the Princip's chief bodyguard, his *secret* bodyguard . . ."

And to overcome his last wavering doubts, she unknotted the ties of her robe and began to slip it down off her shoulders.

The boy fled, taking the knife with him.

A MINUTE LATER she was pouring a dipper of water over stones so hot that they cracked in their iron cradle, she was breathing deeply and sighing luxuriously as steam engulfed her and she felt the sweat start to break through her ingrained crust of dirt. She could sit here and lose more than the stink of her prison cell; she could lose all the distress of the last weeks, all the darkness that had gathered in the corners of her mind, wash it all away and be pure, clean, her father's proper daughter . . .

Sherett cut across her thoughts with a question. "Why did you give that boy your knife?"

"Because he needed it. Everyone in Surayon needs something today," and she wished that everyone's need could be so easily satisfied, or satisfied at all.

"You'd best warn the Princip, or he'll wonder why he's being shadowed everywhere by a kitchen-boy with a dagger in his hand."

"I will, if we see him. He may ride out again, when he and Elisande are finished . . ." And then, because that reminded her of what he and Elisande were doing, which reminded her in turn that she couldn't after all wash or sweat the world away no matter how hot the bath or how dense the steam, she said, "Sherett, what's it like out there? The djinni brought you over in daylight, you must have seen . . ."

"Aye, and been seen in my turn," the woman said, with half a smile that was clearly for something that might have been half funny, on another day. "But yes, Julianne, I saw. I saw what my people are doing, bringing the dry desert to this wet country, covering the green with ash and smoke. They are burning crops and villages, and slaying where they ride: my greedy people, destroying what they cannot take away. And doing all in the name of God, Julianne, to recover the holy places. We say that God chose us from all the people in the world and set us in the Sands to test us, to keep us pure. If that is true, then perhaps God is using us now to test the people here, fetching in the fire and death that we live with daily to see if they are soft or strong."

"Or perhaps that's a thin excuse," Julianne said bitterly, "to justify theft and cruelty and murder, because it was these people who took these lands from your possessing, and you want your revenge."

She expected a sharp rebuttal from her sister-wife, and didn't get it. Sherett only nodded slowly, and said, "Perhaps so. But it is not only the Sharai who are making war in Surayon."

"No, I know. I heard that. There is an army led by Ransomers, come in from the north."

"And more, a party from the east too, following the tribes. A small party, but I saw them. They saw me, too," and that difficult smile was there again, more heard than seen. "They are led by the man you were married to, before."

Julianne stared, trying to make her face out through the veiling steam. "I don't understand. How do you know that?"

"The djinni told me. The Baron Imber, is that right?"

That was right, it was absolutely right; but, "There are two Barons Imber."

"This is the man you married. Your husband, the djinni said. That is not correct, of course, the djinn can be mistaken; but they do not lie, Julianne. It is he."

She sat with the steam and the sweat coursing off her in runnels, with the warmth and the heat of all her Imber memories coursing through her veins, and still she shivered in the chill of this news, still she couldn't believe that she had ever felt so cold before.

THREE

A Hollow Heart, An Empty Hand

IT DIDN'T FEEL like waking, but then what came before had never felt like sleep—more like a grim despair, as though he could have opened his eyes at any moment, but that he could see no reason to. Just as a prisoner in a dungeon knows the crushing weight of the castle rock above his head, just as an exhausted traveller shoulders all the night's sky and drags its burden of stars in his wake, so Marron had felt the insupportable heaviness of a world of ice bear down upon him, cold and grey and mercilessly grinding.

He'd also felt a lashing fire, a fierce vortex that surged and burned. They were at war, the fire and the ice; they fought each other, but their fighting injured him.

If he had any body left to injure, if he wasn't dead already and welcome to eternity. Perhaps heaven hurt, very likely there was pain in hell.

It hadn't seemed to matter. Where everything was distant, nothing could be further off than anything else; he'd remembered a boy from his childhood who had fallen through ice on a frozen winter river, who had been carried like a pale shadow beneath his own feet where he had stood terrified on the glassy, cracking surface. Or perhaps he was that boy, perhaps he always had been.

EXCEPT THAT THAT boy was dead, and he was not. He felt the fire leave him; he felt the cold recede. He thought that his blood ran freely in his body again, at last, and carried him with it, so that he reached all the way to his skin and all of it was his own again, more so than it had been for a long, long time.

A time came when he could reach out even beyond his skin and take note of the world around. He heard voices, though he felt still too far away to listen. He was aware of softness beneath him and warmth above, warmth that lay across him like a blanket. Not desert heat, which he regretted; this was something gentler, that felt to him like something hollow, a mockery-thing, far less than it should have been.

He felt much the same about himself. If he lay still long enough, he thought he might remember all his story, and its proper order; he might know where he was and what had happened to him. There seemed to be no urgency anywhere, in his body or his mind. There was a question that he thought he ought to ask, but he wasn't sure what it was, nor whether it really mattered; it could wait.

So he lay and waited also, feeling as light and hollow as the sunlight, an egg sucked dry. He had come through the fire and the chill; perhaps he was a saint, cast back into his martyred body. Something was missing, though, more than the story of his days. Perhaps he had been a saint and made miracles, and now for his reward he was made to be a normal man, to live without the holy fire in his blood and die at last and never live again. Perhaps he should be content, live hollow and contented . . .

He opened his eyes, because he thought he ought to.

There was a sky of pure pale blue, which was all wrong. There was a sun to dazzle, to make him blink and squint; it had burned the sky white all around the fierce beaten gold of its own face, and all of that was wrong.

Then there was a shadow, a silhouette between him and the light. He felt the dry, warm touch of fingers on his brow, a palm against his cheek; he could smell the spicy desert tang of unwashed robes and a dust-washed body beneath.

"Jemel," he said, recognising the shape of it in his mouth, the meaning in his head.

His own name, "Marron," was given back to him in answer, in a cracked and broken whisper. Now he could see a face in the shadow that hung above him, now that he knew what to look for. A sharp nose, dark sunken eyes, black curls, skin the colour of an ageing bruise: the details of the face, the proud curve of the nose and the gleam of light reflected in the intensity of an eye, were enough to jolt him into a rush of memories. *He is Sand Dancer, of a sort; I am Ghost Walker, of a kind—*

—AND THERE, JUST there it all broke down, as he realised what it was that he had lost, what had been stripped from him, eyes and blood and mind and all.

"Where is it?" he asked, and yes, that was the question.

"I do not know. The Princip took it from you, and healed your arm after he had healed your sickness, so that it could not go back. He sang a *sodar* to make it sleep, and then Lisan carried it when they went away. I do not know where they have gone. Do you want it back, Marron?"

He wasn't sure. *What am I, what are we when I am not the Ghost Walker?* Was Jemel a Sand Dancer still, did his oaths count for anything? And what lay behind the oaths, what mattered so much more—would that endure, or would it be fractured or broken or abandoned altogether, another measurement of loss?

"Do you want me to take it back?" *Do you need me to? Or do I . . .?* Jemel had only ever known him as the Walker, marked out by more than red eyes and an unhealing wound. If he was to be his simple self again, the boy he used to be—well, that boy had been Sieur Anton's entirely, and not Jemel's at all.

Jemel only shrugged in echo of Marron's own confusion and shifted his head a little, as if to break the contact of their eyes. The sun's glare was a sudden, unbearable dazzle; Marron turned his own head to escape it, turned away from Jemel and couldn't bear that either.

He sat up with an effort that left him dizzy and weak, a stranger in his body now. He reached out for his friend's support—and checked the movement abruptly, drawing back his arm. His left arm . . .

There were all the scarred ridges of his wounding, nothing could heal those; but the heart of it, where it had lain open all this time, was sealed over with fresh pink skin. He prodded at it experimentally. It was soft and smooth, untouched by sun or dirt, and the flesh was firm beneath. There was no pain, no matter how he worked it.

Black stars sparkled behind his eyes; his mind whirled. His arms were wooden suddenly, too heavy to hold or move. He felt himself sway, begin to fall, could do nothing to prevent it. Hands gripped his shoulders, held him upright while a strained voice murmured urgently, "You should lie down, you have been very sick . . ."

Healed or not, he felt sick still; even his tongue tingled strangely, and it was hard to speak. There were more questions now, though, and these might win an answer, could at least do no more damage.

He did lie down, though not quite on the pallet. He wriggled sideways—against little resistance—until his head lay nested in Jemel's lap. Then he said, "How did I get sick, Jemel—how could I, with the Daughter to protect me? And where are we now, why did you move me? We were in Selussin, I remember that . . ."

And that name, that memory brought others again, so that he could almost have answered one of his own questions. He remembered faces in a market, a silent threat; he remembered releasing the Daughter himself, and then a cold invasion.

"There was an 'ifrit," Jemel said, "or something of an 'ifrit, some little poison of itself. It found entrance through your hurt, and what you carry—what you *carried* then fought with it, until we brought you here. This is Surayon, the Princip's house. He has freed you from the 'ifrit's shadow, and from the other, too; but Rudel is dead, and Hasan has been gravely hurt, and there is war all around us, you can smell it on the wind."

Marron sniffed for the scent of it, then closed his eyes, shook his head on the Sharai boy's knees and said, "No, I can't. Not any more. I could have done, before."

"You can now. I can. There is smoke in the air."

"You have a desert nose, Jemel, to match your desert eyes."

"Perhaps. The air is dry in the Sands, and scents carry; we learn to read the wind. But these fires are close, even this wet breeze will say so. You could smell them if you tried. Wet your nose with your finger, and stretch to catch the upper air where it moves . . ."

"I need not try, so long as I have you to do it for me. Besides, you told me to lie here and be still. If I sit up again, I will likely faint and you will be angry with me." And then, losing his smile in a moment, before he could even see whether it was returned, "Tell me, Jemel. How is Rudel dead, and Hasan hurt? How long have I been ill, for so much to happen? And how have we come to the Folded Land, and war followed us?"

*   *   *

HE HAD TO wait, while Jemel fetched a beaker of cool
fruit-juice and propped his head up just far enough to en-
able him to drink; and then again for the time it took to
persuade his friend that no, he was not hungry, the juice
was enough for now, he couldn't possibly eat.

At last, though, with his head cushioned once more in
the warm lap and Jemel's fingers playing lightly with his
hair, all his questions were answered—or all except the
one that he couldn't bring himself to ask again, for fear of
hearing himself confess, *I want it back.*

"—AND THAT IS all the news I have," Jemel finished.

"Then we must find more. Is Hasan here still?"

The softest, briefest of chuckles, and, "Marron, he is
asleep on the pallet next to yours. Fling out an arm too far,
and you would hit him on the nose."

"Oh." He didn't turn, didn't look, didn't move except
to say, "How long has he been sleeping, can we wake him
yet?"

"We could, perhaps," Jemel said doubtfully, "but for
what? He knows less than you. The women did not talk
with him long, and told him nothing that mattered."

"Women? What women?"

"His wives. Sherett and Julianne. Lisan sent the djinni
for Sherett—I said that already, weren't you listening?
But then they both left him, and he fell asleep. You should
sleep, too."

No doubt he should, but it wasn't going to happen. He
said, "Well, if Hasan cannot give us the news we need,
let's go and find someone who can. Julianne is with
Sherett; very well. Where are Elisande and the Princip?"

"I don't know. I said—"

"—And you don't think I was listening. I remember,
Jemel. They took my Daughter—no, the King's Daugh-
ter—away from me, and you don't know where they went.
So we'll have to hunt them out. It shouldn't be too hard. I

don't know the Princip, but his granddaughter makes enough noise for two. We'll just ask anyone we meet, *where's the little loud one?* They'll know."

"Marron, you must not move. They said it of Hasan, he was not even to turn his head . . ."

"Well, I've done that and more, I sat up straight, remember?"

"And fainted, when you did."

"Nearly fainted. You held me up. We can do the same again. Slowly, this time. I promise, Jemel, if I feel giddy, I will say. If not, we can go exploring. You won't go alone, I know that."

"No."

"So we have to go together. Unless you're prepared to sit here quietly and watch me sleep while the world burns all around us? Even the women are off doing something, Jemel. Do you want to be left behind?"

"No," again, a fierce whisper.

"So help me up, and we'll see who we can find, and what we can learn."

STANDING TOOK TIME and care, so much of each that he ached for the Daughter's fire in his thin blood and its strength in his weary bones. He felt as though something of himself, all his value had been stolen from him while he slept. He ought to be glad to have it gone, but without it, what was he? Just a boy, an insignificant blade unsure who to fight for and unwilling to kill, sworn to both sides and trusting neither.

Standing now, leaning heavily on Jemel, he looked down on the sleeping Hasan and then out, over the parapet for his first sight of Surayon.

He saw a valley like a garden on a grand scale, green and growing—or rather it had been, and should have been yet. Whichever way he turned, though, west and north and east the air was smudged with smoke. He forgot almost that he had lost the Daughter's eyes; he seemed to see sharply at great distances despite that all-encompassing haze, and what he saw was death and fury.

This was what Hasan had yearned for, he thought bleakly, and Sieur Anton too—a bolt shot at the heart of the Kingdom, a purifying fire, a holy war for each of them although they followed different gods. Try as he might, stare though he did, he could see nothing holy: only men in armour, men in black, men in midnight blue, all blood-swathed and screaming. Three armies, he thought: one was Ransomer-led, one was Sharai and not led by anyone, its only hope for a leader here at his feet. The other must be from Ascariel.

Between them all the Surayonnaise, fighting like farm-ers for their lands and lives. Better if the armies fought each other; that must come, surely, as soon as Sharai tribes met knights of Outremer. However soon, though, it would be too late for Surayon. The land had been blighted already, in a morning's work; another day or two, and it would be destroyed.

Jemel was gazing at Hasan. "I cannot believe that he sleeps in Outremer, while the tribes are fighting."

"You haven't been where he was, Jemel. I can believe that he would sleep and sleep; I wish I could. Besides, bet-ter that for Hasan than to rise up and make a killing choice. This is Outremer, yes—but it is also Surayon. The Sharai have had an understanding with these people for many years. Elisande lived a year in Rhabat, do you re-member? And was not the first to do so. The Princip saved Hasan's life this morning; should Hasan demand a mount and a weapon, to fight him this afternoon? Or should he betray the tribes who trust him, who followed him this far?"

"Hasan should do what he believes is right, what he has always taught and argued for." Jemel's voice was as tight and unforgiving as his face. "It is a coward's way, to es-cape into dreams when the road is hard. He knew that

Surayon was part of Outremer, he has always known that. It was Catari land before, and holy to us."

"And what would you do, if he made that choice and went to lead the tribes? Would you join their slaughter, as you wanted to before? It is a slaughter, Jemel, just lift your eyes and look. Or listen, can't you hear the screaming? There are children's voices in the screaming."

"There always are. Children, women, the old and the sick—they die, whosoever hand directs the blade. That is war, Marron. You know this, you have done this too. You say you will not kill again; I say wait, the time will come. Hasan might control the tribes a little; the slaughter will be worse without him. But no, I would not follow if he left. I followed him once, and Jazra died. I swore then that I would never follow him again, but kill him rather. I was hot then, blaming him for saving me; that oath was foolish, and I broke it. But now he is sleeping in the sun while men die—yes, and children too—and I will not follow him again. A man should not be weak when he is needed. Besides, I am sworn to stay with you, and that oath I will keep, foolish or not."

Marron might have wished the last answer to have come first, but he was glad enough to hear it at all. He nodded his acceptance, although privately he wondered if his changeable friend might not turn once more, when Hasan was awake and in his strength again. That man had a drawing power in his voice and manner, that Jemel had been helpless to resist before.

For now, he just nodded his head towards the open doorway that led off the terrace and into the palace beyond.

STANDING HAD BEEN hard enough; walking was worse, even with Jemel's shoulder as a crutch beneath his arm. He felt absurdly weak, utterly drained and more. He shuffled along like a man old and spent, as though all his youth and vitality had been ripped from him. His body had not forgotten the steely inexhaustibility it had borrowed from the Daughter. With every step he expected to recover it, and with every step he was betrayed into a trembling helplessness.

Probably any man so cruelly reduced would hunger for what he had lost. He couldn't blame himself for yearning to have the Daughter back in his blood again; his soul's freedom didn't seem worth the price today.

They passed through a wide and empty room and came to a corridor that led straight and far, too far, seemingly into the hillside the house was built against. There was still no one in sight, no sound of movement from any of the many doors that opened to left and right. Marron wondered if the entire household had abandoned them to ride off to the war. More seriously, he wondered if he could possibly walk as far as the corridor's end, even with Jemel's support. If he did, and if they found nothing but empty rooms all the way, he was utterly certain that he would not be able to walk back.

Jemel knew; he said, "This was stupid from the start. We should sit on the terrace and wait. The Princip will come soon, Sherett said so."

Even as he said it, they heard voices, down at the further end of the corridor. Marron waited a beat, to know who they were and what they were saying; then remembered that it was the Daughter's trick and not his, to hear such details across such a distance.

So he waited in an ordinary way, as Jemel waited beside him, two young men adrift in a strange house, not at all where they were thought or meant to be. He could have been nervous, he thought, at being found—or caught, he might have said—like this. The boy he'd been, Sieur Anton's squire would likely have ducked through any convenient doorway to avoid it. Now he didn't care, except that he hoped not to startle whoever was coming.

Two of them, stepping through an archway, arm in arm

and arguing hotly. Marron didn't need the Daughter's eyes, nor its ears to identify them now. The one he'd lived and travelled with for many weeks, while the other was actually easier for him to name from some little way off. The squat figure, the barrel chest, the beard—he might almost have thought that Jemel had lied to him, if the beard hadn't been white and Elisande hadn't been so closely in the stranger's company.

"Grandfer!" Her voice rose, easy to hear every word suddenly. "I thought you'd healed him?"

"So did I." It was a fit voice to come from such a chest, from such a man, deep and carrying. "And so I did. He's not bleeding, not possessed, not grey and fading into death—what more do you want?"

"You know what more!"

"And you know what little I had left me, or could afford to give . . ."

But he was talking to empty air; Elisande had disengaged her arm from his and was running the length of the corridor.

She hurtled into Marron, clutching at him, all but knocking him over with the force of her arrival. It was Jemel's wiry strength that held them all upright; that earned no thanks, though, only a glare and, "What were you thinking of, to let him leave his bed?"

"Have you ever tried to keep him there?"

Elisande blushed furiously; Marron felt a little tremor in his friend's arm and thought the Sharai was laughing, deep inside.

Then the girl took his hands in a tight grip, muttering, "Just hold him for a minute, let me work."

She closed her eyes, perhaps to see the better. Marron felt warmth flood into his fingers, into his wrists, wherever her skin touched his. It chased through him, blood and bone, the course the Daughter always used to take; he felt a pang of near-recognition. But this was something far less harsh, sunlight and not fire; what it left in its wake

was not the limitless energy nor the seeming immunity
that he could have borrowed from the Daughter. Rather it
was an awakening, his own strength stirring as his muscles fed, as they drew from Elisande something of what
they had lost in his draining.

Not all: she couldn't give him what had not been his.
Nor could she restore to him the full power even of the
boy he'd been before, the brother Ransomer who would
sweat and endure and achieve through sheer stubbornness.
What he had now, though, what she gifted to him felt like
another miracle, a pulsing wonder in the deep hollows of
his body, a secret flame whose light could not be hidden,
whose source would never show.

"Enough." That was the Princip, who knew that source
too well. Elisande nodded and released his hands, looking
pale and shivering herself now, apparently glad to step
back into the shield of her grandfather's arm.

Jemel frowned as Marron did the opposite, straightening and stretching and peeling away from the Sharai's
supporting hold.

"It's all right, Jemel. Look, I can do this now," standing by himself and smiling at his friend, secure on his own
feet. He could do a lot more; he felt as though he could
run the length of Outremer, race Jemel on a camel, on a
horse, whatever. It wasn't true, of course, he'd fail sooner
than he ought to; it was only with the Daughter's strength
that he could run all day, the granddaughter's wouldn't
sustain him long at all if he were wasteful of it.

"You can, yes," the Princip said, with an edge to his
voice that was patently saying, *and see now, she cannot.*
"Forgive my sounding churlish, Marron, you are very
welcome to Surayon, and to my house; but she should not
have spent so much of her energy where it was not
needed."

"Oh, what, not needed?" Elisande roused herself into
instant outrage, squirming against the arm that held her
pinned to his side. "He was falling down, you saw him—"

"—And could have been picked up by Jemel there and carried back to his bed and kept in it, tied down if necessary, until he had eaten and drunk and slept his way to health again. It would have come, in time."

"He might not have had time," she argued, with that sullen look that said she knew she had lost the point already.

"No, that is true—but if Marron lacked the time to recover naturally, then so will everyone else who comes here in search of healing. And they will come, Elisande, they are coming now. And what will you say to them, to the men with their wounds and the women with their burns and the children with their terrors and their broken bones, when they turn to you and you are too spent to help them?"

"There are other healers," she muttered, twisting again against his grip, this time trying to avoid his level gaze and his steady voice.

"Yes, there are. Some are stronger than you, and some are less strong, and all will be needed—but none among them is granddaughter to the Princip. It makes a difference, Elisande."

"I know," she said, sighing, subsiding. "I'm sorry, Grandfer. But Marron can make a difference too," added determinedly, a new justification. "He's no good to us lying on a pallet in the sunshine."

"Forgive me, lad—but what good to us is he on his feet and twitching with your borrowed strength? As Ghost Walker, he was dangerous to both sides equally; as a boy, he's all bone and nothing."

"He can fight. He's a demon with a sword, I saw him outfence four Sand Dancers at once . . ."

That was the demon with the sword, not me, though it was true that he had his own skills. But he didn't say so, he said neither of those things; he had something else to say that was more important. "Elisande—I will not kill."

"What, *still?*"

"Still."

She glared, with an exasperated affection; he made a helpless gesture, *sorry, but your grandfather's right, I'm no use to anyone . . .*

Surprisingly, it was Jemel who offered a way forward. Jemel the fierce warrior, always ready to kill anything that did not kill him, Jemel said, "The wounded will be brought to this house?"

"Yes, any who are seriously hurt. They'll be looking for me, but I can't be here—no, Elisande, I *cannot!* I must go out to the field again, I've delayed too long already."

"Which field? There are three armies on your land now."

"Each of them in turn. Naturally."

"And do what? Fight and die an old man's death, too foolish to remember that your body is not the force it used to be?"

"Experience is like armour in a battle, Elisande—"

"—Yes, it slows you down—"

"—And I don't plan to fight much in any case, only to organise the defence of my country."

"Oh, that needs you, does it? It's not as if everyone in Surayon hasn't known for thirty years what they should do when this day comes . . ."

"Knowing and doing are different things, when there is fire and death at your heels. I simply have to be there, the Princip has to be seen. And no, you may not ride with me. You have to be here, you're as much a symbol as I am. Rudel is dead, and you are more than ever the continuity of the state. I've indulged you before, but no longer. You stay here, and you help my people, your people—which does not mean wasting what energy you have to make your friends feel better!"

Jemel spoke again, quickly across the seething silence, before the storm could break. "It will not have been wasted. We will ride out, Marron and I, if there are any horses left in your stables; we'll help to bring your

wounded in. Armed men defend the weak simply with
their presence. And if we meet a war-party, well, I am
Sharai and he is Patric; between us we may turn them
without need to fight. Both our peoples have honour
enough, not to attack the injured or their escorts. They
may need only to be reminded of it, in the heat of the day."

More likely, Marron thought, he and Jemel would simply incite extra fury in those they faced, regardless of any
codes of honour. Sharai and Patric riding together, in this
cursed and desecrated land? That was reason enough for
more slaughter.

Still, it was a good idea. Even the Princip couldn't
deny that. He nodded briefly, and even managed a glimmer of a smile as he said, "There are horses remaining,
though they may not meet your standards, Jemel. I've
mounted the Sharai before, and even my finest would
barely satisfy. Now my finest are dead, or ridden half to
death already."

Jemel shook his head. "I wouldn't waste a warhorse,
nor a racing horse. If we fight, we fail, and we will not
flee. Give us sumpters if you have them, they can carry
two at need; give us dray horses if you must. Perhaps we
should take a dray . . ."

"Perhaps we should," Marron said quietly. "Jemel, I
can't ride—Oh. Oh, yes. I suppose I can, at that." A
breath, which didn't help at all, and then, "With your permission, sir? We'll do what we can."

Another nod from the Princip. "Go. Tell them in the
stables—if you can find anyone to tell—that I will come
shortly, and I need my Boucheron saddled and prepared.
No doubt there will be others riding with me. *Not* you,
Elisande," before she could utter the first syllable of the
argument they could all see rising to her lips. "You stay,
and play princess for me as your mother would have done.
Marron, you feel well just now, but you are not. Do what
you can for my people, and by the God's grace I will
thank you for it later, but don't drive yourself into ex-

haustion. There's no more either one of us can do for you today."

"Except one thing," Elisande said swiftly, determined apparently to have some kind of final say, if not the one she'd wanted. "An armed man needs a weapon, Marron sweet, or he may be very scary but he isn't very armed. Esren!"

The djinni appeared at her word in its common form and place, a darkling rope above and behind her shoulder.

Hanging seemingly unsupported in the air below was a sword in a belted scabbard of white leather with silver edging.

Marron would have thought it lost, if he'd had the time to think it missing. His rush of joy at its recovery told him how much he would have mourned that loss.

He spoke his joy in a wordless cry, in a sudden movement that pulled him free of Jemel's restraining arm. He reached past Elisande and snatched for the sword; there was a moment's resistance, and then Dard's familiar weight fell into his hand.

"For a young man who doesn't want to kill," the Princip observed mildly, "you seem uncommonly pleased to have your weapon back, Marron."

"Uh, yes, sir . . ." He was too busy buckling the belt around his waist to worry about the old man's unabashed interest, Elisande's smug self-content, even Jemel's stony silence. They all had their meanings, and any one of them might mean trouble to come, but he could puzzle them out later. He shifted the belt until the sword hung perfectly, put his hand to the hilt and drew the blade a hand's span from its sheath. He wanted to go further, to examine its edge and run his fingers along its chasings, to come that little closer to Sieur Anton. This was not the time, though; he released the hilt and let the sword slide down into its sheath again. In that moment of separation, he remembered again his other, his genuine loss. And looked at Elisande and said, "Where have you put the Daughter?"

"Where it will be safe," the Princip replied brusquely, when she hesitated. "The fewer who know, the safer it will be."

Safest of all if you don't know, that seemed to be what he was truly saying. If safety meant separation, if keeping them apart was its true measure, then even Marron thought that he was right. Already something in him looked at the Princip and thought *thief,* thought *give me back what you have taken from me* . . .

FOUR

A Bridge to Fall

THIS WAS NOT like watching from the terrace, even with the spells of farsight. That was only seeming, a tale told of a battle fought. It was a long, long call from being there, from the taste and the touch, the glamour and the terror of it, the chill of steel and the hot run of blood.

The terrace, the palace lay above and behind them, not so very far in ridden road but all that other, greater distance between the tale and the truth. Up there they had watched and listened, seen and heard; down here they were what they had been watching.

Down here, drifts of smoke on the wind were occasionally heavy enough to sting at their eyes; they had to veil nose and mouth against a fall of dust-fine ash. The sun seemed hazy, high and cool in a thickening, shadowy sky. That was a portent, surely. Death had come to Surayon and spread its hands wide across the valley.

Himself, he rode towards it. His teeth were gritty with the sour taste of burning, his nostrils were stretched for the first scent of blood; the horse beneath him was as jittery as a boy on his first raiding-party, and he was little calmer himself; and yet, and yet . . .

Jemel couldn't help, couldn't keep himself from laughing.

Since the night Jemel had seen him first, running tirelessly with his eyes a smoky red, Marron had always been the Ghost Walker. The name had come from legend, from a thousand firelight stories; the truth of it was still a shadow largely unexplored, known only by its borders. The one fundamental, though, the self-evident truth had always been that the Ghost Walker walked or ran, and never rode. No animal would allow him anywhere near. Horses reared and kicked, camels roared and bit whoever was most handy, and usually Jemel.

So it followed that Jemel had never seen Marron in a saddle, until now. And now—seeing the gawky gracelessness, the shambolic slouch of it, hearing the excuses punctuated by yelps as boy met saddle, bouncing—well, how could he help but laugh?

"You be quiet, you. I haven't ridden a horse in months, and I never could handle a charger, we only ever had ponies at home and I didn't like those. Fra' Piet mocked me for my riding and so did—so did everyone else, I don't need your teasing too."

"This is not a charger, Marron."

"No, it's a raw-boned nag with no manners and nobody could ride it with any hint of style, so stop that giggling and keep your eyes on the road, we could meet trouble any moment."

True, it was a raw-boned nag that Marron rode, but Jemel's mount was worse, and he rejoiced in handling the creature with deliberate, ostentatious style.

But it was also true that they were riding into trouble, and he should be watching for it. Enough of teasing, then. He faced forward to scan the country as he rode, as he chuckled; and it wasn't long before the chuckle died.

This was hard, hard land to read. In the desert, the slightest sough of a breeze might tell him how far he was from water, or how long it would be before a dust-storm hit. The glimpse of a bird could show where camels might find grazing, or where a man crouched in cover. Every mark on sand or rock was a sign that spoke loud and clear, it was writing that said just when it was written, and often who else had read it since.

Here, though, all was confusion. Surayon seemed as empty as the Sands, and he did not believe it but he couldn't read the signs that should tell him otherwise. This was wet country, there were open streams to cross, there was a wide and shining road in the valley bottom that they told him was a river. Look at a footprint in the muddy ooze before a ford, see how water pooled in the bottom, and who could say how long since that print was made? Not he . . .

They had skirted the turmoil that was also Surayon, Surayon-city. War hadn't reached it yet, might not for another day or two, and there were men enough to meet it when it came. One glimpse through the open gates, and Jemel had felt infinitely grateful not to be going inside; walls and roofs made him uncomfortable, people in number made him nervous. Who could use a Sharai boy in a city? Better far if he and Marron rode the open country and offered help where it was needed, where he had it in him to offer . . .

Or so he'd thought. So far they'd found the road deserted, except for the one time when a rising thunder of hooves at their back had forced them onto the verge, to allow the Princip and a party of his men to pass at speed. They wore half-armour, mail shirts and helms, and were mounted on good Sharai stallions, fast and fierce, not the giant destriers commonly favoured by the Patrics. Jemel had seen those horses in the stable yard, and his raider's soul had yearned to steal a couple. It would have been easy, with so few hands to saddle and harness such a number; it would have been gloriously funny, a shocking abuse of hospitality at which his hosts couldn't conceivably complain; above all it would have been utterly and magnificently Sharai, a tale to be told around desert fires till the end of his days.

But he had said *I wouldn't waste a warhorse*, and had meant it too. Instead he'd scoured the Princip's stables and found two ageing saddle horses that seemed to have half-forgotten that they were ever ridden. His was remembering its manners swiftly under his insistence, while Marron's would be ruined entirely if it should survive the day.

The war-party had chased its own shadow into the distance, lost itself in the acrid haze; Jemel and Marron had ridden on slowly, and thought the land as empty as the road. Perhaps everyone had run to the city, who had not run to the war.

Or perhaps these farming folk had clung to their farms, their dirt and weeds; perhaps even now a dozen pairs of eyes were watching the two ride past, perhaps a dozen arrows were aiming at their breasts, *two in Sharai dress, both armed, so casual on stolen horses, they'll pay back the lives they've taken . . .*

He didn't know, he couldn't tell; he couldn't read the country. Even the sky confounded him, shrunk as it was between mountain walls, limited, contained. There was no true horizon here. He didn't understand how people could choose to live like this, locked in, with only a dream of distance. In the desert, there was little that mattered more than that smudged line where sky and sand should meet: it warned of strangers and of storms, of oasis and of bare rock's rise, of any change approaching. These Surayonnaise squatted in the bottom of a well, and their enemies could drop on them like vultures and never be seen coming.

The wind was as mute as the sky; its back broken on

mountain rock, it was warm and damp, weak and shifting, telling him nothing.

Then he thought about Marron and what had been done to him this morning. Himself, he was only far from home and out of sympathy with the land, baffled by its strangeness; his friend was carrying a loss far greater, all the stretch and strength of what he'd borne so long ripped away without his knowledge or consent. If Jemel felt disturbingly adrift in this country, then how must Marron be feeling?

He glanced back one more time, not the hint of a smile on his face or in his mind. His eyes met Marron's—with that momentary jolt that he still couldn't prepare for, when he saw that they were deep brown and utterly human, no trace of alien red—and it was his friend who smiled this time, and briefly they might have been two boys riding anywhere for any purpose or for none at all.

THE ROAD SNAPPED back and forth like a whipsnake's trail as it ran between high walls that broke only occasionally to allow access to fields and orchards, groves of olive trees, long runs of vine. To those who knew and could read the country—those who could hear an invader's footfall in the sudden shriek or silence of a bird, who could smell a horse's sweat behind the perfume of a vineyard in the sun—there must be advantage in such a road, to confuse an enemy and mislead him into ambush. To Jemel it was pure frustration, denying him any glimpse of what lay ahead.

The gentle, steady slope encouraged his horse, where it would have slowed a camel; he did nothing to hold the animal back. Nor did he check behind to see if Marron were keeping up, as his pace increased from trot to comfortable canter.

So he found himself alone as he came around yet one more corner, alone and abruptly facing half a dozen

Patrics who blocked the road from ditch to trickling ditch. In his own land he'd have seen them, heard them, very likely smelled them long before this; here he was all but under their swords already. *Three fighting men, a woman, two children. Her own, by the way they cling—don't discount her as a fighter. One horse, its rider wounded. Blood and pain-sweat, I can smell them now, too late. The youngest man is frightened, dangerous; his father—if that is his father, leading the horse, I think this is a family—his father is disquiet but no worse. Weaponless, though, and his hands busy, in no case to stop the boy if he chooses to be stupid . . .*

And the boy might indeed have made such a choice, he looked as though he wanted to. He was carrying a bill-hook—*too heavy to throw, and if he charges me he dies, I'm not sitting still to be hacked at*—which he lifted threateningly. "Sharai! Father, beware . . ."

If the boy had carried a bow instead, Jemel thought he might have been dead already, with an arrow in his breast. As it was, he had that moment's grace, while the boy made up his mind; just time enough for the father to say, "Hold your hand, Thom. You've seen Sharai before, and not sought to kill them."

"This morning changes that."

"It need not. Use your eyes, boy. Those we fled, that slew our friends and wounded Soren—they came from the east and rode in their tribes. If this lad has a tribe, his robe denies it. Besides, they were mounted on camels, not the dregs of some public stable. Hold, I say—unless you want to find yourself spitted," added shrewdly, with a wary eye on Jemel's ready stillness. "But this is not a good day for a Sharai to ride out alone. Where from, lad—Surayon-town?"

"The Princip's palace," Jemel said softly. "And not quite alone," as Marron finally came trotting round the corner at his back, all out of time with his mount and grunting with the effort of it.

"No, so I see. What's this? Another boy, another cast-off nag, Sharai dress again but not Sharai blood, I think. What *are* you?"

"Guests of the Princip," Jemel replied, seeing that Marron had neither breath nor words. "He sent us to help those on the road, if they should need it—those like yourselves, with wounded in your party. They are ready for you at the palace."

"We saw the Princip a while back, riding north . . ." For the first time, suspicion shaded his exhausted voice.

"He has his country to protect. His granddaughter is waiting in his stead."

"Is she so? I thought she was off wandering, she's not been seen all summer."

"She returned with us today." *And broke the borders, or the borders were broken through her*, but there was no need to say so much.

"Good enough. I'll trust that girl to heal an arrow-wound, and hope her grand-da can do more. We'll need no help to get there, thank you kindly. There are others behind in greater need—but those beasts you ride won't double up with wounded men, and there are dozens that we passed too weak to walk it. Nor are you dressed well for escorts, on such a morning . . ."

Jemel felt a bright cruel bubble of laughter rise in his chest to say that he knew it, he knew all of it. But he was struck by an idea at the same moment, and swallowed the laughter down. "Marron, we could ask Lisan to send her djinni for the injured?"

"Yes—or they could, to save us going back." To the family's bewildered stares, he said, "When you reach the palace, tell Elisande that she could send her djinni to fetch the badly wounded. Say you met Marron and Jemel, and they suggested it."

"Elisande's *djinni?*"

"Yes. Its name is the Djinni Tachur, but she calls it Esren."

"I don't understand. How could she, how could anyone—any mortal—tame or possess a djinni?"

"Did I say it was tame? Go now, go; your man there—"

"—my son, Soren—"

"—your son is bleeding yet." Marron had edged his
horse closer; Jemel could see how he flinched, coming so
near to the stink and flow of blood and feeling nothing, no
responsive surge, perhaps a hollowness at his heart. "Tell
Elisande what we have said and other men's sons may be
saved also, though they lack horses and the time to reach
her."

"Tell her to have it use the carpet," Jemel added, "to
carry them; they'll find that easier. She'll understand."

"BETTER FOR YOU to ride ahead, if that's how these
Patrics react to seeing me. They won't all be farmers' boys
with pruning-hooks for weapons."

"There are Patrics too have crossed the border," Marron murmured. "And I'm a stranger and dressed strangely,
I don't look Surayonnaise at all, and I carry a nobleman's
sword."

"You are still of their blood."

"You think that makes a difference? Marshal Fulke is
of their blood. They're more scared of Outremer than they
are of the Sharai, or they ought to be. They've traded with
the Sharai for a generation, while they've hidden their
whole country from the Kingdom. They should kill me as
readily as they would you, or sooner."

"If you ride first, then I can watch your back."

"Jemel, we'll ride together and face them down together, whoever challenges us. If you can remember that I
slow down on hills, going up or coming down."

THE ROAD TWISTED on, throwing up more refugees at
every turn now. Soon they were necessarily riding single

file again, pushing through a crush of weary, filthy faces; only the badly hurt were mounted, and those on a donkey or an ox more often than a horse.

They gave up crying encouragement to the weak, or directions to anyone. These people knew their way. The wounded were making for the palace, as quickly as they might, riding or walking or carried on stretchers; their families would go with them, or else into the city below. Its walls would protect them, they could help to protect its walls. Good. But they needed no one to shout them where to go, any more than they needed swords to watch them. On this road, they were in no danger.

Except from the sky, perhaps; 'ifrit could fly. Jemel had a bow slung across his saddlehorn, but no blessed arrows. Better not to look for 'ifrit, then. There was trouble enough in Surayon; the tribes were in the east, Patrics in the north and the west, and it was a small, small country. What need 'ifrit in the air, or anywhere? A small doomed country, bleeding already; when the various armies met, it would be drowned in blood. Not all its own, but enough, oh God, enough. This land would be rank for a lifetime. There were places of great slaughter in the Sands, where dry bones still rolled in the wind. Here they would rot and stink, and poison all the water that this greedy country claimed.

THERE WAS WATER everywhere. He saw it, heard it, smelled it, breathed it. His horse trod in it; there was mud in the ruts on the road and mud in the ditches, the earth wet enough to ooze openly under the sun.

That and the noise ahead should have warned him, even before the walls fell away to open grassland and a road that ran straight at last. He should have been prepared, though nothing, he thought, could have prepared him truly; only enough that perhaps he could have pretended, he needn't have sat staring like a slack-jawed lackwit.

Jemel had seen the Dead Waters, but they were just another wonder of the Sands. Besides, they didn't move, except when the djinni moved them. They only lay like a salt plain, vast and glimmering and useless, harbouring nothing good. Or had done, till Elisande came to interfere. They might grow sweet now, he supposed; then they would be a wonder indeed, so very much water and all of it to drink. Then let the Beni Rus and other near tribes look to their borders. So much water must spell a great quantity of war.

There was less water here, but even so he had to sit and stare. He had seen an inland sea, but he had never seen a river. Neither had he ever seen a bridge. He knew the words from stories; he had seen aqueducts and castles, and thought he knew both how water would flow within a course—slowly, quietly—and how men would build a crossing-way above it, strong and straight and practical.

But this was Surayon, and he was wrong and twice wrong.

THE HEADWATERS THAT fed the river rose high in the mountains, up where only goat-paths and foolish children climbed. Snowmelt and spring rains would bring a torrent in their season; even here in summer's lee, Surayon never ran dry and neither did its river. There was always rain, blowing in from the sea and caught by the mountain wall. The Sands were dry because Outremer was not, and this was the wettest of all of Outremer. If the rains should fail, there were still springs and hidden lakes above, lakes that froze in winter and glared back at sunlight so that they could feed frosty streams with their meltwaters all summer long. Such streams plunged toward the valley, young and hectic; met each other, and became a rabble; heard others like themselves, and raced to meet them too.

And so soon, very soon, all come together, they made this river that Jemel sat staring at: this riotous roaring body that flexed ice-green muscles and spat a bitter, glittering froth, that even at this dead end of its season was still a fury, that threatened to reach out and snatch him in. Go any closer, he thought he'd be sucked in simply by the noise and the rush and the irresistibility of it. At this distance, with hands gripping saddle-horn and heels clamped hard into his horse's sides, he still felt dizzy, unrooted, plucked at, dismayed.

He didn't think to wonder what men might call the river. It was a wild thing and far beyond the impertinence of naming. As well name the lion that kills your flock at night, the eagle that takes a lamb, the sun that drops you dead after it has drunk all your water from your skin . . .

And then there was the bridge.

Something broad and solid and built entirely of stone Jemel would have looked for, knowing how the Patric mind turned always to weight instead of speed, how they felt that a castle conquered a land. Squat heavy legs he would have looked for, driven deep to deny the force and chaos of the river, armoured perhaps at either end with turrets, embrasures, gates. Serviceable and ugly he would have expected it to be, defensible in Patric terms, which meant standing and standing and never giving way.

Instead he saw a bow bent against the sky, a challenge against all reason.

Before the road could reach the river, it met a stone embankment that lifted it into a smooth, steep climb. Leaping from that pier's end came the bridge itself, a tracery of beams interlocked to form a single graceful, high and unsupported arch that bent too steeply and stretched too far. It spanned not only the river, but a wide margin of land on either bank; Jemel could see no reason for that, unless it were the simple reason that they could do it. They could build so high and so strikingly and therefore they had done it, for their own triumphant pleasure and no more. Which perhaps was more djinn than human, and certainly not at all Patric.

Thin but constant streams of people were trailing in from west and east, some on foot and some on horseback. Where they met at the bridge, armed men were taking their horses from them. The impounded beasts were tethered in lines beneath the bridge's arch. Close beside them Jemel could see a few figures lying in the grass, men and women too exhausted or too badly wounded to go further. Children could be carried in a man's arms or a woman's at need, but these would need stretchers if the djinni didn't come for them.

He and Marron rode slowly on towards the bridge, shifting their mounts onto the grass to leave the road free for refugees. Some were burned and smoke-stained, some were bleeding or had bled; all looked numb, defeated, too worn even to be afraid. Scanning the sky and—at last!— the far horizons, Jemel saw firesign everywhere but nothing more, no fighting.

Two men from the bridge's guard came walking towards them, hands on sword-hilts, wary of strangers in Sharai dress. With an effort, Jemel kept his own sword-hand in plain sight on the horse's reins.

"Who are you, and where are you bound?"

"Guests of the Princip," Jemel replied economically. "Where bound? I think perhaps here. He sent us to watch the road, and to help the wounded; but they need no help that we can give, and that road watches itself."

The one man smiled thinly, while the other went on watching. "Aye, we've had thirty years to build for this day. The croplands are labyrinths, both sides of the valley. They'll slow down any army."

Slow, yes, but no more than that. Not halt, and not defeat. The Sharai liked to fight in the open, on the move, on horse or camelback; they would hate that maze of walls and shadows as much as they hated siege and castle warfare. Hate it or not, though, the tribes would enter the labyrinth and take it, field by field if they needed to. It could no more be defended than could the Princip's palace. And the town of Surayon had walls, but no other fortifications: no keep, no castle, nowhere to make a stand. And yet they'd had thirty years, and knew that this day must come . . .

"Are all your defences designed only for delay?" he asked, as soon as the question occurred to him. It won him a suspicious scowl, but after a moment he got his answer too.

"Well, if the Princip mounts you, he must vouch for you—though I'll dismount you myself, in a moment. Yes, lad, they are. We couldn't ever fight and hope to win, there aren't enough of us and never will be. We could build a castle stronger than Roq de Rançon, and it would still fall in the end. So we delay and delay, and pull our people back into the high vales, where the roads don't run. There are stronger defences there, walls from cliff to chasm, and no space for siege-engines to reduce them; those we can hold for a while."

"And when they fall? Or when there is no food, when your stores are gone?"

"Then we're gone too. Princip's guests or not, I'll still keep some of our secrets in the folds of my own mind. But they won't have the massacre they've come for, neither your people nor his," with a nod at Marron.

It is the Patrics who seek your deaths, Patric—my people want only the land and the holy places . . .

But at that moment a woman came shambling towards them, her head swathed in a crude blood-soaked linen bandage that came down to cover one eye and half her cheek, but still couldn't cover the whole of her hurt: he could see the clotted tail of a curving slash reach out from below the bandage, almost to the corner of her mouth.

He didn't need to see the way she shied in a touch of pure terror, that moment when she lifted her gaze from the road to see who sat the horses. After one glance Jemel could name the weapon and the blow that had done that to her.

Head-cut from a scimitar, from a mounted Sharai, and he could have been ashamed of all his people, except that shame would be no use to her, nor him, nor anyone. He sat quite still, watching as she edged past on the further side of the road, as she lowered her head and trudged on to face the hard climb up to the palace and some measure of healing, though she would carry the scar for life and had probably lost the eye already. Then he turned back to the guard and said, "You might have given her a horse."

"She's fit to walk, if barely. Horses are reserved for fighting men, that's why we're here. We'll take yours, too, if you've no better claim to keep them."

The guard was already reaching for his bridle. Jemel would have nodded and dismounted with no argument, except that just then there was a shout from across the river.

He looked, Marron looked, the guard turned to look— and no question now of handing the horse over, bow-backed nag though it was. It was still a horse. The guard's hand fell away and he ran for his own mount or any, shouting to his confrères while he ran; Jemel slammed his heels in hard, and came easily first to the bridge.

On the further bank, the slow line of refugees had become a turmoil, a hectic race to cross the river. The guards on that side were at the horse-lines, fumbling with saddle and harness. It was riders that had made the people flee, that had sent the men to horse and kept Jemel in the saddle: riders breaking out onto the grassland, with swords in their hands that gleamed not at all in the sunshine, that were dull and stained with use already.

There were not many of them, a dozen or so. They were Patric, of course, mounted on heavy Patric horses. No surprise in that. But the officer who led them wore white dress with a black cloak thrown over, though the black was ripped and the white was darkly marked; the men who followed him wore black entirely, in sign of their brotherhood.

Jemel could name the brotherhood; Marron could probably name the men. He had belonged to their order, had been a brother among brothers and was still not properly free, although they had cast him out. They would burn him as a witch, Jemel knew, if ever they could catch him; Marron might see some dark justice in it if they did. Worse, he might almost welcome his capture, if it could lead to his meeting with the knight Sieur Anton d'Escrivey.

Worse yet, Jemel had sworn an oath to meet with Sieur Anton d'Escrivey on his own account. He could not be ungrateful to see the Ransomers in the field. If those ravens were abroad in Surayon, Jemel might contrive to find his man. That might even be Sieur Anton on the destrier there, a gift already given, if Jemel could believe it hard enough.

Oath clashed with oath, ringingly in Jemel's exhausted head; he rode on, to the stone footings of the bridge and so up.

First cobbled ridges in the stone, then fillets of wood laid like ribs across the planking gave purchase to the horse's wary hooves. Slowly was the only way to make the climb in any case, against the surge of terrified foot-traffic. The bridge rose and rose, the people surged past; at last he reached the crown of the arch and checked the horse. There must be an end to this flow. Let it dwindle and die, let the animal see where it could safely set its feet for the descent, let the riders see that the bridge was defended.

Let Marron come up to join him, if Marron came. It would be a choice, perhaps a statement: *I ride with you who are my brother* or *I ride to face them who were my brothers* or *I ride to seek him who was my master,* any of those or all.

The riders were still some distance off, but coming

straight towards the bridge. Hoping to take it, no doubt, and to hold it; looking upstream and down, Jemel could see no other way to cross the river. This would be pivotal, then, its defence crucial to Surayon. He sighed softly, thinking that this was not why he had come to Outremer, nor why he had brought Marron out of the palace today.

At his back, he heard the slow sounds of a climbing horse. It might be Marron, urging his mount up with difficulty and determination; it might not.

He sat without turning his head, watching the riders close, watching the last of the refugees scatter before them.

"Ransomers." A voice at his back, and it was Marron, of course it was.

"Yes."

"What will you do?"

Jemel laughed, he couldn't help it. "I will fight, of course. I have fought Ransomers before." *And lost Jazra to them, and found you.* The debts were complex and confused, running both ways; it was simpler far to fight.

"For Hasan, you fought before. For his visions, his grand dream. Will you fight for the Princip now?"

"The Princip has Hasan. That makes it easy," which was not true, but easy at least to say. "What will you do?"

"I don't know."

"They are killing these people, Lisan's people, who have given us sanctuary."

"Yes." And he still couldn't or wouldn't kill them, even now and even so; that was inherent in his voice, in his stillness, in his sheathed sword.

"If they find you, if they capture you, they will kill you. With fire, I think. You said you have seen them do that."

"Yes." And he still couldn't or wouldn't ride away, keep his distance, run and hide.

Jemel would make a stand with what few Patrics here could swing a sword, warriors or farmers. They would struggle to hold the bridge, because that was such a Patric thing to do; he could almost think like them now if he tried hard. They would struggle, and they would die. They would lose this bridge, and die trying to save it; and he would die beside them, because he had no better sense.

Or because that might be Sieur Anton in the black cloak with the bloodstained white beneath. If not the knight might still be somewhere there, north of the river. That thought alone might be enough to hold Marron; it might be enough to hold Jemel. Something held them both, or they held each other. They held the crown of the bridge until they heard more horses coming up behind them.

"What are you waiting for?" one of them growled. "There's but half a dozen of our men out there against twice that number, and none of ours is a soldier trained . . ."

"All the more reason for them to take the first shock," Jemel said softly. "If you must lose men, better to lose the weakest. They will break the force of the Ransomers' charge; we will meet those who come through, and perhaps we will only have to face one each, or one at a time. But we are not helpless, even here."

He lifted the bow from his saddle, ready-strung. It was heavier and clumsier than he was used to, but he could draw it well enough; and this horse might move like two gawky boys in a mareskin, but when it stood it did stand remarkably still. The quiver hung beside his leg, Sharai-style. Patrics might carry theirs on their backs; his people planned always to fight from the saddle.

The knight, the officer might yet be Sieur Anton, and should not die by an arrow. Blade to blade they must be, when they met. He had sworn it. Jazra's shade would be watching him from Paradise; he could be forgiven many things, anything—Marron was not even a case for forgiveness, the question didn't arise—but not that oath. There must be a meeting and there must be a death, blood to pay for blood and loss for loss. That it would be Marron's loss was a strange by-blow, fate's malignancy, a bitter thing for both of them; they did not speak of it. If they had, Jemel would have said that Marron had lost his Sieur Anton already and long ago. It was true, it was inarguable—and yet it made no difference. Just as Jemel carried lost Jazra in his heart, so Marron carried the knight.

And when the knight is dead, when I have killed him, Marron—will you swear an oath against me in your turn?

That was why they did not speak of it, there were too many questions they dared not ask. That might even be the true reason why Marron refused to kill, to make it possible for him not to kill Jemel.

Who sighted now, drew—to the chin with the bow at an angle like the horseman he was, not straight and to the ear like some mudfoot Patric—and shot, watching the arrow carefully in its flight. Like the bow, it was longer and heavier than he was used to; no great surprise to see it fly a little shorter, drop a little sooner than he'd intended. It didn't reach the rider whose heart had been its aim; it took his horse instead, full in the chest and sinking deep.

The horse plunged to its knees, to the ground, dead in a moment. Its rider was flung forward and to the side, directly under the hooves of his confrères who charged beside him. Another rider fell, as his horse stumbled; only one of the two men came to his feet again, and he seemed dazed and hardly dangerous.

"A good shot."

"A good weapon," Jemel grunted, already drawing again.

Two men down had not checked the charge; neither would the unsteady line drawn up to challenge it. Warhorses against hacks and nags, it was a battle lost before the men were measured. When the lines met, that would mean an end to archery and a time to ride, a time for swordwork and sweat, to set one more nag against a destrier and test Sharai swiftness against Ransomer weight.

Time yet for one more shaft, though. He picked his man and shot, and this time kicked his horse into motion while the arrow was still in flight, barely troubling to watch as it took its man sweetly in the throat.

The horse was nervous on the downslope, wedging the toe of each hoof firmly against a cross-piece before stepping forward with the next. It would be more nervous in a minute, Jemel thought.

Onto the stone footings at last, and now he could sling his bow across the saddlehorn, urge the beast into a reluctant gallop, draw his scimitar and scream exulting as he plunged headlong into the simplicities of battle. The men in black were to kill; the man in black over white was most liable for killing; the blade in his hand was for killing with, so long as the horse between his knees could hold him up.

THE GLITTER OF steel in sunlight and the grate of edge on edge, a blade to meet his and the shock of it jarring his body, all but lifting him out of the saddle; his horse stumbling and fighting the bridle and having to be hauled around, the Ransomer's swifter to obey but so much heavier to turn, so that neither could strike again before the other; and so they traded blows, hack and thrust and parry, while the warhorse bit and kicked and Jemel's nag struggled against his control until he was almost praying for the Ransomer to slash its throat for him, save him the trouble.

It sank abruptly onto its haunches, screaming its pain as an iron-shod hoof connected. Jemel saw the great sword lift above his head. But he was so slow, this Ransomer, as slow and heavy as his sword, his horse, his thinking . . .

Jemel dropped the reins, put his hand on the saddle-

horn and vaulted as the nag surged up again beneath him.
His own strength and the horse's rising threw him high.
He swung one leg across the hindquarters of the warhorse,
just as his shoulder struck the Ransomer in the chest,
below the upraised sword-arm. The force of it knocked
the man loose from his stirrups, almost knocked him from
the saddle altogether. Briefly both were fighting for balance, rather than fighting each other; the Ransomer even
dropped his sword, letting it swing loose on its lanyard,
while he clutched at mane and reins to haul himself upright again.

Jemel's legs gripped hard on the horse's flanks; his left
arm took a grip around the Ransomer's ribs and pulled
with a will; he almost expected the man to turn and thank
him.

Instead the man died, as Jemel's scimitar moved
feather-light across his exposed throat.

It took only a moment to fling the body down, another
to slip into the saddle. The stirrups hung too low and the
harness was too clumsy for a light-bodied, light-fingered
Sharai boy, but never mind that. The man he wanted, the
black-cloaked officer was riding him down already, his
darkened sword extended like a lance as the massive destrier hurtled across the ground. No hope of countering
such a charge; Jemel's blade would snap if he tried it, just
an eye-blink before that great sword skewered him.

At the last moment, then, Jemel flung himself down,
wrapping both arms around the horse's neck and sliding
half out of the saddle to keep its body between him and
the blade.

As soon as he'd felt the wind of its passing, he slithered
upright again. One vain slash back at the destrier's crupper, and he was dragging his new mount's head around to
follow, not to be a standing target twice. The destrier
would be slow to halt, slow to turn; when it did, Jemel
would be right there, eye to eye and blade to blade.

And was. The two blades clashed and rang with the

force of the impact, deadening Jemel's fingers. Sword and scimitar locked hilt to hilt; time for one quick glance at the knight's face, and no, it was not Sieur Anton. No matter. This man could die now, and the other later.

Or, of course, Jemel could die now and the other not at all. Steel battered against steel; on a Patric warhorse he was trapped into fighting Patric-style, and his opponent was stronger, experienced, fast. In the end, the simple strength should be enough. Jemel blocked a storm of blows, but he couldn't block forever. Those rare chances he had to cut or thrust, his blade was fended off with a twist of the wrist, a sweet timing that seemed almost contemptuous. He had killed Sand Dancers, but it seemed he could not kill even this one Ransomer, who was not the one he wanted; and he had been so urgent once to kill them all. He bared his teeth in a savage grin, reminded himself that the stars did not in fact turn around his head however often he'd felt certain that they did, and hacked two-handed at the Ransomer's unbreakable guard. His arm was too heavy now for any grace, for any speed or elegance. This was survival or else it was the other thing, and he thought he knew which. It was a matter for regret, and Jazra would be angry, but—

BUT THE RANSOMER was backing his horse abruptly, where he should have been pressing forward; staring past Jemel, over Jemel's shoulder and up, with an appalled look on his face.

Jemel glanced behind him and was entirely still for a moment, forgetful of Ransomers and war, of friends lost and left behind, forgetful of everything that he knew for certain about the strength and reliability of the world.

While he fought, the river had been rising from its bed. It thrust into the air like a dreadful snake, the waters woven together into a long and sinuous body of black that rippled and sheened with all the dark strength that he had sensed in it before. Now it was striking out, rebelling, uprising with a will and a wickedness that reminded him forcefully of the Dead Waters when the djinni had been trapped within them . . .

Except that he could still hear the rush of water on rock, the grinding of rock on rock within the water. No, this could not be the river risen. Which made it a creature risen from the river, 'ifrit; and its snake head stood as high as the arch of the bridge, and there was a figure on the bridge, a boy on a horse, not moving.

Just where Jemel had left him, Marron sat trapped between impossibilities, the shards of broken oaths waiting to pierce him on either bank. He could go neither forward nor back, and so he had gone nowhere; but if he stayed where he was, then that snake was going to eat him. And there would be another oath broken, Jemel abandoned by another oath-breaking boy; Jazra had left him that way, dying where he had promised not to.

Move, ride, run . . .! He ached to cry out, but he had no breath to do it, and he was too far from the bridge in any case. Marron would never hear above the roaring of the water and perhaps the pounding of his own desperate blood, or else the screaming of his horse. Marron's blood was a great uncertainty; the horse Jemel thought he could rely on.

IT DID SCREAM, he could see that and hear it too, thin and high enough to sound even above the tumult of the river, as the fighting failed all around him. Whether the 'ifrit heard, he couldn't tell. They seemed to live in silence, only death dragging any kind of noise from them; perhaps they had no sense of sound.

Eyes were enough. Those smoky, sunken lights glowed like irons in a fire, showed it a view like Marron's Daughter-tainted sight, perhaps, sharp-drawn but all in red, all hues of blood, whatever there was to kill.

Bent at the neck like a hook, like a column of water forever falling and forever failing to fall, it turned its head towards the bridge and couldn't fail to see Marron sitting there: a victim, a sacrifice, a boy rapt by the prospect of his own death coming.

Marron wouldn't scream, any more than he would fight. Jemel would do both on his behalf—and had the blade to do the fighting with, ready blessed for the occasion, more use than Marron's precious Dard—but lacked the time to get there. And the mount: his stolen warhorse stood fixed beneath him, all four legs braced and trembling now that it had seen what stirred in the river.

The horses picketed beneath the bridge were lathered with terror, rearing and plunging in their lines until they wrenched pegs from the ground or snapped the ropes that held them and went galloping blindly off into the haze.

The one horse above them, on the bridge was the only one that Jemel cared about. He saw it scream again, its ears flattened to its skull, its head flung high and lips drawn back as though it were half stripped of flesh already, displaying all the bones beneath the skin.

Then, blessedly, its terror restored its wits. It bucked once, while Marron clung frantically to mane and saddlehorn; the sharp whipcrack sound of its own hind hooves striking the planking acted as a spur, to send it plummeting pell-mell down the bridge.

As it skidded headlong from wooden arch onto stone footing, the 'ifrit struck.

It coiled back the immense length of this body it had made, and then hurtled forward: like a wilful hammer, like a snake balanced on its tail and using its head to batter.

It didn't stoop on Marron nor his horse, nor any of the fleeing horses. Neither did it bring its crushing weight down upon the men who had been fighting, who fought nothing now but their own horses' need to run, Ransomers and Surayonnaise and a single rapt Sharai.

Instead it rammed its jawless head against the timbers

of the bridge, just at the height of the arch, and just the once.

The walls of the Roq were perhaps the strongest thing built, certainly the strongest that Jemel had ever seen; he thought the walls of the Roq would have cracked and crumbled under that assault. Not all at once, though, not shattering in a moment, as the bridge did. It disappointed him; he thought the beams should have held together until they splintered, but they flew apart like blades of dry grass lifted on the first breath of a wind.

The 'ifrit drew back, reared up, for a moment was terribly still; Jemel saw how its hot eyes surveyed the river's banks, and he drove his heels so hard into his mount's ribs that the startled warhorse had leaped into a gallop before it truly knew that it was moving.

Marron had, of course, fallen from his horse. The only surprise was that he had clung so long: long enough to fall on cobbles rather than planks. He stood on the bridge's surviving footing like a man abandoned, alone on a knoll of rock. Like every man there—every man but Jemel—he was staring up at the 'ifrit as it stared down.

"Marron! Here, to me . . ."

Blooded scimitar into his left hand, the hand that held the reins; his right stretched out and down to seize Marron's wrist as the horse thundered past. Saren boys played these games for fun, only realised later that they were battlefield training.

Patric boys, perhaps, never played these games at all. This boy was late in reaching for the grip, slow to jump, a dead weight that almost overtoppled them both before Jemel could haul him up and leave him belly-down and kicking across the horse's crupper.

A slow, steady draw on the near rein to wheel the horse around, not to let it run into the mists and smoke of the river and the day. By the time he was sure of it, Marron had swung one leg across the barrel width of the horse's hindquarters and pushed himself upright, pale and distraught but somehow almost laughing.

"I forgot," he gasped, working his way over the cantle so that both boys were squashed into the big Patric saddle, wrapping his arms tight around Jemel's waist for more support than he should strictly need, "the Daughter would have made the jump easy, but . . ."

"But you don't have that any more. Besides, the horse would never have come near you, if you still carried it."

"That's what I forgot. One of those, both maybe," and he really was laughing, sinking his face into Jemel's neck and his teeth into Jemel's robe to silence it. His own robe was sodden; even his hair was wet and chill. "I almost forgot it was a horse I was sitting on, until it threw me off. Then I forgot everything except—well, that, there—and then I saw you coming and I was going to leap up swift and easy, just as I could have done any day since we met, and the God's truth, Jemel, I miss it so . . ."

Jemel shook his head, *later, we can discuss your idiocies later. If we have the chance, we may all be missing it soon. And dying for the lack of it . . .*

Some men had died already in their own brute squabble; others would die soon, that much was clear. The 'ifrit stood high and then fell, dropping its head like a rock driven by a terrible weight of water. Like a rock with eyes and with intent, it picked out a still-tethered horse and came down with force enough to drive its own broad snout an arm's length into the ground. Jemel didn't want to see what remained of the horse in the bottom of that pit, as the 'ifrit reared up again and cast about. Its skin had the slickness of water, nothing clung for long; it scattered earth and grass with the slow swing of its head, a great worm seeking fodder.

This time it found a man unhorsed, afoot. He was running, but his legs were far too short for the work, or else the serpent-spirit was too long in its body, far too long. It stretched, it seem to hang a little in the air and then it

struck the man just as it had the horse, so violently that a
ripple flowed back all along its length. It couldn't really
be made of water, surely, but it did seem so.

Then its head arose, and there was no man now, only
whatever mess lay compacted in the hollow.

One of his confrères, one of the Ransomers was charging the beast, determined or despairing. He rode forward
at the gallop, driving his horse so hard that it had no
chance to bolt or break. It looked half mad already, eyes
rolling white and its skin shining sickly, stretched tight to
show muscle and tendon wherever it wasn't coated with
foam; but it ran obedient to rein and spur, directly towards
the 'ifrit.

Jemel looked for the other Ransomers, and saw them
massed uncertainly around their officer. He thought they
would charge all together, once they saw another man
down. They must rescue or revenge, if they had any honour. Or die trying, of course, which they would do.

Not his land and not his people, this was emphatically
not his fight. He was glancing about for the Surayonnaise
when he felt Marron's arms uncurl from around his waist
and heard the sound of steel scraping from scabbard.

He twisted in the saddle to stare in bewilderment at the
glittering purity of Dard drawn and deadly, except that
nothing in Marron's hands was deadly now.

"Marron, what—?"

"Will you sit here and watch them be slaughtered?"

"I was slaying them myself, five minutes since. And
you were watching."

"Jemel, that's an 'ifrit, and they don't know how to
fight it. And they are men, brothers. Ride, damn you!"

"Whose brothers? Not mine, I am Sharai. And you are
renegade, they'd burn us both."

"They would, aye. And if they were Saren, Jemel,
would you still not ride?"

He opened his mouth to say so, and could not. The

Saren chief wanted to kill him, but if they were Saren, or Beni Rus or any of the tribes—yes, he'd ride.

Even so, "Not you, Marron. You won't kill it; you can't kill it, with that sword. You can't even hurt it. What are you thinking?"

"I can batter at it," grimly smiling. "Poke and prod."

"Marron, *look* at it . . .!"

Plenty to look at suddenly, as the charging Ransomer closed with the 'ifrit. He stood in his stirrups, his straight arm extending his sword-point beyond his manic horse's head. For a moment, as the 'ifrit seemed simply to lie waiting for his strike, Jemel wondered if the man might not carry the luck of the ignorant with him. One good strike to the eye would kill this or any 'ifrit. The Ransomer might not know that, but any warrior charging such a beast must surely aim for the eye . . .

The 'ifrit lay like a snake along the ground, its unseen tail still in the river; and it lashed its body like a whip across the grass, knocking the sword-point aside as though it were a blade of straw and striking the heavy warhorse hard enough to smash every bone in its legs, so hard that the impact hurled it high into the air. Its rider flew from the saddle, fell as it fell, and must have broken bones himself in his falling. Perhaps too many bones, perhaps a fatal number; he lay still after, while the 'ifrit rose up to loom large above his body. It swayed its massive head from side to side, very like a serpent watchfully possessive of its prey.

"Well?" Marron hissed, in Jemel's ear. "Now will you ride?"

"For what? He is dead."

"Not yet, not necessarily."

"White bones, not even walking."

"Then ride for a glorious death of your own. Why not? When were you ever so shy of it?"

When I found you at my back, but it was hopeless to say so. Jemel sighed and kicked the horse forward, thinking that this was not such a terrible place to die, nor such terrible company. He could go to Paradise hand in hand with Marron, leaving their bodies under the shadow of the 'ifrit; Jazra would be welcoming.

The 'ifrit's skin glistened and ran. Its head had stopped its swaying, and the gaze of both unblinking eyes was focused directly on Jemel. That towering head blocked the sunlight; Jemel held his breath, waiting for it to fall.

In the moment before it did—at the delicacy of that point where the world is toppling beyond fate's measure, where destiny can be fixed by a breath this way or that, where what will be irrevocable, irrecoverable, irreconcilable is still waiting to occur—he turned in the saddle, gave Marron a hard shove and watched him fall to ground.

Flinched as he hit, then shouted, "Watch over the Ransomer!" That man was lying still, hadn't moved, needed little watching. Jemel's abruptness had simply freed him to tackle the 'ifrit in his own way, without that draining, distracting urge to keep Marron safe at all costs.

He wasn't safe now, of course, there was nothing safe about being on foot beneath the brute power of an 'ifrit in its strength, but Jemel was hoping to divert it with his scimitar's edge. He looked up to find that poised and perilous head—

—AND FOUND IT turned away from him, saw the savage eye fixed on Marron as he ran towards the sprawled black body of the Ransomer.

Didn't have time or breath enough to curse. He wheeled the horse with a brutal wrench and forced it down to the river's edge, to where the vast mass of the 'ifrit's body emerged from the water and rested its weight on the bank.

Perhaps one day he would learn to leave the thinking to others, leave his wild ideas to blow away on the wind. For now the wind of his own wild speed was in his hair as he crouched low beside the horse's neck and screamed encouragement into its ear, as he beat it on with the flat of his scimitar, as the dank darkness that was the 'ifrit's shadow above and below them gave into the damp darkness of the living wall that was its body directly ahead.

Jemel let the reins slacken in his hand, he gave the horse its head. Its body veered heavily, its hooves bit deep into the turf, it managed—just—to keep its balance and its speed; it swerved past the rising column of the 'ifrit's body, close enough that Jemel could have kicked the thing.

Instead he swung his scimitar, putting all his strength into a single backhand slash as he passed. This close, he could see that the 'ifrit was clad in scales: uncountable scales, small as his fingernail, each one gleaming wetly even in the shadow, each one doubtless impervious to any common blade.

His blade was nothing extraordinary, though it was well-made, and he kept it wickedly sharp. It was uncommon only in the one thing, the blessing that overlaid its edge. Jemel hewed at the 'ifrit with a young man's desperate strength, his last hope to save his friend. He hewed and felt the blade cut something, cut into something as though through hide and into belly-fat, resistance followed by soft sucking matter. The mad speed of the horse beneath him tugged it free with a jerk that almost snatched the hilt from his hand, that wrenched his weary arm from wrist to shoulder.

Then he was hauling on the reins again, hauling the horse's head around, turning his own head to see.

A slim straight figure standing above the fallen, the glitter of a sword raised high to poke and prod, the dark swaying shadow over all: Marron stood like a symbol of defiance and should not have lived so long, should not be living now except that the 'ifrit was turning away to gaze down at its own body, turning to find whatever small thing had committed this outrage.

Jemel could be defiant too, standing in the stirrups and waving his scimitar; but that was gesture only, his eyes and thoughts were furiously busy. Marron had held off the 'ifrit somehow, for too long to be understood. He himself had hurt it, enough to distract if not to harm; he saw water gushing from the darkness of the creature's body, like a spring discharging from a basalt pillar.

It had been smoke before, he'd never seen them bleed anything but smoke and decay had followed, disintegration. How was this one holding so much water in its gut?

No matter how. What mattered was that head, those eyes that pinned him with their hot stare, the long body twisting back on itself to crush, batter, pulp him into this wet earth and leave nothing worth saving, nothing worth the journey back into the Sands.

But he stood as best he could in the low stirrups and yelled, whirled his scimitar, pointed it at the thing's dull snout. If he could only hold firm as the 'ifrit drove down, it would impale itself before ever it reached him. The vast weight of the thing would still fall entire on his head, but perhaps the 'ifrit would be dead also, or hurt enough to die.

He had time for so much thought, and more yet. Puzzled, he stared up at the 'ifrit where it bulked huge in the sky above him: huge but not growing, not filling his sight, not falling. Huge but growing smaller, receding, drawing back . . .

He must have been right, then, it was afraid to skewer itself on his scimitar in trying to reach him. It saw doom in some shadowed future path, and so it turned away, and so once more Jemel did not die when he was ready to.

But it had done the same with Marron, pulling back from his raised sword; and that was only Dard, a weapon of fine work and lethal edge but it might as well have been a muddy stick, raised against an 'ifrit in its strength . . .

No matter. Jemel was alive, and that mattered; Marron was alive, and that mattered more.

And Marron was standing guard above a fallen Ransomer, and there were half a dozen mounted men riding towards him now and going to reach him before Jemel could get there; and they were all Ransomers, and that mattered most of all. Jemel couldn't imagine what he would say to them, except that it was likely to be something stupid, dangerous, disastrous. His name, perhaps, and his history . . .?

If he lived to do it. The 'ifrit still loomed above the gathering men; but Marron kept Dard aloft, even as he and the Ransomer both were boosted up onto borrowed horses, and somehow Dard was keeping the monster from its strike.

Jemel was riding one-handed himself with his scimitar held high in the other, more a reminder than a real threat as his eyes moved constantly between the black above and the black ahead, the creature that could kill in a moment and the group of men on horseback who were bearing his friend away.

They cantered beyond reach of the 'ifrit and drew rein on the road. With Dard no longer waving above their heads like a needle of light to stitch the eye, Jemel couldn't find Marron among them. He didn't know whether his friend still sat another man's horse or whether he'd slid to ground, gratefully or at a sword's point. All he did know was that there was a body of men between himself and Marron: men he'd been fighting with, brothers to men that he'd killed. And he was Sharai, and he was in Surayon. They ought, he thought, to be merciless.

He pulled gently on the rein, easing the lathered, exhausted horse down through its paces to a steady walk; he wiped his scimitar on the saddlecloth and sheathed it at his side. Sitting straight in the saddle, proud and calm, he rode towards whatever doom they held for him.

*   *   *

WEAPONS DRAWN, BUT not raised against him; faces watchful, wary but not he hoped judgemental, in so far as he could read Patric faces, which was not so far at all.

First a silence, and then a voice:

"Sieur Parrish, Fra' Colcan, brothers, this is Jemel of the Sharai, and you have seen what a warrior he is, what a foe even to that devil . . ."

Marron's voice: he tried to peer through the shifting hedge of bodies, but was distracted by another, bitter and resentful.

"A fine warrior, aye—he killed Sim, and Breck too if those were his arrows come from the bridge."

"Leave be." The knight came shouldering through his men, his authority as heavy, as forceful as his destrier. "We killed our share."

"Not of his people. And what's he doing, fighting with the heretics? He'll not be alone, make no doubt of that. If we take him back and put him to the question—"

"Leave be, I said! You, Jacquel—I'll have silence from you, or we'll all hear you after service tomorrow night. Unless you'd rather follow the Sharai, and ride alone against that—thing?"

"I'll do that, sieur," sullen but determined, from a broad, scarred man in his middle years. "I'm not afraid."

"Then you should be," Jemel said softly. "Has Ma— my friend not told you what that is?"

"'Ifrit, he said. And so? Demons die before the true faith, as heretics die in the God's fire and unbelievers at the sword's edge." He hefted his own sword significantly; Jemel moved not a muscle, answering the challenge only with his stillness. "I say I'm as fit to face it down as any hell-damned Sharai boy—that's if the devil-dealing boy didn't summon the thing himself. Would you trust him, sieur? Or this dog of his, this cur who came to feed on our wounded?"

Now Jemel's hand did move, despite all resolution. It gripped his weapon's hilt and would have drawn it, but that the knight forestalled him with a gesture, *patience, leave my men to me . . .*

"Who came to stand over our wounded, Jacquel, and protect him from the 'ifrit. See the world as it is, man; there is honour even here, however tainted. Yes, I will trust these men, both of them, though I think you might be wrong about who dogs whom. It would honour you to do as the Sharai has done, it would honour any man. I will not order you to it, but—"

"You should forbid it, rather," Jemel interrupted. "Not you nor any man can ride against that and live."

"What, only you, Sharai?"

"Yes, though I intend no insult by it."

"What else is this, but insult? Our horses are as fast or faster; that's Sim's stolen mount beneath you now. Our sinew is as strong as yours—"

"Stronger," Jacquel growled, "he's a mocking puppy, nothing more."

"Stronger, sure," Jemel admitted, "and yet the 'ifrit would kill you, where it holds off from me who hurt it once and from my companion, who has not hurt it at all. The virtue lies in our weapons, and those we cannot share with you."

"Our swords are as sharp as yours, and better made."

"Doubtless so, and yet they will not bite that hide. No normal edge, no point will mark it unless the weapon's been blessed by an imam. Mine is, yours are not and cannot be. You saw how it scorned your own man's weapon," with just a flick of his eyes to find that man, laid on the grass now, pale and unmoving, "and you saw how it feared my blade, how it withdrew. It's too big, though, a scimitar alone can't hope to slay it . . ."

"Nor scimitar and sword together," Marron said suddenly, pushing through the mass of men. "But, Jemel, you saw how it held back from me, and Dard has never been touched by one of your imams. I said a prayer over it myself, just now, as I was standing there; and the 'ifrit had been coming for me, and it stopped at that moment, as I blessed the blade . . ."

Jemel shook his head, bewildered. "You are no priest. Not even of your own religion."

"No—but I was a brother once, of this Order of Ransom," said proudly, defiantly, staring about. *Doom,* Jemel thought grimly, seeing how the faces changed. "We are all—I mean, I was consecrated to the service of the God, as all the brothers are. That's as good as being a priest; we can lead services at need, say a prayer over the dying on a battlefield to haste them into heaven—and bless a weapon, too."

"How did you know the blessing would hold?" A man might trust to such a thing and find too late that it was no more than empty words, spoken over unheeding steel.

"I didn't, but the 'ifrit thought it would. If I was wrong, we both were."

"You say any brother of the Order can act as priest?"

"If I can, then surely any. I was cast out, I no longer follow the teachings of the priests, and yet the virtue holds."

Jemel turned to the knight again. "You heard. He speaks as true as he knows; if he's right, maybe none of us need die this day. Say a prayer over your weapons, bless each separate blade, dedicate it to your own god's good and maybe, maybe we can fight that creature, if we fight it all together."

The knight smiled thinly, and shook his head.

"Not me, lad. I'm no brother, sworn to the Order and the God. We knights take different vows, and mean them less, sometimes. Fra' Colcan!"

"Sieur?"

"You are the men's confessor; that is as good as a priest. Come, bless my blade, then all the rest." Then, as the other man hesitated, "Where's the harm? A Sharai's idea, true, from a recusant's suggestion; but no matter for that, it would still be a prayer to the God. If it means no more, there is still no hurt in it. We can flee that demon, or we can fight it; I for one do not mean to flee."

"Sieur, I don't know what to say."

"You heard the preceptor bless us all, before we rode. You have heard prayers and blessings every day of your life, man. Is it so hard to find a few words now, when you need them more? Here is my sword; come, put the God's light into its steel, to set against the blackness of that soul-less thing. Or would you see a Sharai boy better armed for the fight, and the only one still living when it's done?"

"No, sieur . . ."

The older man laid an ungloved hand on his officer's blade, ran the tip of his tongue across his lips and began to whisper.

"Louder, Fra' Colcan. I want all the men to hear it."

Jemel did not listen, as the Ransomer's voice rose in a hesitant petition to his god. He was wondering how to extricate Marron and himself from among these men when—if ever—the 'ifrit was killed or driven off, now that the bridge was down.

Only a bridge, he thought, *it only came to kill a bridge*—except that Marron had been on the bridge, and perhaps it had come to kill him? If so it had failed twice already, once on the bridge and once on the bank. Even without his blood-companion, Marron was proving extremely hard to kill; Jemel intended to keep him so.

"Look," one of the Ransomers muttered, pointing back past Jemel's shoulder. "It's coming out of the water."

The 'ifrit looked more than ever like a giant worm, creeping up out of the river and shimmering darkly in the sunlight as it dragged itself across the grass. It was vast, massive like a living wall, flexing like a whip; slow, though, slow to move under all that rippling weight of water. Swift to strike, they'd all seen that, but not made for progress on dry ground. A man on foot could outrace it, if he were not rigid with fear; on their horses they could ride in circles and torment it like hunting dogs around a bull antelope. If their weapons were potent after a Patric blessing, if their horses would obey . . .

"Good," he said. "It made itself for water; it's too stupid to know how weak it is on land."

He drew his scimitar, but the Ransomer knight was ahead of him, snatching a newly blessed lance, tucking it firmly beneath his arm and urging his horse into motion.

Draw its attention one way, strike from another, strike and run, wheel back and strike again—a Sharai party wouldn't need to be told. He hoped the same was true of these men. It was too late now to teach them desert fighting. And this was a desert spirit despite its watery body, made for desert men to kill. He kicked his horse forward without a backward glance, permitting himself just the slightest huff of relief when he heard the pursuit of hooves at his back.

They rode to the 'ifrit's other flank, yelling and waving their weapons. Before they could close to striking distance, though, the 'ifrit was moving, snake-swift suddenly where it had been worm-slow before. Its body coiled for strength and balance; its head struck out towards the knight. Blunt black vastness thrust towards slender steel-tipped lance, and then reversed itself shockingly, making a brutal lash as it had before, flailing round at Jemel's small group.

They lifted steel against it, all they could do, flimsy pin-prick weapons against unconquerable bulk; and just before it reached them, the 'ifrit reared, snatching its head into the air so that it skimmed just above their points' reach.

It does, it fears those weapons now . . . Jemel yelled exultantly, to encourage the same understanding in the Ransomers; then he urged his reluctant horse in closer.

The Ransomer knight was charging in earnest now, sods flying from his destrier's hooves as man and horse thundered towards the knotted body of the beast, the lance before them like a thorn thrust at a waterskin.

The 'ifrit turned its head, seemed poised to strike down, ruthless and unanswerable—and then did not, tried rather to slither away. Too late: the knight drove his lance home with a cry, with all the strength of his arm backed by his horse's weight and speed.

Jemel's breath fled from him in an explosive sigh as the lance's point sunk deep, half a shaft's depth into the great barrel thickness of the 'ifrit's body.

Water spurted from the wound it made, such a forceful jet that it soaked the knight in a moment and all but knocked him from his saddle. The next moment, his horse finally succumbed to terror. It reared up screaming, forelegs threshing the air; half-fallen already, the Ransomer clung desperately to the arched neck. Now was the time for the 'ifrit to strike back, before the knight could recover and draw sword against it. Jemel caught his breath again, watching for the monstrous head to fall even as he lashed his own mount with the slack of his reins.

The other Ransomers were already committed to a charge, driving in like a spear's head to slash and hew at the 'ifrit's flank. Its writhing scattered them in a moment, but where it writhed it sprayed water from half a dozen wounds. Its head twisted about, abandoning the knight in search of this new threat but not striking at it, fended off by a hedge of glittering steel.

By the time it turned back to find the knight again, he had recovered seat, reins and stirrups, steadied his frantic mount and drawn his great sword.

Either it had achieved what it had come to do, or else it had failed and lost its chance. Whichever, it sought to turn, to retreat into the river. Jemel had reached it now, though, and knew his own best way to hurt it. He galloped past it as he had before, closing so swiftly that his horse barely had time to register its fear before they were away; and as he passed, he cut forward from the shoulder, hacking down.

A man, any animal of flesh would have been laid open

to the bone by such a stroke. The 'ifrit had no flesh, no
bone; there was only the water that came gushing from a
great rent ripped in its shimmering skin. The weight of it
fell on them both, Jemel and the horse. Cruelly cold and
drenching, it was too much for one of them at least. The
horse tried to swivel sharply away from the looming, lashing body of the 'ifrit; its hooves slipped on wet grass
when it was unbalanced already, and it came crashing to
earth.

All his life, Jemel had had ponies and horses fall beneath him. He was slipping his feet free of the stirrups as
soon as he felt the horse's shoulder go; before the animal
hit ground, he was out of the saddle and rolling, one arm
flung out to keep his scimitar from slashing him.

He rolled twice and came to his feet on the third roll,
muddy and soaked but barely bruised, blade at the ready.
The horse was still struggling up; Jemel let it go, less use
than his own feet now. The twisting coil of the 'ifrit's
body loomed above him, spewing water; a little distance
off was the Ransomer knight, also dismounted, standing
close by the monster and simply chopping at it two-
handed.

The skin still rippled, but it was flaccid now, hanging
in wrinkles where it had been firm and full. Jemel thrust
his scimitar in and sawed like the crudest of butchers, seeing it bulge and split, seeing how there were almost two
layers to the hide before the water spilled out to spoil his
sight of it.

The monster's tail came flicking around, in a last desperate attempt. With its former strength and speed, that
blow might have killed them both at once, would certainly
have broken bones and left them helpless; but they met it
each with his sword's point and felt the shudder that
racked the creature.

It was hard to stand in sodden clothes on the slipperiness of mud and force tired muscles into another stroke
and yet another, when every stroke was followed by an-

other bitter rush of ice-cold water. They endured, though, watching each other now as much as they watched the 'ifrit. Jemel felt a smile rising even through the filth of the work; the Ransomer was not so much older than himself, and neither one of them was ready to slack before the other did.

It was butchers' work, but at last the 'ifrit lay slack and leaking from a hundred punctures, like a water-skin pricked by a swarm of sandflies. It was enough, Jemel thought. He waded through the muddy run-off to the creature's head, gazed for a moment into the abiding glitter of its hot eye, and thrust his scimitar in to follow his gaze.

A whistle shrilled for a moment, and was cut off. The fire dimmed and died around Jemel's blade as he withdrew it; curious, he touched his hand lightly to the steel and found it hot beneath his fingers. Clean and dry also, as though he'd sunk it into the Sands at noon; and yet the 'ifrit was full of water, and that was so cold . . .

The glimmering black body of the 'ifrit clouded over, turned to mist and faded with its death. All its remaining water was left behind, the 'ifrit simply the living skin that had contained it. Jemel was deluged, knocked from his feet with the force of it, spluttering beneath it for one terrible moment before it could spread out across the wide grassland and let him come slowly to his feet. He had been sodden before, wetter than he could remember; now, smeared all over with liquid mud, he felt as though the wetness had soaked all the way through to the dry desert soul of him.

That must have been why he was laughing.

HE SQUELCHED OVER to where the knight was struggling to rise under the weight of chain-mail and mud, under the exhaustion of a day's fighting, under the paralysing grip of his own all-consuming laughter.

Jemel reached his left hand down, gripped a gauntlet

and hauled mightily. Felt his feet start to slip, just as the knight came up; for a moment they hung in balance, each dependent on the other. Their legs scrambled for purchase and found it, they saved themselves with an ungainly lurch together and still managed not to let go of each other's hands, neither of their weapons.

Briefly they stood eye to eye and grinning broadly; then the knight took a pace backwards, released his grip and bowed formally.

"My thanks, for your sword and your wisdom too, for knowing how to meet it."

"That was Marron's wisdom, more than mine," and he was already looking around to find his friend, to be sure of him, left alone with enemies all over. He seemed well, but more than that, he seemed distant; too much so. Like the creature that Marron used to carry in his blood, Jemel could go only so far from him and be comfortable.

WHEN THEY FOUND him, Marron was laughing too; possibly laughing at them both, though his eyes were fixed on Jemel. He was on his knees beside the broken man he'd helped to save. There really shouldn't have been anything funny in that, but he was definitely laughing, though he did it as quietly and privately as he did everything.

"Mud-babies," he said, in response to Jemel's stare. "We had a story when I was growing up, where a barren woman makes herself a family of babies from the river's mud. She loves them dearly, until her carping neighbour tells her that they're dirty. So she fetches a bowl of water and she washes them, and they all dissolve to mud again. You look just like a mud-baby, I'd be afraid to wash you . . ."

The Sharai told the same story only drier, with a single baby made from sand and spittle. Perhaps all the stories would be wetter in a country like this, where they could let so much water run to waste.

"The 'ifrit nearly washed me into the river," he grunted, scowling at Marron for his mood. If ever there was a time to be serious, to be vigilant, to watch every word, this must be it.

"You pricked it like a water-skin, it dribbled itself to death."

"I think it was a water-skin," he said, "I think it made itself that way, just a skin and filled itself with water, to be long enough to reach the bridge. Those we fought at Rhabat must have eaten a lot of rock to make the size they did. This one lacked the time to feed itself, perhaps."

"It might have been smaller and done its work as easily," the Ransomer said at his side. "That bridge was built to fall; I was sent ahead to capture it before they could knock out the pins that held it from collapsing. My commander will be displeased with me, but even he didn't foresee a demon rising from the river."

I think the demon foresaw Marron, standing on the bridge; and so it made itself so long, to strike so high and have a chance at him. Though why it would, when he is harmless now . . .

"Tell your commander of this," Marron said, perhaps not so harmless after all; he did after all know the ways of these people, as Jemel did not. "Tell him that these demons, these 'ifrit are the true enemy. Tell him to bless his weapons and to hunt 'ifrit. Tell him there is more virtue in cleansing this or any land of such monstrosities than there is in hunting men who say their prayers another way than he, more honour in this fight than in burning women and children, tell him that. And say that Marron said so."

Jemel flinched at the name; the Ransomer seemed not to react to it at all. "I do not think that I will tell the marshal what you say, but I might tell Sieur Anton."

There was a stillness that had no connection with the

wind, a chill that was nothing to do with ice-water still dripping from their clothes. Jemel felt it in Marron, and in himself; each of them was suddenly very watchful of the other, though their eyes they kept fixed on the Ransomer.

"Your man here," Marron said, speaking just as carefully as the knight had before him, "he could live, but he needs urgent care. He would die before he reached your camp, if you tried to carry him. He needs healing, and we can fetch him to it; but you must trust us, and those whose land this is."

"Trust him to Surayonnaise sorcery, you mean."

"Yes. If you want him to live."

"Sieur, no!" That from one of his men behind. "We should kill them both, the Sharai killed ours . . ."

"And would you see Tryss die, after what's been done to save him? By these men, as much as ourselves?"

"We've only his word for that. Tryss is tough . . ."

"Not too tough to break. You helped bear him back from the demon's shadow, you know his hurts. The boy's right, we have no infirmarer fit to heal those. Give me your word that he'll be returned to us unharmed, lad, and you can have him."

"Returned and healed, I swear it."

"Marron," Jemel said, "how can we take him? How can we go? The bridge is gone, and we cannot cross that water."

Which was good news for Surayon, perhaps, that neither could the Patrics, or this army of Patrics, these Ransomers. There was another army to the south, of course, come from Ascariel; and then there were the Sharai to the east, who might be on either bank or both. When all those armies met, Jemel thought, there would be a killing great enough to dam even this river, if it were not blocked already with the dead of Surayon.

But Marron only smiled, and said, "Esren."

It sounded like a summons, though spoken quietly, as Lisan spoke it. Jemel looked instinctively for a distortion of light in the smoky air, and could not see one. But he saw the Ransomers look wary, and back off up the road; he heard Marron say, "Yes, keep your distance—and put up your weapons, you could do great damage here. You too, Jemel."

He slipped the point of his scimitar into the sheath on his belt and slid it home. Then, only then did he turn, to see a carpet waft its way towards them, hovering at knee-height above the torn and trampled grass. He could have laughed again, perhaps, at the absurdity of it, except that he was not given the time.

"Esren, take up Jemel and this wounded man. Take them to Lisan, at the palace."

"I will, Ghost Walker."

That was wrong, he was not Ghost Walker now; but there was more wrong than words could cover. Jemel met Marron's steady gaze and was startled one more time by the soft unexpected brown of the eyes; startled into stammering as he said, "What, what about you . . .?"

"I am not coming."

"Marron . . ."

"I have to speak to him, Jemel."

"About what? Peace, no more killing? He will not hear you."

"No. About war, and slaughter. He will hear me, I think. Tell the others, Jemel; there are other armies on the march, other commanders who need to hear. Esren, take him now."

"No!"

But there was a band of solid air about his chest, a weave of wind that he could neither find nor fight. The djinni lifted him onto the carpet as a man might lift a struggling babe, and set him down beside the broken Ransomer, and carried him away so swiftly that he barely had the time to watch his friend dwindle out of sight, out of all staring.

FIVE

Little Lights

TIRED OF CAUTIOUS counsels, Imber had struck out wild and chancy, and taken his little army with him.

Had struck out wild and chancy and wrong, and was paying for it now, finding it priced in equal parts shame and frustration.

Had overruled Karel to do it, in front of his cousin's own men, and so shown himself to be callow and foolish and unfit for any command, all those accusations that Karel conspicuously did not level against him. He felt them all the more keenly because he had to make them all himself.

It had all been so clear to him at the time, at the noon to which this was the sunset. They had trailed the Sharai army all day, like carrion crows drawn to the stink of smoke and blood. Sharai were swift about their work; the Elessans could have followed from the mountains to the sea and found nothing but leavings, gleaned not a life from the ruins.

And so, when he had seen how the river turned in a long loop ahead of them, Imber had made a decision. The Sharai forces were keeping to the north bank; he and those he led would cross by the arching stone bridge he could see just ahead and cut across the narrow span to meet the river returning. That way they might hope to get ahead, if they pressed hard now.

He had been deeply pleased with the plan and with himself, and furious when Karel rejected it. No point in getting ahead, Karel had said. Better to sneak up behind, though it took days to do. That was the chance for a small force to do significant damage, in the dark and by surprise. Besides, it was stupid to take a chance on unmapped country. How did he know there would be a bridge downstream, to bring them back to the north bank and the enemy?

Of course there would be a bridge, Imber had snarled, this was farming country and the river was unfordable. He would stake his life and honour on there being a bridge; and Karel might be older and more experienced but Imber was the Baron-heir and would be obeyed in this, the men would follow him . . .

And so they did, and Karel too, wary and unhappy. Imber had led them across the river, across the neck of land beyond and so back to the water—and, of course, there had not been a bridge.

From there to here, there had still not been a bridge. He had been disbelieving at first, and then outraged; how could people live, with their land so impassably divided?

"Carefully," Karel had answered, with a light touch to his voice that only emphasised his abiding anger. "If you lived in Surayon, would you not be careful? The people may have their own ways to cross—tunnels, perhaps, or sorcerous devices—but they have ensured that an army does not."

Certainly, they had done that. The Sharai army was on the other bank, and he had no way to come at it; only a handful of bowmen, and Karel had told them to save their arrows. The Sharai had arrows to spare, it seemed, and sent a flight over at intervals. Karel kept the march out of range and sent men running to glean those shafts; he told Imber to be grateful for his enemies' generosity.

The tribes were facing some resistance now; watching from his distance, Imber saw squads of mounted men meet and part and meet again, leaving some of their number fallen at every meeting. He saw men afoot ambush camel-riders, and die largely. He also saw what was no honourable warfare, what had to be sorcery: gouts of fire flung from the hand to sear and burn whatever flesh it touched, man or camel. Instinctively he made the sign of the God to ward off evil, though none had been flung towards him or his men. They had been ignored, indeed. They had found no one on this side of the river, only homesteads abandoned, barns and stables deserted, flocks of sheep and goats wandering untended.

All Imber could do was to match the Sharai, to keep pace. Through all that was left of the day he had done that, and now as the sun set he could still only shadow them. They made camp in the last of the light; so did he. They scavenged food and firewood from a farm but camped on open ground; so did he. It was the Sharai way in any case to scorn buildings and sleep beneath the stars, but here there was good sense to it, not to be surprised within walls that could burn. Imber understood that, after Karel explained it to him.

In truth, it was Karel who chose the site, set the perimeter guard, made all the decisions for his own men and the ragtag brigade that followed them. Publicly he deferred to Imber, and that was salt on the wound; privately he made suggestions, and Imber was far too sick with himself to argue. Besides, Karel was doubtless right, right again . . .

Even the sunset was a vivid desolation, fierce reds and oranges, colours of burning. He was glad to see the last of its light leave the sky, though the stars offered him small comfort, glimmering through a murky haze.

There was a fire at hand, the men's company, and roasting meat; there was another fire, strangers' faces, the peasant army he had enlisted at Revanchard. He could sit among them and learn their stories, as a good commander should. There was a tent where he could be alone, to sulk or scowl or sleep; there was always Karel, who would always talk or listen as he chose.

But there were also fires like distant flecks of gold, and that was the Sharai beyond the river, and he thought their lights were mocking him, *here we are*; there were other, duller glares behind, which were the blazes the Sharai had set in corn and cabin, barn and barley-field. Those accused him, *they are here, and this is what they did, and where were you?*

He could settle neither at one cookfire, nor at the other; he couldn't play either the popular young lord or the determined captain, not tonight. No more could he retire to his tent and lock himself away behind canvas walls. They were too restrictive and too thin, both at once; they would keep him in but not keep the world at bay.

Restless and angry with himself even for being restless, for giving so much away, he paced away from the firelight with a muttered word to Karel about making a round of the pickets.

They'd been set at all points of the compass on this hostile ground, two experienced men to each and no lights permitted; but it was easy enough to find them when he knew where to look, when he'd had a voice in placing them. He had no trouble in slipping by.

AT THE MARGIN of this meadowland, the ground had been divided by dry stone walls into a myriad small fields. In the last few miles, those walls had risen higher and higher, to stand above the head of a mounted man.

He didn't understand the walls—what sense was it, to build so high and make more shade for crops that loved the sun?—but he could use them now. Karel had distrusted them deeply, seeing their rare entranceways as snares or sally-ports. Imber didn't believe in hidden hordes. If Surayon had an army, they must surely have met it by now; it wouldn't be lurking while its country burned.

He walked westerly along the wall with his left hand brushing the rough dry stonework, his eyes growing sharper as he left the lights of the camp behind him. It cost an effort not to strain them by peering ahead in some hapless search for redemption, for justification, for a bridge.

The treacherous river was a glimmer in the corner of his eye, the voice of it a whisper against his thoughts, as the smoke in the air was a whisper in his throat to say that war was here and he was a part of it.

Not far ahead now was the next opening in the wall, giving access to the fields beyond. It would be darker in there; the darker the better, to suit his mood. He wanted to pace, and out here there was nothing to make him turn, he might walk all the way to the far marshes and the sea.

Distress always had him yearning to be on his feet. His wedding night had been a torment to him, lying cramped in a cot in the preceptor's study and painfully, brutally aware of Julianne being equally wakeful in the next room. Worse than the ache in his muscles had been the ache in his heart, and both had been urging him up to outpace the dark, the one thing that he would not and could not do to her.

He couldn't have done it tonight either, anywhere in camp. Out here and unobserved, he could pace till dawn and be grateful.

He paused in the entranceway for one last look across the wide empty pastureland, and saw that it was no longer empty.

Saw something moving, something so dark and low

that a distant sentry might easily mistake it for a drift of
smoke, a flock of ground-running birds, an eddy of wind
stirring the grasses.

Standing closer as he was, alert as he was to every nu-
ance of light and shade, he could name it for what it was,
which was unnameable: a creature but nothing natural,
nothing of the God's making. Something come out of the
river, he thought; something heading certainly, directly for
him.

It was black as a beetle is black; its body shimmered in
the starlight. It was swift, too, as a beetle is swift to scurry.
He couldn't see how many legs it had, but many, he
thought. Too many, he was sure.

He gripped the hilt of his sword where it was hanging
at his belt and gave thanks for that much sense. Only a
fool would have slipped away from his company on hostile ground without a weapon; but then, only a fool would
have slipped away at all. Surely only a fool would not
now shout, to draw friends to him . . .

None the less, Imber did not shout. He stepped cau-
tiously through the gap in the wall, never taking his eyes
from that rapid shadow. The creature's body was seg-
mented; it stood as high as a man's waist, perhaps, and
had eyes that glowed red in the dark, mouth-parts that
champed together as it ran. At least he could see no more
of the creatures crawling up from the river's bed. Just the
one, and coming straight for him: he didn't believe in coincidence, nor in ill chance.

He did believe in spirits, since he had met his first. It
was nothing but wisdom, to be afraid of what was coming;
in his wisdom, he stepped back into the shelter of the high
wall. Once out of the creature's sight, he ploughed heedlessly through a flourishing crop of millet, towards an
opening in the wall opposite.

Looked through, and of course it only led into the next
field. But that one too offered an onward path, a further
opening. A man might choose rightly or wrongly, but once

he'd chosen he should stand by that choice. In woman, or
in war: which was after all why he was here, how he'd
found a war while he was looking for his woman. He'd be
as steadfast in the one as in the other, which for now
meant steadfast in flight. If the monstrous thing caught
him before he found safety—if there were any safety from
that thing, any safety at all in this cursed country—then
he'd fight, because he must. Until then, he would run.

And did run, through the crop to the next gap; and
paused there to look back, and saw no sign of the creature
following. Went through thinking that perhaps he did have
a chance, perhaps it would grow confused within this
maze of walls and lose his trail. Tried not to think about
the djinni, how impossible it was to imagine that spirit
confused.

Glanced up at the sky, within its sudden square horizons—and was suddenly confused himself, reeling almost, as though the ground beneath his feet had shifted
sharply out of true. Turned itself around entirely, indeed,
because all the stars lay backwards overhead, as mind-
twistingly wrong as a river that ran uphill . . .

No. Absurd. Not the ground, not the stars: it was himself all turned around. High walls and speed and fear together must have confounded his sense of direction. That
way lay north as it always had, the stars said so; which
meant he was facing south, which was a place to start
from. The way out of this field lay to the east, and he
should take it quickly, before the scuttling demon caught
him up.

And did, and found himself facing three blank walls,
and thought he had run himself into a trap; except that as
he twisted around in desperation, he saw another way out
in the same wall that he'd just come through.

That shouldn't be possible, there had been only the one
opening on the other side; and when he ran through he
was in a field of sunflowers, where he certainly hadn't
been before. And he looked up, and again the stars were

lying wrongly strewn across the sky, and there was that shuddering sense of dislocation before he could pull his mind into line with them.

He was beginning to understand. There was a spell bound up in these walls and fields, like the greater spell that had hidden Surayon for a generation. That had lost a country; this would lose a man within a labyrinth and keep him lost, turning him more dizzy at every doorway.

Then he saw the creature he was fleeing. He saw its silhouette blank out the stars as it rose above the wall ahead, flowed over and ran lightly down. Still on a direct bearing, entirely unperturbed by magic, still heading straight for him.

Imber could climb walls and hope to see a way out from the top; but he couldn't climb as the monster did, as easily as running. It was coming through the sunflowers, the blooms were high enough to hide it but it must be close, it must catch him in a moment.

He turned and ran, back the way he'd come.

It led him further into confusion, into fields he had not seen: more crops, more doorways, more moments of jolting shock as the stars realigned themselves at every turn. His head spun, his muscles ached, his breathing laboured as he drove himself on and on, faster, harder—and often, often he saw the creature that he fled, ahead or to one side or the other, always coming over a wall with that smooth scuttling run that spoke of infinite stamina, infinite knowingness—*I will always find you, little mortal*—and infinite patience, *you cannot always run.*

Soon he found himself stumbling over his own tracks in the soft earth, but they were no use to him, going this way or that, no kind of guide. The sweat ran on his skin, the air stung his throat; his legs trembled beneath his weight and he all but fell as he plunged through one more opening.

*   *   *

PLUNGED FROM NEAR-DARKNESS into soft and simple light, and all but fell again from the simple shock of it; and did fall to his knees—more in wonder than in worship, though only a little more—when he saw who stood there among the broadleaf greens.

There were two figures in the light. One was a boy who held a lamp, a page in service to his mistress; the other was Julianne.

They made a strange and troubling tableau, standing with their feet in leaves that were green where the pool of lamplight fell, that turned silver under the stars and black beneath the walls. They looked as though they stood on the stillness of the ocean, as though they were statues cast in light against a darkness that only they could hold back, and only for a time, what time they lingered here. He did not think they would linger long. Not for a moment did he think that Julianne was here to be rescued, by him or anyone.

She smiled at him, and gestured: *stand up, come closer.*

He did both, slowly and reverently, which might equally have been said *slowly and fearfully,* because that too was true. He felt as though he were approaching some sudden manifestation of the God, a revelation to be both feared and revered.

When he was near enough, she reached out a hand in a way that was all wife and nothing saintly. Their fingers met, and gripped: fumblingly at first, and then with a solid certainty. He might have crushed her hand between both of his; he might have dragged her to him, crushed her slenderness against his weight; he might have crushed any resistance in her, to claim her for himself. He thought there was permission, implicit in her touch.

He did none of those. He let her choose how tightly she held him, not tight enough for passion, never tight enough for him. He felt a tremble in her fingers and thought that she was fighting her own instincts, holding back.

He stood and gazed at her. His lips shaped her name

without breath, without sound. He marvelled at her as he always had, at her height and beauty and the straight gaze of her measuring eyes. Only when the boy shifted at her side and all the shadows danced, only then, reminded too late, did he snatch a breath against the startlement of finding her here and croak, "'Ware, run, there's a demon, I'll face it while you flee . . ."

His arm had pointed back, behind him, through the opening, but the monster came over the wall as it always did. This was like a child's dream, being hunted by relentless evil that would always, always reach him in the end. Except that the thing was real and really here, and so was he, and so appallingly was Julianne.

He pushed her and the boy behind him. It had followed him this far; perhaps he was all it wanted. He could see the thing more clearly now that he was no longer running. If he'd ever felt a moment's shame at how he'd fled it, he could abandon that. Some creatures were not made for men to fight. This wicked beast had horns and claws and antennae like whips; its glowing eyes were shielded within plates of black and gleaming armour. Its innumerable feet marched forward like tattooing-needles, swift and sharp and deadly.

"Run," he said. "Julianne, run—and you, boy, go with her. This thing is mine."

"If yours, why should we run?" she countered stubbornly. "Imber, has that blade been blessed?"

"What?"

"By a priest, a man of faith sworn to the God . . ."

"No." What was she talking about, why was she talking at all, why was she not in flight?

"Then put it up, it'll do you no good. That's an 'ifrit, and no mortal sword can cut it. The knife I carried is blessed, but . . ."

"But I have that, my lady." The boy, his first words of the night, and Imber was almost too distrait to hear them.

Until all the shadows shrank and turned and stretched

at once, as the lamp was lobbed high over his shoulder and flared as it fell, splashed like a coughing ball of fire onto the monster's head.

The creature—'ifrit, she had said, and perhaps he should have named it himself, he surely should have known—reared up higher than a man, legs and antennae waving wildly while the oil blazed between its eyes.

A small body hurtled past Imber, chased by a voice, Julianne's, shrieking as he had meant to shriek himself:

"Roald, no! You can't—!"

But he could, or he thought he could. And he was a boy, with a lady to defend and a knight to watch him do it; she had no hope of calling him back. Imber recognised the impulse even as he started forward himself, too slow, too late again. He was vaguely aware that Julianne was shouting something at his back; it might have been a name—*Esren, Esren, damn you!*—but it meant nothing to him.

What he saw meant little more. The monster was demonseed and horror, all the terrors of all the stories of the dark; the boy was just a boy, a rough-clad serving lad with a poniard in his fist. He'd likely never used a knife in his life except to cut himself a trencher from the loaf, and the thing he fought was vastly bigger than himself and vastly malign. There was a smell this close, a dry and dusty odour, the spice-smell of the desert; Imber's soul abhorred it, even while his mind found a memory, the scent of the djinni that had sent him here.

The boy Roald was daunted by nothing, not the smell nor the sight nor the size of the 'ifrit. He simply ran at it while it was still erect, in pain or shock from its burning; he held his blade high and two-handed—his tiny blade, it seemed, against the looming black of the monster's belly and the waving menace of its legs—and plunged it home.

And it sank home where it truly looked as though it shouldn't, as though that shimmering black armour ought to shrug it off without a scratch; sank haft-deep through the belly-plates of the beast as easily as though it slid through the mirror surface of a pool. Roald screamed in triumph and dragged it down like a slaughterer's man opening an ox, and Imber looked for the slipperiness of guts to come tumbling out of the rent he made.

Nothing did, unless there was a little smoke or steam, a sudden mistiness around them. The creature had fire in its eyes; perhaps its guts were smoking. Perhaps its guts were smoke.

Roald was at it again already, slashing at its threshing legs as though he were lopping branches with his father's billhook.

It had legs enough and to spare, though; the knife was simply too short to do it much harm. The boy was doing brave work, but it needed a man with a man's strength and steel to finish the task.

Imber had an executioner's time to set himself, time to swing. He brought his great sword scything round with all the power and timing of a lifetime's training, backed by his long hunt and his bad day and his own determined fury, not to disgrace himself before this girl, this stranger his wife. There was a sweet edge to his blade; it ought to shear the monster's body half through, given how easily the boy's small knife could cut it.

The edge met the armour and didn't cut, didn't shatter, didn't mark; it simply stopped. Stopped dead, as though he'd been trying to hew granite. The jar of its stopping snagged every bone in his body, numbed his arms up to his shoulders and snatched the air from his lungs again; the blade rang falsely and dropped from his helpless fingers.

Stunned, bewildered, he was as checked as his blade: standing useless, only peripherally aware of Julianne's bellow from behind, "I *told* you, your sword's no good! Back, both, the knife's as bad . . ."

Roald wasn't listening. He was still there, still hacking, a close arm's reach from the 'ifrit; and the 'ifrit was poised like a snake on its tail, and it seemed to Imber as though the whole world were equally poised and still, waiting for the strike.

Imber fumbled on the ground for his fallen sword and lifted the point again against the 'ifrit. Perhaps he could thrust it into a wound that the boy had made before him, if he couldn't cut through that impervious shell; see what damage a length of good Outremer steel could wreak in a demon's innards, if once it could get in there . . .

Still slow and shaken, though, he couldn't come at it soon enough. Something had got through to the boy, Julianne's sudden silence perhaps where her voice had never reached him. He turned his head upward, and must have seen two baleful eyes of fire: eyes that must have swelled against the glitterdust of the sky behind, as the creature's head drove down.

No telling whether he saw the horns that impaled him, throat and belly. Perhaps the double blow came so swiftly that he felt nothing, neither cold nor heat nor terror as he died.

The creature's head flung sideways, flung the broken body off; and then it turned, to find Imber. Its speed was gone, though, it was floundering almost on its belly from the loss of legs and substance where Roald had hewn at it; and Julianne was calling again, and this time Imber would listen.

"Its eye, Imber, strike at its eye, that's all the hope you have . . ."

And her hope also, for she lacked even a knife to meet it with, she'd said so. She used to flee from him, now she depended on him; that firmed his double-handed grip, steadied his nerve and his trembling muscles, gave him safe footing and a clear gaze.

He tracked the swing of the creature's head, trusted his lady's word and waited his moment, which was just that moment before it thrust itself forward to destroy him.

He plunged towards it, all his weight behind the blow.

The creature seemed to rise to meet the blade, so perfect was his timing or so gracious the hand of the God at his back.

His point found the sunken socket of the 'ifrit's red eye, and all the length of his blade followed it down. Down and down, while his body twisted to avoid the reaching horns; he felt the quillons grate against its shell, and then a terrible wrench on his shoulder as the creature hurtled abruptly upwards, hissing like water on a fire now, like water falling over broken stones.

He let go of the sword's haft, or felt it slide from his grip rather, as he fell hard on his back. Lay gazing up at the black shadow of the 'ifrit's bulk as it eclipsed half the sky, half the stars that he could see; it was a shadow that swayed, that was going to topple at any moment, and when it did it would topple towards him, land atop him, crush him entirely out of life, and there was nothing he could do.

A moment before it fell, Imber remembered what the djinni had said to him on that first far day. *Great peril,* it had said, and he'd thought it meant at Revanchard, he'd thought himself too late to save her. He felt that a price had been paid tonight, innocence and honour, and it was a small price for her life and less than she was worth.

And then the 'ifrit began to fall; and as it fell it faded, so that he could see the stars through its body like jewels through a thickness of veils. Brighter and brighter they shone while the dark came down like a curtain falling too slowly, losing all its rush: a curtain of finer and finer fabric as it seemed, more and more sheer, until when at last it touched him it was only smoke drifting coldly in the windlessness, drifting and dying and gone, and his sword fell down heavily beside him as though a cloud had held it for a time and dropped it now, weary of its weight and pointlessness.

*   *   *

HE LAY STILL for a while, wondering how long he had been dreaming, just when he had parted company with the reality of the night. Then he tried to sit up, and the sharp ache in his shoulder, the soreness down his ribs and spine, the slow exhaustion in his legs all said that there was no dreaming here: that he had fled a monster, he had met Julianne, he had seen evil dissipate in death.

So he sat up despite the pain, and looked around. He was looking of course for her, and found her of course where she should be, where she had to be because she was Julianne: not with him but with Roald, kneeling above the boy's body, cradling his head in her lap while her hair fell down to hide his face and her own.

If Imber could sit, Imber could stand, or so he told himself. And so did; and if he could stand, he could walk, and so did. Slowly, totteringly almost, but thinking to stoop on the way to retrieve his sword and the dagger also that the boy had used. *Blessed,* Julianne had called it, and so it had proved. With his sword in the one hand, with her magic dagger in the other, he'd still place his body between her and any peril that came at them, whether it was another 'ifrit tonight or a Sharai warrior tomorrow, a conjuror from Surayon in this strange valley or his own raging uncle at his own home in Elessi . . .

He could do that, he could stand against any danger and live or die on the hazard, because he knew what to do and why he did it. He didn't know what to say to a weeping girl—this weeping girl, his wife—where she crouched over the body of a boy who'd died for her sake.

Soon, though, she would have to lift her head and look at him. Because she was Julianne, because he was Imber. Because they were married, in every way except what the law allowed to married love.

Because she had to do it, so she did; and, "I met him today," she said, her voice hoarse with shouting, thick with tears. "Only today. He insisted on coming with me. I

said, I said it was only to escape the kitchens for an hour;
he was so angry . . ."

He died with honour; I am glad he came; both were
true, but impossible to say. Nor could he reach to touch.
The gap between them was small, but unbridgeable.

"Julianne," and it was something even to speak her
name against that gaze. "Julianne, how are you here?"

"How?" A dead note to the repetition, to match the
corpse-light in her eyes. "We were brought."

By whom? Who had fetched her from the castle, where
was her allegiance now? He would not ask, not yet. "Why,
then?" A girl and a boy, unwatched in the heart of a war—
it was unthinkable.

"Why? To talk to you, I thought. I'm not sure now . . ."
And her eyes strayed back to the body she was nursing.

"To talk to me? But—you couldn't know, how could
anyone have known . . .?"

"The djinn know the future, Imber," as her hands
stroked the hair back from the dead boy's brow. "Some, at
least. Not everything, not enough; but enough at least to
put us in your path."

And in the 'ifrit's path also, so that Roald died. That
was so clear, neither of them needed to say it.

But, "What have the djinn to do with this?"

"It was a djinni brought us here."

He'd have liked to close his eyes to think the better, as
he had done all his life. That was a child's trick, though,
and he was a man grown. A man grown and married, desperately parted from his wife and bewilderingly reunited,
and he could not close his eyes to her face. But a djinni
had brought her here, and a djinni had sent him in pursuit
of her; and that djinni, his djinni had named itself as Esren
Filash Tachur, the strange words were branded in his
memory, and he had heard her crying "Esren!" as he
fought . . .

He thought that the djinni had placed her in the peril
from which it had sent him to rescue her; or placed her

here, rather, where he would lead the peril to her and then
rescue . . . "What could you tell me, Julianne, that a
djinni could not? Why do this," *risk a girl and kill a boy,*
"why fetch you here?"

"I was to tell you—oh, that there was a greater danger
than the Sharai, greater evil than the Surayonnaise abroad
in this land. Well, that you have seen. Which I expect is
why it fetched me here, to be sure that you would see. And
survive, to say what you have seen." Her voice had passed
beyond bitter, into some depth of cold savagery that he
had never thought to hear from any woman, never mind
his gentle, politic Julianne. "I was to tell you also that
there is an army come up from Ascariel, hastily gathered
but more potent than this raggle-taggle that you lead.
They are to be found to the west, along the line of the
river. There is no way to cross it now, I was to tell you
that. They lack a commander of rank, and will listen to a
lord of Elessi. And if there's a priest with them, have him
bless their weapons. Have him bless yours, twice over; it
works, you saw . . ."

"I did—and this is yours, my lady." He handed her the
knife and saw her shudder in the starlight before she took
it, the haft still warm from Roald's tight and clumsy grip.
Warmer than his hand, perhaps, by now. "But I will not go
any further west, now that I have found you. I have what
I came for. We'll leave this cursed land, I'll take you
home . . ."

"No," she said, soft and determined. "I am not free to
leave—and nor are you, Imber. We've all of us been
fetched. Besides, you could not cross the river now. The
way you came is barred, and there's no path through the
mountains south."

"What, shall I go west, then, and take command of an
army? This is a bad night to ask it, but I will if you are
with me, Julianne. You're free to go where I go, nowhere
else. You are my wife."

"And another man's," she said, confirming the impossible with a sad little smile, "and can follow neither of my husbands now. No, don't touch me, Imber. There never was any force between us, and will not be. Esren . . ."

This time it came, the djinni, a suck of darkness and a glitter string, starlight caught on a thread and spun around velvet.

"Esren, take us back, Roald and me."

"Julianne, wait!"

"For what?" It seemed to him that she was half gone already, more than half, although she hadn't stirred from where she knelt; she'd moved no more than the boy had. "I can't take you with me. Find your own role, Imber—go back to your people, warn them, lead them, be aware. And don't slay any more innocents."

"I have not—" he began, and then thought that perhaps she meant Roald, and wondered if perhaps she was right. And said instead, "Julianne, I'm lost in here. There is a curse on these fields, they lead me all awry . . ."

"Call it a blessing, for those who live here. But there's a trick, they have to tend their crops." And she smiled, just a little, as she said, "When you pass through a gap turn left, keep your left hand on the wall and follow it around to the other opening. Even if that's directly opposite, even if it's only three paces to your right: always turn left, and always follow the wall. That's all, that will see you out." The smile vanished all too soon, as she added, "Roald told me that, while we were waiting. Now, please, Esren."

And he thought she rose up and flew like a witch, with the boy's body in her arms; except that he would not believe that of her, and it was hard to see with the sudden swirling lights and the suck of the dark that seemed to close around her, so perhaps it was all an illusion of the djinni's.

One thing was no illusion, though, that she was gone. If it weren't for the aches in his body and her words bright in his head, he might have thought her an illusion altogether, just a fever dream.

But she had been his Julianne, and she had been there. The crops were flattened where she'd sat; there was the stickiness of blood on the leaves where Roald had fallen. She was his certainty, his rock. If she held true, then so did all about her. There was the 'ifrit, the boy, the news, the message; the urgency of the message confirmed by his own experience, brutally driven home by the boy's death. Even Julianne could never have persuaded him, he thought, if he hadn't seen for himself. How was he to persuade his cousin Karel?

Well, he would confront that when he came to it. He had to get there first. He put his left hand to the wall and leaned against it for a moment, dizzied by memory or anticipation, both; then he straightened, took a glance upward to see how the stars were set, and started walking.

✠ ✠ ✠

BHISRAT WAS YOUNG to be sheikh, but the Saren were an exceptional people and he was an exceptional man.

Also he was a proud man, although there was nothing exceptional in that.

Tonight he was an angry man: cheated of his proper authority, betrayed by something he could not understand and so humiliated in front of his peers, the sheikhs of other tribes. They mocked him with their silence, and he could do nothing. If he spoke, if he gave a moment's notice to the issue, they would mock him with words instead. Then he would be forced to fight, and so his name would be written in infamy, as the man who lost his tribe in war and then in fury turned on other sheikhs and so lost the war for all the tribes.

It could happen, it was there to be done. Already half the men had forgotten why they were here, whether that be to recover Hasan or to recover the land, drive the Patrics into the sea. They were content to raid and burn, to fight whenever they could find a fight. Not finding fights enough, they were close already to fighting each other over a word or a gesture or a bolt of looted cloth.

Without Hasan they made a poor army, an ill-disciplined mob; and the sheikhs who led them were little better. The council could not meet without arguing, nor keep its arguments a secret, with firelight and wind its only walls. Let one of those arguments come to steel and there would be no Sharai army, only a dozen tribes more at war with each other than they were with the Patrics, though they fought on Patric land.

So Bhisrat held his peace against the silence, which was almost but not quite worse than spoken taunts; and he sat with his face to the fire, keeping his back ostentatiously turned to the high walls of the field-maze, where the dirt-grubbing Patrics laid their deceiving traps for honest warriors.

He had men watching the walls, of course. It was not true that he had lost his tribe: only the best of the tribe, the finest, the pride of his blood. And it should not have happened, it bewildered him, and so he was raging.

In Hasan's absence, no sheikh would risk giving orders to another, *scout that way* or *search there*. Instead they vied for the place of greatest danger, sent their men to outrace others to the fight, made promises of blood now and loot to follow.

There had been disappointingly little of either, this whole day's march. A Patric troop tracked them on the wrong side of the river, and could not be closed with; this morning they'd met farmers and peasants largely, as easy killing as their flocks and as poor as the land they tilled. There was better fighting and better raiding in the Sands. Much better raiding, now that all the fighting men were here. It couldn't be long before one tribe or another would think of that, speak of that around its fires, slip away before the dawn.

Determined that it should not be the Saren, Bhisrat had led them in a furious race to find the fighting men of

Surayon. They had found only skirmishes and traps, tricks
and sorceries that stole his tribesmen's courage and his
own pleasure in the chase.

When the walls rose up around the fields, the good running was squeezed down towards the river, but there was
no one to run after. The cursed grubbers laid ambushes,
appearing suddenly from behind the walls, shooting arrows or riding down stragglers and then vanishing into
shelter again.

Of course he'd sent men in to flush them out, like dogs
who put up finches for the hawks. When those men didn't
return, he'd listened to the clamour of his people and let
larger groups go in search. He'd warned them to beware
of lurking magic, but still he'd let them go.

And had waited then, with what remained of his warriors, while the other tribes caught up; it had been their
passing taunts that sent a number more into the maze of
fields intemperately, in ones and twos into the unyielding
silence.

AND NONE OF them, not one had yet come back.

So he sat at the elders' fire, with his back to the wall
behind which he had lost the pride of his tribe; he kept his
own pride in check, not to be known as the man who
wrecked the hope of all Sharai; he pretended to listen to
the older men's talking while he waited for news, any
news from what Saren he had left to watch the wall.

There was news, other news from other tribes, where
they watched other borders of the camp. Things moved in
the dark, they said, that were not men. They had shot arrows without result; none was willing to venture out, to
try what a scimitar could do. Bhisrat thought that the fate
of the vanished Saren was perhaps weighing on their
minds, turning common cowardice into good sense; it was
good sense not to say so, though.

For as long as he could, he kept silent. His control was

only broken when there was a stir in the half-light beyond
the fire; when there were voices raised in startlement, crying out in disbelief; when two figures came stumbling
awkwardly out of a deeper dark.

They were awkward because they leaned on each
other—no, because one leaned and the other had to support him, even while he carried something heavy in the
opposite hand. Their sudden appearance was shock
enough; it was their recognition, though, that made men
cry aloud.

One of the figures was Hasan, and the sight of him
raised joy that spread like a fire through the camp, that
was as quickly followed by fear. He needed his companion's strength to walk, he was pale and scarred and terribly weak who had always been so strong and masterful,
master of himself before he mastered any man.

That companion, with his one arm wrapped around
Hasan and his other raising high the vile thing he carried—that was the tribeless boy, the oath-breaker who of-
fended all the tribes but the Saren specially, he who
followed the bastard Patric Ghost Walker and should have
died twice by now, twice at least. And he had given a finger to join the Sand Dancers and still he was let live, he
was let walk into camp as into Selussin and Rhabat and
this folly had to end, how long must Bhisrat endure it . . .?

The boy walked into the firelight, into the heart of the
elders' council, and didn't even pretend to be there simply
as a prop to the sick Hasan. He settled his master carefully, to be sure—but then he straightened himself and
turned a full circle, showing what he held to every man
that watched.

It was a ghûl's head, female and monstrous. Hewn after
death, it must have been; Bhisrat guessed furiously at
what blade had been used to do the work, and saw his
guess confirmed as the nameless, shameless boy dropped
the head and then knelt beside it, with Bhisrat's own good
knife in his hand.

There would be no honour in slaying the boy, it was only a necessary duty owed to the dignity of the tribe, a restoration. He would do it in the Sands, on Saren land and under Saren eyes. Even so, this blatant parading called for some response. Half the men around him were waiting for it, he thought, even while they babbled questions at Hasan and were entirely ignored.

"Enough!" he cried, into the general clamour of rising voices. "There are many questions, and we will ask them all; but first, Hasan, tell me how it is that you allow that outcast to strut so at your side? This is the third time he has forced himself into our councils. His arrogance will earn him brief reward, but I do not understand why you give him your support."

"It was rather the other way about," Hasan said softly, drily. "And is that your chief concern, this night? Well, let it be. He is here because he has something to show you, that I think you ought to see."

"A ghûl's head? I have seen one before."

"Not the head alone, something more."

"You could have shown us yourself, why let the boy bring it?"

"He slew it," mildly.

"Better it had slain him, saved me the work."

"See him as a prop to my weakness, if that is easier for you, and a bearer of burdens. I could not have carried that head tonight, and you need to see it. All of you need to see it. Show them, Jemel."

The boy wrenched open the dead thing's mouth—too long for a human jaw and too pointed, but still disturbingly female—and slipped the blade inside. His hands worked, one gripping while the other sawed; they emerged with the tongue of the ghûl hanging like a miscarried foetus, dark and dripping.

"So the boy is an incompetent butcher. And what?"

"Look . . ."

The boy himself had still said nothing, and he said

nothing still. He probed the point of the blade into the heavy wet meat of the tongue, found something, grunted his satisfaction.

And cut it out, and held it up for all to see: not a growth, nothing that could be natural even to so unnatural a thing as a ghûl. A small stone, a large seed: something like an olive-pit, except that it was itself the size of an olive.

"What is that?"

"A spell, an enchantment; a whip, perhaps. Break it, Jemel, or Esren leaves you stranded here."

The boy placed it on a broad, flat stone near the fire, that had been used an hour before for baking bread. He still held the dagger, Bhisrat's own blade in his other hand; now he reversed it and brought the pommel slamming down. Bhisrat cried out in protest at seeing his knife so abused, but this time he was ignored.

The little thing had been a stone indeed, and had broken open under the blow. Stained dark on the outside by the body or the blood of the creature it had inhabited, it showed its golden heart in the firelight. Now half a dozen voices asked the same question again while the boy went on silently, heedlessly ruining the dagger's fine hilt, using the weight of it to crush the stone to powder.

"What *is* that?" the voices asked, and answered themselves in a ragged and rising chorus. "It's a stone, that's all, just a piece of rock, what was it doing in that thing's tongue, what's this about?"

"It was fetched over from the land of the djinn," Hasan said; and quiet, tired as he was, his voice cut through the sheikhs' uproar as they all sought to outshout each other.

They gaped at him, so many fools with their beards hanging loose. Bhisrat wore no beard, but still he could feel his own startlement writ large on his face in the firelight. No way to recover that, only a brief opportunity to seize leadership again, before another man stepped into the silence.

"Hasan, I—we—do not understand."

"It is, it was a pebble from the land of the djinn," he said again, more clearly, "fetched over by the 'ifrit to make the ghûl a tool to their will. There is some virtue if you would call it that, some glamour in the rock of that place, that gives it power here. The 'ifrit have used it to bind a djinn, the same that brought us here—but you know that, you were in Rhabat and saw what came of it. They use it also to bind ghûls. Those are ghûls that haunt the borders of your camp tonight, but they are ghûls with a stronger mind behind them. They are being driven against you, and it's the 'ifrit that drive them. I do not know why, but the 'ifrit have attacked us before; they have attacked others along this river this day."

"It is obvious why," Bhisrat growled. "The 'ifrit are bound or in allegiance to these Patrics of Surayon, and are sent against their enemies."

"It was the Patrics of Surayon that saved my life today," Hasan returned mildly, "and an 'ifrit that threatened it."

"Seeming so. And as a result you come to us, you are returned to us—to say what? I do not think to lead us to Ascariel, or to plunder. Have they turned your head, Hasan?"

"Have they? No, I don't believe they have. You are right, though, Bhisrat of the Saren. This much I am convinced of, that the 'ifrit are the greater enemy and the greater cause tonight. We must fight and defeat them before we think to fight further for our land, that the Patrics stole from us. Not to forget that, but to put it aside for now; and if that means we must fight alongside the Patrics for a short time, then let it be. When men ride out against the spirit world, they do well to ride in numbers."

Bhisrat snorted, was ready to say that the Sharai were too wise to be so trapped. He was forestalled, though, by the oathbreaker.

"Bhisrat of the Saren," the boy murmured, loud enough

to carry. "Yes, indeed. And where are your Saren tonight, Bhisrat? I remember all their faces, and I don't see any of them hereabouts . . ."

He could not have seen in the dark, in the crush of bodies packing in around the firelit circle. He must have known before; and of course he did, because he had come with Hasan, which meant he had come from those Patrics who had snared the Saren in their cursed labyrinth. True warriors of the tribe, of the Sharai, and they were being sneered at by this boy of shifting allegiance, who had long since forgotten how to spell his loyalty or what oaths he'd broken and to whom.

Bhisrat's roar of fury was building in him like sand blown in a storm. He must break his own oaths now, at any moment, he must draw his scimitar and smite that reckless, feckless boy's head from his dishonest shoulders, let it fall down beside the ghûl's and lie there, kind by kind . . .

But again Hasan cut in, just a moment before Bhisrat must have lost control; again the breathy fragility of his voice was somehow a quality that must be listened to.

"Jemel, enough. Don't be petty. Go and fetch them now."

"Very well, Hasan."

With half a smile and a mysterious glance that was meant surely to infuriate further, as it surely did, the boy rose easily to his feet and began to walk towards the wall that hid the ensnaring maze. Bhisrat stood four-square in the boy's path and—almost choking on the effort to speak, grinding the words out—he said, "You know where they are."

"Oh, yes." For a moment, he held that same mocking smile; and then, relenting, "They are not dead, Bhisrat, only lost and wandering; and they have been my brothers all my life, till now. I will fetch them out."

"They are my tribe, outcast. I will fetch them."

"Oh? Go, then," with a courteous gesture. "I will wait with Hasan; he needs me, if the Saren do not."

"You know I cannot fetch them without help."

"And you should know that I will not help you to fetch them. What, shall I lead you through your confusion, while you dog obediently at my heels?"

That was another reason to kill the boy, that insult flung so casually. But the tribe's safety lay between them, in this strange and unknowable land; he swallowed his fury and said, "You need not watch your back, so long as I walk behind you. When I kill you, trust that it will be face to face and blade to blade, as I promised before."

"That was not my concern; I had not thought to fear my own knife at my back." *Even from you* was not spoken, it did not need to be. "What I fear rather," the boy went on, raising his voice and looking around, playing to his listeners now, "is seeing you restored to the trust of your tribe, as you come from the dark to lead them free. A sheikh should be wise and temperate, and you are neither. I care yet for the Saren, and I would not see them endangered at your hands. You have lost them once on this adventure; where will you lead them next? Or send them, rather?"

There was laughter all around. Some must be at the very idea of a Sharai sheikh being wise or temperate, that was a known joke, but most of it was purely aimed at Bhisrat.

"Stay, Bhisrat," Hasan said mildly from the fire. "Let the boy fetch your people; he has your blade for his authority, they will follow him out of the trap they're in. Stay, and aid our councils here. We need wisdom, we must talk about the threats we face and how we're best to meet them."

He had no choice; he stepped aside and let the boy slip smiling into the dark. But his voice would be wasted now, as his searching would have been before. Every time

Hasan mentioned wisdom, he knew, everyone who heard would remember the oathbreaker's jibe.

And the boy was right, Bhisrat would lose more than the respect of other sheikhs by this night's work. The Saren too would be eyeing him askance, and less inclined to listen or to follow. Tribes had risen against their sheikhs before now; and that boy would provoke them mightily as he led them out of the labyrinth.

Oh, they were clever—but there would still come that moment, a circle of bodies and a stretch of sand, where the boy met Bhisrat's steel and choked on it. That would make much worthwhile.

In the meantime, Hasan was tipping the baking-stone towards the fire, brushing the golden dust of crushed stone into the flames like so much wasted flour. It was not such heavy work, but the strain of it showed; another man asked him why he did it.

"The djinni would not come, while even that dust lingered in the air."

"Djinni? What djinni?" A hundred voices now, hushed by his gesture as they always had been.

"This," he said; and, "Esren . . ."

The djinni came like a break in the darkness, like a fault in a rockface that showed the glitter of hidden wealth beneath. Bhisrat heard the rushing whisper on all sides, *where has he been, that he comes back with command over the djinn?*

They were fools to be impressed, twice fools to trust him now. He had been with sorcerers, and there were too many spirits in this story. Bhisrat smelled the stink of betrayal in the air, and dared not say it against so many true believers.

"Esren, when Jemel comes out of the fields with the Saren lost, I want you to take him back to the palace."

"He will not want to go."

"I know that. Marron went with the Ransomers; this is his stubbornness, that he means to go with the Sharai. I mean him to go back, he causes nothing but division here. Tell him Marron will return shortly."

"The djinn do not lie, Hasan."

"I hope that it will not be a lie."

"Neither do the djinn hope. I cannot see what Marron means to do."

"Well, tell him nothing, then—but take him anyway. Regardless of his protests. Lisan told you to obey me, not him. Take him away from here and back to her."

Hasan was speaking to the sheikhs now, speaking of 'ifrit, but Bhisrat would not listen. He had his own thoughts, his own suspicions; he should make his own plans, if he could only find some men to follow him.

✠   ✠   ✠

RONAN DE MONTCLAIR had looked for miracles and wonders ever since he came to the Sanctuary Land, and had been sadly disappointed for more than twenty years already.

He'd learned to live with older men laughing at his fancies, and boys too, boys born in Outremer and wise within their world; before long, he'd learned to keep his dreams private even from his friends. He'd never learned to stop looking. The priests' teachings and the old legends both were burned into the bone of him. He knew that the God had walked this country and blessed it in His passing, and he believed also that there were spirits and demons here that his homeland had never seen. He watched trees and rocks and rivers, he prayed with his eyes on the stars, and he had never yet seen a shadow not cast by the sun, a shimmer not made by wind on water or a fire not struck from a flint. He had sat on his horse on a hilltop and seen what he thought was the gleam of sunlight on the domes of Ascariel, the God's own city; but he had never come closer than that far view, and even he couldn't read a distant glitter as even the promise of a charm. That had been

when he was a youngster still, a squire in his lord's ret-
inue. Now he held his own land in his own name, directly
from the Duke. It was what he had come for, but it had
made a farmer of him, where he could have been a knight.
He had earth under his fingernails and his feet had
sprouted invisible roots, which his father might have
called a miracle indeed, but he would not. Married with
children, twice tethered to his holding, he still prayed at
all the proper hours and at other times too, when he was
abroad in his fields; he still watched for strangeness, for
any sign that creatures not mortal had visited his land; he
still saw nothing but what he had always seen: the actions
of light and weather, the flights of birds, no angels.

It was good land he was granted, fertile and well-watered. It should have gone to a man of better blood than
his, but that it lay close to the road north and the northern
border of the dukedom, that strange dislocation where lay
the Folded Land.

He had never gone that far, either, not though the ride
would promise a touch of magic at its end. Some wonders
were accursed, and he would not willingly seek them out.

He could face them, though, if the need arose. When
messengers rode wildly south from the border's guards,
when a small and hasty army came marching north in response—*the way is open, Surayon lies where it always
lay; to arms, to arms and march!*—he didn't hesitate to
join it. All of Outremer might be vulnerable to the Princip's spellcasting; his own land was vulnerable to any evil
that might have been breeding in darkness this thirty
years. The Church might call him, his liege lord might
send him, but he rode for himself and his family.

From the moment they crossed the border, he had expected sorceries to be levied against them, fiends and
ghosts and foulness; all day and half the night, he had
again been disappointed. He had seen houses, herds and
crops, and he had seen them all laid waste. He had seen
groves and orchards that reminded him of his childhood

home; he had seen men at the trees with axes and with fire.

Nor was it only trees that suffered, or only crops and cattle. Those same axes had hewn at men; those same flames had burned women in their cottages, women and children too. Ronan had no wrath, but his own fear survived; he had watched every death warily. He couldn't believe that these heretics and sorcerers would simply die as they did die, like farmers and families or any mortal folk.

And yet they had done that, they had died and died, and fought with little more than swords and courage first. There had been a few balls of fire flung, that had burned hotter and longer than an oil-flame ought; but he had been a soldier before he became a farmer, and he had seen such things before. If there were magic in these fireballs, he couldn't distinguish it from the science of the artificers he'd served with, who could compound pitch, naphtha, sulphur and charcoal into a murderous firepot.

It was hard to rejoice, where he felt little better than a bandit falling on ill-defended farms. He was a farmer himself now, and recognised the land-love that could set a man with a billhook against a troop of horse; he was married now with children, and recognised the protective terror that could throw man and then wife against a hedge of blades, hoping to turn them from a baby even where there was no hope. A part of Ronan was disappointed that his captains had led him to this slaughter. A smaller part of him, little more than a whisper in the uttermost privacy of his skull, was disappointed that the Surayonnaise showed no vestige of their much-vaunted magic. Never mind his lifelong yearning to see signs and wonders, he would have welcomed the sight of women and children vanishing into a veil of mystic smoke, if it could save his having to see them trapped behind a curtain of fire, nothing but their voices rising free.

They'd made camp at sunset, on a low knoll that they could encircle with thorn and brush for a crude palisade.

Ronan had tried to eat with the others, but had found fresh-killed meat too hard to swallow. And the fires too hot, too bright with faces and the crackling, snapping voices of the day's dead calling to him, asking questions for which he no longer had an answer.

So he had walked away: had made his way past the guards at the cut-thorn hedge and out through the narrow wynd they'd left in case of need. With his back turned to fire and company, he'd walked far enough for folly, and further yet.

And stood now amid the tough grasses of the river's bank, gaping at what he'd been waiting twenty years to see, what he'd been ready for all day until this moment, what he had feared and dreaded and yearned for all at once.

He saw magic, he saw what was impossible, what he'd previously found only in tales that he'd barely more than half believed. It didn't seem so much moment by moment, it wasn't half as portentous as he thought it ought to be; and yet the whole of it, the thing itself left him shaking, gasping, reduced to a child too stupid to feel terror in the face of what was wonderful and dreadful both together.

It started with a light against the dark, a warm bright glow he should have welcomed, except that it came from no source that he could guess at and burned nothing that he could see. It was just a light, a line of light like a rip in the fabric of the night, that spread wider like a door opening and spilling glory.

It was right in front of him, not ten running paces ahead; it lit all the grass between them and none beyond, as though there truly were a door in a wall of dark and the light it spilled could fall only towards him.

There was, of course, a figure outlined in the light. There had to be.

A figure of dark it was: a shadow that grew sharper, that loomed larger, that came towards him like a demon rising from the depths, quite unhurried.

Ronan should perhaps have run, but he'd been told all his life that wickedness had wings to outspeed a racing horse. He might have cried out for help, he should certainly have prayed to the God to shield him from hellspawned creatures, but there was a weight on his tongue that might have been terror or might have been doubt, though it felt more like simple wonder. His thoughts trembled on a hair, on a razor's edge. Here was what he'd looked for all his life and what he most dreaded, both together and somehow quieter than he'd ever imagined, a man walking through a door and how could he kneel to that, how could he scream at it? He'd always thought that magic would be huge and fiery, not cool and small and simple . . .

The figure moved forward and was a man. There was relief in that, but—of course—a hint of disappointment too, a sense of something missed. Ronan found it hard to remember even that he ought to draw his sword. It was a second figure that reminded him, following the first out of the light: this one a young man fumbling for his footing, turning his head as though he found it hard to see quite where he was, or how he had come there, or why. And he overtopped the first man by a head and had twice the breadth of shoulder, and was a warrior, no question.

A warrior, following a sorcerer—Ronan did draw his sword, and he drew his breath also to shout the great alarm to rouse all the camp behind him. But the sorcerer lifted his hand, and Ronan felt that weight pressing on his tongue again, except that this time he felt it truly, like a pebble in his mouth. Gagging, he lifted a finger to pluck it out, except that there was nothing there: only his silence, his emptiness of voice.

"Easy there," the man said softly, when Ronan might have turned to flee. "You've nothing to fear of me, nor of my companion. We too serve the King. This young lord is Elessan, and his family name is Karlheim; that should be enough. He is not meant to be in this war, so we will not declare him further. My own name is Coren de Rance, and I am the King's Shadow in Outremer."

The walls of night were dark and high, but there was starlight and there was riverlight, and Ronan thought that together they were enough. An honest man himself, he believed in honesty writ plain to see in others; he did not, could not doubt this man for a moment. He sheathed his sword, bowed to the lord, might have knelt to the Shadow but that the man's swift gesture refused him leave to do so.

There was to be no more magic, it seemed, unless there were spells in words alone. The King's Shadow said, "Come: if you have no duties of watch or guard, will you take the two of us to meet with your commanders? There will be hard work in the morning, and the news of that should be broken now, to give all possible time to prepare. And be easy, man—the work may be hard, but at least it should be cleaner than the work you've done today. Enough of burning, I say, and enough of slaying the innocent."

Something turned in the river, something rose like a rock so that the star-blanket broke and flowed like shards of shimmer falling, fleeing the great dark that divided them. Ronan touched a useless hand to a useless sword and said, "Of course, my lords—but come quickly, if you will. I cannot protect you here."

"Nor we you," the young lord said softly, his eyes on the same massive disruption in the river, watching as it sank and was gone, as the waters settled again above where it had been. "Perhaps all the men in your army cannot protect you, or us, or each other; but that we will learn in the morning. For now, let us go and surprise some few of those men, before something comes to surprise us altogether."

Ronan led the way, as was proper, but he couldn't keep from glancing back as he went, both at the men and at the river.

"They always said this place was cursed." He said it aloud, if quietly, only for the comfort of hearing his own voice; and of course he was answered, by the King's Shadow himself.

"They did say so, and they were wrong. Surayon is endangered, as it always has been. That same danger threatens us, all of us, from the Kingdom to the Sands and further, to Marasson and the lands beyond. Not a curse, though, and not attached to this small land. Surayon is only a focus, it draws the attention of the world and worse, the powers beyond the world."

And where was the God, where was His shielding hand? Not here, Ronan thought, not poised to shield him.

✠ ✠ ✠

EVEN BEFORE HE turned, Anton knew—or told himself so, at least, in his later solitude.

There was something in the stillness, in the silence, in the utter sense of a world in wait. He couldn't mistake that for a moment, he who had lived with his own waiting moment by moment through month after month of moments.

And so he had turned, and so he had seen Marron, and there had been no surprise in it at all. Or so he told himself later, when such a thought might have seemed a comfort, if he had needed comforting.

For now, tonight, he felt the impact, the weight of the moment before he knew what it meant: like the stillness that presages a tremor in the earth, like the sudden suck of air before a conflagration. Understanding broke over him like a wave of water, brutal and destructive; and so he turned, and so he saw Marron.

HE TURNED AND saw Marron and was barely conscious that the boy was not alone, that he and the boy were not alone together. His tongue reached for words, and for the moment could not find them; which proved to be a blessing, because the man who stood with Marron spoke first and gave Anton time to remember that some things should never be said in public, some things should never be said at all.

So he listened and said nothing while the other man spoke, while the boy stood mute.

The man spoke of monsters, of dark terrors in the world, of greater evils abroad than the heretic Surayonnaise or the unbelieving Sharai. He spoke of evil at the bridge, he warned of evil in the morning, and Anton believed him without question. Outremer was the land of miracles where the God had walked in flesh and sorrow; he had himself seen wonders and terror at the castle of the Roq, so why not here?

But all the wickedness, all the devilry he'd seen had pivoted around Marron, had come from the boy or else followed in his shadow.

Anton commended the man and his troop for their good work in surviving, in helping to destroy the creature they'd encountered, in returning to bring the news. He spoke not a word of blame for their failure to preserve the bridge intact, the task he'd sent them to achieve; he promised to consult with his commanders on how best to meet the challenge of the dawn.

Then he dismissed the man and all his other auditors, the curious circle of his confrères and their squires, their pages and servants and hangers-on. They moved not far off, not far enough, but they did move.

He daren't take Marron inside his tent; his reputation couldn't afford it. His reputation couldn't afford even this, a quiet talk in the open, in the firelight, before men came to arrest the heretic, the sorcerer, the traitor. That would happen; already men would be racing to the marshal and his priestly officers. The boy had no chance of leaving as he had come, quietly and unchallenged. He had no chance

of leaving at all, and surely must have realised that before
he came.

And yet he had come, and must have had a reason,
which could not be any of the reasons Anton had to be
glad to see him come.

So Anton's first words to him could have been, should
have been, must have been to ask why he was here; and
yet they were not.

"Do you think you will be let leave this place?" he
asked instead; which was almost but not quite another
question altogether, *do you think I will let you leave this
place?*

Marron smiled thinly. "I come and go," he said, the
first words that Anton had heard from him since the world
changed. It was astonishing that his voice was even recog-
nisable, let alone so resonant of the boy he used to be, so
redolent of the summer that had been. "Not always at my
own choice, but the Ransomers do not hinder me."

A soft hint there of a night at the Roq, slaughter and destruction, broken gates and broken minds to back up broken oaths.

Now Anton could, did, had to ask, "Why did you
come? Not to gloat, not to flaunt your powers," *not to kill
and kill again to prove them, surely not that,* "so why?"

"Because it matters, what he just told you," with a jerk
of his head to signify the man just gone, "because you
have to listen, and you have to be ready. The people of
Surayon are not your enemy, sieur; nor are the Sharai. I
have been with both . . ."

"And you too are our enemy, Marron. Your words
prove it, if proof were needed, but it is not. Do you imagine that I or any of us have forgotten what you did at the
Roq?"

"No, sieur. There was a madness that night, in me and
in others. I am clear of it now," and his hand moved to
touch his arm, a healed scar where there had been a living,
livid wound. Anton remembered that; he had made the

wound himself. He was glad it had healed now, but couldn't read the gesture otherwise. "If you spend your days killing men of this country and men of the Sands, if you waste your strength and your steel's edge, you will die the quicker when the 'ifrit choose to meet you. You must be ready, and you must understand them when they come. Have your blades and arrowheads blessed by your priests, you can do that . . ."

"I cannot order such a thing done, Marron. It would have to come from the marshal; it is a matter for the brothers, not the knights."

"You will die without it," said bluntly, coldly, mercilessly. "Even the best sword, even Dard would be nothing, would be a willow-wand unblessed against these creatures. Trust me, sieur . . ."

"Trust you? How?" And that was said just as bluntly, just as coldly, just as mercilessly, and it won him the silence that he'd sought, his only defence against that voice. He needed not to listen, not to hear; otherwise he was lost. "Do you still carry Dard, do you still dare that, with all your history in your hand?"

"In my hand and blood; but Dard has a history of its own, sieur," *in your hand and blood,* which he did not need to say, "and I carry it regardless. Carry but do not use, I will not kill again. I have not, since that night."

"Those who carry a sword should be prepared to use it."

"So I'm told," with a soft laugh, "so another one keeps telling me. But for yourself, sieur, for Outremer, for all that you believe—be ready to kill 'ifrit, rather than men in the morning. See your weapons blessed, by men who can still be holy, and warn your people that there are beasts abroad. They fly, they swim, they come out of the earth; they are devils, as the Church has always taught us."

"And so are the Surayonnaise, and so are the Sharai, as the Church has always taught us; heretics and unbelievers,

greater dangers even than devils. And you are in league
with all of them, Marron."

"Not quite all, sieur. Only with the Sharai, and the
Surayonnaise. And you. Esren, take me away from here."

And Esren did, if Esren was a glimmer of gold against
the night, sharper somehow than the firelight, a twisting
string of brightness that appeared behind the boy's shoulder a moment before he was lifted cleanly away into the
darkness and out of sight, a bare minute before a troop of
brothers came running from the marshal's tents with their
weapons drawn and their faces grim.

"Too late," Anton murmured to their leader. "Take me
instead, I have words that must be delivered to our masters."

Words that were nothing, ash and shadow, and what did
he care? Monsters could come and drag him, drag them all
to hell, and the world's loss would be less than his tonight.
He touched his sword Josette and vowed that she at least
should be blessed before the dawn, because he could do
no other. If Marron had foresworn killing, that was all the
more reason to kill, or ought to be. But he would do it
dryly, with dust upon his tongue; there could be no virtue
in it, where there was no hope.

SIX

Blood Follows the Blade

SHE HAD SEEN dawns in the desert, she had seen the sun rise over vast waters and distant ranges, she had seen storm-dawns and dust-dawns and dawns so peaceful that even the birds had seemed surprised and hushed by the mystery of the moment. Here was something different from any: slow, slow light, shapes that loomed out of shadow but no sun yet and not for a long time yet. Perhaps she should not call it dawn at all when it was as deceptive and elusive as the djinn, creeping like water between rocks, insidious and secret. She used to appreciate that, to proclaim it as an image of Surayon itself, cloaked and masked and inescapable, its influence seeping throughout Outremer.

No longer. The gates were down, the barbarians were riding and shadows offered no protection now. She ached for light and could not have it, could only see it like a rim of fire where the sun burned on the mountains' peaks all around. She didn't want to think about fire.

She didn't want to think at all. For a girl in that condition, there could be little better than a rage slow-stewed overnight, with a convenient friend at hand to stoke the fires beneath it this early morning.

"Elisande . . ."

"What?"

"Call the djinni."

Call it yourself she wanted to say after last night, when it would come to her friends and take them wherever they wanted, when it would not take her a frog's leap from her grandfather's hall, although she had both begged and commanded in her exhaustion. But Julianne wouldn't take so much licence this morning, whatever she had taken last night; Elisande contented herself with a surly, "To what end?"

"To the end of taking you—or both of us, if you will have me—somewhere other than here, to do something other than stare at the creep of day."

"Yesterday you added your voice to the others', to have me stay exactly here while you all went off to do other things."

"That was yesterday, and your staying was as useful as our going; how many people did you heal?"

She didn't know, she couldn't count; all she remembered was the ache of her body and the giddy maze of her mind as she poured herself into one stranger after another and still could never meet the need. "Not enough," she said, shrugging, "and there will be more today. What makes you think I will be let leave, when I am so useful here?"

"I don't believe there will be many more wounded brought to us. Those who could flee have fled; the men who rode out in the dark"—the Princip among them, laying stern injunctions on his granddaughter not to follow—"will live or die in the field. That's where we should be also. Heal them where they're hurt, if we do no more than that . . ."

Elisande gazed up at her friend and said, "Have you talked to your father about this?"

"No," with a half-smile that might have meant anything. "I am a married woman, a twice-married woman; I am no longer in his care. I might ask my husbands, either of them—but I would need to find them first."

"We would need the djinni to take us, first. We'd never get past the men at the gates, I think they have orders to watch for me."

"We've found a way out when we've been better guarded than this, my love. But let's try the djinni, it's so much easier."

The day Julianne found it easy to be carried by a djinni would be a rare day indeed. Elisande gave her another thoughtful stare and then summoned the djinni, "Esren," with almost no expectation at all.

She was almost surprised, then, when it came. She still expected another refusal when she said, "Esren, take us— oh, I don't know where. Take us somewhere we can be useful."

Last night it had simply refused to take her anywhere. Today she felt its grip, she felt her body rise; and then, only then was she struck by another thought, an entirely new thought, "What about Marron, should we take him too?"

The question was aimed at Julianne; it was the djinni that replied. "I have told him already, it will be better if he is here."

Better for whom, she wondered, and for what?

✠　✠　✠

MARRON SUPPOSED THAT he was not the only one who had not slept the night just gone. He had seen watchmen come and go, here on the roof; he had seen the Princip and a handful of his officers on the terrace below. He had seen

Jemel, but that was only in his mind's eye: a warm body lying in a warm bed, waiting.

Waiting in vain. He had come from Sieur Anton; he could not go to Jemel. It really was as simple, as insurmountable as that.

He gazed out at the inclosing darkness of the valley walls and wanted to have the Daughter back, to show him what he could not see. At the same time he was deeply grateful to be free of it, to feel the aching misery in his bones and the hollow yearning in his belly and to name them weariness and hunger, nothing more. To be human again was to be false again, and there was great relief in that.

Streaks of colour in the sky, colours that were not red: dawn was coming, the sun was rising out there in the world. Not here. He'd faced Sieur Anton; he could not face Jemel. Now he stood facing cold shadow, a dull and murky dawn. He stared north and could see nothing, and wished fervently to have the Daughter's eyes again, if only for a while.

If he went down to the terrace he might see better, but one thing he had seen even before the dawn: Elisande's slight figure swathed against the chill, watching and waiting as he was.

If he couldn't go to Jemel, if he had spent a long night not going to Jemel, he certainly couldn't go to Elisande.

He could have gone out, away, alone; he could have run off, to take all his troubles somewhere they could do less damage. Somewhere they could damage only him. He would have done that, surely, when he was younger—three months ago, one month. Perhaps a week, a day. Yesterday, he might have done that. Today it wasn't possible.

Besides, the djinni had told him to stay here. Others could leave, others were leaving—below him now there were voices, Elisande and Julianne: and the tall girl was saying what the short girl wanted most to hear, and she of course was arguing against herself and would lose in the end because she wanted to. Not he could leave, though, the djinni had all but said so. *Stay in the palace, if you cannot cross the worlds,* it had said.

Oh yes, he'd snarled, *stay safe while others die. Of course.*

I did not say so, it had said, unbearably calm. *If others must die in the morning, you may still die in the afternoon. If the battle is lost in your absence, be sure that death will seek you out regardless. I will not take you to meet it; there is no need. You were better to remain here.*

And do what? Stupid with worry and weariness and temper, he'd heard his mouth shoot the question before his mind could stop it.

I will not give you answers, the djinni had said mockingly. *Seek your own. But seek them here, if you value anything that you have found here.*

He didn't understand it; he lacked not the courage but the knowledge to defy it. Instead he stood and watched while the girls left, while they were lifted and carried by an unseen power on an invisible wind towards the dull glimmer of the river far below; he stood and watched and made no sound when a last group of horsemen rode out to seek the war, and there was one in Sharai dress among them who didn't need to cast back his hood or turn his head for Marron to feel that jolt, that physical pain that came with a night's separation and a weight of words unspoken, impossible to speak.

✠   ✠   ✠

JEMEL HAD PASSED the night as a betrayed man must, or thinks he must: alone, awake, afraid. Small wonder then that he had risen before the dawn to escape a bed too wide, the absence that he had shared it with. Marron had come back from Sieur Anton; Marron had not come back to him.

So he had risen into darkness, and carried the darkness

with him where he went. In that dull, bitter mood, stubbornly ready with a few sour and unequivocal words if he could only find Marron to say them to, he had found others instead and been offered a fight instead of an argument. Had accepted heedlessly, almost joyfully; had run to fetch weapons, all the weapons that he owned or claimed; had returned to find himself being led—not without some sideways glances among his new companions, but led none the less—into a place he had never, never thought to enter.

He had broken into the priests' house in Selussin, climbed the gate and bullied the guards and burst into the chiefs' private council; here there was an ever-open door and a welcome carved into the lintel, and still he would not have dreamed of coming here, would not have dared to cross the threshold uninvited.

Even invited, even ushered inside, he half thought he would die regardless. Walking stiff as a brand through the doorway of a Patric chapel, he thought he might burn as a pitch-soaked brand can burn, seemingly from the inside. Their god was fierce, Jemel knew that from Marron, who had confirmed a hundred rumours true. They did burn children; they had done that at the Roq. Marron might blame the Ransomers and the cold hearts of their leaders, but Jemel was free where he was not, Jemel could blame their god.

He glared a challenge at the ceiling, and found his eye snared by decoration: figures painted in red and gold and green, pictures that perhaps he could read. He stared upward as he walked, and so walked solidly into the back of the man ahead where he was kneeling, and would have sprawled ungainly on the tiled floor if he hadn't been caught and held by the belt, by the man behind.

"Easy, boy," in a rough rasp. "I don't care whether you give the God your prayers, but give Him honour at least in His own house."

"I meant no dishonour," hissed between his teeth as he

wrenched himself free, ready to start the day's fighting here and now. "I was—"

"—Staring up at the saints, I know, instead of watching where you walk. All the Catari do it, when they come in here. I don't care if you gawp, and I doubt the God does either; just don't tread all over Markam as you go, it's disrespectful."

To the god or to the man, that wasn't clear. But just then Markam rose, and Jemel could see what the Patric man had been about. Not praying, or not only praying; he had laid his weapons on the floor before the altar, the latest in a line of bows and blades.

The Princip had given orders last night, that no man go into the field without his weapons blessed. If Hasan had tried the same, he must have failed. The Sharai were his to lead, perhaps, but not to command. Even if he could find an imam, the tribes would never stand in line to have their weapons touched and prayed upon. They would laugh, rather. With a day's burning and looting at their backs, their robes rank with dried blood, an army or two ahead of them and a river to fight over, more good water than any of them had seen in their lives before, what need an imam, a blessing, a warning to beware? They'd know where their blades were bound; come the battle they would rely on a strong arm and a scimitar's edge, as they always had. Jemel thought they would die in numbers, as they so often did.

Here, these men were very much for the Princip to command. They had brought their weapons to the chapel, laid them on the floor; they looked to him to do the same. Would a Patric blessing hold, on a Sharai blade that was blessed already? He didn't know, but now would be a good time to find out.

He had a bow on his shoulder, and a quiver of arrows hung Patric-style at his back; he set them on the tiles beside the scimitar. There were extra knives in his belt; he added those. And felt the weight of one more at the back, heavier than he would have picked out for himself. He drew it forth and added that too. With a priest's blessing on the blade, perhaps the merest prick would act on Bhisrat as it would on an 'ifrit, slide into flesh as if it were nothing but smoke, seek out the soul of him and send it down to hell . . .

Except that there was no priest. Rather, one of his companions stepped forward; not even their officer, just one of the men. The others bowed their heads and responded in quiet, firm voices as he led them in prayer. Jemel couldn't follow the words any more than he could understand the rituals: the turning and bowing to east and west, to where the dark rose up at sunset and where it retreated come the dawn. It must be retreating now in the world outside this windowless chamber, where the views were painted to show another world entirely. Perhaps all religions looked toward a world not real; but then, Jemel had walked in a world different from this and had found no gods in it and little enough else.

The man who led the prayers reached down to touch and bless the blades laid out before him, but what power did he claim, to give them virtue? When he was done, Jemel retrieved his own weapons and examined them suspiciously. They were as heavy to his hand as they had been before and as sharp to his finger's touch, as bright to his eye and nothing more. That was right, a blessed blade had no extra shine; even so, Jemel thought he would be riding into battle like his fellow Sharai, with nothing to rely on but the strength of his arm and the edge of his scimitar, the speed of whatever broken-down animal these men could find to carry him.

✠ ✠ ✠

"ESREN."

Elisande said the name softly, where Julianne would have expected her to scream. The djinni had lifted them up like the hand of hope, like a promise; and it had brought them—well, it had brought them here. To this.

"Esren, I said to take us somewhere we could be useful."

"You did."

Elisande gazed deliberately about her, and so did Julianne; it was irresistible.

They were standing on an island, rough rock and wild grasses. The icy rushing river divided itself about them, north and south; on either side the stream was too strong to swim, too wild to row or raft, far too broad to leap. Either side might have been bridged, but neither was.

An unexpectedly patient Elisande—*diplomatic, perhaps I should say, and can she have been learning lessons from me?*—took a second glance around, just to make the point the stronger, before she said, "I do not see what use we can be to anyone, if you abandon us here with a gulf on every side."

"Of course not," the djinni said. "You lack the sense." Which might have been a common insult, or else a plain statement of fact; the djinni was quite capable of either.

Whichever it meant, the familiar Elisande would have taken it as insult, and laughed. This one seemed to take it the other way; at any rate she nodded, and was silent. And looked about her one more time, as though she were struggling to see what was impossible for her; and shrugged at last, and said, "Very well, Esren. Leave us, if you will."

It would and it did, although Julianne did not believe it had been waiting for permission.

In its absence, Elisande reverted. She gave a huge groaning sigh that had nothing of patience about it, stooped to heave a rock up from the ground at her feet and hurled it into the swift bitter water that encompassed them.

"I could kill it," she said conversationally, above the splash. "If I had the strength, the speed, the skill, whatever it takes, the *knowledge*—I could kill that spirit, and feel not a moment's guilt."

Julianne smiled. "Of course you could. And you do have what it takes. It's never said so, but I think a blessed weapon will kill a djinni as easily as an 'ifrit."

Elisande touched the knife in her belt, in a moment's pure startlement; then she scowled, and said, "You call that easy? You want to go up against those monsters with just a dagger in your hand, blessed or not, you're welcome to it. I'll stand back and applaud."

"Of course you will, what else? But we won't be going up against anything, 'ifrit or djinni or plain bad man, so long as we're stuck here on our own. We need them to come to us for slaughter. How can we best arrange that, do you think?"

"Don't ask me questions, it's dangerous. As well ask the djinni—or better, it might have an answer to give you. For a price. I have none, but I'll charge you anyway. Tell me why that creature put us here."

"I'd need to be a djinni myself to know that, sweet. There must be something, though—something to find, or something to wait for."

"What do we do, then? Wait, or look?"

"Look while we're waiting, don't you think? It passes time or saves it, and either one is useful."

WHAT THEY SAW was a broad, flat stretch of meadow grasses, studded with boulders and meadow flowers, rising to a peak of rock at the easterly end. Isolation had kept it wild, and there was a beauty in wildness that the tamed acres on either bank could never hope to rival.

Beauty had no use today. There was grass, there were rocks and flowers; no matter how careful her inspection or how free her imagination, Julianne could find no value in any of it.

She looked and thought, and watched her friend; and

when Elisande flung herself down on her back, full-length in the deep sweet grasses, she said, "Secret tunnels? Hidden caves, long-lost treasures of the family?"

Elisande snorted. "With magical properties, no doubt, that will drive all enemies back beyond our borders and ensure peace forever? Sorry, no. We don't have legends in Surayon, only the knowledge that we found or worked out for ourselves. Some of that we've hidden from the world, but not from ourselves; we don't bury secrets. There's nothing here but what you see," grass, rocks, flowers.

"So why did Esren bring us here, and why leave us?"

"Julianne, I still do not know. I have looked, and not seen; I have thought, and found no answers. Now I am waiting, as you told me to."

Fighting, she was, to find some surviving shard of that brittle patience she'd had with the djinni. But fighting was no way to win patience, and patience was no prize to Elisande. Julianne waited in an entirely different way, to see what would happen when her friend gave up the fight.

✠ ✠ ✠

COLD HAD NUMBED his fingers to all feeling; long standing had stiffened his knees. Cramped and awkward legs were slow to hurry, down the narrow turning stair. He leaned his shoulder to the wall and slid as much as stepped, then felt the slide run away with him and could not catch it, only saved himself on every step with another reckless stumble forward.

When there were no more steps, he could not stop himself, but someone else could stop him. He came charging out of the stairwell, almost flying, utterly beyond control—and his lowered head plunged into something resilient just as he heard a bark, a yelp, the strangled rush of breath forced out by violence.

So rather than sprawling full-length and slamming up hard against the opposite wall, he fell in the tangle of another man's fall. An elbow caught him above the ear, just payment for the stomach-butt; otherwise he came to ground far more softly than he deserved.

He felt the man's chest stir and heave beneath him; he felt stiff embroidery against his cheek and had just a moment to understand that this was a man of rank who was lying here, winded and still half-crushed beneath the weight of the idiot who had brought him down . . .

Marron scrambled up, already stammering, desperate beginnings to an apology he couldn't begin to shape. Then, seeing who it was who lay like a broken poppet on the floor at his feet, he fell abruptly and entirely mute.

"Marron." The voice was cautious, on a breath that laboured for comfort and had not found it yet. "Was there some reason for your, uh, urgency—something seen from the roof, that will not have been seen from the terrace?"

"No, sir." Confession at least came easily to him; he'd been trained to it all his life, and it was good to tell a simple truth for once. "Only I was hungry, so I went too fast on the stairs; and my legs were stiff with too long standing in the cold, so I lost balance, and—"

"—And you found your landing in me. I understand you perfectly. It may be that some mystical power impelled me to walk along this corridor at precisely this moment, purely in order that I might save you a cracked head. Don't you think?"

Marron thought that this was a strange morning to be making jokes. If the man was joking. It was almost impossible to tell.

"Still," Coren went on, "I'm relieved to hear that you've recovered one normal human appetite, at least. It grew wearing, watching Elisande and Jemel between them take note of every mouthful. I don't suppose that sword at your belt signifies that you've also recovered a willingness to use it?"

Marron shook his head. Dard was his, a gift, and so he wore it; but what it signified was another gift that he had, a gift for killing, with or without the Daughter. He wore it as a reminder, not to use it. Of all men, he thought, the King's Shadow should understand. Wasn't the King the same, in that he kept the Kingdom as a reminder not to rule it?

"No. I could wish that you were more surprising, but then I suppose you would be less Marron. I was myself heading towards the kitchens, to see what a man might glean after a long night's plotting. Shall we go together? We could pause by my daughter's room on our way, and ask if the girls have any appetite for food."

"Uh, sir, the girls . . ."

A soft thread of a sigh, and, "Yes, Marron? What of the girls, what have they done this time?"

"Well, they're not there."

"Ah. Again, I'm afraid you don't surprise me. Where are they?"

"I don't know. The djinni took them from the terrace, but it didn't say where . . ."

Another sigh, which carried another wealth of meaning. "Very well. If the djinni has taken them, no doubt it will find some way to set trouble stirring. Though either one of those two is capable of stirring up trouble enough on her own account, let alone the two of them together."

"Sir, I don't believe the djinni means them any harm."

"Do you not? Well, no. Neither do I. That does not mean that harm will not result. The djinn have their own interests, which seldom coincide with ours. Witness how that one plays with Elisande, and with the oath it swore. I could wish that my daughter were more reluctant to be played with, but I trained her to be a piece in a wider game. If it is wider than I had imagined, I suppose I have little to complain of. I set her loose on the world, entirely as she is; my fault, then, if she wreaks havoc where she passes. But it's hard to be philosophical after a long night and before breakfast. With me, Marron, if you please."

"Sir, I can bring you what you want, in the solar, or—"

"—Or anywhere else I can be cold and alone while I eat, as befits my station? Thank you, Marron, but no. We are soldiers and comrades today, you and I. Comrades eat together, soldiers always seek the warm; which in a great house like this must always mean the kitchen. If you don't know that lesson, learn it now."

Marron did know it, of course he did. He was a little surprised that his companion knew it first, until he remembered that the King's Shadow had earned that title by fighting all through Outremer. Coren might have been a lordling once and become a diplomat later, but he was truly a soldier between the two. The broad blade he wore today was no courtly weapon, all jewels and inlay, show without strength. Rather it was a plain man's sword, the scabbard stained and the hilt rebound with wire, the form and weight of it a generation out of fashion. No smith would make such a blade today, but any soldier would respect it. If Coren had fought his way from Tallis to Ascariel, then this was the weapon he had fought with.

Clearly, he intended to fight with it again today. Only Marron wore a sword and would not use it.

STAIRS BROUGHT THEM down into the cavernous, low-arched spaces that were the cooks' domain, where they found no cooks; found no women, no pages nor scullions nor anyone at all except a group of men-at-arms with bandages, bruises, bloody scabs to show why they clustered round a table's end in their lord's palace. Marron tried to seat the King's Shadow, tried to fetch him bowl and spoon and beaker; Coren would not allow it.

"I said, boy, we stand on equal terms today. As we did in the desert—which is what this palace and this valley will become, if the various passions of the various men out there come together this day. They will make a conflagration between them, and it will be generations before anything good grows again in Surayon."

"Does the King not support his own armies?" Marron demanded, stooping before a fireplace to ladle two bowls of porridge from where it boiled in a cauldron above a bank of smoking turves. He drew a dipper of molten mutton-fat from a copper pan beside the fire and added a glistening stream to each bowl, while Coren filled two beakers with beer from a keg. "Or his own priests?"

"They are the God's priests, not the King's."

"They fight for the Kingdom. The Ransomers do."

"They do—but few of the Ransomers are priests, and those were mostly soldiers first. I can't answer your questions, Marron, I'm not a djinni. The King gives his support where he deems that it is needed, or so I assume. He does not explain himself, to me or any man."

"No, but you speak for him. I thought it was your job to explain him to other men," *to me* . . .

A soft laugh, and, "Would you ask me to explain what I do not myself understand? Well, yes, you might; but the King is kinder, or simply not so young. No, no, Marron. My task is to speak for him the way your mouth and tongue speak for you, no more than that. Without thought, without argument. I am more of a servant than you have ever tried to be. And a better one, I think; at least I've never run from my master."

Another day, Marron might have choked on his porridge. Without thought, without argument? This man, of all men? This morning, even a smile eluded him. Nor would he be eluded. "You have not run from your master, but you deal with his enemies."

"Do I?"

"You are known and welcome here in Surayon, which has sealed itself off from Outremer in rebellion; and I met you in Rhabat, where the Sharai were planning war against the Kingdom . . ."

"And where I was arguing as best I could against it. All

of Outremer deals with the Sharai, Marron, and the Sharai deal with Outremer. Trade with the left hand, battle with the right, it's an old saying; it's old because it works. I know men who will tell you that warfare is just another form of trade. I know two girls who will tell you the same thing: one because I taught her so, the other because she's always known, except that she believes that it's better expressed the other way around, that trade is just another form of warfare. As for Surayon, it has never rebelled against the King; neither has he ever turned his face against it. He has always tolerated squabbles between the states."

"This is more than a squabble, sir!"

"Is it? It's the prime of all squabbles, rather—a family of children, all with knives. Brothers and cousins, and the land too small to satisfy—that's how Outremer was made, how we raised an army in the homelands forty years ago, from quarrelsome sons who would otherwise have been killing each other over their fathers' fiefs. A little sunlight and a priest's blessing don't change a man's nature. He may say he does a thing for the greater glory of the God, but actually he does it for land, for territory, for borders: for somewhere he can stand and say, *this is mine, and all that is within it comes to me.*"

"The Sharai don't—"

"Marron, do you lack eyes, or is it simply common wit that's missing? The Sharai do, exactly. They don't farm, and they don't build; but you've travelled in the Sands, you've seen how the tribes defend their territories. Neither is Hasan any different. He's a visionary, but his vision only amounts to more land for the tribes to fight over. He wants a Sharai kingship across this country, but he doesn't want to rule."

"Like the King, then?"

"Mm? Oh—is that how you see him? The King rules, he just doesn't govern. And see him or not, everyone knows that he's there. Hasan doesn't want to live in Outremer, nor do any of his people. They'd be quite happy to leave it to other Catari, or to us if we were peaceable and paid our tribute duly. Then each tribe could raid the others' camel-trains, and they'd be entirely content."

Marron opened his mouth to murmur that perhaps that would be better than an unseen King and a cruel, frightened people. Before he could say it, though, another voice cried, "Ghûl! Ghûl!"

Every eye was drawn to the doorway, to the skidding broken sounds of a man plunging recklessly, helplessly down the stairs with no one to run into at the foot.

He fell hard on naked flags and seemed barely to notice it. His hands like claws had hauled him up the nearest pillar before any man could reach him, so that he stood on his feet again to point, wildly behind him.

"Ghûls! In the yard, in the stables . . ."

In the stairwell too, to judge by the sounds he pointed at: slow clopping and vast breathing, as though there were pack-mules coming down the steps.

"Where are the guards?" Marron murmured, standing shoulder to shoulder with Coren and stepping forward while the wounded men scrambled to arm themselves with kitchen-knives and cleavers.

"The guards are gone to war, Marron. These few came in late and exhausted. The Princip gave them what healing he could, but he daren't spend all his strength, or all his daughter's either. They're probably still too much hurt to fight."

They looked it, certainly; it showed in the way they struggled to look strong, with their assortment of cooking irons. Too weary, too hurt or too stubborn to flee, they would die here in the Princip's kitchen unless someone else could shield them. And who was there? There was Coren, who had powers as the King's Shadow that Marron couldn't guess at, but seemed rarely willing to use them. As a man he had a sword and a lifetime's experience, but the length of that lifetime must tell against him now; he was old and tired and no more fit to stand alone against ghûls than those other men were fit to stand beside him.

And then there was Marron, young and fleet with food in his belly, with a fine sword apt for his hand and that hand well-trained for fighting. What did it matter if an oath was broken casually, for little reasons like the lives of strangers, so long as it was kept where every little thing mattered hugely? The gods or luck or bloody fate must care for Jemel and Sieur Anton, because he could not; perhaps the djinni would care for the girls; Coren could surely care for himself. That left these men, who held their lives too cheap to run. These Marron could perhaps care for, because he didn't even know their names.

Perhaps.

The more noise there was in the stairwell, the more quiet and still they were in the kitchen. If terror was a weapon, then sound was its keenest edge. A clear, brisk rattle like hooves in a stableyard was half smothered by the wet rasping weight of oxen's breath, the muted rub of hide on stone. Then, at last, there was darkness moving in the shadows. Huge, ponderous figures bent below the stairs' low ceiling, squeezing through the archway, straightening slowly in so far as ever they could stand straight.

Three, just three of them. Split and shredded rags were clinging to rough hair and skin; they must have dressed and shaped themselves as women, to seem like belated refugees.

Marron stepped forward and monstrous heads turned to eye him, still roughly human, except that no human was ever so crudely modelled: a gross body bowed and its brutal arms swinging below its knees, its head stretched and distorted, more horse than man if horses ever did have lions' teeth . . .

They carried no weapons, and needed none: only the strength of those long, long arms and the claws that tipped them, the bite of their heavy jaws, their weight and reach and simple savagery. Marron felt more than small against them. He felt delicate as parchment, fine-drawn as an inkline, Dard like a slender nib to write their story. He could write it as he chose; ghûls were deadly but clumsy with it, awkward in their bodies and slow of thought. Marron could call a dance of steel and blood to proclaim the triumph of man above beasts and demons, that cold and killing touch where civilisation meets barbarity. There were only three and he could kill them all, if he could only choose to do it.

He raised the sword that he had sworn not to use again and walked forward, crying back over his shoulder as he went.

"Lead the men away from here, Coren. You can do that, while I delay the ghûls." The King's Shadow could walk through walls and take others with him, through solid rock and distance. Marron couldn't even walk between the worlds any more, and missed it badly.

"Marron, remember, kill with a single stroke; a second will only heal the harm of the first."

"I have not forgotten."

Ghûls were rougher-made than men, more brutal, spirit wrapped in something closer to original clay than mortal flesh. They did bleed like men, but likely not to death, he thought. He could hew and hope, at least, where he could not hew to kill. *And if one looks to be dying, well, I can hew it again to let it heal. And then again, to hurt it . . .*

It was an absurdity, a madness. But it was his own madness, a nonsense of war when war was a madness in itself. He ducked neatly under the flailing club-like claw of the nearest ghûl, hesitated just a moment and then struck hard and clean.

Dard bit, seemed indeed to leap forward in his hand in its eagerness to bite after a long fast. Bit deep, for blood and meat together: drove in beneath the swinging arm, high and rising into the massive creature's chest. In a man, the point must have erupted from neck or spine; in a man, it must have been a mortal blow. Marron gave the blade a twist and still thought the ghûl would survive.

A gush of hot blood drenched his hand, soaked the sleeve of his robe, stinking mightily. The ghûl staggered before him, both hooked claws lifting; Marron sidestepped watchfully and called back over his shoulder, "Get you gone! Why do you linger?"

"Lack of confidence," Coren said quietly at his back, "and rightly so, it seems. You could have killed that thing, and did not."

"Hurt, dead, what difference to you if you're not here? Muster those men together and leave this to me."

"Some difference to you, perhaps, if I'm not here. But, Marron, look . . ."

The ghûl he had maimed was slumped against the wall now, sliding down it, leaving a dark wet streak where its sodden mats of hair rubbed against white plaster. But the second beast was crouched above its brother and impeding the one behind, blocking its way between the long kitchen tables. Marron gaped in bewilderment as the one ghûl raked a claw across the other's throat, opening a wound that could bleed only in a dribble, as there had been so much blood lost already.

Or no, not that. It bled and then it did not bleed, so swift to close that only a dribble escaped. And the wound that Dard had made, wide and wet, that closed also; and the creature that had been so hurt rose up strong and fresh.

"They are not stupid," Coren said at his back. "They may move more slowly than you do, they may even think more slowly—but they do think, and they are as wily as any man. And they know what they are, as well as we do."

"Well, then . . ." Could he hurt them all, so badly that they could not hurt each other? It seemed unlikely. But he was still quicker, he could worry them, distract them, draw them to himself and so do well, do something good this day and have nothing to worry him at the end of it. "Best take those men away swiftly."

"I'll take you first, Marron. You matter more."

To whom—his friends, Surayon, the Kingdom? "Not any more. The Princip took what mattered from me," and stowed it somewhere in the palace. He had no feeling for it, no sense of where it might lie.

"You could matter as a swordsman, if you chose."

But he had made that choice already, and didn't mean to change it. Being a swordsman in the only way he could, he stood with Dard raised and ready, watching the gap between the heavy tables, the only way the ghûls could come at him, one by one. He thought he could hurt them, one by one; they could heal each other, but only one by one. That must buy time enough for Coren to open his hidden gateway and escape with what little garrison was gathered here.

But, *they are not stupid, Marron*—and he had forgotten it again. Two of them laid their brute clawed hands suddenly atop those refectory tables and vaulted over on long stiff arms. Scrubbed timbers creaked; one snapped, late and uselessly. The ghûls had swung themselves half across the kitchen in one simple movement. Their hooves skittered on the flags of the floor; for a brief moment they looked likely to fall, and did not.

Stood now within a long arm's reach of the wounded men with their pitiful kitchen-weapons; and ghûls have long, long arms.

POINTLESS FOR COREN to bellow, "One stroke only— one stroke!"

Where one stroke of knife or cleaver could never kill, could barely cut tough hide; where the beast seemed barely to register the blow, even with a heavy blade buried deep in flesh and bone; where dying seemed almost a duty, why worry whether you hurt or healed before you died, why not simply chop and chop?

They did that, those men, those doomed men. They chopped and hacked with a will, with that heedless energy born of utter despair; and, one by one, they died.

Marron saw the first death, even while he was trying to watch everything that happened, everywhere. He saw the last of the ghûls—its rank hair glistening, sodden with its own blood—watching him, his sword, the movements of his head and hand; he saw Coren doing nothing, only standing back and watching, that big blade wasted in an old man's hand who apparently had no strength to wield it; he still saw how the first man died.

One great arm swung, a claw struck and clung hold; the other arm reached out to take a more brutal grip.

One twisted, nut-knuckled hand circled the man's upper arm, the other his neck; there seemed no effort in it, as the ghûl pulled its two hands apart.

The man had dropped his little knife, long since. Now he arched his back and gave himself over entirely to screaming until the screaming stopped, snapped like a string, and the room was emptier for lack of it and the man who made it.

It seemed quiet then, but not for long. The ghûls were among the men, and Coren made no move; apparently there was only Marron to prevent a slaughter. He had a ghûl of his own to face first, though. To face again, to strike again: to kill or not to kill, as his hand or mind allowed.

He meant to maim it, as he had before; its companions were too busy now to heal it. But he was prevented, forestalled. The ghûl's eyes that had been sheened with a cunning intelligence were suddenly dull, as though it had been cast into shadow. It swung its arms randomly as though it groped for what it could not see, blundered directly into a pillar and clung to it.

Marron spared a glance for Coren, who said nothing but, "Swiftly, swiftly now . . ."

He was swift, and thinking even more swiftly than his feet could run. He ran not directly towards that reckless mêlée where men ducked and rolled, stabbed and gasped and died. He ran instead towards the cooking-fire, where it lay smouldering beneath its turves, still hot enough to boil porridge and render mutton-fat. On the way he slammed Dard back into its scabbard and snatched up instead a bleached and age-worn timber from the ruins of the table.

Cold ashes grated beneath his boots; no one had swept the hearth today. The pot-boys were gone, fled or dead. Julianne had borrowed one last night and brought only his body back. She had cried for him, he remembered, when she had not for Rudel.

Marron thrust the splintered end of the plank through the blanket of turves, deep into the glowing heart of the fire. Left the other end jutting out and reached for the handle of the porridge-cauldron, where it hung from a pot-hook beneath the great manteltree.

Hot iron seared his palms. He hoisted the weight of it, cauldron and bubbling contents together, and felt it score through to the bone. It was only pain, though, and he could endure that almost with welcome, almost with contempt. What matter one more scar where he carried so many, one more hurt when he had known so much? This was a simple thing, a mindless thing, another trivial story written in his flesh.

He pivoted on his heel like a dancer. The cauldron whirled at his arms' length, and barely a drop of the porridge spilled; wet though it was, it clung to the smoothness of the pot as he turned and turned.

Twice around, thrice around while it rose higher, travelled faster, burned deeper into his hands; and then he let it go.

Felt it tear free of his flesh, and did not care. Watched

it twist in the air, watched as it struck heavily against the hideous skull of a ghûl; saw the porridge flood out before the cauldron fell, a steaming grey coat flowing down over the creature's hair and hide.

It howled even while he went on turning, stooping back to the fire and seizing hold of another scalding handle, this time the pan that held the molten mutton-fat.

Loose enough to run down over the ghûl's body, thick enough to cling, the porridge had made a grotesque capering fool of the creature. Half blind and terribly scalded, it danced its agony, moaned the song of it, entirely disregarding the small men who were falling back around it, gathering up their small weapons and waiting their moment to close in again.

One blow harms, the next heals—but not now. Magic or simply mystery, that was still a rule for clean strikes, for individual wounds. That ghûl must have monstrous blisters swelling already beneath its monstrous hide; neither spell nor nature could count the harm it had taken now.

Or so he hoped, so he—almost—dared to expect. Let the men do their work, with whatever blades they had gleaned. No warnings this time except a hoarse cry, "Way! Make way there . . ." as he plunged forward to hurl this second pan.

Not trusting to aim or luck a second time, he came close enough to smell the second ravening ghûl, the rank rancid fur of the beast and the taint of human blood that smeared it. By contrast, the dense odour of the mutton-fat was herb-sweet: *a perfume for the stinking,* he thought as he finally let the pot fly.

This time he screamed himself when the handle ripped out of his hands, but the ghûl screamed louder. Marron didn't wait to see if this one also danced.

He went back to the fire to retrieve his plank of splintered table-wood. It was cruelly rough and heavy to his seared hands, but that was a petty cruelty, it lacked malice and intent; he lacked neither as he drew out the smoking end and whirled it around his head to make it flame.

Whirled the brand and flung it, straight and true, so that its blazing made a spear's head of light that flew clean towards the ghûl's heart.

And yes, it did know what was coming, and the noise it made was pure wordless terror. Too near to dodge, it tried to knock the brand aside. A neater creature with a quicker eye might have done that, but its own clumsiness was its betrayal. Its clawed hand met the flame, rather than the wood behind; its first tight, sharp little cry at the heat of it was lost in a soft, eruptive sound as the fire caught and gripped it, flowing up the length of its arm and so all over. Dags of hair drenched in hot oil made simple wicks; Marron had known it, and the ghûl did too.

It had never seemed so human as now, when he could see only the dark shadow of its shape at the heart of a living pyre, when its agony made an animal of it, as it would have done of any man. Marron had seen boys burn at the Roq; now he saw a ghûl burn in Surayon, and he could see little or no difference, except that this time he had set the flame himself.

A voice at his back said, "Your sword would have been kinder."

It was true, and he knew it. He said, "So use yours. I have not been trained to kindness."

And then turned round, because he'd sooner see his shame reflected than in the raw, in the raw burning flesh of the ghûl as it howled and capered like a king's fool at a feast. Coren had used his sword already; the blade of it showed darkly stained in the flickering light, and the ghûl he had mazed lay slumped at the foot of its pillar now, a spreading pool at its neck like the stubborn shadow of a head gone missing.

Marron might have cast about to find the head itself, but Coren gave him no chance.

"Oh, no. Even you have to learn to live with your

choices, Marron. If this is how you choose to step aside from your oath, then so be it—"

"I didn't kill them," in a dishonest, defensive mutter.

"—And yet one is dead," with a gesture towards another bloody corpse more crudely butchered by the men around it, "and the other is dying," with a sudden tug on Marron's arm that pulled him out of the way of a stumbling, tottering inferno that was the ghûl aflame, and at the same time turned him round again so that he had to face it, "and both because of what you did. Is it the fire that kills, and not you? As well use your sword and say that it is the blade that kills, and not you. Marron, I am sorry that you must lose one more thing that means so much to you. You may be the lesser for it, you will certainly be changed again and I have enjoyed knowing you as you were; but this is war, and all men lose in war. Kill that beast, and have done."

Marron found that Dard was in his hand again. There was nothing now to stop him, and almost nothing to feel: only a slight hesitation which might have meant *how am I going to tell Jemel?* and which was swiftly overtaken by another thought, one that gripped his mind even as his body did its work so that in fact he barely noticed the moment when he did finally kill again.

Two rapid paces and a lunge, like an exercise in drill, a thing that his body could do without his mind's attention; a wash of heat against his face, the least hint of resistance as Dard's honed point met the dark shadow at the heart of light. It was a neat kill, a sweet kill. His uncle would have applauded, and Sieur Anton also. Jemel would have been satisfied with the result. Coren said nothing, even after Marron had withdrawn his blade, had straightened and turned to face the older man.

His to speak, then, his to say his thought aloud.

"You made me do that."

"I invited you to do that; you should not have needed the invitation. It was cruelty, to let the thing burn."

"No. You made me do it, from before. From the moment they attacked. You stood back and did nothing, but you could have done . . ."

"I could not come to the men, to lead them out."

"You did not try; but not that. You could have defeated the ghûls yourself, before they hurt a soul. You could have mazed them all as you did the one that came at me—and even that," realising it as he spoke, "you did not maze the first time, you hoped that I would find the heart to kill it. When you saw that I would not, not in my own defence," working this out almost on his fingers, spelling his thoughts aloud as they came, "you thought I must for the defence of others, you thought I could not bear to see men dying badly. So you mazed that one that might have prevented me, but did no more than that. Men died, because you wanted to see me kill."

"I wanted to see them saved," the King's Shadow said softly, neutrally, "and you were the one best placed, best skilled to save them. This is no time for delicacy, Marron, we cannot afford to have you so fine-spirited. We are at war; why do you assume that you can stand aside from all the killing, or that you will be let stand?"

"Why do you assume that I will kill for you?" Marron returned, equally softly, trying for an equal neutrality. "Jemel is of the Sharai, and my own people—your people—turned me out."

"Fight for us, fight for the Sharai, I do not care; fight for yourself alone, or for those you love, or for those who love you if you can distinguish between them. We will none of us fight each other today. Tomorrow, surely; but today there are monsters abroad, and we can all fight together. You *know* all of this, Marron, why are you being tiresome?"

"You told me that a young man should not get into the habit of breaking his vows; and then you forced me to it, when it was convenient to you. If I am tiresome, perhaps

it is because I am tired of being used, your tool or anyone's else."

His heart was in his mouth as he said it. He was appalled by his own daring, unless it was stupidity, or both.

"And yet I will use you when you are apt to the occasion. It's a wise man's habit, Marron, and an old man's
necessity. Some things I can do, but many things not, or
not as well. And I cannot afford, this world we have made
cannot afford to have you stand idle by. We need every
man who can wield a blade, and you do it with an uncommon grace and purpose. With the Daughter in your
blood, you were too dangerous to be let loose. Almost too
much so to be let live—which you knew, I think, and
hence that famous oath of yours. But you are yourself
again, and nothing more; and you are a trained fighter and
a skilled fighter, and we are needful of you. This is why
you came to the Sanctuary Land, Marron, to honour your
father and defend your people . . ."

And to serve the God, but Coren wisely did not mention it, which was perhaps the only wisdom that he
showed in that little speech. For a man with his reputation,
he was displaying a wonderful lack of understanding.

"I came with my friend," Marron said, "and then I
killed him. Too many men died at my hand, or for my
sake, and so I forswore killing; and now there are more
dead, and these too can be laid at my door. What am I, that
men should die for me?" There were half a dozen men
dead, to make a killer of him. He might as well have killed
them himself. It was a poor bargain reckoned in simple
numbers, a monstrosity by any measure. He went on, "At
least they can lie in a place of honour, away from—
those," with a gesture towards the dead ghûls. "And we
can help take them there, not leave it all to their confrères," all of whom had been wounded even before this
day began. Most had fresh hurts now, or else what had
been half-healed was opened fresh again. Marron knew
too well how that felt.

"There is," a sharp look suddenly, the slightest hesitation, and, "no place, Marron. No appropriate place, in the way that you are thinking. The Princip does not favour pomp and formal rites; neither do his people. Let them see to their fallen according to their own customs."

Marron looked the King's Shadow in the eye and called him a liar, as directly as he dared. "You fetched the Princip's son home, and a place of honour was found for him to lie. Julianne took her serving-boy to the same place, when she brought him back last night. I don't know where that is, *I don't know where they lay precious things in this palace, things they want to preserve out of the sight of men,* "but these soldiers will. Their fallen friends can lie there too, with the same honour, and I will see them so."

Briefly, he thought that Coren would argue further; then that he would forgo argument and strike him instead, knock him unconscious or spirit him away in a haze of gold.

The man was all King's Shadow now, though. He seemed to weigh all the likely consequences, all the possible mischances, and at last shook his head in a gesture of surrender.

"Even without, you are not in my control and never were. Well, go your own way, lad, do what you think you must. This is beyond me, for good or ill; I will not interfere. Be careful, though, and think what you are doing."

"I have been careful," Marron said softly, "and there is blood on my blade, where I had sworn there would not be. There will be no more," *unless it is my own.*

"And that should teach me not to dice for a man's soul, is that it?"

Marron looked deliberately towards the bodies of the fallen men. "Not when you dice with others' lives. You won the game; what did they lose, who were not playing? More than my oath you have broken here, and you had no

right. Even the King would have no right. You might tell
him that."

"I might. I might indeed, if I live to speak with him. It
is perhaps less likely, if you will not fight for us."

"Enough." Marron said it, heard himself say it. Rage
burned brightly, and at the moment, oh, he was raging. "I
may kill again, for you or for others. You said it yourself—*if once, why not a dozen times more, a hundred?*
You also said that you would hate to see it, and you might
do that also. I do not know; am I a djinni, are you? But
now, let be. I will help these men with their dead, and then
I will do—what I will do." Which would involve finding
Jemel, finding Sieur Anton, both of them and hopefully
not together, a valley's width apart; that much, he was
sure of. What more, he could not say. He was not a djinni.
And the djinni had said that he should stay within the
palace, but perhaps it had only meant until now, until this,
so that he could kill these ghûls? Or so that the King's
Shadow could manipulate him into killing these ghûls, so
that he could be asked to kill again? Or—

Well. He could spend a lifetime trying to outguess a
djinni. He would do what he meant to do, and then he
would leave the palace and seek out his friends, and never
mind what the djinni had meant or what Coren wanted. He
was not fool enough to think that he could rule himself,
now or soon or later; but he could have the shadow of it,
he could seem to be free, and that mattered.

✠   ✠   ✠

OUT IN THE valley's breadth with his back to the palace
and his face to the wind and riding, riding at last with a
good horse beneath him; unsure of whom to fight or
whom to kill, but certain that there would be blood on his
blade before sundown; for the moment he could be glad
enough to be here and not there, with these strangers and
not with anyone who loved him.

The valley could give no distance, no sense of space to a tribesman from the Sands, who had scoured all the desert from the height of the Pillar of Lives. It was trying as best it could, though, high mountain walls dropping and drawing back as they rode westerly, giving the sky more room to spread. Giving more room to the river too, making a wide and worrying road of water off to his right. It shimmered and danced, it was always moving; it snagged and snagged at the corner of his eye. Its urgent strength kept him continually anxious. An 'ifrit had lurked within it yesterday, maybe more than one. He was ready for another, but he distrusted the river on its own account. So much water so ill-contained, so lively; he doubted its obedience, its willingness to stay within bounds. Doubt was good, though, it was a distraction as welcome as the horse he rode and the speed of his riding, the men about him and the certainty of war.

And the wind, the wind that was too cold and far too wet, heavy with the scents of strangeness. There was all the stink of yesterday's burnings there, but that was a stale smell, flattened by more water than the river could justify; and there was a sharpness that overrode it, an edge that he could taste against his lips. It tasted like tears.

Salt, and water: an immeasurably great mass of water, too far to see or hear but the wind was bringing word of it. This was the sea, that he had heard tales of but never thought to reach and never wished to. Marron had crossed it, by his own report: a journey of weeks in a boat, a little bobbing hull of wood like a nutshell in the jaws of God . . .

Jemel shivered; he would cross the Sands on foot with a leaking waterskin, sooner than go to sea in a boat.

He would not see the sea this day, at least. He had that comfort. Surayon had never reached so far. The river splayed out, he'd been told, as the mountains fell, and a broad salt marsh lay between the valley and the coast, where sea and river mingled. There was a road that hugged the foothills, and men seldom strayed west of that unless they chose the nutshell ride and took a boat to sea.

When Surayon was Folded, that road acquired a Fold of its own. Marron had told him of it, carefully not saying from whom he had heard the story. Jemel knew: silence, namelessness meant Sieur Anton.

But the road was open now, it led into Surayon like a woven thread and not through it like a stitch in a hem. An army had marched up that road yesterday, one of the armies that had come to harrow the valley. Jemel could not reach the sea today if he had chosen to; half the fighting men of Outremer lay between it and him.

THE FORMAL FIELDS and their defensive, deceptive walls had been left behind. As the mountains diminished to north and south, so too did the walls; as the valley broadened and stretched itself, so too did the fields. Now they rode through olive-groves and pastures, there was sheep-dung in the turf and ought probably to have been the sheep themselves cropping in the shade, except that war had come to Surayon and the flocks were taken or fled.

That was the only way that he could see the war, in its absences: no flocks of sheep or goats, no women fetching water from the springs, no idle men or boys at play among the trees. As he could hear it only in its silences, no voices on the wind, no birdsong. The harsh sounds of crickets he could hear, louder than they ought to be against the hush; anything more clever than a cricket was gone or simply beaten down by dread, by the taint of wet smoke encroaching.

There was nothing to be seen but the low shoulders of the hills outflung in scarps and vales, these gentler slopes he rode on, groves and orchards and sweet green forage. Nothing was burning in his sight, though he stood high in the stirrups; there was only the smell of it like a song to destruction, a promise of what he was to find.

That smell must be reaching further than he'd thought. Surayon was small, the pip within the lemon. But they had been riding since dawn, looking for the war and had not found it. That might be just as well, as they were ill-provided to face an army. Two dozen men, well-mounted but lightly armed: this was going Sharai-style, good for tribal raiding in the Sands, but his companions were Patric and would not understand the way of it. Patrics rode in battalions and fought like chained lions, face to face until one fell. They would think it shameful to strike and run as the Sharai did, but this band was fit for nothing more. Perhaps they might come upon other Surayonnaise, before they met the army out of Ascariel; perhaps they might make a little army of their own. If so, Jemel would still not stand and hack in line. He could ride scout, stand off and use his arrows, harry the enemy's flanks . . .

Or none of those. Riding in the stink of war with weapons at belt and back, it was hard to remember that they might not fight with those they went to meet.

If they met with anyone. There was still nothing to be seen as he guided his mount between twisted trees to the crest of another rise, a running rib from the southern hills. Gazing westerly, he saw land roll and roll into a far-distant haze; he thought he might almost see a gleam at its heart, sunlight dazzling on immeasurable water. If Marron had been with him and no one else, if things had been utterly other than they were, he thought that one or other of them would have said the word, and they would have ridden on together until their horses were knee-deep in an ocean.

He turned his head away, and found Markam ridden up beside him.

"You promised me a road, from south to north; you promised me an army, and I do not see either one."

The smile he got in response showed no teeth, and no humour. "Patience, hornet. You see that shale cliff, a league to the west? That marks a break in the hills, and a long vale running southerly. That's where the road lies, and that must be where the army lies; they have made a scorched hell of the vale," and now there was a pure fury in his voice, "and have spent the night sleeping in their own creation. For now, we will ride on towards the road. If we meet a scouting-party before we come to the vale's mouth—well, perhaps we will see if a desert hornet deserves its reputation. The Princip could have no complaint if we were attacked."

He was eager for a fight, and made no attempt to hide it. Jemel thought he would be equally glad, for very different reasons. He had no love of this ravaged land and nothing invested in it; only a raging distress that was easier to handle if he called it simply rage, and would be easier yet if he could stop thinking at all and channel it simply from his heart into his hand.

And then he could, and did; and there was nothing, nothing at all to be glad about.

THEY CAME OUT of the ground, out of the harsh and sour soil. No grass could grow there in the trees' shade, nothing grew but the trees themselves and those had to reach far down between the rocks to find anything good to feed on. Embittered by a lack of care, that soil could have nurtured nothing but the twisted olive and its black thoughts.

Nothing till now. Now the ground, that soil, those rocks all shivered beneath the gathered horses' hooves, startling beasts and riders both. Jemel had heard tell of tremors in the earth that could rattle mountains till the land slipped, shake buildings into dust, rip cracks open wide enough to swallow camels and their burdens too. He gave the stories little credence, preferring the certain knowledge of his own feet: that sand might shift on the wind, shale might slip under a man's weight but what lay beneath was immovable with age and mass and endurance, all the potent majesty of rock.

His horse danced, or the ground danced beneath it. It whinnied with anxiety, and he had to bend low over its suddenly sweating neck to reassure it, when he felt most like crying out himself with shock and fear. There was a terrible wrongness to this. He could see dust rising in wisps, like steam forcing from under a pot-lid. He could see the hard-baked cracks in that crusty soil stir and widen, he could see great plates of earth pull free of rocks they must have bound like mortar for a century or longer; he saw a gnarled and blackened tree-root twist as though the olives themselves were coming alive within this living land, as though they would pull up their deep-delving tap-roots and join the march of armies. Perhaps they would, perhaps the trees would be the Princip's last defence, a long-hidden sorcery of horror.

But the soil seemed to upwell suddenly, all along the ridge where the horses fretted; and then it burst open, shattered, erupted into clods and dust. It broke like eggshell before the many-headed battering of innumerable serpents, all coddled as it seemed in the same deep nest. They hurled that smashed shell high, and Jemel had just a moment to see them clearly before the debris fell back in a blinding, unbreathable cloud.

Thick as his thigh they were, and black as the olives' thoughts. They flowed up and out of the darkness like those thoughts made viable, twisting and glistening like the distant river as it picked itself apart like so many silverdark threads fraying into the marshland ahead.

Serpents did he name them, in that moment of their eruption? They had mouths like serpents, though their teeth were something other, unnatural needles and far too many of them, no mortal creature could eat with teeth like that. They broke out like a knot of vipers, bodies all tangled together, and they surged apart something like the river indeed, what had been one becoming many, a twisted rope in all its separate threads; but these threads were obsidian and they looked as hard as stone, as flexible as wire, as swift as a whip.

Even those needle teeth were black, and the brief glimpse he had of a gaping throat behind, ridged like a dog's. Then the choking murk descended, most of it crumbled into a bitter grit that stung the eyes, invaded nose and mouth and stifled breath.

Jemel had lived through a three-day sandstorm once, and lesser storms were commonplace in the deep of the desert. For this, he needn't even think of hood and veil; it would pass, and worse things would happen before it did.

Worse things were happening already. Horses were screaming, beyond where he could see. A man's voice joined the screaming; there was no terror in that cry, only pure agony, the voice of courage driven beyond extremity. Those teeth were finding out their targets in the filth; 'ifrit were feeding.

No question in his mind, but that these were 'ifrit. All but buried in all that black, he had seen hints of red like jewels aflame, eyes hidden deep where it would take a long needle to come at them. He could see them still, flashes of fire through the dust as the serpent-beasts quested for men.

Or for horses. His own mount reared, its forelegs kicking wildly as though it scrabbled for a safe stand in mid-air; something worse than the lack of one made the animal topple suddenly sideways, made it crash hard to ground, made it scream.

Jemel was off already before it struck. He felt more than the thick shaft of the bow beneath his back, in that tumbling roll; there was sharp rock and shifting clods of earth, but also there was something fat and hard that moved beneath his weight, reacted to it, reared up against it. He must have rolled clean across the body of an 'ifrit.

He went on rolling downslope, letting his body's weight carry him until he fetched up against a tree and had to stand. Battered and unready and half-blind, he must stumble to his feet, set his back to the tree and draw his scimitar. No hope of standing off to use his arrows in this mêlée, in this confusion of dust and bodies.

He squinted upslope and saw a dark shape looming, shining eyes and jaws agape ahead a bulk of shadow. It made a darting jab towards him, all teeth and throat.

Not he but his body ducked aside, he couldn't help it. He felt a blast of cold air above his head, the tree shake at his back as the monstrous beast slammed into it.

His eye was measuring, even as his body moved— thick as his thigh, had he thought? Thick as his chest, rather. He couldn't see how long; too long, though, several times his height and this one at least would look better for being shorter.

He was poised and set, his scimitar drawn back and both hands on the haft. He didn't pause, but he did pray; even as he swung, he prayed that all men's prayers might be equally effective. The grumbling and greedy Selussid priest, the Ransomers who were priests and killers both, the Surayonnaise this morning who was no kind of priest at all: they all prayed differently to different gods, and who could say whether Selussid and Surayonnaise might not have undone each other's work, the prayers of one nullifying the prayers of the other, one angry god blunting where another had made sharp . . .? He had no way to tell, except by learning; and so he swung, and his blade met the glossy black hide of the 'ifrit.

His blade met its hide, and bit; bit and sheared through, driven by all the strength he had in arms and shoulders, all the exultant power of his body as he felt it sink deep, deep into the body of the 'ifrit. The Selussid blessing had held, or else the Surayonnaise, or both together. The serpent-beast spasmed on his blade, coiled and twisted and tried to tear it from his grasp. Jemel turned the point inside the great gashing wound and heaved like a man at a hunt, opening up a carcase with his gutting-knife. No entrails gushed out but only smoke, as though all the solid heft of the creature had coldly and instantly burned to an insubstantial ash. Its glowing eyes faded, and were dull; its hide—its carapace, perhaps, hard as shell and smooth as shell, and yet it had been as supple as snakeskin—dulled also, as though there were smoke within the gleam; and then it dissipated and was gone, and left him with nothing at all.

Now he could look around and see an image of hell. Not a horse had broken free to escape the ridge, not a man remained mounted; men and beasts lay everywhere, dead and dying, broken and ripped asunder.

And yet there was hope, there were men still afoot and still fighting, cleaving brutally amid the carnage.

But even a blessed blade, even a twice-blessed blade took time and effort to slay one of these serpent-things, and there were many of them and more coming. The earth still churned, the rocks themselves were shifting with its movement, trees that had stood a thousand years were falling as new demons erupted from their roots.

Two more were coming for Jemel. He couldn't even go where he was most needed, to the heart of the battle; he must guard himself and fight his own fight for his own survival.

He set himself against the tree again and met the first serpent's hurtling charge with his blade between its teeth, felt those lethal needles rake his arm even as the fire died in its eyes, too close to his; and heaved arm and blade sideways, all the strength he had, so that the scimitar cut its way out of the first dead 'ifrit even before it had faded, and cut savagely into the second before it could strike.

That one took more killing, he took more hurts; and when he next had time to look, it was sweat that was stinging his eyes now and there were fewer men still standing, still fighting, and it seemed an inexhaustible number of the monsters to oppose them.

He stumbled over the broken ground to help them, though all the help he could offer was to draw some few of the creatures to himself, to his own slaughter. His mind had narrowed with his eyes; his focus was so intense it was almost painful. There were 'ifrit to kill with this wondrously heavy scimitar, that grew heavier yet with every blow and yet less potent, which was strange but didn't matter, it meant only that he must strike again and yet again. And duck, too late because the creatures were moving more swiftly now, and that one had scored his shoulder; but the sharp sting of it was a spur and he'd seen horses spurred, the Patrics did that in their armour and he knew what it meant, it was to drive the horses harder and so he would be driven, another blow and another and this blade of his must be drinking the deaths of these endless 'ifrit, absorbing all the weight they lost, it was so heavy now he could barely lift it, and yet he must . . .

AND DID; AND fought on and on, and soon there were no coherent thoughts at all but only the necessity of movement, the planting of the foot and the swinging of the arms like a peasant, like a farmer with a scythe, no art or grace but only death in his blade and death in his mind's eye, his own death looming and as many others as he could make beforehand.

For a short while he was aware of another man beside him, shoulder to shoulder; they could hew together, and guard each other against the worst. Too short a while: there was a sudden flurry of bright black bodies, and when he had the time to glance around, his companion was gone, a sudden absence at his side that seemed the worse because Jemel had never had the chance to learn his name.

IN THE END, at last, too soon it came. There was a trembling weakness in his arms as he raised the scimitar, he nearly lost his grip on the haft which had grown slimy with his blood, he saw the point slip low when it needed not to do that, it needed to stand high and firm and yet he could not lift it. And there was a fresh 'ifrit directly ahead of him and all he could see were the eyes of it, hot and draining, sucking, leeching the last of his strength as though it would kill him before it even touched.

He wished he had time to feel sorry; he thought that with a little time, he would remember what he had to feel sorry for, why his death must be a sadness. At the moment it eluded him.

But then the death eluded him also, strangely. He saw a sudden dark flower in one of those glowing eyes, and the glow went out before the 'ifrit crashed into him. He fell, of course, and the creature fell atop him. But those teeth that should have ravened at his throat lay still and sharp against it, not cutting in the least. And then there was no weight, the thing had vanished; and instead there was a standing figure against the sky, a silhouette to block the sun, a voice; and it said, "We came too late. I am sorry. How many are your dead?"

Why, only me, he wanted to say; but he couldn't find a voice of his own to say it with, and before he did he remembered that there had indeed been others, and perhaps they were all of them dead, and only he not. Which would be a thing to be sad about, perhaps, though not the chiefest thing, he thought.

He struggled to rise and could not until the man stooped to help him, to lift him with an easy heave of the arm.

"Steady now, lad. This was a heroic battle, you've earned your pride but don't overdraw it, lean on me . . ." And then, more slowly, "Wait—these others are of Surayon. Do the Sharai fight beside them now?"

"Against this?" Another voice, whisper-thin, without a drop of blood behind it; it was an effort even to turn his head, but Jemel had to see. Three men sat on the turned earth and passed a waterskin between them. All of them were pale and bleeding, but all were alive and seemed likely to stay so. Not alone, then; it was good not to be alone, though there was a tremendous sadness in it. "We all fight beside each other, when we fight a thing like this. What, would you let us stand alone?"

"I did not. Those were my arrows saved you, blessed by my own priest; and be glad there were that few of you standing, that we could use the arrows. Otherwise you'd none of you be standing, we could not have come in time. But I had not realised the Sharai . . ."

His voice trailed away, or else Jemel stopped listening. He was a man, a Patric in a black cloak over white; and Jemel knew what that meant, and he remembered something of his sadness, and the causes of it.

His scimitar was in his hand yet, he had not let it go. Now he strained to lift it, shimmering clean blade and blood-sodden haft, he struggled to point it towards this man his rescuer; and he said, "I have been looking for a Patric man. D'Escrivey, his name is. He is a Ransomer, he wears your dress. Are you d'Escrivey? You might be. I might be seeking you . . ."

A soft, puzzled laugh, and, "Aye, lad, you might—if I were he. I am not; my name is Karlheim, of Elessi. I served my year with the Ransomers, no more than that. Is d'Escrivey here? I have not heard. You'd do better to seek him northerly, that's where I last saw him. But you're going nowhere yet. Come on, you little infidel, put up that hero's sword and lie down with your friends there, take some water, you've lost half the blood your god has given you. Which was probably the only half you had left anyway, by the look of that scar on your throat. Steady, there, don't give me one to match it; I told you, I'm not Anton d'Escrivey. Though I'd like to know what he's done to upset the Sharai. He upset all of Outremer long ago, but I hadn't realised his ambitions ran so much further. Perhaps you'll tell me later. For the moment I have an army to move and I don't know the country; but I guess I'll ask your companions about that, because I don't think you'd be too much help there, would you? As a matter of fact, I think you're asleep, unless you're dead already. Which would be a shame, because I'd like to see you meet d'Escrivey. Give me some help here, someone . . ."

☒   ☒   ☒

EVEN FROM THEIR island, from this lowest point in all the princedom, the girls had a view of the valley. Its gentle rise on either side of the river meant that the swathes of open pasture, the defensive walls and the settlements beyond the walls, Surayon-town to the south with the Princip's palace behind it, everything was laid out for them here, between the rushing water and the crowding trees of the mountains' early slopes. Julianne knew nothing of the land, except what she could see; nothing of the people, except what she had seen. Whatever lay further that she had not seen, however, she thought that this vista embodied the heart and the soul of Surayon. Unless the Princip was his country's soul, but she thought them much the same: open, warm and welcoming, but with rocky heights where she dared not tread, hidden places she could not even see, traps and snares where she could not find her way without a guide.

Today it was a heart in ashes, a soul at war. There was smoke in the air, though that might still be from yesterday's burnings. One house could smoulder for days unattended and dozens, hundreds had been put to the torch as the invaders passed through. And there were dozens, hundreds of men Julianne could see coming and going, riding westerly or easterly alone or in small bands, some few afoot; even at the limits of her sight or the valley's turning she could identify Sharai and Patric by the dress they wore, and she could see how they kept their distances, how none of them closed for battle.

This might be news worth the telling; but when she looked around for Elisande she found her still busy, still muttering to herself, head down and almost on hands and knees among the grasses.

". . . Is this bloodwort? Yes, it is. Good for clotting, if there were enough to pack a wound, which there is not, and time enough to let it work, which there will not be. Still, pick it, save it, someone might prick their finger . . ."

Elisande had decided that as there was no other conceivable use for this fleck of land in mid-stream or for these two girls upon it, and as Esren had brought them here to be useful, therefore it must intend them to tend the injured. It was her one known talent, after all; and Julianne had learned by helping her, they had been sicknurses together in the Roq and in Rhabat. No doubt Esren would ferry the wounded across the water as they fell. In the meantime, she would scour every green and growing thing for any medicinal effect whatsoever. This was a safe place, which might be why the djinni chose it; and she was a skilled healer, which must be why the djinni chose her; but still there was an element missing, and she thought it must be some potent hidden herb.

Or so she was pretending, at any rate: gazing at the ground with a fierce focus, refusing to look up or around as she picked and poked among the damp and heavy grasses, hoarding a poor harvest into the gathered belly of her skirt.

Julianne turned back to her vigil, looking for patterns in the movements of men and seeing none, living breathlessly from moment to hopeful moment until a sudden unexpected noise made her twist around sharply, and the words she might have been thinking to say unravelled themselves entirely as she went.

The noise came from Elisande—of course, there was no one and nothing else here that might have made it—and it was, startlingly, a laugh.

At least a sort of half-laugh, a choking, coughing sound of self-mockery. She had laid out all her gleanings neatly on a stretch of trampled grass, and now she was sitting back on her heels and looking at them, looking up at Julianne and back at her herbs again.

"I'm sorry, my love," she said softly, not laughing now. "That was pathetic."

"Do you think so?"

"Do you not? Look at it, an hour's labour for this . . ." Her fingers played with what she had collected, lifting and letting fall. "Any abandoned croft could show a better crop, and what, I'm going to heal half an army?"

"We don't have an abandoned croft, Elisande. All we have is what you can find, because I don't know a simple from a, from a—"

"Simpleton?"

"Anyway, you may not need to heal half an army. The armies have decided not to fight."

"Have they? Truly?" A sudden heedless scramble to her feet, scattering half of what she had worked so hard to gather; she stared, stood on tiptoe as though an extra inch would show her a deeper truth, shaded her eyes with her hand and stared again.

After a while, though, she shook her head and sank back, sank down, sank almost utterly. Briefly Julianne felt a cold fury, only that she was not certain who to be so angry with: herself for raising such a fragile hope or Elisande for doing nothing to keep it perilously aloft, for so easily allowing it to fall.

"That's not peace," she said. "That's reconnoitring. They're sending out scouts, watching each other, waiting to strike . . ."

"I didn't say peace. I said they'd decided not to fight. They're not waiting to strike, they're just waiting. Watching each other, of course, but expecting something else to happen. It's better than yesterday, love. Would they have waited even this long, if they'd met yesterday? If they'd had a chance of meeting, two armies from Outremer and the Sharai?"

No, of course they wouldn't. There'd have been no

courtesies of war: only a yell of hatred, a holy curse on all unbelievers and a thundering charge from either side, from both. And they'd have ridden over Surayon and hardly noticed as they trampled lives, hopes, an entire people into the bloody dust.

They might yet. They would yet, if nothing else did happen. It was strange, disturbing to find herself yearning—praying, almost—for an assault, for men to die; but it was the only way she knew to stop them killing each other. She trusted neither side in this undeclared, unconvincing truce. It needed one hothead, one holy fool, no more than that . . .

Elisande shrugged, the closest she could come to *perhaps you're right, perhaps it's too early to despair.* She gave a despairing look to the tumbled herbs that represented all her morning's work, another to the fertile but barren island on which they'd been marooned, and moaned. "There has to be a point to this, there must be something that we're missing."

"Must there?"

"Yes. *Yes!* Esren said we'd be of most use here. Didn't it? Or did I dream that?"

"You know you didn't dream it, sweets."

"Well, then. That's what it said—and the djinn know these things, Julianne, it *knew* we'd be useful here . . ."

It knew they would be useful, but it didn't tell them how. Likely both parts of that were significant. It wanted—or needed?—them to work it out for themselves. Or else to fail, perhaps that was their usefulness? Like leaving Marron at the palace, if only to stop him making matters worse elsewhere . . .

Elisande had abandoned the muttering and the search for herbs, but not the search for meaning. Julianne had nothing to offer, no inspiration; she turned her attention back to the riders in the valley, north and south.

*   *   *

OF COURSE THE story changed, because it must; of course the change was for the worse, a degradation, a loss of hope. She thought it had never been otherwise, and never would be. It was the nature of humankind to hope, the nature of hope to fail, the nature of the world to decay. All life was a losing struggle. *God is history*, she thought suddenly, startling herself into a soft cry; she hadn't re-alised that she or anyone was fighting God, but the con-clusion was irresistible. The djinn had foreknowledge, and even the djinn were fallible and so mortal; what else could be eternal than the sum of what had happened, the exactitude of knowledge—and how could she or anyone resist the past, or what it taught?

"What?" Elisande looked up from the depths of her si-lence, which had dragged her deeper and deeper down as though she sat in the bottom of a well, unreachable.

"Oh—uh, look. If there was a truce, it has been bro-ken." She didn't want to confess where her thinking had brought her. This was what had led her there, this was what mattered more: death had come back to Surayon, re-freshed.

FOR SOME LITTLE time now, she had been watching an army emerge onto the northern flood-plain. No more scouts, no more reconnaissance—here were men in num-bers, sure of their strength. Most wore black robes, though there were colours among them; their officers had black cloaks thrown over white. They were the Ransomer army come down from the Roq, swollen by recruits en route as a river swells and swells in time of flood, between its ris-ing and the sea.

They came down the single narrow road between the high-walled fields; they issued out in pairs abreast and spread across the grassland like a flood indeed, a slow-seeping darkness that invaded the bright green like a poi-son. She had been guest of the Ransomers, she knew some of their intimacies at first hand and had heard tell of others. They were the last people she liked to see within these borders. Better the Sharai, who would pillage, burn crops and houses and move on, leaving a corruptible governor behind to levy later tributes. That was slavery; but Ransomers would burn the people too. And build castles on the heights, and stay, and never trust because they never could. Their hand would always lie cold and heavy across this narrow, tender land. She tried to imagine a lifetime lived in its shadow and shuddered, and yearned to see the army of the Sharai come out of the smoke to the east there, to drive the Ransomers back. It was there, she knew, she had seen outriders come and go; she thought she could see a darker shadow building, the massing of the tribes.

If they fight, we all lose, she reminded herself fiercely, but thought they would fight regardless. She had no faith in these men: not in either of her wise and foolish husbands, let alone in any man else. Never mind their intentions, she thought that one or another of them would fling a blade or let an arrow fly, too soon and at the wrong target. There were too many blood-debts on either side. Each had its history, of cruelties and dispossession; each had its god, and as she had learned—or perhaps decided—those were the same thing, indistinguishable.

That was her fear, and there was only one way to avoid it: that both sides see men die, and see who killed them.

She waited, breathless and fearful, while long files of riders unwound across the plain; she watched a patrol detach to follow the line of the field-wall easterly, towards the hidden Sharai.

She thought she knew what she had to fear. She thought her Hasan would appear from the smoke, riding alone with the tribes behind; she thought some high-minded Ransomer—Marron's Sieur Anton, as like as not: there was a man who carried his nobility in every haunted muscle of his body—would go to meet him, man to man and face to face; she thought they would speak with cour-

tesy and respect on both sides, and somehow there would
be words said that must reluctantly, regretfully be answered with steel. She thought they would fight, because
that was the style of the day. Hope must fail, men must be
weak.

She watched the men ride the wall and saw that she
was wrong, she'd been too subtle and too grand. No meeting of proud captains, no honour; that was a girl's fancy,
a nursery tale, no part of war. Instead there was simply a
boiling, a sudden rush of shadow through an opening in
the wall, and the fighting had begun.

Men on foot should not, could not stand against horsemen. She knew that from her earliest schooling, from before she knew that she was being schooled. And yet these
half dozen in their black robes swirled around the riders
and their beasts, and one by one the horses fell. Then it
was black against black, Patric against Sharai; and when
six men were left standing, they were not Ransomers. It
ought not to have been possible, but—

"Sand Dancers," Elisande said beside her.

"How can you tell? From here? Are you counting their
fingers for them?"

"They killed the horses. Besides, those robes are black.
But why are they here, and what are they fighting for?"

"Sweet, I don't know. I never have known. Theirs is
another war altogether, it seems to me."

"Well, there are few of them; and here come the Ransomers for vengeance."

Indeed, a squad of horsemen was cantering along the
wall, two dozen or more with a cloaked knight prominent
among them. She said, "The Ransomers won't care about
the niceties, black robes or blue. They have seen Sharai
slaughter their brothers; there will be no truce."

"Likely not. I never had much faith in it. But they can
kill Dancers, and welcome so."

"If they can kill Dancers."

"Why not? We did. Those riders were surprised, and

led by a fool. It's been how long, six hundred years that the Dancers have lived alone in the Sands? I'm sure they killed the odd braggart for reputation's sake, but reputation is all it is, Julianne. Reputation and good training, but the Ransomers also have both, and the Ransomers have been fighting for forty years. The Dancers haven't faced a real enemy in ten times that long. None of these living have risked their lives till now. They will not stand. Besides, they are Sharai; they are not stupid. Strike, and run . . ."

And so they did, back through the opening in the wall, where the horsemen could only have followed them slowly and one by one. Their leader had better sense.

"Perhaps they'll lose themselves, and starve," Julianne muttered vindictively.

"Not they. Dancers think round corners; they'll know the secrets of those walls. Or they'll climb straight over them, as your 'ifrit did. Not your foolish boy . . ."

She meant Imber, of course, not Roald. Julianne still felt a pang, though she hoped her face had not shown it. Roald was dead, and laid with honour with his Princip's son; let him lie. She stared into the distant haze, watching for Hasan and desperate not to see him.

"Look," Elisande said suddenly, startled. "There, the Ransomers . . ."

The horsemen were milling chaotically around that narrow opening. Not trying to go in, but what, then? For a moment she thought that they were somehow knocking down the wall. But then she saw a great section topple and fall—and it fell outwards, towards the Ransomers. Whose horses were backing, wheeling, kicking and rearing, caught in a crush and close to panic.

It was hard to see, but there was black against the green, there were dark shapes gleaming in the sunlight as they came through the field's trampled crop and over the rubble of the wall. There were riderless horses running free, their discipline as broken as their harness. Others were dead or dying; she saw one and then another seized and drawn down. There were men on foot amid that desperate madness, then. If any could find space enough to stand and keep their feet against the buffeting bodies, the noise and terror; if any could survive so long as this, survive at all against marauding 'ifrit with strength enough simply to push a strong wall over, where it lay between themselves and their prey.

"ELISANDE, YOUR EYES are sharper than mine. Can you see how it goes there? They are killing each other, look . . ."

"I daresay they are," Elisande replied in a voice so strange, so distracted that she might as well have said outright, *I do not care what is happening, and I am not going to look.*

Julianne turned and saw, and understood.

Marron stood there, on their island, where he had not been before. Nor was he alone. He held Jemel in his arms, but not the Jemel that Julianne could have wished for, grim-eyed and fearsome and fierce. This was Jemel hurt, atrociously hurt, unconscious; his robe was clinging wetly to his blood-streaked body where it was not hanging in rips and shreds.

Marron lifted his eyes to gaze at both the girls. Deep crimson red they were, as though Jemel's blood had dyed them so, or else he wore them as a badge of war.

"Oh, Marron . . ."

Was it Elisande's voice, that despairing sigh, or was it her own? She couldn't tell.

He didn't seem to care, either way. She never had been sure how much of him was Marron and how much the Daughter, when they shared one flesh like this.

"Jemel needs your healing," he said to Elisande, as though she could not have seen that for herself.

Was it only Julianne who thought, *again?* Perhaps it

was. Elisande's authoritative hands pulled open the tattered robe and moved rapidly, assessing from one torn wound to another, while her voice was weak, almost whispering, chasing after what was lost already.

"How did you find him? Or us?"

"It knows," he said, "I could feel where he should be. I had to take him from some Patric men, but they gave me room enough. Then I felt where you should be, and I came. Can you heal him?"

"Easier than last time," Elisande said. "He's not so very dead. There'll be more scars, but you won't mind that," *you carry scars enough yourself*, her voice implied, *and not all on that tender skin of yours*. "But, Marron, the djinni would have taken you to Jemel, brought you here, you didn't need . . ."

"I am not finished yet," he said. "Your father wanted me to fight, Julianne, he forced me to it; now I can, if I have to. If I must break one more oath, it may as well be broken beyond repair."

"That may not be all that is broken. Grandfer might not draw it out of you again, he might not be able to . . ."

"I have not said that I would ask him to. I did not ask before; how can it matter now? See to Jemel, Elisande." And he pulled a dagger from his belt, pricked his arm, let the Daughter flow.

Swiftly then, while his eyes were his own brown, Elisande chased him with one more question. "Where are you going now?"

"To find Sieur Anton," and there was none of that chill, despairing certainty in his voice, only a determination so strong that yes, he would sacrifice anything, more even than he had given already if he had indeed anything more to give. "Look after Jemel," and this time it was a plea, or as near as he could come to it in the moment before he opened a blood-red gate and stepped through it into a golden light that folded itself around him and was gone.

✠   ✠   ✠

DISTANCE WAS NO trouble, time was no concern. He ran only because running was there to be done, and so he did it. He could have run forever; he might yet run forever, if his running fetched him no reason to stop.

He was aware of but did not feel the warmth of the world around him. He had fire in his veins that flowed to match his running, and he had a cool stillness in his mind that matched the static precision of his thoughts.

He ran over dust and rock, under an opal sky. He was alone, if not unobserved; there was a glitter in the air about him that was more than the eternal gold, an occasional line of darkness in a shadowless land.

He ran quite untroubled by his awareness of trouble in the other world. This time around possession had been invited and had driven deeper, with a sharper edge; he carried twin souls within this single body, himself and another that was not him, not male, not human. In this world, it was ascendant by right; in the other, only by his gift.

When he—they—had run enough in this world, the prick in his arm came without his thinking, he didn't need to, it did the thing itself; and then it left him—but not entirely, not now, some vestige still remained, the coolness of the shadow cast—and pain flooded in, more pain than ever such a little cut deserved, and far more blood.

And it made a doorway for him, he didn't need to think about that either; and he stepped through and swiftly took it back. He could lose himself in what possessed him and find a terrible comfort in the red cast of its sight, the ice and hammer of its thinking. Why be what he had been before, when he could be this strong, this safe, this simple?

THERE WAS A battle at a little distance. This was what he had wanted to see, or else what it had wanted him to see;

he would have found it hard to say which was true, or more true. He did not try; it did not seem to matter.

There were men in the battle, and horses, and 'ifrit. He had a cold certainty in his head, an utter knowledge that Sieur Anton was among the men. He would not have been brought here else. No need for him to scan the horsemen for one who wore white beneath his cloak, although he did.

Sieur Anton was still mounted—of course, he was still mounted!—where many were not. His stallion reared and screamed, blind with terror, lashing out at man or monster indiscriminately. Not so the knight, whose blade Josette was neat, vicious, lethal. *Blessed Josette, who has said a prayer over you? Did he do so himself, in his virtue?*

Men were dying and horses too, but Sieur Anton would survive this. That was axiomatic.

Sieur Anton might survive alone. No men were riding to his reinforcement; all the troops on the grassland were fighting now on their own account, clustered around the road that had led them down from the northern hills. There were 'ifrit there too, and broken walls, an ambush well repeated.

This one had cut the Ransomer army in two, north and south of the walled fields; the 'ifrit had severed its spine as it marched that narrow road. Or crushed it, rather: he climbed up fallen rubble to the top of the long boundary wall and saw the proof of their power, laid out before him like a map written upon the land.

How many 'ifrit there were, he could not tell. They had struck all along the length of the road, where it was contained within those sheltering, concealing walls. The sudden collapse of so much stonework must have accounted for many of the brothers or their mounts in the first moments of the attack. He could see men, horses, weapons lying scattered in and among the heaps of rubble. Those fallen would not fight again. Some few men were heaving themselves free or trying to, hauling or dragging at stones they could barely lift; some few horses were kicking where they lay or struggling to rise, falling back with broken legs and bloody froth at their muzzles; most of the bodies were simply bodies, no hope of life in them.

Even the collapse of so long, so high a run of walls without warning could not bury an entire army. There were pockets of fighting all along the road, but this was nothing like the disciplined drill of the Ransomers in their troops, nothing like the way they had fought Hasan and his Sharai at the Roq. Disorganised, disrupted, distressed; ill-led through sheer confusion where they were led at all, where their officers or confessors had not been killed already; vulnerable, unready and afraid, the knights and brothers of the Order were fighting, yes, but they were dying too.

He saw men charge hopelessly into reaching jaws, saw them crushed and broken, hacking at the chitin that gripped them as they died; and where their blades sliced through that chitin, he thought they might be dying with a sense of satisfaction, at a victory dearly bought.

But the 'ifrit could lose their jaws and still kill men. They had taken an insect shape, as they so often did, to haunt the nightmares perhaps of those who escaped them; fear was a weapon as deadly as any. These insects were monstrous, with great plates of chitin—fit for pushing walls over—above their deep-set eyes, and vicious spurs projecting from their shell all around. Men with swords would find it hard to come close enough to harm, even where their swords were blessed. Except by hurling themselves into those cruel jaws, of course—and that still left the 'ifrit with the speed and lethal sharpness of the claws that capped its many legs, with the crushing power of its armoured head, with its questing intelligence that sought ever new ways to kill.

There were ghûls too, coming from the fields behind their masters, the 'ifrit. They didn't join the brutal little battles that were like knots on the string of the road; instead they made their way along that string, long arms reaching for the wounded. Man or horse, it made no difference; those claws could kill, and did.

He saw what was happening and knew what would come, what must come unless help came first and swiftly.

Alone, he would have gone himself to help, and so died at Sieur Anton's side, perhaps, or struggling to reach him. He was not alone, and did not run to help, but ran to fetch it. Along the tops of the fields' walls, leaping the openings, undistracted by the slaughter close below him, he ran as though on solid ground, and left all the fighting behind him.

He ran, and came to the final wall and the trees beyond, the first thin forest of the mountains; and here he found the remainder of the Ransomer army and their new recruits, gathered in rank and waiting while Marshal Fulke paced with his officers.

PACED AND PRAYED at a little distance from the grooms who held the horses, and cast sidelong looks along the empty road. He might be waiting for news to come back before he sent his next divisions down; he might have sent outriders to learn why there was no news, and be wondering now why he had no outriders. Certainly he knew that all was not well. He was an alert man, a wary man; he paused in his pacing the moment he saw movement, a runner high on the walls. He spoke swift words to his generals and sent them to join their divisions, not to have all the army's heads grouped together where they might be cleaved with a single blow. Other men came running at a signal, archers among them. This was no messenger of theirs for sure, this boy in a Sharai robe who was so fleet of foot, so casual of his balance on a height.

*   *   *

HE WAS INTERESTED to see how near he could come before one of them knew him, and whether they would see his eyes before they saw his face; and, in either case, whether any man would shoot an arrow before he came close enough to speak to them.

Or after.

HE HEARD THE pound and suck of his own body, wetly working; he heard the thud of his feet striking ground as he leapt from the wall, and then their steady rhythm on the earth, and the earth's reply; he heard what they thought he could not possibly hear, their voices at this distance. He heard:

"Magister, it is a demon, see its eyes! The Sharai are possessed, I always said it, let me shoot . . ."

And he heard:

"No, Magister, that is not Sharai. That is the heretic squire; he that passed himself off as a brother first and then Sieur Anton took him, but he showed himself friend to both Sharai and Surayon. His dress betrays him, and his being here; what evil else he has done, I dare not know, to make his eyes glow so. He comes as a messenger, but there is nothing he should say to you; his words are poison and deceit. His death is decreed, demanded . . ."

And he heard:

"No, let him live for now. If he acts as messenger, I should like to know from whom, and why."

"We have no friends in this country, Magister, to send us messages."

"All the more reason to hear what he has to say. Quiet now, say nothing to him; this is for me alone. If he has come here to learn, better that he has only one guarded voice to learn from; wickedness is subtle, too much so for you lads. Just keep your arrows nocked and watch me, be prepared to kill him at my gesture . . ."

* * *

SO THEY CAME to stand face to face, and within almost a sword's-strike distance; and if ever he could have lost his sense of distance, of being far away and untouched even when he was closest, this should have been the moment and the man to make it so. Fulke's clothes were rank with blood and smoke; his gaze was fixed, his mouth was set and grim. There was no mercy in him, for a rebellious land open to his harrowing nor for a people who had abandoned true religion in the very heart of the God's own country.

Marron had feared and hated him, when Marron was alone. But Marron couldn't find himself, or his passions. He felt disinterested, unconcerned; he said, "You are waiting for news of your men. I bring it to you. Those on the road are lost. You may yet save some of those who have reached the river, but you cannot go this way."

"Magister, he is a demon, he lies, you must not listen to him . . .!"

"Be silent." Fulke didn't turn his head to administer the rebuke, didn't shift his gaze; he went on staring levelly, with a slight frown and no sign of fear. "What are you?" he asked, directly but musingly, as though it was a question he was putting to himself, to his own wide knowledge as much as to the figure now before him. "Once, you were a boy; I remember him. Then you were traitor, renegade, apostate, and I hunted him and lost him in the hills. Now, though—now you come back with hell in your eyes, and I wonder what you are, what you have become . . .?"

"I am wiser than I was, when I was a boy. Else I would not offer you this news. If you wish to save any of your men, Magister, you will take them to the river by another way."

"What, have the Surayon sorcerers set a devilry to work upon the road?"

"Not the Surayonnaise, but there are demons, yes. The 'ifrit are waiting for you, and killing as you come."

"We were told our weapons would be good against 'ifrit, if we said a blessing over them."

"So they are, or can be. Are they good against stones? The 'ifrit have collapsed these walls atop your men, and are destroying those who survived."

"Then we will ride to their assistance."

"Then you will die, as they are dying. The road is a trap; it would be folly to follow the dead."

"Then perhaps we should pitch our tents here and go no further. Any 'ifrit that ventures this far we can despatch, to protect the world beyond; meanwhile they will do our work for us, in scouring this polluted land."

"And will you abandon your men, to share the fate of those who belong here?"

"You said my men were lost already."

"Those on the road, I said. Those who won through to the river, some of them may be saved, and the world with them."

"The world, I think, can save itself, with the God's guidance; but I cannot reach my men except by that road, which you tell me I may not use. Your advice is a snake that eats itself."

"Not so. There is always more than a single road."

"Not in this pass, and I have no time to go back and ride around the mountains, west or east."

"You have candles, you have priests. Open the King's Eye and lead your army through; you know the way. All hope dies else."

Hope for whom, he did not say; perhaps he could not. Perhaps he did not care.

✠   ✠   ✠

JEMEL HAD KNOWN this before: the desperate sense of being trapped in his own body, breathless and panicking and utterly unable to save himself.

Usually it was a dream or a half-dream as he drifted towards sleep, and he would jerk himself out of it with a cry. There would be Jazra, or latterly Marron, and being awake would be a fine thing then, being vulnerable would be easy, no harm in the world.

Once before, it had not been a dream. He had felt himself fall and fall into some deep place inside himself, from where he could never climb out. But Lisan had come to find him, and bring him up again. She had mended what was torn in his throat, and he had opened eyes on a golden world and the naked body of a girl who was not his own. An imam might have thought himself in Paradise; Jemel remembered only doubt, wondering where Marron was, why not there?

Now again he was held in that waking nightmare, his body somehow robbed away, only a dead cage around the quick of him.

He lay helpless and irredeemable, and nothing changed; he felt as though he hung on the point of death like a moth on a thorn.

Except that he was neither helpless nor irredeemable, only that he could neither help nor redeem himself. He felt her come, whom he had not dared to hope for: fire against his ice.

She walked in the ways of his body, and made herself free of them. Where she went, he felt the warmth and power of her passing; he followed eagerly, tirelessly, riding gladly on the surge of pain because pain is a measure of time and he was back in the blood's beat of his body again. He followed her up until she left him, and then he tried to follow her out.

And so felt her first, warm and firmly pressed against his skin, wherever she could reach; and so defined the limits of himself, rediscovered that he had skin because that was where she ended, and so he began.

So his eyes opened and he saw her eyes, her face just a moment away from his. No smile, only a fierce determination, a glare that would not permit him to be weak. He could feel a tremble within her, as though she'd physically dragged him further than her strength could bear.

He could also feel that she was naked, he could see it as she pushed herself suddenly away from him, but no matter for that. It had been so before, the last time she saved his life; it meant nothing. What he needed to know, he could not tell by looking.

Lisan stirred, struggling to sit up; Julianne appeared at her side, to lift her onto her knees and ease a robe over her head. The smaller girl looked grey and ill, her familiar ferocity floating like a scum atop extreme exhaustion. Julianne fussed with her dress briefly, then produced a flask and held it to her lips.

Lisan drank, then spluttered.

"Julianne, how did you—? I thought it was water!" She ran her hand across her face and licked it, to salvage what she could of what she'd spat or dribbled.

"I know you did," smugly. "I fetched it before I came to you this morning, I thought we might have need. This is all I've brought, though, so don't waste it. If you're going to cough the rest of it around, you shall have water. Will I fetch some, or do you want to drink this decently, like a civilised woman in company?"

"Give me."

Julianne gave her another drink, then brought the flask to Jemel. At that moment, his last doubts faded. Not one of their Patric wines, if she would offer it to a Sharai; only one possibility, then.

"Please . . ." he whispered, trying to haul himself upright, falling back.

"Easy, Jemel. I'll help. Here . . ."

An arm slipped under his shoulders, a quick heave and the tall girl lifted him as simply as she had Lisan. His head lolled disgracefully against her shoulder; he scowled, tried to straighten his neck and found that he could not.

Julianne laughed in his ear. "Don't be afraid, you'll be running around quarrelling with everyone again soon enough. It's only weariness, and weakness. You must have been in a terrible fight, there were so many wounds on you; Elisande's only healed the worst of them, all she had the strength to cope with. The rest I've patched up myself, in mortal fashion. With no proper dressings. You'll yelp when they're changed; best ask me to do that too, you won't want Marron to hear you. But at least you're not bleeding any more. You're an awful colour still, worse than she is, and she doesn't look good. You need to rest, that's all. Now stop talking so much, and drink . . ."

He opened his mouth, obedient as a child, impatient and greedy as a child; she set the flask's lip against his and tipped gently.

Bitter and sweet in subtle balance, herbs and fruits: potent beyond medicine, the *jereth* coursed down his throat like a renewing draught of the desert. Gold for the Sands, green for the oases—and it was in the gold that the sweetness lay, he thought as he always had thought, and bitterness in the green. Green could be for all the wet lands now, and gold could be for the land of the djinn, which was nothing but gold; understanding changed as the world changed, as it grew wider.

The Patrics had never understood *jereth*. They drank it for a drink, and nothing more; they had never considered its meaning. Blood-dark in their glass goblets, it showed them nothing of its sources; they misunderstood its making and its uses both, the sheer burning power of the thing. Even Lisan: she wanted more, but had no true idea why she craved it so.

He felt that first mouthful lying like a liquid fire in his belly, like gold transmuted into oil, as though a lamp's fuel could contain its own flame. Let his body only absorb it, and he could shrug off this dreadful feebleness; he could draw strength from *jereth* as the Sharai had done for many, many generations. Properly taken and properly appreciated, *jereth* would drive back weariness, stiffen aching muscles and lend as much support to flagging spirits. It had saved many a life in the Sands; many a man who had lost his water and been given up as white bones walking had walked into his camp fully fleshed and lucid, thanks to the little flask he kept within his robe.

Already, simply from the taste in his mouth and the knowledge of its being in his body, Jemel could lift his head, straighten his spine, look around him. Julianne looked a little startled at the change; she would be more so shortly.

He touched his tongue to his lips, to catch what drops had slipped from the flask or from his own loose mouth before he'd swallowed. For a moment he closed his eyes, savouring, welcoming. Not to judge: this brew was not of Saren making, but that was immaterial. It had come into the world, and come to him. Besides, he was no longer Saren himself.

Words were still difficult; he should probably drink water to ease his throat. But he would have to ask for it, apparently, neither girl had thought to pass a skin. If he had to speak anyway, he might as well ask his real question.

"Where is Marron?"

Not *where am I?* or *how did I get here?* or any of the other puzzlements. He thought they could all be answered by the one, or else they did not matter.

The girls looked at each other. It was Elisande who won that exchange, or lost it; she said, "He went north." *Where you cannot follow him* was inherent. Neither one of them needed to glance at the raging river, or the great gulf between here and the bank. He had seen it already, and was starting to answer *where am I?* on his own account. On an island, clearly, surrounded by a terrible force of water. The spray of it was cool on his skin, hanging in the air like a mist that the sun could not burn off.

He looked to Julianne, who had an overrun of words where Lisan hoarded hers as close as water. He supposed that in this country, no one would hoard water; but words were treasures, meanings were gifts.

"Marron brought you to us," she said, speaking hurriedly against his silence. "He said he took you from some of our people, but none of your hurts were sword-wounds, so you cannot have been fighting them?"

"I was fighting 'ifrit," he murmured, remembering. "Many 'ifrit like serpents, or one that had made itself many; I do not know if they can do that, but they each seemed small-minded, easy to kill. It was only the numbers that defeated us. We were defeated, I think. I fought beside your people, Lisan, but they were mostly dead before yours came, Julianne. Perhaps they rescued me. I was small-minded myself by then, I could not think; only remember that there was a Patric I had to fight when I was finished with the 'ifrit, or they with me. I thought I had found him, tall and white and cloaked in black, but he said not, he said his name was Karlheim . . ."

Julianne gasped, but quite silently; he only felt it because she had her arm around his shoulders still.

It was Lisan who pressed him. "Was he a young man, blond-headed?"

"I suppose. He wore a helmet, and all Patrics are blond to me."

"Was he hurt?" That was Julianne, picking at the ground like a child, trying to look as though it mattered not at all.

"He seemed well. I did not kill him, at least. I thought I might die in his arms, which was very wrong." And something else was wrong, too. He was coming at it all askance, but in the end the most sidewise shuffle must bring a man to the place where he must stand. He said, "Marron came to fetch me? I do not remember that."

"You had swooned before he brought you here," Elisande observed neutrally.

"Before then, I think, before he found me. How did he find me?" Jemel didn't believe in the calling power of love; he had heard of too many men and women too who lost themselves in the Sands, searching for those who were lost already. Besides, this was Marron. There was no telling whom he would have called for, or whose calling voice he would have heard.

"He knew, he said. Where you were, where we were. And so he brought you."

Which was all the answer he needed, to all the questions that he needed to ask. Meanings were gifts and gifts could be poison, did they not know that, these girls? He'd no more asked them than he would have asked a djinni, *has Marron taken the Daughter back?*—but they'd told him regardless, and now he had that to deal with as well as another certainty. *He went north to find Sieur Anton. Once he'd found me* . . .

"Give me more *jereth*," he said.

"Oh, no," Lisan objected. "It's my turn, if either of us is to have treats."

"Not a treat, it's needful. You don't know . . ." He would pay for it later, he would overtax his body to the breaking-point, but he had somehow to go north.

"Give it him," came another voice, unexpected and startling, none of theirs.

Briefly they stared at each other, then around the tiny flat landscape of the island where nothing could hide.

Nor was it in hiding, only small and unlikely and hard to see in the bright light and the dense spray from the dashing river. Elisande found it first, but seemed to have lost her tongue with the surprise of its arrival; she simply gestured, and then glowered furiously up at where it hung like a trick of the sun in the wet air, betrayed by water-drops.

It was Julianne who spoke to it; Jemel saw no need for conversation, it had said what they should do and he thought that ought to be enough. But they were Patrics, and they were girls, and so they would be elaborately cautious and take terrible risks and never know it. Even

Elisande, who thought herself so wise in the ways of the desert and its peoples—even she was a child at play among scorpions, when she dabbled with the djinn.

"It is unusual to see you, Djinni Tachur, where you have not been summoned."

"It is impossible to see me, Julianne de Rance, where I do not wish to be seen. But time presses, the river is in flood and cannot be Folded away. Give the boy what he wants; and Lisan, do you be ready to follow as he drinks. It will take you deep, so keep a thought always for your way back."

"You mean—I have done all I can for Jemel, for anyone just now. I have no strength left . . ."

"That is true, but you need none. Enough of healing, he will endure now; but wake the *jereth* to reinforce his spirit, or he will sleep when he must needs be fighting."

"I don't understand. He should sleep, he's exhausted and he's lost more blood than I thought a thrifty Sharai would carry with him. I don't know of any other cure but sleep."

"Not a cure, no—but a crippled man may ride a horse, and so travel far and fast. Wake the *jereth*, Lisan. There is good cause to do it."

"Maybe there is, but I don't know what that means. Find someone else to ride your horse, and let Jemel rest."

"There is no one else. Follow as he drinks, you will know what to do when you see it. It takes only a touch."

"Do it yourself, then," but her reluctance was suddenly unconvincing, stubbornness for the sake of show, no more.

"I cannot touch him, or he dies. You know this."

Yes, she knew—and he had had enough, more than enough of all this talking while Marron ran wild somewhere out of his sight. He snatched the flask from Julianne and upended it into his mouth.

No more than Lisan did he know what the djinni meant; no more than she was he going to ask. But he felt her hand suddenly on his chest, and that was welcome. He felt her spirit, her awareness slide in under his skin, and that was oddly welcome too. She was become a familiar stranger in his body, alien but recognised.

He felt the moment when she met the *jereth* and touched it; he felt the change. Always before it had seemed like a fire contained, sunlight held in glass. Now abruptly it was a fire released, coursing through all his body at once, a spark that became an inferno. He thought his hair should be ablaze, his ragged blood-soaked garment charring as he stared. He thought everything he looked upon should burn.

Lisan made a soft and sudden noise, fell away from him all in a rush.

"What did that *do?*" she demanded, if a shocked whisper can be demanding, which in her it could.

"What did *you* do?" Julianne countered, when it became obvious that neither Jemel nor the djinni thought the question addressed to them.

"I don't know. Touched the *jereth*, as the djinni said. Things look different in there, and it seemed broken, somehow. Unwhole. So I touched it as if it were damaged tissue, to start the healing; and a touch was enough. I don't have a word, for what it did. Or—yes, I do. It un-Folded. Like that, like a bud opening into a flower, as big a change as that. I don't know what the flower is, what it turned into, what it does. What it's doing to Jemel . . ."

What it was doing was just what he needed. What it was burning to generate such heat, how much and how long he would have to pay later: these were questions that concerned him no more than they did the djinni. Flesh was a tool, and he would use it until it was entirely broken. He wondered if this was how Marron felt, sharing his body with the Daughter. In Jemel it could not last, he would burn it off like oil in a lamp and miss it badly when it was gone; to have been gifted this and more, and to have it always within reach, always there to call on—that would be a prize to kill for. Jemel felt not invulnerable but something close to that, powerful beyond measure. For how many generations had his people been making the liquor and trading it for common things, for cloth and gold and spices? All this time, all those long lives wasted, when they could have driven the Patrics into the sea long since, with an army that had drunk of this. They could do it in a day.

But not today. Today there was only him that knew, and the girls who might be guessing; today there was another fight, and there was Marron somewhere in the midst of it. Marron in pursuit of his Sieur Anton, which was a chase that Jemel would very much like to join.

He stood up, swift and sure. Both girls were staring; he thought that one at least might be looking to see the colour of his eyes. *Green and gold*, he thought, and smiled privately: gold for the fire in his bones and green for everything that grew and changed, that included him. One was sweet and the other bitter, and both were strong; mix the two together—in a barrel, in the mouth, in him—and it should be no surprise if they came out the colour of blood. Perhaps his eyes would be red after all, to say so. Perhaps he and Marron could find each other out in the dark, by dint of how their eyes shone crimson.

He and Marron could find each other in the dark anyway, simply by reaching. He meant to keep it that way.

He said, "Esren, take me to where Marron is."

The djinni said, "What you have now, you should not waste. I will take you where I choose."

"That's not what I—"

He felt the djinni's grip close around his chest. He felt himself lifted; he felt so potent and so furious, he thought he might fight with the djinni first before ever he came to the men. He did move his hand towards his scimitar, only to find the belt slack of its weight, the scabbard empty.

Lost in his fighting before, or taken since? Taken by the Patrics or deliberately left behind by Marron, who

wished so fervently that neither one of them need fight?
Any of those might be the truth of it; the reality was that
he was being carried to a war, and he was weaponless.

Not quite weaponless. The bow was gone too, but he
still had a quiver full of arrows over his shoulder; his dag-
gers were gone, but he still had the sheikh's knife tucked
into the back of his belt. He'd meant to keep that for
killing the sheikh; he might need it sooner now.

He might have used it now to unpick the intangible
seams of the djinni's mortal body. He might have done
that out of simple rage, except that he was not born a fool.
Angry men were careless men, and careless men were
dead men in the Sands.

Besides, the djinni was carrying him high above the
river. If it dropped him now, he was a dead man indeed.
Dead and messy in the grass, or dead and lost, dead and
sodden and drowned in the river, meat to feed its marshy
fish . . .

Do not drop me, djinni. But it would not, or it would
not have picked him up; just as he would not kill it while
they flew, or it would not have picked him up. Just as
wherever it was taking him, that mattered, and what he
did there would matter too.

His eyes had always been sharp, but up here he felt
truly eagle-sighted. There was the interlocking pattern of
the walled fields, a bewildering maze even from above;
and the broad river margins were dotted everywhere with
men and horses, living and dead. And with 'ifrit, all living. And then there were the smouldering ruins of yesterday's burning, and the wooded slopes behind the walls,
and the canyons and blind vales that ran up deep into the
mountain ranges, where the people of Surayon had taken
shelter. . . . One man could hunt another for a week in this
country, and never meet him. Jemel would need the djinni,
it seemed that he would need to persuade the djinni; at the
moment, he was persuaded that the djinni needed him.

It allowed him just a minute of that high view, perhaps

to impress on him how lost he would be without its help. Then it swooped low over the grassland, low and fast, picking a weaving route between the knots of fighting men and spirits.

There were 'ifrit everywhere, so black they swallowed sunlight where they did not shrug it off like water. There were men who were organised in opposition, in defence, and men who were not; men who were effective, and men who were not. So far as Jemel could see, they were all dying anyway. Even those not crushed or bleeding to death, not dangling screaming from the jaws of a demon—even those who were strong and determined, still mounted and fighting well with weapons that were fit for the work, Jemel thought that they were white bones walking, only that they hadn't realised or accepted the truth of it yet.

There were too many 'ifrit and too few men, that was all. It was a time to stand off with arrows, strike and run in the Sharai way; but these were not Sharai. Nor Surayonnaise, who were not too proud to learn from other peoples. These were Patrics, mostly Ransomers in black, the army that had come down from the north.

The djinni carried him among the fallen, where the crippled horses in their agony moved him more than the men; it skirted every scattered battle until at last it brought him to the ruins of the field-wall. No wall now, only broken stands of masonry and mounds of fallen rubble. There were still 'ifrit seething out from behind the wreckage, but here at least they had met men who could stand against them. Unhorsed but organised, a troop of Ransomers was holding the line with savage determination.

It was a line of dead horses they were defending, the great chargers of the Patrics hauled bodily into a rampart. It gave them an illusion of shelter, at least. That was pure Patric thinking, they always looked to build and to hold ground. Even now one of their knights was leading a sortie across the horseflesh barricade, seeking to drive back or destroy the 'ifrit between there and the rubble of the fallen wall. He would make his stand, because he knew nothing else to do. He was doing it well enough, to Jemel's inexperienced eye; while he and his companions hacked and danced and set steel edge against chitin—steel and blessed, and the blessing was the sharper edge, cutting clean and deep—others had tumbled over the awkward barricade to heave and drag at yet more corpses, to keep the ground clear and build up what defence they had. If they built it higher in their minds than in reality, so much the better. Patric soldiers found the same comfort in a wall that the Sharai did in a horse and open land to ride it.

There were men astride the rampart with long spears, jabbing and thrusting at the encroaching 'ifrit. One came too far, too eager for blood or else simply pressed forward by its nestmates. That time the spear was driven home with a fierce cry, and sank deep into the creature's head between its bright eyes.

The fire in them faded, that iron-hard body dissolved into smoke and was gone. No exultation in the Ransomer, though; he simply hefted his weapon and stabbed again, towards the next 'ifrit.

It was that discipline, that grim resistance that had held the line. Jemel guessed that it would hold as long as the knight survived who led them. He was the pivot their fate would turn around; his men were strong as a body, but they would be lost without him at their head.

No fine swordwork, no fencing down there among the 'ifrit, no neat defence and sudden thrust. It was more like axework, hew and guard, block and chop. The knight seemed to be everywhere: leading his men in a swarm against a single 'ifrit and delivering the final killer blow himself; letting them fall back while he watched their welfare, while he protected one who was injured all the way to the rampart; rallying the remainder with a cry and urging them on again.

Jemel barely noticed when the djinni's grip loosened from his body. He was aware of stone beneath his feet, but only peripherally; he took a pace forward to see better and found his foot reaching into emptiness, clear air.

Startled, he looked down and discovered himself to be standing on a surviving remnant of the high wall, just where it broke and fell away. He glanced around, and could see no sign of the djinni.

What, was he meant to go down and find a blade, join his rampaging strength to the Ransomers' stubborn discipline? Well, perhaps, but he saw little point in it. One more man could make small difference; it seemed a waste of *jereth* and of himself. Worse, it seemed a betrayal of Marron and of all the oaths he'd sworn.

Still, any fight would be better than none. He sighted the ground below him in readiness to jump—and stilled abruptly, shrank back as black-clad figures came slipping along the wall directly beneath him.

The Ransomers wore black, they wore hoods, and so did these. These were no Ransomers, though. Even looking down, Jemel knew what they were. He knew them by their dress, much like his own but for the colour, and his was dyed darker by all the blood he'd lost to it; he knew them by the way they moved, desert steps even in this lush grassland; he knew them by the curve of their scimitars that no Patric would carry, that no Patric bar Marron could fight with; he didn't need to see their hands and count their fingers.

Neither did he need to understand why they were here. They were Sand Dancers; that was enough. Dancers and 'ifrit belonged together in Jemel's mind, for all that the Dancers were his own people and had sworn their lives to goals that he had long sought himself. They should be sworn to Marron, but Morakh had tried to kill him too. More than enough . . .

He slipped over the wall's side, to climb down secretly; they were alert to the wind's breath on the grasses, they would hear if he jumped. As he went down, he let hands and toes find their own grips on the stone. His eyes were following the Dancers.

Following to where the wall of horses met the fallen wall of stones, in an angle of rubble and blood. Ransomers were there, lifting the bodies of their fallen brothers over; when figures in black robes and hoods came to join them, of course they were greeted as welcome, as relief. How else?

Those men learned their mistake, but did not live to profit by the lesson. The Dancers left them lying, and moved on.

What their purpose was—beyond the simple killing of Patrics, always a priority for Dancers—took Jemel a moment longer than it should have done. He was distracted by a sudden doubt, a question, recognition: one of those men was not a Dancer. He was not even wearing black, only a robe as blood-dark as Jemel's own. Easy to see how it had got so stained, he joined the slaughter with a will; but even from the back, Jemel knew him.

And was sworn to kill him. Suddenly, though, it seemed to matter not at all how the man died, so long as he did die. Jemel would not be jealous.

Why and how the sheikh of the Saren had joined himself with the Sand Dancers—outcasts, by tradition and his own word—were questions to be addressed later, or not at all. He was here, he was among them, he was slaying Patrics; and the Dancers' path was cut directly towards the Ransomer knight.

That man had drawn his sortie back to the rampart; he had taken over one of the long spears himself and was balanced lightly on the heaped corpses, holding the resurgent 'ifrit at bay. Not once did he look behind him, for aid or retreat or for further trouble coming.

Perhaps the djinni had a sense of humour after all. There wasn't only the one man here for whom Jemel felt that shudder of recognition, nor only the one whom he had sworn to kill.

For the moment Jemel left the sheikh's knife tucked firmly into his belt. Lacking any weapon else, he pulled one of the arrows from his quiver. Gripping it halfway along its shaft, he stole up behind the last of the Dancers in their cautious file. His bare feet were noiseless on the trampled grass, he didn't breathe at all; even so, the Dancer began to turn. Wary, prepared, deadly, and just a moment too late: Jemel pounced at the man's first movement. Like a cat's, all his body was fluid and grace in motion. It was a gift of the *jereth*, nothing of his own, but he rejoiced in the sense of perfect balance, the stillness at the heart even as he flung himself through the air.

An arm round the throat, tight, to choke back any cry; legs round the waist to pull his victim off-balance and backwards, so that they fell together and the Dancer's arms flew wide and useless, no chance for him to use his bloodied scimitar.

And as they fell, already Jemel's free hand was using the arrow, thrusting it deep and deeper into the Dancer's eye, all the strength in arm and shoulder to drive it in through the socket to find out the brain, and twisting as it went.

THE MAN MADE no cry, he died as silently as he had killed; Jemel saw none of the other Dancers glance back.

He stooped to pick up the fallen man's scimitar, and hurried after the next in line.

Properly armed, he took less care to be quiet. Perhaps he wanted this one to hear and face him, to fight for life. It was battle, it had always been battle that made his heart sing. If the song were bitter these days, he took that as a sign that he had left his boyhood somewhere in the Sands, or at the Roq, or given it to Marron, who had lost it.

The Dancer did hear, and did twist around to meet his

attack; and the man next ahead checked swiftly at the sounds of steel grating and sliding against steel. With no secrecy left for Jemel, he was determined that there should be none for the Dancers either.

Evenly matched and fighting for his life—like fire and ice, he thought, hot youth and cold experience—he drew a breath and screamed. High and shrill, louder than the knight's hoarse voice yelling directions above and beyond him: loud enough to have every man's head turning that could hear.

The Patrics on the rampart heard, and turned. He had, he thought, just saved the life of Sieur Anton d'Escrivey, or at least given the knight the chance to save it himself. Now he could concentrate, he could focus on keeping his own skin whole and making the Dancer bleed. If he was capable. Even with his body exultantly alive, preternaturally alert and swift, he was beginning to doubt it. This was like fencing with Marron, an impossible struggle against an opponent who knew his every move before he made it, and knew a wicked counter when it came.

He was equal to every one of those counters, though. In other circumstances, Jemel thought they could have fought till sundown, and all night too. But he had no time for swordplay, simply for the vicious beauty of the thing. There were 'ifrit massing behind this horseflesh barricade, more elsewhere; Marron was at large somewhere in the valley, he knew not where or doing what, only that it would be something foolish and dangerous and he wanted desperately to share it; this was a Sand Dancer he was fencing with, and he wanted to see him dead in the grass, a long long way from any sand to dance on.

So he let the curved blade twist in his hand, to turn and catch around the other man's. With the two locked together, he stepped forward and rammed his knee hard into the Dancer's crotch. These men trained all their lives, but they trained with steel; he'd grown up in the Saren caves, fighting with everything bar steel, because a blood-feud would mean deaths that the tribe could not afford.

The Dancer gasped, choked, wrenched his blade free but had no strength to use it; Jemel slashed with his doubled strength, saw the black robe part and the flesh beneath it, saw the blood gush out.

Saw the blood gush and stop, too soon. Saw the man still standing, when he should have been sprawled on the ground, dying or dead already; saw the wide open wound close itself again.

Saw the man smile thinly and step forward, raising his blade like an invitation, *let us fight*.

Something in Jemel nearly broke at that moment. He was close, as close as ever he'd come to running from a challenge. Anything mortal he would fight, and gladly; anything spirit, he would try. But something that dressed itself in mortal flesh, something that bled and yet could stop the bleeding, heal the wound in moments, something that a blade could never kill . . .

He might have used the *jereth*'s gifts to his eternal shame and disgrace, by fleeing faster than a mortal body could; except that his mind was so tumbled over by the shock of it—and all the thoughts that came tumbling after: Marron and the Daughter, Elisande, a black hand whose touch could heal, images that made no picture he could understand—he only stood and gaped.

And might have died so, gaping yet, except that there was a bright flash from above, a flare of reflected light that snagged his eye; and the Dancer slumped abruptly, and fell in a huddle where he stood.

On the horse-wall behind him, a Ransomer jerked his long spear free from between the body's shoulders, and directed the point of it suspiciously towards Jemel.

He backed away, but not from the spear's point; from the body, rather, humiliated by his fear but fearful yet.

"Beware, beware of that," he stammered. "You cannot kill it so easily . . ."

"Can I not? Looks dead enough to me." The spear jabbed and twisted, to make sure. The Dancer's body jerked; Jemel almost squealed, almost scuttled further off.

The Ransomer laughed scornfully, then sobered in a moment with a glance over his shoulder, to where 'ifrit were pressing forward.

"Quickly, boy—why should I not skewer you also? You are Sharai, as he was; and he was killing our men."

"I am not of them," though he had no way to prove it. "We fought, you saw. I cried out to warn you . . ."

"You cried out because you were afraid. That's what I heard, what I saw."

If he could have reached the man, Jemel might have killed him. Instead he stepped back, and no matter what the Ransomer thought about his courage. Once out of the spear's jabbing range, he could look along the curve of the rampart and see what good—what other good, beyond that spear that had saved him—his screaming had wrought.

There were more spears at work on this side of that wet and slippery bank of bodies, and swords too. Once alerted, the Ransomers could outmatch their assailants in sheer numbers; and it seemed that where their blades cut or stabbed, the normal world applied. Jemel saw one man die, and not recover from it. Then another, and that was enough for the rest; they flickered out of sight, reappeared some distance off across the plain, beyond anything but arrow-range, and these Ransomers seemed to have no arrows.

Jemel had arrows, but no bow. He was casting about in hopes of finding one when he remembered, realised, saw what he'd forgotten.

The Saren sheikh might walk and slay with Dancers now, but he was still no Dancer. He couldn't work that trick that took them walking between the worlds, winking in and out of view, here and then not here, not available for killing. He was very solidly there, facing a dozen swords alone.

He should have died then and there, and so stolen another of Jemel's oaths from him; but he cast one glance up at the sky and then turned to run, away across the grass towards the Dancers.

Several of the Ransomers started after him, but found themselves quickly called back. Jemel still had his spearman on watch; he had also just spotted a line of weapons laid out beside a line of dead men. Honour to the fallen, an armoury to him; but first he glanced up at his wary guard and said, "Tell Sieur Anton d'Escrivey that he owes me for a death, and perhaps for a life too, and that I will claim for both when this is over."

Startled, the man stared down at him. "What do you know of Sieur Anton?"

"Enough that I mean to kill him—but not yet. Wish him joy of the 'ifrit, and much honour—and tell him my name is Jemel of the Sharai. Another day we will meet, if God allows it."

And then, without so much as a glance along to see if the knight were watching, he turned and ran in his turn: first to that place of the dead, where he discarded the scimitar and seized a bow instead, and then away on the sheikh's trail, leaping through the grass with great strides. He could have matched Marron's speed, he thought, and his endurance too, so long as the *jereth* lasted; he could match the fleeing sheikh also, but could not catch him. They seemed to be pacing each other with no gain, except that with every step they drew closer to the distant Dancers.

Jemel felt that as a gain. He was grinning savagely as he ran, as he breathed, as he felt the pulse and fire of his blood; he would lay down some bodies on his own account, a line of honour to show the Ransomer knight, Marron, anyone. To show that spearman, if he survived to

see it. Was that a scream of fear, did he think? Well, he
should learn—

AND THEN THERE were distant cries behind him, that
were shock and fear indeed. He wondered if the 'ifrit had
broken through, but did not pause to see; he kept running,
and saw sudden shadows overtake him on the grass.

His eyes were dragged upward in simple startlement.
He saw black shapes against the sky, and remembered
'ifrit in flight; and tried to set an arrow to his bow-string
as he ran, and nearly tripped himself. Stumbled but kept
running; and saw monstrous creatures swoop low ahead
of him, to snatch up the Dancers where they stood.

Not 'ifrit, these were ghûls with wings, slaves to their
spirit overlords. The Dancers didn't try to run, or to resist;
they looked as though they had been waiting for exactly
this.

Another ghûl, lower and closer; this one swooped on
the running sheikh, and took him as an eagle takes a rabbit. Jemel cried out in frustration then and did stop running at last, did nock his arrow to the string; and was
bringing the bow up to aim a desperate shot when he felt
a tremendous blow on his back that should have flattened
him, except that great claws had curled around his body in
that same moment, and so he was lifted up and swept
away.

THERE WERE SEVEN ghûls, and four men: two Dancers,
one sheikh, and Jemel. He could still count at least, despite the bruising strike, the buffeting flight, the shock.

He could look down and see the river, the plain, the
war far below him; that battle already behind him and the
mountains rising ahead. After a little while, he preferred
to look forward. He did not think the ghûl would drop him
now, but it was less reassuring even than the djinni. Be-

sides, it stank, and groaned to itself with every effortful stroke of its wings that sent another blast of foul air down into Jemel's face.

He watched the ghûls, and the men they carried; he saw them suddenly stretch their beating wings wide and soar, rising like vultures on an uplift of air.

His own ghûl did the same, and he felt the change immediately. Flight was smooth and easy now, he wasn't being shaken flesh from bone. And there across the mountains was the margin of the Sands, his own country like a glimpse of blessing . . .

He ought perhaps to call the djinni, try if it would wrestle him from the ghûl and take him back. But his mind was working at last, catching up with his body: seven ghûls, and four men. At first he hadn't thought at all, he'd been as stiff and stupid as a rabbit in an eagle's claws. Then he'd assumed that he was of course a captive, a rabbit in an eagle's claws, being carried off to imprisonment or death.

There was little sense in that, though—he had no value as a prisoner, and why delay his death?—and ghûls were notoriously slow of mind, slower even than he had been, and less likely to catch up. He thought the ghûls had been sent by 'ifrit, their masters, to collect whoever survived among the Dancers and the sheikh. Death defied foresight, they wouldn't know how many. He thought they had seen men in Sharai robes, running from the Patrics; if those big horse-eyes were sharper than they looked, they might have checked for maimed hands, missing fingers.

He thought they had seized him alongside those he chased, mistaking him for just another Dancer; and now were carrying him to wherever the Dancers were being sent. Out of the valley, and into the Sands: he didn't understand it, but no matter.

He had a tight grip yet on the Patric bow, and arrows in his quiver. He knew he could trust the arrows, where the abandoned scimitar had betrayed him. These long glides gave him a chance to aim; the ghûl's tight grip held him steady.

It might of course realise what he was doing, and simply let go. If it did, he would shriek for Esren and see what befell, whether he did. But he thought the ghûl would not open its claws. Dull terror and enforced obedience, the stone in its tongue—he was sure that it had one—would keep it numbly on its course, whatever he did.

He hoped.

He held the bow horizontally against his locked left arm, and drew it to the chin. With his first shot, he thought his strength and eye would be good enough, he'd been shooting from the saddle all his life; he loosed at the nearest of the Dancers and saw his arrow drift wide, far wide and fall uselessly lost to the sand below.

One he could afford; more would come expensive. He worked another carefully out of the quiver and nocked it to the string, puzzled and thinking hard. He'd missed by so much, an unblooded boy could have done better. As an unblooded boy, he had certainly done better from his first day with a bow.

He had stood on towers and on clifftops, and felt winds when the air below was not moving at all. Up here, he thought there must be a wind indeed: wind enough to give the ghûls lift, despite their weight of men. His movement, the Dancer's movement, he had allowed for both—but the air between, that must be moving too, and fiercely.

He drew the bow again and this time made allowance, an estimate—a wild guess in truth, he could do no better—for the wind's strength. And loosed, and saw the arrow fly; and saw it strike, hard home into the belly of the Dancer.

That man screamed and writhed around the shaft; then something seemed to leave him quite abruptly, nothing that Jemel could see, but it was not quite like a death, and the abandoned body slumped in the ghûl's talons.

The ghûl flew on, unheeding.

The other Dancer, the sheikh, both had heard the scream; they stared around, saw the man dangling, saw the arrow.

And could do nothing, they seemed not to have a voice between them to cry to the creatures that bore them, if crying would do any good. Jemel took another arrow, and a careful aim. It was less than a perfect shot; it struck not the Dancer, but the ghûl above. The creature bellowed, and buckled, and fell out of the sky.

Jemel watched it shrink below, and thought he saw it drop the Dancer as it fell. It was possible, he thought, that they would both survive the drop. Not likely, but possible. If so, though, they should still be separated and alone in the Sands, a long way from comfort. No trouble to him, at least.

And then there was the sheikh, and Jemel would not kill that one with an arrow at a distance, though he had countless opportunities as they flew.

THEY FLEW, AND as they went he used his remaining arrows to pick off the other ghûls one by one, till there were only the two left, his and the sheikh's. They paid no attention to their nestmates' sudden falling, slaved as they were to a distant will, a single driving urge. There was a mission here, Jemel thought, and it was the sheikh's now to perform; the ghûls were only beasts for transport.

The Sands were broken up with outcrops, ridges of black rock rising. It was hard to be sure of his ground from this unimagined angle, but he knew their direction from the sun and thought he could recognise what tribal lands lay below. He had travelled those lands once with Jazra and again bare weeks ago, with and without Marron.

Then he saw a landmark that was unmistakable, and he knew exactly where they were and where they were heading, though not why.

*   *   *

THE PILLAR OF Lives rose like a pinnacle above a ridge
of rock. From a distance it might have been a natural finger of stone upthrust, one of the many bizarre formations
that God had set in the desert. Come closer, though, and it
could be seen to be man's work entirely, built of countless
gathered stones into a needle shape, an arch for an eye and
then a high, high tower.

Jemel knew it well, he had climbed it once and left his
own contribution, his own stone at the top.

It was the top of it now that the ghûls brought them to.
Brought them and left them, dropping them heedlessly
onto the uneven surface and then flying on without ever
touching the rock themselves.

Jemel was the swifter to recover, if only barely; he
would just have had the time to fling himself onto the
sheikh's back and sink the man's own dagger into his ribs.

He was curious, though; he wanted to see what the man
did, why they had been brought to this of all places. The
Pillar of Lives was a Sand Dancer creation, one stone for
every Dancer who had ever taken the oaths and forfeited
a finger in signature. It was also the place where Marron
had first learned to control the Daughter, where he and
Jemel had first stepped through the eye into the land of the
djinn.

The sheikh got to his feet, with never a glance towards
Jemel. He walked the few paces to the pillar's centre,
where a few stones rose in a cairn. Topmost of those was
the one that Jemel himself had laid there, one that he had
brought back from the other world and carried up here in
defiance of the Dancer Morakh and everyone else, in defiance of the world it had felt at the time; and it was that
stone that the sheikh reached to lift.

He staggered, under more than the stone's weight; his
face was suddenly flushed and glistening with sweat, and
his breath came in brutal gasps. He lurched towards the
pillar's edge—and stopped, finding Jemel suddenly between him and the drop.

"Take another," Jemel said softly. "You can cast down any stone else, you can dismantle the Pillar entirely and consign every man that helped to build it into hell, for all I care—but not that stone. That's mine, my oath, and it stays here until my word is broken. Put it back."

The sheikh seemed not to understand the words, not actually to hear them; his expression didn't change, until he set down the stone quite carefully at his feet. Then the twisted pain left his features, and they fell into a neutral, assessing stare.

For a moment his eyes seemed entirely black, and Jemel couldn't suppress a shiver.

Then the sheikh drew a scimitar, and Jemel laughed.

"Those don't work," he taunted, "didn't you know? They cut, but it doesn't keep. Besides, you and I, we have a promise to meet. I have your knife, you have mine . . ."

The sheikh responded not at all to that, only moving forward with the wary confidence of a skilled swordsman. Better than skilled today, Jemel thought: inhumanly strong, inexhaustible, as the Dancers were.

As he was himself, today.

But he had no sword to meet and match the sheikh's blade, only a heavy knife that he found ill-balanced and unnatural in his hand. This couldn't be a fight. He tossed the knife in his hand, and then from one hand to the other, testing the weight of it and its balance in flight; then he took the blade between his fingers and cocked his arm, cocked all his body in readiness to throw.

An alert man, a watchful man can dodge a thrown knife, if he sees it thrown. Less easy from this close distance, perhaps, but the sheikh was alert, watchful, would be abnormally fast. Jemel feinted once, twice; the sheikh swayed side to side, never fully committed, eyes never leaving the hand that held the knife.

Then Jemel made his move. One more feint and he threw not the knife but himself: he rolled forward over the cobbles while the sheikh's arms were both stretched out to

the sides, while his scimitar was so far out of line. Rolled
inside the reach of that scimitar and came neatly to his
feet like a tumbler at a fair, with the knife gripped by its
haft now and the blade a bare hand's-span from its
owner's chest.

A bare hand's-span, and then not so much; then nothing at all, less than nothing, buried its own length deep between his ribs.

Jemel thought he would not recover from that. He
twisted the blade in the wound in any case, for satisfaction's sake; and saw more than the life-light die in the
sheikh's eyes. He saw a wisp of black smoke eddy from
his lips and seem to quest a moment before it dissipated
into the heat of the desert day.

JEMEL THREW THE body over the edge after he had
stripped it of anything valuable, silver rings and orna-
ments, a buckle of gold. Then he restored his rock to its
place on the cairn's height and stood staring at it for a
while, wondering what was its importance here; remembering how Esren would not come near any rock fetched
to this world from the other, for fear of being trapped
again as it had been in the Dead Waters.

When he was tired of puzzling over that, he gazed west
and southerly, feeling the *jereth*'s edge begin to fade now,
so that his sight was little better than it ever was. That was
very good, though, and this was a high spot, and the desert
air was clear; he would see someone coming from a distance, from a great distance off. Whether it was a figure
running or a figure flying by a djinni's courtesy, he would
see it against the sand or against the sky, so long as he was
looking. So he would look, and so he did, and gave not a
thought to leaving this place, to seeking water or shelter
as any man of sense would have done. He looked for
someone to come, and when he was tired of straining his

eyes to see a dot that was not there, he turned back to his stone again and looked at that, and the puzzle of it.

⛸   ⛸   ⛸

JEMEL HAD DROPPED the flask after he had drained it. Julianne picked it up after he had left.

A last sticky dribble was pooled in the bottom. Julianne was curious but reluctant; Elisande insisted; the flask was at last uptilted, and the residue dripped out onto Julianne's waiting tongue. One precious, cherished moment to linger over the taste of it in her mouth, and she swallowed.

Elisande was there, at her side and somehow inside her also, both at once. She felt her like a sprite, a spirit of mischief: wicked but not malign, alien but welcome, tender and sharp and surprising.

Then Elisande touched the *jereth* to life inside her, such a tiny drop of it there was, and it was like touching fire to the finest tissue, a flame that overswept everything at a gasp, except that it left no harm where it had passed. Rather it lingered, consuming only what was drab or weak or tired in her. She felt unexpectedly well, and better than well; she felt bright and clear, as sparkling and as strong as the water in the river: fresh from a mountain spring, deep and full of character, understanding the darkness and breaking into light.

She felt Elisande slip outside her skin again, and could almost have gone with her, simply for the fascination of the thing. She thought she could see how it was done now, she thought she could do it herself at need. Another time, though: for now she had her own whole body to explore. She felt as though she'd barely been here before, as though she'd lived all her life in purdah and was suddenly free of the harem and all a busy city lay before her.

She became aware that Elisande was looking at her a little doubtfully, a little quizzically; she laughed, and found it unexpectedly hard to stop laughing.

"I'm sorry," she said. "This is . . . a revelation."

Elisande shook her head. "And all this time we've just been using it as a drink. Think how much we've wasted . . . But no one ever told us. Can we use that as excuse?"

"Sweetheart, I don't believe that anyone knew. Even the Sharai who brewed it. Jemel was—startled, wouldn't you say?"

"Mmm. Jemel had a flaskful. If it's done this to you, what in the world has it done to him?"

"And where's he gone, and what's he doing with it? I thought that djinni of yours had taught you not to ask questions. There's no point in them—or no point in putting them to me. I can't give you answers."

"Are you sure? Have a look, see if you can't spot him. He went north, and he's chasing after Marron."

The suggestion was absurd. However much the valley was laid open around them, however much the war was displayed in smudgy smoke and distant figures, it would be impossible to tell individuals at this distance. Hard enough, almost impossible to say that those to the north there were Ransomers, hard beset by 'ifrit . . .

Except that it wasn't impossible at all, now that she looked more carefully. Those were clearly Ransomers, the dress was unmistakable, and the way they fought. She could see that as clearly as she could see Sieur Anton, filthy with blood and work, standing high on a mound of dead horses and exhorting his troops to another greater effort, she could almost hear his voice . . .

It wasn't possible, and yet she was certain. She could see what forms the 'ifrit had taken, where they had been evil shadow-shapes before, blurred and unreadable; she could see how the men had built themselves a crude defencework of slaughtered horseflesh, which Sieur Anton bestrode with the artful balance of a natural sailor; she could see every separate man fighting for his life or his brothers' lives as they sought to keep the 'ifrit penned in.

She wondered why the spirit-creatures didn't break out further down the wall, where there were no men to oppose them; and even as she wondered, she saw the wall bulge and fall at half a dozen sites at once, and a horde come forth.

Julianne gasped at the size of that army, so many, enough to swamp all the defenders she could see. Those Ransomers must be lost, surely—unless the hard work of last night could pay off even at this late hour, this desperate time. There was a movement, a line of darker blue amid the blue smoke-haze horizon to the east; it broke through and rolled in across the plain, like a ripple of shadow sliding across the still surface of a pond. Behind it came another such ripple, and then another.

Julianne stretched her new acuity of sight to another degree of impossibility. Beside her, Elisande didn't need such clarity of vision.

"It's the tribes, Julianne. The tribes are riding." And then, a moment later, "Can you see him?"

It was Jemel she was supposed to be looking for, and she didn't misunderstand her friend for an instant; the question was *can you see Marron?*

And when she answered, "Yes," she knew that she would be equally understood. She didn't need to add *of course, Hasan is leading, where else would he be?*

"That's good," but it wasn't, plainly it wasn't. Elisande wanted to be Jemel, invigorated and away to search for the boy they both loved. She'd had to give the best gift she had to her utmost rival; she'd had to give the last least trace of it to her friend, who would of course misuse it in searching for the wrong man entirely. The wrong men: Julianne turned and gazed southerly, searched all the southern slopes of the valley from riverspout to marshbeds, as far as she could see in every direction, far up into the trees beyond the palace, and still could not find her Imber. Jemel had suggested that he might be far to the west, beyond where the valley bent; she tried to bore her sight through the elbow of ancient rock, but even these new eyes would not oblige her there.

Even so, "This is like standing on your grandfather's terrace," she murmured. "I can see whatever I want to see. How did you know?"

"Because everyone gets what they want, except me." Then Elisande laughed at herself, and the laugh was as bitter as her words had been. "No, but I could feel it flower inside you like it did in Jemel. So he can pretend to be Marron for as long as ever it lasts, and you—you can stand back and watch, and understand it all."

"Is that what you think I do?"

"I know it's what you're best at. It's what your father trained you for."

It was true. She should have been a woman high at court, scheming and manipulating behind a curtain of modesty and obedience, dancing men to her father's tune. Because it was true didn't give it any sweeter a taste. "So what would the *jereth* have given to you, Elisande?"

"What, if I didn't have to give it all to others? I don't know, my love. Not the thing I wanted, that's for sure. Not any of the things I want, my country safe and my father living and . . ."

A wave of her hand implied a whole list. She didn't name Marron; again, she didn't need to.

"It might have given you what you most want on this island."

"What," ruefully, "Marron back, and free of the Daughter? I don't think so, Julianne."

"No, I meant an understanding why we're here, why the djinni left us here."

"Something to do, you mean—it's you who always wants to understand it. And haven't we answered that anyway, wasn't I here to heal Jemel and wake the *jereth* in him, so that he could go and do whatever heroic thing he's doing?"

Julianne had seen him suddenly, thought she had,

snared in the claws of a flying ghûl: not so heroic, more doomed to die.

She didn't mention it to Elisande. She might have been mistaken, after all; she might have been deceived. Instead, "I don't think so. That you could have done anywhere, Marron would have sought you out wherever. I think this place has a purpose, and so do we."

"To sit and watch, most likely, while everything happens all around us. It's very good to watch from, you said so yourself, like Grandfer's terrace; and now you've got the eyes to see with. You'd better tell me everything."

Elisande could see most of it for herself, but Julianne was happy to oblige. It gave her the excuse she needed to stare and stare, to watch her man at work, at war.

One of her men, at least. There was still no sign that she could see of Imber.

THE GREAT WAVES of tribesmen had broken up rapidly, even before they met the 'ifrit, as soon as they had seen them. Those who had raided horses yesterday were faster anyway than those still on camelback, and so outpaced them with something like excuse; but there was nothing about the Sharai that could make them fight in regiments. It was like watching surf rise and shatter against a rocky shore, she thought: all that power, all that waste and loss.

Small groups and clusters of dark-robed men swirled around darker streams, 'ifrit like stains against the green. Even the hottest heads among the Sharai had the sense to stand off at first, to let their bowmen shoot; even Julianne couldn't see the arrows strike and fail, strike and fall. She could see the momentary dismay among the riders, though, the way they checked their mounts, glanced from side to side, watched each other watching them. She didn't need to see the necessary sequel: the spears and scimitars lifted and the voices lifted higher, the mounts urged forward against their terror and the tribes' charge against demonseed, against all good sense or understanding.

It was courage flung down like a banner underfoot to ride across, a bridge into disaster; it was an idiot made of honour. They rode in screaming, and she thought she could hear their screams on the breeze, so much passion, so much fury. They learned quickly that there were other ways to scream, and other causes for it.

The trouble was, of course, that the Sharai travelled with no tame imams. Never mind all Hasan's warnings and wisdom of last night, never mind their own experience of spirits in the Sands; they had precious few weapons that were blessed, and no one able to work that minor miracle for them.

They might as well have thrown stones from a distance and charged with willow-wands for sword and spear. No matter how well-aimed the arrow, unless it struck an eye it would glance off uselessly, and they must needs be close to shoot so well from horseback. By the time they got that close, any man of the Sharai wanted his scimitar in his hand; arrows were for hunting, not for war.

So they wasted their arrows from too far off, and then they charged; and few of them came close enough even to batter at impervious shells with blades that had no cutting edge for this. They rode into a hedge of claws and jaws, of piercing and tearing, of death dressed in a dozen sharp arrays.

The lucky were shamed by their horsemanship, or by their camels' training; their mounts bolted before they came in reach of the 'ifrit, and they were carried a long way towards humiliating safety by animals that simply could not be ridden back.

Hasan, of course, was not lucky, not so lucky as to be safe. Of course he had a horse; and of course the sheer ferocity of his will was enough to drive it through its fear. Followed by his own small knot of Beni Rus, who would blood their mounts with their own blades if need be, Hasan led the tribes against the 'ifrit invaders.

"He knows that he must," Julianne whispered. "They would charge, with or without him; they would never follow him again, if he did not lead them now. So of course he must . . ."

So of course he did, knowing that many behind him would die in this charge, and knowing that he himself was better equipped to live; his blade had been blessed, long since. He had slain 'ifrit before, and ought to have had little cause to fear. Julianne feared for him, though, very greatly.

"Strike and run, that's how the Sharai fight; and if he only would . . . But he's forgotten all he ever knew, or else he's just too stubborn to live. See, his blade cuts, but one blow won't kill the creature, a monster like that, it needs hacking to pieces; and the man who rides at his back and strikes after him, useless, he might as well be a poppet with a sword of wood and silvering. And Hasan knows that; he's already turned and gone back, see, but his horse is so slow, he's having to fight it all the way; and the man's dead or he will be, there's no point in going back. But he will, he'll go back and back, and he can't guard himself forever. He was so sick only yesterday and he hasn't had any *jereth*, or if he had you weren't there to magic it for him . . ."

And she could hear the near-accusation in her own voice—*why weren't you there to magic it for him, why here for Jemel and not there, or why didn't you do it last night in the palace when there was all the* jereth *in the world and all the time too and you could have made a demigod of him, so strong, he could have led the world . . .?*—and tried to choke the words back before she said them, too late to stop the feelings from showing through; and when Elisande said her name, "Julianne," in a dry dead voice she thought her friend only meant to quarrel with her, nothing more than that, a distraction from watching her husband die and another way to pass a dreadful time.

But she turned in any case, if only to demonstrate how utterly she was not going to quarrel; and Elisande pointed without words and without dramatics, just the gesture, nothing more.

Away to the south, from beyond the elbow where the valley turned, a party of Patrics was riding. They were approaching the river at an angle that would bring them to the bank almost opposite the girls on their island. They had scouts and outriders, they were military in their formation but certainly not Ransomers, nothing uniform in their dress and little sign of discipline in their riding; and they came at a pace that was too slow for soldiers with any real purpose in mind, somehow solemn and distraught both at once.

Among them, led by a man on foot with his head respectfully hooded, was a horse that might have seemed riderless on any other day, to other eyes than these. Or it might have seemed simply burdened, carrying a sack of grain or a side of beef, perhaps, wrapped against the dust of its journey.

Wrapped and knotted tightly with a rope, tied firmly to the saddle of the horse; but it was too fine a horse to bear such burdens, gleaming white in the hazy light.

Elisande had recognised the horse. So too did Julianne. The two of them had spent a hot afternoon riding beside it, riding in disgrace and towards retribution, towards a marriage long ago.

Julianne, the Baroness von und zu Karlheim choked, and wheeled round; but that way there was nothing she could do but watch her other husband die, watch him give himself to death again and again, knowing that the gift would not be spurned forever. Besides, she was a married woman, twice-married and both to soldiers; she would not disgrace either the one who was somehow still miraculously living, nor the other. She should be embarrassed to have her friend see her turn to find a living man, when his comrades were bringing her the dead.

All unwittingly bringing him to her, she was sure, they could not know that she was here; nor would they have chosen to fetch him to her, if they did. More likely they were looking for help and hoped to find it, some way to cross the river.

If they could see what had befallen the Ransomers, they would not be so eager. But they were coming, all innocence, they were bringing her Imber to her as Marron had brought his Jemel to Elisande. This time there was no help, no hope, neither one of them could give breath to the dead; if they could, they could not cross the river to achieve it.

That was suddenly somehow the worst of it, the greatest outrage: that fate or freak chance was bringing her boy dead to that bank there, bare yards away, and she was here and could not cross the water to receive him.

She cried out to Esren, to carry her across; the djinni did not come. Elisande tried, sharp and demanding, still with no response.

"Elisande, you have powers that I do not, that I don't even understand. Can you not—oh, build a bridge, raise the river-bed, still the waters into ice, something?" *Surely something, or why else are you here?*

"No, my love, none of those. I'm sorry." She didn't sound sorry, only distracted; and went on, "Julianne, Esren lied to me. No matter how it squirms this time, it did lie when it made that oath. It swore to come to my calling; it has not. But the djinn cannot lie, that's—that's inherent, fundamental, sewn into the fabric of the world . . ."

"Then the fabric of the world has a snag in it. But Esren was desperate, when it made the oath. And mad, I think. Perhaps it still is mad. And it had been cut off from, what does it say, the world-web for so long—"

"Weft, the spirit-weft."

"—Yes, that. It says it's crippled, it still can't see the

future as other djinn do. Perhaps it couldn't foresee that it would break that oath." Though it had seemed to guess well enough in other matters, when it wanted to. She thought the simpler explanation was the truth, that it had simply lied. And if in that, in how much else, how often?

"Something else it said," Elisande murmured, in a tone of wonder. "Something else, that wasn't true either . . ."

"Well, what? And what of it?"

"Never mind for now, love. Don't make me say it, I don't want to listen to myself or I'll never believe it. Just let me think, let me work . . ."

THERE WAS WAR on the north bank, that much she could see. Thanks to the *jereth*, she could see very clearly, and she didn't want to. Every time she looked, every time she risked a peep she thought she'd find herself a widow entire, not the demi-widow that she was now. On the south bank, no war that she could find; only a funeral procession and an army in disarray, *they have lost my man, and they don't know what to do without him.*

It was true, or it seemed to be. Some little distance behind the advance party that bore the body, a whole parade came trailing into view: all men, all mounted, with a great variety of weapons, it was undoubtedly an army but it seemed entirely purposeless, a snake without a head. It needed an enemy to fight and a leader to command it. Lacking both, it seemed spiritless also, exhausted by its loss. And by whatever battle had brought him down: many of those men were freshly wounded and ill-patched up, and there were empty saddles as well as other bodies. They all looked weary, and wary also, though it was the grass they watched as they rode over it, rather than the horizon where an enemy might lurk.

Julianne wanted to cry out to them, to warn them to beware of walls and water. She was quite pleased, quite relieved to find that she could still care that much; though it was a distant, detached sort of caring, nothing at all like the passion that was driving Elisande as she stamped about the island building little cairns of stone and gleaning tinder.

Julianne had passions of her own, but they were not rooted like her friend's. Perhaps she lacked depth, foundation. Perhaps that was why she could love two men at once. She might have proved fickle and loved neither one of them for long; some people might be grateful that they died before she could shame them. She might be grateful herself, in years to come. Not now. Now she saw her Imber's slack cortège, and could not bear it; she turned around, and saw a miracle.

Just for a moment she saw a hint, a glimmer of gold in the air and beneath the grass, as though an image of the djinn's world had been overlaid on this one. She saw a great shadow moving to obscure the gold, a mass of black that brought her nothing but despair; she thought it was another army of the 'ifrit, coming out of that world into this.

Then the gold was gone, not so much in an instant as in a succession of instants, like a line of bubbles bursting one after another; and there indeed was a host in black, but not 'ifrit. They were mounted Ransomers, and Marshal Fulke was at their head. On his saddle-bow was a great candle of twisted wax in black and white spirals, echoed by the spiral of the smoke that twisted up from the wicks of it.

The marshal stood in his stirrups, gazed about him, started calling orders back along the column of his army. Troops broke away as he directed them, charging towards the greatest concentrations of 'ifrit—which brought them also inevitably through the greatest concentrations of the Sharai.

Julianne saw black sweep past midnight blue without a pause, apparently without a glance; she also saw the opposite, she saw black and midnight blue together in swift conversation.

The first time she saw a Ransomer spread his arms wide to encompass all the Sharai within his hearing, lift up his head and voice—that was the first time today that she wondered if she were simply dreaming all of this, all the day's disasters. Easier to believe that than this, that out of all of Outremer there was a man to be found in Ransomer dress who would call down blessings on the blades of the Sharai.

And yet there was, and more than one. She could see it happen again and again; she could see Marshal Fulke himself, still erect in his stirrups, pronouncing a general blessing on all in the field and all the weapons they bore, if only they fought 'ifrit.

She stood in a valley where sorcery was mundane, quotidian; she had seen miracles worked by holy men, and by conjurors, and by faith alone; she could not believe in these blessings. How could a Sharai give credence to the word of a Ransomer? And if they doubted even as much as she doubted, then how could the blessing possibly give an edge to their weapons?

And yet visibly, incontrovertibly it did. Those few Sharai archers with any arrows left tested them suspiciously, and saw their shafts strike 'ifrit chitin and sink in to the fletching. That was good enough. One more time the tribes attacked, in the eye-bewildering patterns of ride and counter-ride that could so baffle an enemy he might die without ever understanding which direction the blow would be coming from.

The 'ifrit seemed not to be baffled, but they died in any case. Blessed blades bit deep, to hew off threatening claws or simply thrust through the carapace to seek whatever lay inside, in lieu of heart and lights and liver. Julianne thought that was where death lay buried, and swords or spears freed it; she always had thought so, and no priest nor warrior, philosopher nor poet had ever managed to dissuade her. Babies sometimes brought it out with them; her own mother had died that way, and Marron's too.

She saw the 'ifrit driven back through the breaches they had made in the enclosing wall. She saw men follow and fell anxious again, thinking that they would lose themselves in there where the 'ifrit would not, and so the tide of the battle could turn again.

But there were men of the Sharai, unmounted men running and climbing up onto the tops of the walls, to be both guards and guides. How they knew to do that, she couldn't tell: whether someone had warned them, or whether they had learned a humiliating lesson for themselves. Imber had learned it, but that was knowledge wasted . . .

Sharai and Ransomers both rode into the maze in pursuit of the 'ifrit, often side by side; Hasan, of course, was among the first to do so, to ride out of her sight and so give her imagination time to feed her fear.

She turned south again, to confront what was no fear at all, because who could be afraid of the truth? The cortège was closer now, and the men seemed more like farmers than warriors, scanning their fields for rabbit-sign or insects. Except that no farmer had ever been so frightened even of a plague of rabbits, a locust-swarm. Something lurked, something was expected . . .

Something erupted from the ground around them like a thousand massive serpents. Their mounts reared and plunged; a few trained warhorses lashed out with their forefeet, but no one it seemed had thought to bless them or the plates they were shod with. Where they struck, even razor-sharp steel had no effect, though the same blow would have ripped a man's leg open and shattered the bone within.

The men reacted wearily, hacking down from the saddle, hewing at the creatures as they rose. The horses were dragged down, one by one; most of the men jumped free, though some were too slow, falling with their beasts and being either crushed or snared amid the writhing demon-snakes.

Those who could made a stand in twos and threes, back to back and using their blades like scythes, cutting swathes through the encircling creatures. Like farmers again, Julianne thought, surrounded by some wicked living crop that was tearing itself free from the soil, discovering mouths and teeth . . .

For as far as she could see, all that army was under attack: fighting, screaming, dying. She wanted to stand witness to every man there and his individual death. One scream, though, gripped her ice-hard, froze her gaze. One scream among many, and just a horse that screamed; she had a care for horses, but not overriding her care for men. It was only that she saw which horse was screaming.

Imber's horse, that carried Imber's body: it leaped and kicked, but there were snake-things swarming over its quarters now, binding its legs and fastening great sucker-jaws onto its flesh. The burden it carried was flung madly from side to side, straining the ropes that held it. At last it slipped and hung mockingly, revoltingly half-free for a moment before another sprawling lurch from the horse shook it loose altogether.

It fell to ground, into the midst of the gaping horror; now it was Julianne's turn to scream.

That caught Elisande's attention, and more than hers. There was a soft glow in the air suddenly, between herself and Imber's wrapped corpse, right on the river-bank there and still a fair way from the fighting. It was her father, coming as he so often had throughout her childhood, quite without warning when she needed him the most.

Coming not quite far enough, offering her something short of what she wanted.

"Father, fetch me over to that bank! I have to . . ." She couldn't say it quite, her throat was too full of sobbing, but that alone should be enough. She never wept in public, and he knew it.

"You have to do what?" He spoke as softly as ever; she heard him more clearly even than usual, despite the roar of the water between them and all the sounds of battle behind.

"Imber's horse," she said, with a desperate gesture, "he's dead, and it fell . . ."

"And what will you do, about either?"

She stood already in winter's hand; those few words were colder by a distance, more bitter to receive. "I am his *wife . . .!*"

"Perhaps. He would have said so, at any rate, and that is good enough. But even so, Julianne. Man or horse, a body is a body; concern yourself with the living first."

"They will *eat* him. . . !"

Shockingly, if shortly, her father laughed. "No, sweet heart. They will not eat him. You can find him later, if you live. Far more useful now to help Elisande, and try to ensure that you do."

"Help Elisande . . .?" She gazed around, feeling almost stupid with grief and despair. Elisande was striking fire from a flint; looking past her, Julianne saw the Princip standing on the further bank, as her father was on this. It came to her that this was no accident, these men too had come to help Elisande.

"Elisande? What can I do?"

"Well, you can stand in the wind's eye for me, till I get this sodden stuff alight," in the familiar growl that could always uplift her heart. "Wet grass, wet air, how's a girl to make a fire . . .?"

Julianne wasn't clear quite why she wanted to make a fire, but knew better than to ask. There were mysteries abounding here; these close folk would give her less than a djinni, she suspected, nothing for her questions and a payment to be demanded anyway. Better to make a virtue of not wanting to know, of being a married woman quite unsteeped in magic.

Or, indeed, a wind-break. Elisande could draw light

from the air at need, but she still needed flint and tinder to conjure a true flame. Julianne crouched down with her back to the river's spray and pulled threads from the inner hems of her robe, winning a frail smile and, "That's a desert habit, it's why the Sharai wear rags. Have you been in the Sands, lady?"

"Once or twice. I met my husband there . . ." *One of my husbands, the one who has the advantage now, if living is an advantage in a world where men die when you love them.*

"Well, never mind, my love. One has to meet them somewhere." Her eyes held a different message, compassionate, distracted. It was her fingers that truly mattered, teasing those threads into cloudy puffs of fibre and looping them around her feathered twigs before she went to work again with flint and steel.

This time her sparks settled and caught in the fluffy stuff: a glow, a hesitant twine of smoke, a bold but tiny flame within the shield of her cupped hands. They held their breaths together; at the first faint snap of green fibres parting, they both exhaled together, both turning their heads away from that precious flame to do it.

And caught each other's eye, and giggled together as if nobody's heart were breaking, and then fed the infant fire with shreds and shavings like two maiden aunts determined to see a precious child grow fat.

"Why do we—you—need a fire?" That question that she wasn't going to ask: it just slipped out while her guard was down, while they were just two girls together and all their attention was focused on not losing this tentative little flame.

"I need a source, a power I can work with. Grandfer used the river, but I'm not so good with cold and wet. He always did say I had a desert soul."

"Is that why you went to live with the Sharai?"

"Not really, no. I loved it, but he'd have sent me anyway. Ruthless, like your father. They use us, any way they choose . . . How much pain can you stand, Julianne?"

An infinitude . . . "As much as you can load upon me."

"Truly?"

"Truly. That and more." *See me standing?*

"Good. Because I have made this fire, whole and strong"—it didn't look strong to Julianne, it looked shy and reluctant; but this was ritual, there was almost a chant to the way that she was speaking—"and now it has to be divided, and you must do that work. It must be carried to all the cardinal points"—north and south where the old men waited, east and west where the river ran: her hand gestured to the little cairns that she had built—"and set to burn there with a memory of what it was before, a single point of light. I can teach it to remember, but not do that and carry."

"How shall I carry the fire, Elisande?"

"In your hands."

Of course in her hands, in her cupped hands. They had no firepot, no shovel; and how could it hurt else?

"It'll go out."

"No. I can keep it now; you only have to hold it. I won't let it feed on you, but it will hurt."

She nodded. Heat did hurt. Many pretty things hurt, she thought, if you came too close, but some you had to cradle.

"Be ready now, let me just speak to it a minute . . ."

And Elisande did speak to the fire, though Julianne didn't know the language; she thought it brightened, whitened, stiffened under just the impact of her voice.

"Now, Julianne. Scoop your hands right underneath, don't let it scatter . . ."

It didn't want to scatter now, despite its being made so scanty. It felt light but solid between her palms, like a ball of glass.

Light and solid and hot, like a ball of glass newly blown. Anywhere else, any time else she would just have dropped what she carried, before her skin could blister. Here, now she set her teeth and tightened her grip and followed Elisande.

Who seemed to her to walk deliberately slowly, but perhaps that was ritual again, pacing to her own blood's beat; or else it simply helped to keep her mind in focus. Julianne could focus too. All she had to do was lift her head and see where men were fighting for their lives, where her man had done that thing and lost, and lay neglected. That was a burning focus, and a sharper pain. Let her flesh blister and scar; she'd wear it as a reminder, every time she reached or touched or gripped a thing, that once she'd been twice married and had lost the first and sweeter, lost her boy . . .

What she felt here was pain, pure and meaningless; that in itself was a strengthening, a gift. She could do this, she could carry a thing that was too hot to carry; which being true, she could also certainly bear a thing that was too heavy and too hard to bear. Or else turn it around, look out across the river, look in vain for Imber's body; and she could do that, she could endure the loss of him twice over. Which being so, she could undoubtedly endure this simple and uncomplicated pain, she could carry this fire for Elisande who so much needed her to do it.

SHE COULD, SHE did. To the first cairn, and let a segment of the bulb-fire fall away between her fingers when Elisande sang to it; wait and watch while it spread out across the little heap of stone and flourished there, burning rock and air.

And so on to the second, thinking that she could smell her palms begin to cook.

To the third, and she thought her bones were steel, and glowing, and shining through her skin. She thought her joints were locked and solid, she couldn't drop the fire now if she had chosen to, she'd have claws for hands forever.

To the fourth, and she couldn't see the river's banks now, couldn't hear the water. Elisande had to guide her, a hand on her rigid arm to push her forward, a tug to stop. Her greedy body had seized her, wrapped her in itself and in its agony, so that she could barely remember her husbands' names and not think at all about them. That part of her which was grateful for this was very small indeed, and very deeply buried.

She had to trust that fire flowed across that last cairn; she could not see, could not stand to look. She twisted in a hobbled dance, too racked to be still, too breathless to scream. All she could think was to throw herself into the river, if only she could find it. Distantly, though, she felt someone grip her wrists; faintly she heard a voice, "All done now, sweet, all over, trust me now . . ."

And there was a cooling somehow within her burning bones, a soothing from the inside out; and then a wordless whisper in her head, a voiceless song that eased her dizzy mind, calmed her breathing, laid her down in damp sweet grass—

—AND WOULD HAVE sung her to sleep in another moment, except that she understood it just a precious moment too soon for Elisande, just in time for her. She forced her eyes to open and stared up into her friend's, bare inches away and just where she had thought to find them; said, "Don't do that, Elisande. I don't want to sleep, I want to see."

"Nothing to see, precious, nothing that matters. They just need salves now, but not till they've been cleaned and it's too soon for that, even if we had the necessaries. Let them rest, don't look . . ."

"Not my hands," she said, with terrible patience. "I can't feel my hands." *I can't feel anything*—but that was a lie, even though she didn't say it. She only wanted it to be true. "I want to see what you're doing; and I want to see what happens." North and south, to her Imber and her Hasan and all men else, and Elisande's precious Surayon also.

"Unh. All right, then, sit up and be good. And still don't look at your hands, keep them in your sleeves. Promise? Or I'll knot them there . . ."

She made the promise carelessly, literally not caring. What need beauty, after today?

Elisande helped her into a sitting position, with a bare stub of rock to lean against.

"Comfortable?"

"I'll keep. Time won't. Don't waste what's most valuable."

Elisande shook her head. "I had to break a while, to let myself calm down. Nothing's more calming than a little gentle healing."

Nothing was more exhausting by the look of her, vast eyes in a bloodless face, a tremble in her fingers where they still touched and fussed over Julianne. She was in no condition to make a major working—but there was no one else to do it, and so she would. Julianne had a great respect for Elisande's endurance. She kept going where men and lesser mortals fell and failed. Imber had fallen, Hasan might fail yet; perhaps only Fulke would be triumphant. And still she thought that Elisande would endure. Outcast and homeless, what was indomitable in her would sustain the rest; and if nothing else, she would have Julianne for company. Widow and orphan, together they could chase a myth of rest over all the world, and never pine to catch it . . .

If, if, if. Even the djinn could not see that future, there was too much death in it. For now, Julianne was helpless. She settled herself more comfortably against her rock, cradled her hands unfelt, unseen within the long charred sleeves of her robe, and set herself to watch.

*   *   *

THE FOUR CAIRNS were flaring brightly, beacons of white unnatural flame. Elisande walked over to the first, on the northern bank; she thrust her hands deep into the light—Julianne gasped, but why should Elisande spare herself, who had not stinted to use her friend?—and drew it out in strands and cables, ropes of shine that flexed and flowed and seemed to live between her fingers.

She gathered them all into a hank between her hands, and flung them high and far.

For a moment they hung in the air, and Julianne feared that they might fall back, that all her friend's strength might prove not to be enough; or else that the wind would catch and scatter them, they'd fall into the water and be dragged to loss.

Those weaves, those plaits and cords of light hung and twisted, turning contrary to the wind, seeming to quest rather than drift. Then they stretched themselves across the river in a high arc, sprung and vibrant like bent sword-blades, steel under tension. White-hot steel was what they looked like, and Julianne knew how that felt in the hand, but the Princip lifted both his big hands and caught hold of those intangible cables as they came to him. And knelt, and plunged them into the earth; and they held there, binding bank to bank with a fiery and impassable bridge.

Elisande left it so and turned to the south, to Julianne's own father. As she went by, Julianne glanced at her friend's hands. No hint of burning, not so much as a reddening in the skin. It had been live fire in her own, a natural and wild thing; now she supposed it was something other, cool to the touch, fit to be gripped and spun and not to burn. Which would be why Julianne had had to carry it, she supposed, because Elisande needed nimble fingers for this as well as a dreadful concentration.

The same dabbling of those fingers in the fierce light, the same strands drawn out, flung up with the same force; they found the King's Shadow ready to receive them. Now the island was poised at the centre of a double arch,

like the grip of a recurved bow such as they used in
Marasson; like a strung bow, it seemed almost to vibrate
with possibilities.

Elisande went to the west and there, when she had
woven her glittering cables, she flung them high and far
again; only that this time there was no waiting hand to
catch them. Only the river's rush, and Julianne had been
afraid of that.

No need. Again the ribbons and streamers of light stiffened and arched and plunged down. This time they wove
themselves into the water's turbulence, so that Julianne
could see bright threads amid the spume and the darker
currents, running down and down and out of sight. She
turned her head to follow when Elisande went easterly,
and saw the lights flow upstream with the same ease, the
same high disregard.

It felt then as though the island were no longer fixed to
the river's bed, but hung rather from these white wires,
quivering with a quick anticipation. The river's noise
couldn't actually be quieter, but she had to strain to hear
it.

A snag of movement in the corner of her eye drew her
attention to the southern bank. Her father had sword in
hand now, and he was battling with a sudden rush of those
black serpents. As he killed them they faded, like 'ifrit;
but there were so many of them, and they came on and on,
and how many could one man kill before they over-
whelmed him . . .?

It was a little while before she realised that he had been
expecting this, waiting for it: that he was defending not
his own life, but Elisande's working. The Princip was
doing the same on the northern bank. No question that his
opponents were 'ifrit, and several of them. Great scuttling
creatures with burning eyes and pincers snapping at his
sword-arm, they were trying to avoid the blade but trying
more crucially to pass him by, to reach those cords of
light.

Julianne turned back to Elisande, willing her to hurry, or there would be two more great names among the dead of the day. Whatever she was doing, it was pivotal; the 'ifrit betrayed themselves with this sudden assault. The battle on the north bank might be as good as won—thanks to Marshal Fulke, and she hoped, she did hope to have the chance to force herself to thank him—but that on the southern bank was equally well lost, she thought. Give the 'ifrit a foothold in Outremer, and men would never prise them from it.

Something surged in the water, that was not itself water nor rock; she glimpsed a body, long and sleek and black where the light danced against it. *Hurry, Elisande . . .*

Elisande threw her head up, stretched her arms out, turned slowly full circle. All her arcs and cairns, her threads and skeins of light pulsed gently, throwing strange patterns of glare across her skin. She drew both arms up, moving like a dancer to some heavy, stately music that Julianne could not hear; her hands came together in a silent clap that would not disrupt the music, and the world changed.

Julianne's body shook in response to a thunder that had no sound, only impact. It felt as portentous as an earthquake, except that the ground did not shake, just her . . .

NO, NOT JUST her. Elisande looked more than shaken. Not dancing now: terrified, rather, terrified and helpless. Like a child who has done something terrible and crucial, and is only now feeling the weight of it. She stood still, hand to mouth, staring all around her; Julianne was looking only at her, and was none the less aware that a power beyond measure had seized the valley at her friend's asking, remade it . . .

Had Folded it, in fact: folded and refolded it like a map refolded to hide something crucial in the crease, and she and Elisande were there in the fold of it, they could see the world as it was and the world as it appeared to be also, without themselves being anywhere within it.

Julianne ran to her friend; the two girls held tight to each other, and Elisande whispered, "Did I, did I do that . . .?"

"I don't think so, no. I think someone, something else did that, through you. Who do you think you are, girl, the God's own self, to go making or unmaking His needle-work?" It didn't matter what she said now, it was only words, and Elisande wasn't truly listening.

Julianne wasn't truly speaking either, not speaking her heart. Her heart she thought was in her eyes, just as her friend's was: bewildered, scared, not daring to be triumphant.

THEY COULDN'T STARE forever at each other, learning this new world only through flickers of reflection. They had to turn, to look, to see. At least they could turn together, arms still tightly bound around each other's bodies; that was something to cling to against the impact of the moment, that they still each had someone to cling to.

They could look east or west and still see the river where it ran. They could see all the visible course of it and guess the rest, from lost sources high in the dim purple shadows of the mountains to its far flat mingling with the sea. Directly north and south of them, there were the high and stony banks that contained its fierce rushing; beneath their feet was the island, and Elisande's magic could shift that no more than the urgent water could, not one finger's width along the bottom.

And yet, and yet: they could look out and see another world spread like a tapestry over this one, if tapestry could ever be so real, threads and stitchings confused with rock and sun and water.

They could see wide grassland north and south, and no river to divide it; they could see armies north and south, and no river to divide them either. Elisande had Folded the river entirely out of the valley.

More than water parted around the island now, and ran seamlessly together again. It seemed as though the valley did the same, so that where they stood was a loop knotted out of a thread, still a part of the whole but separated from it. They could stand and watch, but from here they could not touch; all that was left them now was witness.

North and south, two men were fighting for their lives. They needn't protect the spellcasting any longer—the girls still stood in a matrix of light, like spiders at the heart of a burning web, but those threads had pulled two hems of land together, and the stitching was hidden from the world around—and the Princip and the King's Shadow were fighting on the same ground suddenly, where there had been a river to divide them.

Neither man was fool enough to fight alone, where he could stand back-to-back with a companion. It was Julianne's father who moved, who leaped away from a rage of serpents when the Princip cried, "To me, Coren, to me!"

A few long strides should have brought him to the river; they brought him first to the boundary of Elisande's Folding, where he had stood himself to catch and hold the light. Julianne couldn't tell what he saw there, but it delayed him not at all. He bounded across that line, and for a moment she didn't know where he was. He seemed to be briefly in neither the one world nor the other, before he came from nowhere to land cat-footed on the northern bank.

Nothing so unusual in that. He was the King's Shadow and he worked the trick repeatedly, stepping in and out of nothing. But he was her father, and he was old and tired and hurt; there was blood on his clothes and his skin, and none of it had come from what he fought. He might have gone all Shadowy and walked away from this at any time, and had not for Surayon's sake, for the Kingdom's, perhaps for the world's.

At least the two old men could help each other now. King's Shadow and Princip of Surayon, old comrades and old friends: they stood shoulder to shoulder and pressed forward, stubborn determination a good substitute for the strength and speed of the young men they used to be. The 'ifrit seemed to have lost their frantic purpose, now that they could no longer reach the Folding. They fought only because they were being fought, or because that was what they did, or Julianne thought so. And they died also because that was what the 'ifrit did when her father fought them, when the Princip did.

She took the time for one anxious glance back, the other side of that impossible line where the Fold made a tuck to stretch one world tight across the looseness of another. The serpent-beasts clustered there were making no attempt to cross it. Stared and twisted balefully, rather, as though they yearned to cross but could not.

There were 'ifrit in the river still, trapped in the Fold with only two girls to oppose them; she could see them when the broad stillness of their backs broke the roiling of the water. If they rose, they could destroy this Folding in a moment. She and Elisande could not resist them with a bare pair of knives between two, and she could not say where the world might go then, only that it would follow a different and a darker path.

Elisande had seen them too, of course. "Why don't they attack," she asked against the silence, almost petulantly, "why didn't they attack before we did this? They must have known it would happen, and it would work against them when it did, so why didn't they try to stop us?"

"They did not and they do not because I am here, and they dare not."

It was a thin voice, a cold voice for all that it came

from the heart of the fire; and it had a body of sorts, there was a fiery spirit rising . . .

"Esren."

"Indeed."

The djinni it was, learning it seemed from Julianne's captivity and reversing the 'ifrits' own trick, keeping them at bay by its simple presence here.

Quickly Elisande said, "I wasn't asking you." Julianne thought that was ungenerous. If the djinni had truly kept them safe, and so perhaps saved Surayon, she thought Elisande should begrudge it nothing: service, freedom, whatever it might desire. And disguise the gift as carelessness, a heedless question demanding a price, why not? For herself she had less cause to be grateful, she was uncertain what, if anything, had been saved for her.

But the djinni said, "Do I need your permission to speak?" and there was a silence that was almost palpable, a shock of stillness that could have changed the world again.

"No—but that was a question, djinni, and I have answered it."

"Nothing matters," the djinni said, "further than this. Here, at this point, now. Stand and look, Lisan of the Dead Waters, and see what you have done."

She had pulled living water out of the valley, unpicked it from the tapestry, joined two battlefields into one. Beyond where her grandfather and his old friend were fighting, there were riders coming: men driving frenzied horses past the edge of terror or exhaustion, men whose mounts would carry them now into the mouth of hell, would chase death till they caught it.

Men, Ransomers, who chanted prayers as they rode; Marshal Fulke led them with his hood thrown back and his pale cropped head like a summoning in the sunlight, like a beacon, bright against black robes.

They chanted prayers against evil, and they rode down the 'ifrit and hewed from the saddle as the creatures tried to flee, too late and surely knowing so. Fulke's own blade bit deep through chitin and into whatever served as heart or life's blood to a spirit in a mortal frame. Then, as the 'ifrit's body dissipated into dust, he turned his horse towards the Princip.

His voice was still murmuring, prayers to the god who had condemned this old man and all his land for heresy. His sword was in his hand, and his face was grim. Elisande gasped; Julianne wanted to scream. Specifically, she wanted to scream at her father. *Don't let him, you're the King's Shadow, he has to listen to you. Stand in the way, if nothing else, push that stupid stubborn old man behind you . . .* Elisande had seen her father die, in one brutal moment; now her grandfather stood in the same danger and under her eye again. If necessary, Julianne would push that stupid stubborn girl behind her, not to let her see; but she wasn't sure, she didn't know Fulke's mind, she couldn't read him.

Fulke kicked his horse forward, the King's Shadow stood like a shadow and did no more than the Princip, did nothing at all.

It was a slow ride, though, not a slaying speed. One man might kill another slowly, but not on a battlefield. Fulke came up to stand his horse beside, above the Princip. How did he know him? Not by description, surely, when he hadn't been known or sighted outside Surayon for thirty years. Not by his dress of battered leather and chain, any old soldier with a life's supply of stories could boast as much; not by his noble bearing and haughty demeanour, for he had none.

However it was, Fulke did know the Princip. And did and must still want to see him dead, that was given, it was required between those two men in this world. But the world was fractured, and darkness spilled in through the cracks; Fulke did no more, no worse than to speak.

"There are demons abroad in this country."

"There are." With a look that seemed somehow entirely

level, although he was gazing up; with an unambiguous directness that made no compromise and allowed no doubt, that included both the 'ifrit and the Ransomers.

"Then let us be about them."

With no more than that, Fulke rode his horse hard at the boundary, disappearing entirely for that instant as he passed through the Fold. He recovered himself and his horse and began to slash at the serpent-things that swarmed about him, even before his men had ridden through to join him. Watching him as he fought, though, Julianne still thought that salvation might be an impossible stretch. Wherever she looked, men were fighting; but wherever she looked there seemed to be not enough of them, never quite enough. Fulke's army might win in the north there, with the Sharai to help; but Fulke himself had left them, and had taken too many men with him and yet not enough to win the south, and it was a law of history that a force divided was a force betrayed. Surayon needed more, and she couldn't see any hope of finding it in all the wide valley, until she saw movement in the shadows of the hills. She thought that must be more 'ifrit, she thought they were endless, innumerable, doomed to win. She knew that simple counting decided most battles, heroes seldom had a chance.

But the shadow, the shadows, the long lines of shadow resolved themselves into people in the sunlight, a steady stream flowing down from the mountains and breaking out across the plain; and for a moment she didn't understand who they were. She had seen the Ransomers, the army from Ascariel, the Sharai; she had seen Sieur Anton and Marshal Fulke, her husband Hasan, she had seen the end of her husband Imber; who else was there who could come to battle willingly, leading such numbers?

Elisande's trembling tension, her expressive silence gave her an answer, or part of an answer. All day she had watched other people fighting over her homeland, and she had done what she could to help; now it was her own people she was watching, and there was nothing more that she could do. These were the Surayonnaise who had been fighting Ransomers and Sharai just yesterday; also the Surayonnaise who had been fighting no one, who had retreated to their holdfast in the hills. Someone had gone to fetch them, had blessed their weapons and brought them out for this last throw . . .

Someone who Julianne could see quite clearly: someone tall and brightly blond who made her heart ache for her lost man as he rode to and fro, as he marshalled his unlikely troops and led them forward against serpent-beasts and worse.

And she watched him despite the pain of it, unless it was because of the pain, because all she could do for Imber now was hurt. She watched him as the slow time passed, as more men died and women too, but the serpent-beasts fell before them. She watched him and watched him and could not have said, could never later say when it was that her mind understood what she was seeing.

It was later and a lot later before she understood what else it meant, that his beloved cousin Karel was dead in his place, dead on Imber's own horse. What she knew now, all she knew now was that Imber was not dead after all, that she was not a widow in either side of her life.

She watched with more shivering intensity even than Elisande at her side, suddenly desperately fearful that he would die now under her eye. Not even the sudden recognition that Sherett was there too, leading a small regiment of women, not even that could distract her for longer than it took to be amazed, to stare, to turn back. When he was at bay, when his reckless youth and determined ferocity had led him too far forward of his followers, when she had to look away she'd look for Hasan to the north, and see him too fighting, killing, surviving while men and monsters died all around him; and when she'd had her dreadful fill of that she'd turn again to see how Imber lived and

killed, and how he rallied these who were not his people
in this that was not his land.

And she would love him, as she loved Hasan who was
moulding all the tribes into an army even as she watched,
who was making one people of the Sharai, and she knew
what he would want to do with them and loved him none
the less.

But they were two men, and each of them loved her
and would not, could not brook the other. More than a
river ran between them. They were hot with slaying, fierce
in victory; she could see nothing else now, but she saw
them perfectly. And had her own touch of djinnish foresight, as she saw them meeting on this field of battle, with
the last of the 'ifrit slain between them. Each with a blade
in his hand, each determined to claim her and to allow no
claim else . . .

She waited until it was clear that they would destroy
what last 'ifrit remained, that the Sharai and the Ransomers and the Surayonnaise between them all would win
this day if not the next. And then, as the two men her husbands came closer and closer, she pulled herself away
from Elisande and ran from one cairn to the next, and
kicked them down. She scattered light and magic, let it
lose itself in nothingness, brought the river back into the
world so that the valley truly had two sides again, and she
had a man in each.

The End of All Roads

THIS IS THE *Dir'al Shahan in Ascariel, that was their greatest temple when the Ekhed governed the city. It would have been destroyed when the God gave us victory there; but the King decreed otherwise, and took it for his own. Now it is his palace, and the seat of his power.*

MORE THAN THAT: it was his home, his shelter and his symbol. For many people—for the lucky ones, those who had seen it, those who had walked the streets of the golden city on its golden hill—it was what they saw when they thought of the King, because they had no other image for him.

It was not the building set highest on the hill, nor was it the tallest, nor the most grand in decoration. Once, yes, once all three, but that was long ago. Now it was only the oldest, and that only by default, by destruction of what had come before. It stood on a broad platform of stone to-

wards the summit and was made to look small by the size
of that platform, which might have contained three, four
such buildings and still have left room for an army to
march between them. There stood a temple complex ded-
icated to a god forgotten before the Catari came, before
the Sharai found the Sands, before the Ekhed rode north
to rule until the Patrics drove them out. Legend said that
the djinn had removed the temples overnight and left the
platform bare; the imams said that too, or else they said
that a tremendous storm had levelled walls and buildings,
had ground the rubble to dust and swept it all away. In either case, they said it was at the will and instigation of
their god, who had decreed a temple to his worship to be
built there in its stead.

And so it was: high shielding walls of stone about a
central court, with domes and minarets to rise above the
blank faces of the walls, to be tiled and gilded to gleam in
sun and starlight to declare God's glory in this holiest of
cities.

THAT WAS THE Dir'al Shahan as it was made, as it was
meant to be. Years passed, decades, centuries. There was
a palace built that stood higher on the hill, whose garden
wall enclosed the peak itself, as though the Ekhed could
possess the Mount and all it stood for; there were temples
built whose towers rose higher, as high as their architects
had dared to dream. Still the Dir'al Shahan was the glistening jewel, the Eye of God, the utmost point of the cre-
ated world; when people spoke of Ascariel—as they did,
everywhere in the world, in terms of hope and longing—
it was the Dir'al Shahan that they meant, even where they
did not name it.

And then the Patrics came from their homelands far
away to claim the city, to seize it with steel and pay its
price in cruelty and death. They displaced the Ekhed,
slaughtered the imams and their congregations, filled the

temple courts with bodies and washed the stone facings with their blood.

After the horrors of that time, once the bodies were limed in their pits and the stains and stinks of death were scrubbed away, the man who had led the Patrics took the lands he had won for his Kingdom, the Dir'al Shahan for his own.

In all the years since then, he had not been seen outside the silence of its walls. In forty years the gilding had peeled and tiles had slipped, rain and sun had done their work to dull what had been glorious. Desecrated by its occupation, shabby by neglect, it had become a monument to absence, of god or King depending. Still and nevertheless the Dir'al Shahan was what people meant when they spoke of Ascariel. They might come on pilgrimage, they might pray in all the holy places, they might fast and scourge themselves in the new-built temples to their own true god; it was the Dir'al Shahan that filled their dreams before they came and their eyes after, their thoughts always. Some, many thought more about the King than about the God. Even those who came and looked and went away disappointed because it did not glitter in the sunshine so brightly as it did in their imagination, even those who would rather see the building razed than restored— they all found that the one thing had turned into another thing, that they could not see those walls and domes and minarets without thinking about the man who sat within, whose reach extended as far as he could throw his Shadow, and that was far indeed.

IN FORTY YEARS, the King had not come out. Neither in forty years had any gone in to him, except his servants and his Shadow at his call.

Now there was a party going in, and not by invitation. The Shadow was there, and the Princip of Surayon, come to visit his old friend all unexpected. The Shadow's daughter and the Princip's granddaughter, they were there. The two sons-in-law of the Shadow, they had come this far but declined to go that little step further, through the doorway of the Dir'al Shahan. Imber would not cross the threshold of his King without a direct summons; he was sure that his wife ought not to do so either, he feared for her dreadfully and had told her so, but could not find in himself the authority to forbid her. Hasan looked at the high gate and the higher wall and could not see any palace for any King. What he saw was a great temple overrun by unbelievers and deliberately corrupted, rank in its ruin. What had been sacred could not be made secular, only profaned. He would not step through that gateway while any temporal power sat beyond, be it Patric or Catari or the Ekhed returned. Nor would he have stepped through it while the imams held sway, because their god might be his god also but their worship was not. He disliked buildings, distrusted walls; like the Ransomers, he would burn the Dir'al Shahan sooner than he would pray there.

Like Hasan, the Ransomers looked at the palace and saw the temple; they felt the sacrilege of it like a chill in their bones in the sunlight. Not a stone of it, not a timber nor a scrap of plasterwork should have been let stand. None the less, there was a Ransomer going in. Bad enough to bring heretics and sworn enemies within the walls of the city; he could not countenance letting them within the walls of the palace unwatched, unguarded, armed. Marshal Fulke would risk whatever wickedness the bones of the building still sustained, to guard his King against whatever wickedness the Princip and the girl might yet have planned.

He felt soiled in his triumph, he felt the God soiled in His, that it should be followed by this capitulation of honour. His only comfort—small and bare that it was, cold comfort—lay in the absence of the heretic and traitor, the apostate boy who had once worn Ransomer black. That boy was still an element in this story, camp-fire rumour placed him here, there, all over; Fulke would not be content until he had placed him squarely in a fire's heart and seen him burn. Had he been found at any point from Surayon to here, Fulke would have burned him regardless of truce, safe-conduct or King's command. The King himself, in his person, could not save that boy. Fulke held vengeance in his heart like a treasure, but he was glad not to have spent it yet. Let the Ransomers find the boy quietly, privately; let them deal with him in their own way, within their own strong walls. No public eye, no glare of argument, only the traitor and the men he betrayed and the God to witness.

Ransomers and Sharai and Surayonnaise had made uncomfortable companions on the slow march south, and they were uncomfortable companions still; there had been no bonding along the way. All the separate peoples held themselves apart, as they had fought in the valley, as they had buried their dead. The bulk of their armies they had left in the valley, camped north and south of the river, east and west of the plain, where each could see which other broke the truce. Only these few, these watchful wary few had come to Ascariel, and the Sharai, the Surayonnaise emphatically wished that they had not.

Fewer still were going further, in through the gate of the Dir'al Shahan. Those few were meeting now, solitary walkers coming together in the shadow of the wall. The King's Shadow, who knew this place of old; the Princip of Surayon who had known it also but long ago, at the Conclave that had given him his country; the two girls, and Fulke whom they did not trust. None other. There should have been one other, the girls thought, one at least, but Marron was not here. Marron, they supposed, was with Jemel; and the two boys together—together with the Daughter, which was a different thing, a greater and a worse—they might be anywhere. They hadn't been sighted since the battle. At least no one had found their bodies, but that was small reassurance, when they had a whole other world to lose themselves in and no one to fetch a message home.

The girls might have been angry with the boys, if they weren't so worried. They might have been more worried still, if they weren't so nervous. The King was a mystery, he lived in closer seclusion than the strictest religious; and yet they meant to walk in on him unannounced . . .

As far as they knew, they were unannounced. He could hardly be unaware that they had come; his Shadow might have warned him days ago, that they were coming. Julianne's father was maintaining a magnificent discretion, saying nothing at all of any consequence. What that meant, even Julianne couldn't guess. Perhaps he knew that they'd be welcome within; perhaps he knew that the gates would not be opened, the walls could not be climbed.

Perhaps he knew nothing and had simply travelled in hope and with no expectations, as they had.

FIVE FIGURES, BUT they had walked two and two and one across the wide open stretches of the pavement, coming from different directions under a white sky and a sun of burnished copper: the old men, the girls, the Ransomer. That was how they stood before the gate, grouped but not together, not one group and not at all with one intent.

"Do we knock?" Elisande asked, deliberately savage, fiercely unfunny.

"No," Coren said. "We wait. When the King is ready, he admits us."

"If he will," from Julianne, the most doubtful, the least determined.

"He will," and that was her father and her friend, speaking together but still not with one intent. He meant that he was sure of his ground, of his master; she that she was sure of her own purpose and the strength of it to carry her through to where she meant to be, face to face with the man she'd come to see, whether he chose to have it so or not.

"How long does he usually make you wait?"

"Julianne, I don't usually go in by the gate." He said it with that long-suffering tone universal among fathers. She flushed, and was suddenly glad of Elisande's heat to distract notice from her own.

"You could take us in, then, couldn't you? Of course you could . . ."

". . . But of course I won't. Quite so. I'll stand with you at his gate, for as long as you choose to linger; I won't help you break into his privity."

"I could summon my djinni, have it carry us through."

"You could summon it, yes. Would it come?"

"I don't know," in a sullen mutter.

"No. Well, why not try a little quiet patience? I've never known the King be wilfully discourteous—"

"—Unless you want to count forty years of silence," which came from the Princip, unexpectedly taking his granddaughter's part against his friend's, "which has always seemed discourteous to me." *Specifically to me* was how he meant it, meaning that the King's voice raised on his behalf could have eased a generation of pain and fear.

"Was I so silent?"

"On Surayon, yes. And were you so very much him?"

"If the King chose not to speak of Surayon," Fulke hissed, as though even the full use of his voice in this company was too much taint, came too close to a contact he could not bear, "might it not be because speaking was so unnecessary, because his subjects could see for themselves what was rancid, and smell for themselves what was corrupt?"

"When the Church Fathers could see it and smell it all the way from the homelands, you mean, and so sent you to burn it out?"

"But this is his Kingdom," Coren said swiftly, his voice just strong enough to stand between them, "and not yours, nor theirs, nor mine. The King makes his own choices—which is why all of us"—though his glance at Fulke corrected that, *most of us*—"are here, to ask questions to which he if any man should have the answers. Otherwise we must ask the djinn, and that might prove unfruitful."

DESPITE THE DOUBTS, despite the bickering, they did not in truth remain long at the gates of the Dir'al Shahan.

Slowly and soundlessly, those high gates drew back. Nothing mystical or potent in it: there were men at either leaf to open them. The men were gowned and hooded in pale yellow. Elisande was not the only one who tried to peer beneath the hanging hoods to see what manner of man it was that wore them; she was perhaps the only one who let her attempts be obvious, and also her frustration when she failed.

As slow and as silent as the hinges of the great gates, another man came to lead them across the court beyond. He seemed to be a man, at least, as the others did. They might be slaves, they might be devotees; they might be lords of the Kingdom giving secret service in some undeclared bond of brotherhood. They might equally well be men of clay, animated by magic.

HAD IT STILL been a place of faith and worship, the Dir'al Shahan must have been the most striking, the most overwhelming of man's work on the earth. Within its walls it was a complex in itself, and all its complexity was a wonder that spoke more and more loudly to the glory of God. There were stairs and archways, lesser temples and rising platforms, all of a golden stone with veins that glittered under the sun; all leading the eye onward and upward to the grand consummation that it sought, the great domed temple with its spiring minarets, needle-fine and sky-piercing. If there were another such dome in the world, none there had seen or heard speak of it.

And the King sat there, or so rumour said and his Shadow had never denied it: *crouched like a toad beneath a stone* some said, or *poised like a spider at its web's heart, waiting* or simply *still as a rock, purposeless, stretching an overlong life still longer, and to what end?*

To this end, perhaps, the end that they had all pursued this far: to answer the questions of his own generation and another. The Princip's country was in ruins, many of his people were dead and the survivors were dreadfully exposed; he trusted the Ransomers' truce precisely as far as he trusted Fulke. And he believed in causes. The 'ifrit had invaded his little land, which was unheard of; they had let the Ransomers in first, and the Sharai had been there to take advantage, and he did not believe that any of this was coincidence. His son also was dead amongst his people, and he had come to ask for explanations. The Princip had all the claims of an old comrade, of a history shared, of hurts taken and gifts received; his granddaughter and her friend had the claims of youth and vulnerability, the rights of the world to come, fresh candles lit from dying flames.

So they broached the King's privity, his sanctity, his dome. His servant led them not to the great closed door but to a long arch, almost a tunnel at one side. In the blackness of its shadow, they found another door; this one stood open, and there were lights beyond.

The servant gestured them through. The King's Shadow was first, and would have entered then but that the Princip delayed him.

"No, wait, Coren. I would see this man's face, before we go further."

"Does his face matter? He serves the King; what more do you need?"

"I saw—" He was not sure what he had seen, but he thought it might have been the faintest gleam of red in the darkness beneath the hood. At any rate, "I should like to see his face."

"Well." Coren raised no further objection, only seemed genuinely bemused. "If he is content to show it to you, I am quite content that you should see it. If the King objects, no doubt he will let us know." He turned to the man and said, "Of your courtesy, sir? Would you lift back your hood?"

The man said nothing, but his hands did what the Shadow asked.

The girls gasped, and so did Marshal Fulke; it was he who said the name.

"*Blaise . . . ?*"

His eyes were dully red, which made the girls draw back, press closer to each other.

"Blaise," the man repeated. "I served you once, when I was Blaise," spoken slowly, as if the truth of this were buried deep, drowned deep in memory's well, "and called you Magister."

"You did. Nor did I release you from my service."

"I was released. I served you, too," the man who had been Blaise went on, turning to Julianne, "and called you my lady."

"You were my sergeant," she murmured, willing him to remember it. "At Roq de Rançon, and on the way there. Do you remember?"

"I remember Roq de Rançon. I served the God there once, till my brothers drove me out. Now I serve the King. Will you go in to him?"

Julianne might not have been the only one there who hoped that his current service was happier than those he had known before. That could almost seem to matter more than how his eyes were red, or why, or how it was that the King came to have such a man as servant.

But then the King's Shadow strode through the brief darkness and into light, and the others followed him; and now for a while they could forget Blaise entirely if they chose to, as they had chosen before.

THIS PLACE HAD been holy to the Patrics since their god had blessed it, choosing this of all the places of the earth to set his foot when he walked as a man. It had been holy to the Catari long before that as the seed of all creation, the first place their god had made and the source of all the rest. Before them there had been others, other faiths—as witness the pavement where this temple stood, wide monument to a forgotten worship—and each had known something different about the Mount of Ascariel, but each had known it holy.

The Patrics who owned it now, who claimed possession of all the Sanctuary Land, maintained that possession by strength of stone as much as strength of arms; they had built massively up and down the land, castles and walls and fortifications. Their architects understood power and endurance and resistance, none better. It took the Catari before them to build for beauty; and here at least, that beauty had been let live.

Fulke would not have had it so. Fulke saw heresy in every curving line, in every gilded word he could not read. He had been offered tutors, but he would not learn the tongue: "We have the language given us by the God; what would I need of another?" In his heart, he had been afraid. There were those who said that to understand all was to believe all; here especially, in this cradle of faith where men could run mad from a simple excess of belief, he feared to find it true. Serving a God Divided—and serving as he had, as inquisitor and judge—he knew the dangers of a divided soul. Better to be ignorant and safe . . .

Now, in this dim and smoky lamplight, he gazed around him, he gazed up and up and was afraid again. He could not understand the messages on the walls, but he could read beauty, he could feel its influence. More subtle perhaps than a sword, but no less powerful in time: and the King had spent years and decades here, had chosen to make his home amid the strictures of a forbidden faith, and the King could surely read them. Like Fulke, he had been a monk before ever he was a warrior; report said that he had been damnably curious even as a novice, always reading, reading, asking questions and reading more. Fulke didn't believe that any man could live among so much beauty and not be swayed.

To Julianne the beauty was a tangible thing, as solid as the tiles of the floor beneath her feet, as fixed as the colours in those tiles, as calculated as the patterns in which the tiles were laid. Men had made this, and her soul rejoiced at their skill. She supposed that they had been devout, inspired; it seemed not to matter any more. There was no worship here now, no habitation for their god or any. Rather it was a man who lived here, and she didn't understand why he would want to, how he could bear to clothe himself in such a wonder or to hold himself alone beneath its majesty.

The Shadow had as many questions as the others, or more perhaps: a lifetime of questions dammed up behind a stubborn determination not to ask, never to ask.

THE DOME ROSE above them, or closed down around them, like a sky at a human scale. Its horizon was glazed in that midnight blue that the Sharai claimed for their own colour: a gift of their god, a sign of his favour and their service. The height of it was lost in a night deeper than any that the Sharai might know, the black of shadow far beyond the touch of lamps. This was a place removed from daylight, with its high doors locked and its walls, its dome unpierced.

There were pillars in a wide slow circle within the wider circle of the walls. There were lamps and braziers everywhere, the air was full of smoke and shifting shadows, a constant tugging at the corner of the eye; there were men like Blaise who moved silently over the dense rugs underfoot, who caught the eye more solidly but were still gone before they had been properly seen; there was no doubt, there was never any doubt where in all this blurring beauty they must go to find the King.

To the centre, of course: to the point of balance, to the focus of the eye, to the heart of what had been so long hidden.

HERE AT THE hub—where it was not at all hard to believe that this was stillness and all the world else spun around it—there was a raised platform, a dais. Once, surely, there must have been an altar here. Now there was an ancient chest of black wood, bound with iron.

On the chest, a man was sitting.

His face was on no coins, neither drawn nor described in any text. Against history's silence, legend had painted him unnaturally tall, which he was not; unnaturally broad of shoulder, which he was not; unnaturally strong and handsome, startlingly clear of eye and voice and skin, and he was none of these. Other legends, Catari legends had him hideous, brutal, deformed by the weights of his own cruelty. They were no more true than the Patric hagiographies. Where the man was not known but his decisions were, where the power of his word abided in the absence of his voice, it was hard to be utterly certain that he was not at least a hand's span higher than his subjects and a little too wide to pass through a normal doorway, one part giant and one part witch, sparks in his eyes and sparks in the tips of his fingers.

There might in fact have been the glimmer of stars shifting deep within the shadow of his eyes, but no greater sign than that. He sat before them like an old man, quite nondescript; there might have been a dozen such men at market in any town on any day, and they might have been peasant or lord if they all dressed as plainly as he did. Not one of them would have stood out among the crowd. This one could hardly stand out from himself, so modest he seemed. And yet, and yet: the girls and Fulke knew him as immediately, as coldly, as certainly as the one man who had known him long ago, the other who had known him then and since. Granted that no other man could have been sitting just here at the centre, the point, the purpose of the world—even so, this one man wore his kingship like a crown.

They all felt the urge to kneel, but none of them yielded to it. Even the Shadow, who knelt to the Emperor of Marasson without an apparent thought: even he stood stern and upright before his own master. His daughter was mildly surprised at it, but they had been friends first; perhaps they were friends still. Or perhaps he was more angry than he let show.

Elisande was less angry than she had claimed to be, more nervous than she would ever admit. A lifetime victim of the legend, now that she was face to face with the King, she found herself entirely robbed of speech. She had intended to be brusque, demanding, uncharitable; instead she was silent like a child, gawping like an idiot.

It was the Princip who spoke at last, and his voice was more tentative than a robust man's ought to be, as though he were feeling his way through the dark towards a long-forgotten doorway.

"Well. It is you, then."

"Indeed. It has always been me."

"Mmm. I did wonder, sometimes."

"Did I give you cause?"

"No, but I wondered anyway. This seems—unlikely," with a gesture round about, "this eggshell. You always loved the world too much to be a monk for long."

"And still do. I am not a prisoner here. Nor a monk," smiling at him gently, "whatever my reputation." Julianne remembered her father saying that it had been the Princip in a former incarnation who had rousted the young man out of his monastery and away from his books, to teach him life and war. It had perhaps not taken too much rousting, to judge by that smile. "I do go out into the Kingdom, in other guise than this."

"Do you? Aye, then, so do I. Or did, while I had a son to guard my borders for me." It was a bleak truth, bleakly said; its reminder of a life lost drew him back from memories of a life long gone. "You know why we're here. How many of my questions are you going to answer?"

"As many as you care to ask. Or dare to. Remember that questions have consequences, and nothing is more dangerous than knowledge."

"I have never forgotten. Even so, I have questions. I risked the journey here to ask them of you; I will risk the answers." He was torn, manifestly torn; friendships are built on familiar deceits, and he feared to break a long, long-lost friendship on the rocks of truth. But his son was dead, his land in peril; either of those must weigh heavier in the balance than a love that had gathered dust for a generation, and the two together were insuperable.

Still he was torn, he did hesitate; and so he was forestalled by someone much younger and much less careful, someone whose heart and mind could match each other in their anger and distress.

"There can be no risk attached to truth. Truth is the best weapon that we have against heresy, and I am not afraid to seek it; the God will watch over me even here in the hall of his enemies."

"I am no enemy to your god, or any."

"You say that, and yet you live, you *live* in this place where the air is still poisoned with Catari incense, where every wall is covered with their foul verses, where every breath and glance corrupt. You say that, and yet you welcome *him*"—a gesture towards the Princip as he would give neither name nor title to one so rank, although they had fought the same enemy a week ago and travelled together since—"as a friend and a subject although his every thought is blasphemous, although he led his people in rebellion against you and against the God . . ."

"Not so," the Princip said, quite mildly. "I never rebelled against the Kingdom. The other states rose up against me, with fire and sword—as you have done since, Marshal Fulke, slaughtering the innocent in the name of your sweet god. I closed my borders to protect me and mine, as any prince would do under such an assault. I was a loyal subject to the King then, and I am still."

"You closed your borders with damned magic!"

"If you choose to call it that. I say with knowledge. And we have gone on learning since; and it is as well for you, for the Kingdom, for all of us that we did so, or the 'ifrit would rule in Surayon by now."

"Can we be so sure that they do not? I hear that they can inhabit men and possess their will. If they failed in their invasion by force, why should they not invade by subtlety? That land is fit for it, where no one serves the true God truly. I saw them in Roq de Rançon, and thought they were demons there; I see no reason to change that opinion, and where better should demons find a home than in the Folded Land?"

"Folded no longer, alas; prey now to every fanatic who sees evil in doubt and wickedness in curiosity. But how did you see them at the Roq? I had not heard that they were active there, except for that one that Julianne drew through into the hermit's cave . . ."

Of course he had not heard, who would not speak to Ransomers on all the long ride here. Fulke said briefly, "I saw them issue forth from the sealed tower. They did not stay; how could they, in a stronghold of prayer and purity? They went to seek a more suitable home and found it in Surayon, until we destroyed them."

"From the Tower of the King's Daughter?" The Princip's eyes turned to the man who had named it so. "When

Rudel tried to lead his party out that way, he found it closed against him."

"Indeed," the King said. "Closed by the 'ifrit, who must have known that he was coming and preferred to keep the Daughter in this world, and out of Surayon. They wanted it for their own man, for the Sand Dancer Morakh."

"He was not theirs at the time, surely?"

"What does time mean, to an 'ifrit or any spirit?" the Shadow asked. "Dangerous or otherwise, some answers are simply too elusive to be gripped; that one I have been chasing for forty years, and not come near. If they knew they would want the Daughter, they would act to keep it close and bring it closer."

"How could they close the Tower, though?" Elisande demanded, finding her voice at last. "I was there, we both were, Julianne and I. It was hard even to get in, harder than it should have been; and then when my—when, when Rudel tried to take us through to the land of the djinn, there was a wall there that blocked us utterly . . ."

"The two worlds do not easily or willingly share their substance," the King said. "The stuff of one has power in the other; it becomes dangerous out of its proper place. Lisan, you know how the djinni Esren Filash Tachur was trapped by a rock from the land of the djinn, and so held slave in the Dead Waters."

She could do no more than nod.

"Similarly, a pebble taken from the other world and set in the tongue of a ghûl will enslave it to the will of the 'ifrit. Do that to a man, or something like it, and you will close his mouth to the world; do it to a gateway, and you close its access to the other world. Jemel did that unwittingly at the Pillar of Lives, when he brought a stone through and set it there. Which is why the 'ifrit had to go so much further, to use the gate at Roq de Rançon. They must have closed that earlier by taking a stone through from this world and setting it in the tower on the other side—or by having a ghûl do it, more likely. They would be afraid of the thing themselves, unwilling to touch it."

"You talk of other worlds than this," Fulke said, "yet I know only of paradise and hell beyond, as the word of the God has taught us. You talk of the djinn and the 'ifrit and other creatures, where I see only demons without souls. You are the man who led the armies here, to win these lands for the God; your faith was rewarded, and the Church has supported you ever since. And yet you speak with His enemies in their own manner, and against His teachings . . ."

"The Princip of Surayon also fought, to free the Sanctuary Land from the possession of the Ekhed princes and their Catari god," the King said mildly, gazing at Fulke with a curious interest. "That's why I gave him land and title."

The Princip snorted. "You gave me Surayon to stand as a buffer between Ascariel and Less Arvon, to keep those hothead fools from making war with each other while the Sharai raged around the borders."

"Well," with a smile, "that too. And it worked, did it not?"

"Only because you fed me to them as a bone they could both gnaw at."

"That would always have been true, whatever I said. The Dukes of Less Arvon, the Great Duke and the Little Duke his son have both of them proved too greedy to look at a rood of land beyond their borders without wanting the profit from it; my own son the Duke here in Ascariel is too holy to believe that his god could possibly want anyone other than himself to govern. You'd have thought he'd want to be here today, would you not? But I didn't need to forbid him. He's occupied already, on his knees in his new cathedral, giving thanks for a deliverance he does not understand."

"He is on his knees and praying, giving thanks—and you are mocking him." Fulke's voice grated at them furiously. "You might have been wiser to have joined him. This man led an army here on a holy quest, but has been long lost to righteousness—and what of you? I hoped not to challenge my King when I came in here, I hoped only to protect him; but I will challenge you now, you give me no choice. Tell me this, straight and true—do you still serve the God I worship?"

"Serve? No. I do not serve. But then, I never did. And for that question, for this answer, I will claim a payment that is already overdue. The war is done; the Ransomers will have no further need for a Marshal Commander."

"I do not understand you—"

Just then, just at that moment, none of them understood him. The King's voice went on speaking but no one was listening to it; their minds were still stumbling over what he had said already, while their eyes were entirely caught up with trying to make some sense of what he was doing now, while he spoke, while his mouth did not move although his face was breaking apart.

". . . You question whether there is truly another world than this, yet you have walked within it. When you open the King's Eye you see as I see, Magister," and the voice was rising higher all the time and losing inflection as it rose, and yet there was still a scalding weight behind that title, "you see two worlds contiguous, the land of men and the land of the djinn; when you walk within the open Eye, you pass from world to world and still you doubt me. Luckily I do not require imagination of my servants. You need not try to run to your men outside, my own man there will prevent you; nor will your Ransomers hear you if you scream."

And yet Fulke did try to run, of course he did; and he had barely made the turn towards the door before his shoulder was seized and held. He struggled to pull free, but Blaise's arm that gripped him might as well have been cast of iron or carved from rock.

"Blaise, man, you were mine before ever you belonged

to that—that creature; remember the oaths you swore to me, to the God . . ."

By all appearances, Blaise had entirely forgotten them. But Blaise, Fulke could hold the others' eyes only for a moment, for a series of moments, glances snatched against desire when Fulke did scream and scream again. Through all of that, it was still the King who drew them, because his flesh was disintegrating as they watched.

Mortal bodies were not made to lose coherence suddenly or from within, except in the patient darkness of a crypt. What they watched here was like all the little secret changes after death happening between eyeblinks, the hand of time scrabbling in a frenzy. The King did not rot so much as crumble, like a corpse that had desiccated in the Sands and turned to sand itself, falling into dust as it lost any memory of itself.

It began in the eyes, where he had kept the only visible sign of his power or his strangeness, a glitter in the darkness, a hint of lights far off and busy. Now they shone and dazzled, and not only within the confines of his gaze; they shone through his skin, they danced in the spaces where his bones ought to be.

Light and shadow: it seemed that his flesh was shaped over something quite other than a skeleton. *I do not serve* he had said, and why should he, when his own body told the whole story of the god that Fulke would have him worship, when he was himself both battleground and battle?

The King had lost his bones to lights; he lost his skin, his flesh to dust. It fell away in trickles and runs, forgetful of its former shape. It seemed golden in the lamplight, and shimmered as it was swept up by the currents of light as they swirled and spun. There was no skull where his face was lost, only the patterns that dust could make in a silent, vicious wind that wound around itself, tightly and more tightly so. It ripped the King's simple garment into shreds and tatters as the fabric fell in upon itself and was snared in the rushing of that wind; it showed its own weave only in the way it drew the dust like a line, like a thread wound round and round a spinning bobbin.

IT MIGHT HAVE been Elisande who knew first what it was; it was Julianne's father who named it.

"Djinni," he said, which was obvious to all of them by then, except perhaps to Fulke.

It gave him no response, beyond its rising like a pillar before them. It stretched itself until it had achieved almost the height and slender grace of the pillars round about, though it still hung poised above the old chest the King had sat on.

"Djinni Khaldor," the Shadow said. If he were Shadow still, if he had a King to serve and chose to serve him. He named the djinni as though he recognised it. "I think you lied to me, djinni. You said 'It has always been me', and that is not true. The King was once the Duc de Charelles, and the Duc was once a young man whom I knew. I will swear that he was a man of normal flesh, whatever they say of him in the wider world; and he was still so, I think, still a man until he came to be King and closed himself into this place."

The djinni said nothing. The man who had been Shadow while the King still had a shadow to cast took a slow, angry breath and faced his betrayal squarely; said, "I have done you service enough in the last forty years that I think you owe me some questions answered."

"You think I lie to you, and yet you will stand and demand answers. Your thinking is as loose as your understanding; you should grip more tightly. *I* think that you have asked me questions enough for one man's lifetime, and that in only half a life."

"I did not know then that you were a djinni."

"You always knew that I was a djinni. What you did not know is that I was also the King. But ask your questions; I have said already that I will answer them. Only the answers may be dangerous to you, because knowledge is always chancy. I will not claim a price, except from Fulke who is paying it already."

No one there said *let Fulke go*, or even thought it; at least one was guiltily delighted to see him held by a djinni's servant, claimed by the djinni itself.

Coren—who thought he would answer after this to no title other than his name—said, "Where is the King my master?"

"I am the King your master."

"Where is the man who was Duc de Charelles before he was King of Outremer?"

"I do not know."

"It's lying," Elisande said fiercely. "Of course it knows, they always know. But Esren lied to me too, and they weren't supposed to do that. I thought the djinn were honest," suddenly accusing, facing the creature where it rose, where it hovered, where it spun.

"I know you did. Why did you?"

Another day she might not have answered, she might have been wise or cunning. But another day she would not have been here in the dim light and the heavy air, watching the way it leaned against the stillness, feeling the way it leaned against the truth.

"Because I have always been told so, because it seemed to be true, because it seemed right that something made of spirit should not lie." Men walked on the edge of darkness always, groping for a path; their only light fell behind them to show where they had been, and they called it memory or history. Or God, Julianne said; lies, said Elisande. The djinn moved in a mist, perhaps, but they stood in a pool of light that fell all ways around them. It would be unfair, it would be wrong to see so much more and not describe it truly.

"Who was it told you?"

"My father," and she said it firmly, determinedly, almost proudly.

"And who told him and his father, who was it told the world?"

That one she had to pause, to glance at her grandfather where he stood mute and impassioned, to think about; in the end there was only one answer possible. "The djinn," she said, chagrined for her entire race, for their innocence and gullibility.

"The djinn indeed. Myself, indeed, I said it. Long ago now; and often since, when men gave me the opportunity."

"What, and were you lying all the time?"

"Perhaps I was," it said, as though that were something it too had to think about.

"Why, though? Why would you do that, great one, do you like to laugh at us little people as you lie?"

"I have laughed at humans, in my time. But perhaps I did it for some other reason; perhaps everything that I have ever done was done to bring us here, to this place and this conversation."

She would have asked *why?* again, but Coren broke in.

"And are you telling the truth now, then? I will risk that, and ask again. Do you truly not know where the King my friend is to be found?"

"Truly, I do not. I have watched many a human die, and I still do not know where their spirits go when it happens."

"Is he dead? Since when?"

"Since he died."

"How long since?"

"Almost forty years."

"Did you kill him?"

"Not by my touch. I came to him, and he died; that was understood. I had foreseen it. So perhaps had he."

Perhaps so; how could they tell, if the djinn could lie?

"What have you done with his body?"

For answer, it drifted a little away, to the further side of the rug-strewn dais. Briefly their eyes followed it, as though it were going to show them; then Elisande made a noise in her throat—contempt or self-contempt, even she was uncertain—and ran forward, jumped up, pulled open the lid of the old chest.

It would have been easily big enough to hold the new-slain body of a man, and a bigger man than the King had ever been. In fact what lay in there, half-curled like a child, was something smaller than Elisande herself, the figure of a wizened thing. She stooped and lifted it out into the light before either of the older men could reach her.

"It's not . . ."

She genuinely thought it was not a man at all, as she lifted it. Too light, too dry, too browned and tough ever to have been human: at first she thought it was another lie, a tease, a dead man sculpted, made, a mockery. Her own father had put a poppet in a cell and made it human-seeming; that had moved, at least, which this did not.

When she saw the skull's shape beneath the leather skin, when she saw how the thin black lips were drawn back from real teeth, she still did not think it was human, or the King. A giant monkey, dried and salted? It was still too small, too twisted surely to be a man . . .

But there was white hair clinging to the scalp of it, and no fur else. And the skull had a human shape, like no monkey that she had ever seen; and yes, it was a man, of course it was, deny it as she liked, she could not change it.

Instead she knelt and laid him on the carpets; looked up at her grandfather, at the father of her friend, and said, "Is this him?"

"Oh, yes," the Princip said, "it isn't lying now."

"It might be, about how he died . . ."

"No." Julianne had seen a man touched by the djinni, she knew what kind of death that was; and there was no visible mark on this body, only the terrible absence of its owner. Terrible and long-term: very soon after he closed the gates of the Dir'al Shahan. Outremer had been ruled by a djinni for a generation. And the djinn were supposed not to meddle in the affairs of men. She gazed at it where it roiled in the dust of its own deception and asked the first question of her own. "Why are you so different? You're not like Esren, even, let alone like the djinn in the histories I've read, or the stories Jemel tells. What makes you play these games?" *Why kill a king, and spend forty years in imitation of him?*

"I am . . . incomplete," it said, with just the faintest hesitation before the word.

"In what way, incomplete?"

"I have given myself away," it said. "Small pieces of myself, to strengthen these my servants in their tasks," and its servants were still going about their tasks in the shadows of the great chamber, no whit disturbed. Marron might have done that too, she thought, with his red eyes and his unnatural powers, with the Daughter slowly sealing him off from the world; she was ahead of the djinni already when it said, "And rather more of me, of my substance went long ago. It is almost its own creature now, though not a djinni, far from that. There are those of my kind who will say that I am no longer truly of the djinn; its absence diminishes me, so that I can do these things and find some amusement in them."

And now, at last, "Why would you want to?" from Elisande, where she knelt still above the body of the King. "You must have known that this would happen, that you would be—reduced," in what was almost cruel imitation, except that she could see no way to be truly cruel to something that had no true humanity, only a decaying of its proper self.

"It was necessary. The 'ifrit meant to take this world from us."

"I thought this world was ours."

"Lisan. We are the djinn. Do your pastures belong to the cattle, does the soil belong to the worm? You may do

as you will, but we are still the djinn. The 'ifrit, though—
the 'ifrit wanted this world for themselves, and they
thought they could take it. We are stronger, but they are
many; they thought we would not fight them. Why should
we risk death, for this crude clay?"

"They thought you would not fight them," the Princip
repeated. "They were right, weren't they?"

"Of course."

"You used us instead, you used men to fight your
spirit-battles for you."

"We cannot meet them in our own form; and if we take
solid bodies in this world as they do, we become as vulnerable as they are. Even a man can kill us, with a blessed
blade. So the King lives in seclusion, and we take what
precautions we can."

"Esren isn't cautious," Elisande said, thinking of Rhabat and the flooding of the valley, an invasion of 'ifrit
blocked by one djinni and a small inland ocean.

"That djinni is unique." *Uniquely damaged* was what it
seemed to mean. "As am I. We are both unlike our kin."

"That unlikeness didn't stop you using my land, my
people for your war." The Princip again, in a rising anger.

"Of course not. Men are always eager to fight. The
Sharai and the Patrics would have fought each other anyway; they would both have fought in Surayon. I brought
you together to let you fight for us."

"And?"

"And what?"

"I thought you would go on to say that now we were all
peaceful together, thanks to you."

"That would be absurd. The Sharai and the Patrics will
fight again; they will both fight the Surayonnaise."

"But not yet," Coren interrupted, over the Princip's
grunt, "not for a while yet. I will be sure of that much.
And don't tell us who will win those fights, djinni; foreknowledge is not a human gift, because it is not a gift to
humans."

"But the 'ifrit have foreknowledge too," Julianne objected. "They must have known that you were leading all our armies into Surayon to face them . . ."

"Of course; but death clouds the image. They knew there would be a battle, and so did we; they hoped to win it, and so did we. They did what they could to keep your armies apart and fighting each other. If the most powerful forces in the Sanctuary Land destroyed themselves, then the 'ifrit could rule unchallenged; we would have nothing to set against them for a generation. Men fight like dogs, they hardly needed to encourage you. And then they are an army in themselves, faith is the only weapon that men have against them; and they hoped to have the Ghost Walker among their ranks, to lead the Sand Dancers and so the Sharai in a holy war. That would have been a triumph. The King's Daughter is a part of me, and they could have used it against me and mine."

"Would the Sharai have followed Morakh? The tribes hate the Sand Dancers . . ."

"If he was the Ghost Walker," Elisande said, "and if he showed them they could drive the Patrics out of Outremer? Even at the cost of letting in the 'ifrit, they'd have followed him."

"We were lucky, then."

"For a while. Lucky often, I think. So many times it could have gone wrong; from that first day where you met us in the road," and Elisande addressed the djinni again, "and started moving us around . . ."

"It started before that," Julianne corrected, "when it called my father away so that I'd be alone on the road, so that I could meet you and then it could persuade us both, without a man there to interfere. Except for Blaise, I mean . . ." and her voice faltered as she remembered, as she glanced aside to see where he stood quite impassive, with the figure of Fulke silent beside him. Pain or terror had broken that one utterly, she thought, unless it was simply helplessness, that terrible weight of certainty, too much for any man to stand against . . .

"I had started long before that," the djinni said. "I knew what I would need, and when need it; I have been preparing this for forty years."

"Julianne, I met your mother on a mission for the King," her father told her suddenly, "and it was I who brought your parents together, Elisande, and proposed the match to your grandfather here, under the suggestion of the King."

Foreknowledge is not a gift to humans; sometimes, neither is its inverse. The girls looked at each other, and it was a shared decision that had them suddenly turning away, walking away, crossing that wide pillared space without a glance back. None of the men there sought to detain them; the djinni presumably had known that they would go.

"EVERYTHING WE ARE," Julianne murmured as they came out into sunshine at last, in the courtyard of the Dir'al Shahan, "everything we do. It knows *everything*. Did it make us, or did it just predict us? I can't work it out."

"I don't think there's a distinction. What are you going to do, Julianne?"

"I don't know. I wish I could spite it somehow, but it's too late for that, the war's over."

"And we won," Elisande said glumly. "But there'll be other wars, it said so. Only we'll just be fighting for ourselves next time, and I don't know if that's better or worse."

"Worse. Definitely. I think . . . And how could we know, anyway? Maybe it's still using us, against the next time the 'ifrit want to fight. Whatever it tells us, whatever it *chooses* to tell us, it knows exactly how we're going to react anyway, so we might as well ignore it and do what we think is right for us, for Outremer, for Surayon . . ."

"Or for the Sharai? You're still married to Hasan, my love."

"I know. And I love him, I want what's best for him and all of us."

"And Imber?"

"Him too. I love them both."

"Tricky. You can't stay married to them both."

"Can't I?"

"Oh, *what?* Julianne . . ."

"Why not? My father'll love it. What better way to keep peace between them, than to have one girl married to the lords of both armies?"

"The men won't accept it."

"I think they will, they'll have to. It's my ultimatum; if either one wants me, they have to be prepared to share me. Neither one recognises the other marriage anyway, so that's not a problem. I can be true wife to each."

"But you can't, you can't have children, not to either one of them . . ."

"No." Traditionally, children sealed an alliance; here it was impossible. She couldn't share either man's bed, not even once, or the whole delicate structure she was trying to build here would come crashing down. She had lied, when she said she could be a true wife; she could be a virgin wife, but nothing more. To sleep with one would be to cuckold the other, by their own laws or any. That would be disaster.

"Oh, Julianne . . ."

"It's all right, sweet. I can find my comforts, be a power in the shadows on both sides, it's what my father trained me for all my life." And Hasan had his other wives, and Imber—well, Imber would suffer and endure, and be noble and honest and not take a lover because she was the one that he loved and the one that he'd married. Mostly, he would suffer; and she'd suffer to see it, and there would be nothing that either of them could do except to remind themselves that it was a small price to pay for peace, for as long as the peace should last. "What about you, though, what will you do?"

"What, without Rudel to kick against, without my country to defend?"

"Surayon will still need defending, I think."

"Yes, but not the same way. It'll be all negotiation and treaties now in the open, secret dealings and distrust in the shadows. We need politicians, and that's not me. And Grandfer needs to find an heir, and that's not me either; I don't want to be Principessa and urgently looking for a husband. You've got the best of them in any case. I was going to say I'd have your cast-off, but if you're not going to be casting one off, then I think I'll just come with you anyway. If you'd like to have me."

"Elisande, I'd love it. You know that. But I won't let you waste your life on me . . ."

"Why not? Waste is my speciality." Her voice was bleak beyond bearing, savage with self-contempt; her desperate anger needed a focus and had found it in herself.

"I think surprising your friends is your speciality. But what will you do?"

"Look after you, sweetheart. See that your men make you happy, as best they can. Oh, it may not be forever—though if you're planning to die a shrivelled virgin, I don't see why I shouldn't be sisterly about it. For the moment, I just can't think of anything better," and even she wasn't sure which way she meant that. "And when we get bored, I've always got Esren to liven us up."

"Have you?"

"For my lifetime, it promised."

"Elisande, I think it was lying, wasn't it?"

"Oh yes, I'm sure it was lying. It'll do what it wants to do. But as Djinni Khaldor said in there, Esren is unique. I think it gets bored too; I think it'll still come when I call it. Sometimes."

"Just to see how it can annoy us, most likely."

But the way she phrased that sentence was a resounding yes, a welcome and a thank you all at once. Elisande grinned and said, "Come on, let's go and tell your husbands, see how they take the news."

ALL THE NEWS, and there was a lot to tell them and a lot for them to take in; but all of it had to wait, nothing could be told or talked about for a little while yet.

There was—of course—a man waiting at the high gate, to let them out of this deceptive palace and into the gaze of all those men waiting and watching. As they emerged, Julianne was struck by a sudden thought. "How do we tell the Ransomers that their Marshal Commander isn't coming out, that Fulke's just one of the King's servants now? They'll think we tricked him inside and killed him . . ."

"Show them the body. Let him come out and wave."

"Will his eyes be red, do you think," *like Marron's,* "like Blaise's?"

"Sure to be."

"Then they'll say he's been possessed by a demon."

"Which is true, or true enough. So all right, let's not tell them anything. We went in all together, and we girls have come out alone; they'll think that's as it should be, except that they won't know why we were allowed to accompany the men in the first place. Leave your father to find a way to deal with the Ransomers. You've got two husbands to deal with, that's enough for any woman. I've got a djinni, and no sense of responsibility."

There was something else that had to be dealt with first, though, something that touched them both deeply and irredeemably.

The sun glared cruelly off the white stone of the pavement, reducing men to mirage, shimmering shadows. The day's heat lay heavy in the air, dulling sounds and senses.

They saw a figure push through the gathered Sharai,

and come running out into the open space between them and other groups. Distantly, they heard him cry a challenge, with a contemptuous insult for support when it brought no instant response.

They saw a man reply at last, striding from the Ransomers, sliding a black cloak from his shoulders as he went, stepping forward in vivid white.

They could not hear what passed between the two, but that was quickly done with; then it was a case of blades, a scimitar for the Sharai and a long sword for the Ransomer.

And both girls could name both men, and one at least of the swords. They scurried forward uncertainly, not knowing how to interfere, knowing only that they must; and were too late already, because another figure came chasing after the first, and he too had a sword in his hand and the girls were old friends with that one.

He used it even as he ran, he used it on himself; and then he flung his body between the two duellists and was impossibly lucky not to find himself twice skewered as he deserved—but he always had been lucky, just as he always had been desolate.

No talking this time, no mediation; all in the same movement, he seized one of the startled fighters and dragged him through a sudden raw wound in the world, a ripped red gateway to a golden land.

And the gateway closed at their backs and and there was nothing there except his blade, which he had dropped as he went through, deliberately or otherwise.

And the one left behind stood quite still for a long, long minute, as the girls did, as did the watching world; and then he stooped slowly to pick up the fallen sword, which was called Dard.

Don't miss the other books in the epic
Outremer series
by

CHAZ BRENCHLEY

From Ace

The Devil in the Dust
0-441-01071-7

Tower of the King's Daughter
0-441-01080-6

A Dark Way to Glory
0-441-01086-5

Feast of the King's Shadow
0-441-01098-9

Hand of the King's Evil
0-441-01110-1

The End of All Roads
0-441-01114-4

"Brenchley's striking new epic fantasy series [is]
a revelation." —*Starburst*

Available wherever books are sold or
to order call 1-800-788-6262